"HAVE SPACECRAFT, WILL TRAVEL" echoes across the universe from hundreds of different planets as earthlings and countless alien creatures ready their ships to embark on vast sight-seeing tours of cosmic panoramas.

Some of them travel to survey the scenery. Others come to seek shelter from adverse environments while some are merely curious. But all of them travel by night and in seclusion. And they all use some variation of the dome-topped disks we know as FLYING SAUCERS.

# FLYING SAUCERS

edited by

## Isaac Asimov,
## Martin Harry Greenberg,
## and Charles G. Waugh

Introduction by Isaac Asimov

FAWCETT CREST • NEW YORK

A Fawcett Crest Book
Published by Ballantine Books

ISBN 0-449-21400-1

Manufactured in the United States of America

First Fawcett Crest Edition: May 1982
First Ballantine Books Edition: March 1983
Third Printing: August 1987

The editors and publisher are grateful for permission to reprint the following:

"WHAT IS THIS THING CALLED LOVE?" by Isaac Asimov. Copyright © 1961 by the Ziff-Davis Publishing Company. Reprinted by permission of the author.

"PAGAN" by Algis Budrys. Copyright © 1955 by Street & Smith Publishing Company, Inc. (now Condé Nast Publications, Inc.). Reprinted by permission of the author.

"THE BEHOLDERS" by A. Bertram Chandler. Copyright © 1957 by King-Size Publications. Reprinted by permission of the author and the author's agents, the Scott Meredith Literary Agency, Inc., 845 Third Avenue, New York, N.Y. 10022.

"SENSE OF WONDER" by A. Bertram Chandler. Copyright © 1958 by King-Size Publications. Reprinted by permission of the author and the author's agents, the Scott Meredith Literary Agency, Inc., 845 Third Avenue, New York, N.Y. 10022.

"TROUBLE WITH THE NATIVES (also known as Captain Wyxtpthll's Flying Saucer)" by Arthur C. Clarke. Copyright © 1951 by Stadium Publishing Company. Copyright © renewed 1951 by the author. Reprinted by permission of the author and the author's agents, the Scott Meredith Literary Agency, Inc., 845 Third Avenue, New York, N.Y. 10022.

"THE LIZARD OF WOZ" by Edmund Cooper. Copyright © 1969 by Edmund Cooper. Reprinted by permission of the author.

"THE GRANTHA SIGHTING" by Avram Davidson. Copyright © 1958 by Mercury Press, Inc. From *The Magazine of Fantasy and Science Fiction*. Reprinted by permission of Kirby McCauley, Ltd.

"THE MERCHANT" by Larry Eisenberg. Copyright © 1973 by HPD Publishing Corporation. Reprinted by permission of the author.

"THE MOUSE" by Howard Fast. Copyright © 1969 by Mercury Press, Inc. From *The Magazine of Fantasy and Science Fiction*. Reprinted by permission of The Sterling Lord Agency.

"THE TIME FOR DELUSION" by Donald Franson. Copyright © 1958 by Columbia Publications, Inc. Reprinted by permission of the author.

"SMALL MIRACLE" by Randall Garrett. Copyright © 1959 by the Ziff-Davis Publishing Company. Reprinted by permission of the author and the author's agents, the Scott Meredith Literary Agency, Inc., 845 Third Avenue, New York, N.Y. 10022.

"ALL THE UNIVERSE IN A MASON JAR" by Joe Haldeman. Copyright © 1977 by Joe Haldeman. Reprinted by permission of Kirby McCauley, Ltd.

To Olga Vezeris
With respect and thanks

# CONTENTS

# FLYING SAUCERS

# FLYING SAUCERS AND SCIENCE FICTION

### by Isaac Asimov

*I* am helping to edit a book on flying saucers? Isaac Asimov? Surely, I am a leading and vocal skeptic where flying saucers are concerned!

Have I changed my mind now? Do I believe in the existence of flying saucers?

That depends on what you mean by the question. Do I believe that many people have seen something in the sky that they can't explain?

Absolutely! Of course! You bet! Seeing something one can't explain is very common. Every time I watch a magician perform his act I see something I can't explain.

However, when I see something I can't explain, I assume there is a perfectly normal explanation, one that fits in with the structure of the universe as worked out by modern science. I don't instantly jump to the idea that there is no explanation short of the supernatural or of some far-out near-zero-probability hypothesis.

For that reason, I have no tendency to explain every appearance of a light in the sky by declaring it to be a spaceship manned by extraterrestrial beings.

Nowadays, in an effort to gain respectability, people who accept the wilder hypotheses about flying saucers call them "unidentified flying objects" and abbreviate it UFO. On numerous occasions, I have been asked if I "believe" in UFOs.

My usual answer is, "I assume that by UFO you mean 'unidentified flying objects.' I certainly believe that many people have seen objects in the air or sky that they can't identify, and those are UFOs. But then, many people can't identify the planet Venus, or a mirage. If you are asking me whether I believe that some mysterious object reported is a spaceship manned by extraterrestrial beings, then I must say I am very skeptical. But that, you see, is an *identified* flying object, and that's not what you're asking about, is it?"

Mysterious objects have been reported in Earth's skies all through history. Usually they are interpreted according to the preoccupations of the day. In ancient and medieval times, and in primitive societies, they would be interpreted as angels, demons, spirits, and so on. In technological societies, they would be interpreted as first balloons, then dirigibles, then airplanes, and then spaceships.

Of course, if they're spaceships *now*, then they've been spaceships all the time, and some people have indeed interpreted Ezekiel's vision in the Bible, for instance, as the sighting of spaceships manned by extraterrestrials.

The modern surge of flying saucer sightings began on June 24, 1947, when Kenneth Arnold, a salesman, claimed he saw bright disk-shaped objects flying rapidly through the air near Mount Rainier. From the shapes he described, the expression "flying saucers" came into being.

Nothing much might have happened in consequence, for wild reports about all sorts of things reach the news media every day and then fade out. In this case, though, the report attracted the attention of Raymond A. Palmer, who was then the editor of the science fiction magazine *Amazing Stories*.

Palmer may not himself have been a piece of broken pottery, but he was certainly not averse to building circulation by means of items that appealed to crackpots. He had shown that in his earlier work on something completely wacky which he called "The Great Shaver Mystery."

Now he took up flying saucers and single-handedly promoted it into an international mania. That is one connection (an important one) between flying saucers and science fiction.

Mind you, I have a soft spot in my heart for Ray Palmer. Way back in 1938, he bought the first science fiction story I ever sold, and sent me the very first check I ever earned as a professional writer. Nevertheless, candor compels me to state that for years after this noble deed of his I never had occasion to believe a word he said.

At the other extreme of the flying saucer spectrum is Professor J. Allen Hynek. He is a respectable and learned scientist who has spent decades examining the evidence and who remains firmly convinced that there is something there. He doesn't accept the extraterrestrial spacecraft hypothesis, but he thinks that something mysterious underlies the phenomenon, which, if understood, may revolutionize science.

However, in all the years he's been investigating the phenomenon, he's come up with—nothing! Far from revolutionizing science, his work has not added one even marginal item to the world of physical science.

Then what am I doing helping edit this anthology?

That brings us to the second connection between flying saucers and science fiction. The whole concept of flying saucers—the whole notion of thousands upon thousands of spaceships hovering about us without ever seeming to do anything or to affect us in any way—has supplied science fiction writers with an endless supply of story material.

All of us have written flying saucer stories. I have myself, and one of them is included in this book.

Generally, we have to deal with a situation in which extraterrestrial spacecraft visit us, but keep out of sight for some reason, or decide not to do anything for some reason, or try to do something and fail for some reason, or fail to manage to convince Earthpeople they are real for some reason.

You see, science fiction writers, being sane and rational, have to find some *reason* for so many spaceships doing *nothing*. Usually the results turn out to be funny, satiric or ironic; sometimes tragic. Very often, they prove to be stories that are entertaining and good—so what we have done is to collect a sizable number of them into one book for your delectation.

Come, see for yourself that every cloud has a silver lining, and that even the silliest notions can undergo a sea change into something rich and strange in the hands of skilled science fiction writers.

*Author of* The Foundation Trilogy (1951–53), I Robot (1950), *and* The Caves of Steel (1954), *Isaac Asimov may be the world's most famous science fiction writer. During his 40-year career, he has produced over 250 books as well as thousands of articles. Indeed, as co-editors we often kid him about being a man who needs no more introductions, since he has written more of them for books than any other three people. In the following story, however, he investigates the introduction of humans to aliens and a man to a woman.*

# WHAT IS THIS THING CALLED LOVE?

## by Isaac Asimov

"But these are two species," said Captain Garm, peering closely at the creatures that had been brought up from the planet below. His optic organs adjusted focus to maximum sharpness, bulging outwards as they did so. The color patch above them gleamed in quick flashes.

Botax felt warmly comfortable to be following color-changes once again, after months in a spy cell on the planet, trying to make sense out of the modulated sound waves emitted by the natives. Communication by flash was almost like being home in the far-off Perseus arm of the Galaxy. "Not two species," he said, "but two forms of one species."

"Nonsense, they look quite different. Vaguely Perse-like, thank the Entity, and not as disgusting in appearance as so many out-forms are. Reasonable shape, recognizable limbs. But no color-patch. Can they speak?"

"Yes, Captain Garm," Botax indulged in a discreetly disapproving prismatic interlude. "The details are in my report. These creatures form sound waves by way of throat and mouth, something like complicated coughing. I have learned to do it myself." He was quietly proud. "It is very difficult."

"It must be stomach-turning. Well, that accounts for their flat, unextensible eyes. Not to speak by color makes eyes largely useless. Meanwhile, how can you insist these are a single species? The one on the left is smaller and has longer tendrils, or whatever it is, and seems differently proportioned. It bulges where this other does not. Are they alive?"

"Alive but not at the moment conscious, Captain. They have been psycho-treated to repress fright in order that they might be studied easily."

"But are they worth study? We are behind our schedule and have at least five worlds of greater moment than this one to check and explore. Maintaining a Time-stasis unit is expensive and I would like to return them and go on—"

But Botax's moist spindly body was fairly vibrating with anxiety. His tubular tongue flicked out and curved up and over his flat nose, while his eyes sucked inward. His splayed three-fingered hand made a gesture of negation as his speech went almost entirely into the deep red.

"Entity save us, Captain, for no world is of greater moment to us than this one. We may be facing a supreme crisis. These creatures could be the most dangerous life-forms in the Galaxy, Captain, just *because* there are two forms."

"I don't follow you."

"Captain, it has been my job to study this planet, and it has been most difficult, for it is unique. It is so unique that I can scarcely comprehend its facets. For instance, almost all life on the planet consists of species in two forms. There are no words to describe it, no concepts even. I can only speak of them as first form and second form. If I may use their sounds, the little one is called 'female,' and the big one, here, 'male,' so the creatures themselves are aware of the difference."

Garm winced, "What a disgusting means of communication."

"And, Captain, in order to bring forth young, the two forms must cooperate."

The Captain, who had bent forward to examine the specimens closely with an expression compounded of interest and revulsion, straightened at once. "Cooperate? What nonsense is this? There is no more fundamental attribute of life than that each living creature bring forth its young in innermost communication with itself. What else makes life worth living?"

"The one form does bring forth life but the other form must cooperate."

"How?"

"That has been difficult to determine. It is something very private and in my search through the available forms of literature I could find no exact and explicit description. But I have been able to make reasonable deductions."

Garm shook his head. "Ridiculous. Budding is the holiest, most private function in the world. On tens of thousands of worlds it is the same. As the great photo-bard, Levuline, said, 'In budding-time, in budding time, in sweet, delightful budding time; when—' "

"Captain, you don't understand. This cooperation between forms brings about somehow (and I am not certain exactly how) a mixture and recombination of genes. It is a device by which in every generation, new combinations of characteristics are brought into existence. Variations are multiplied; mutated genes hastened into expression almost at once where under the usual budding system, millennia might pass first."

"Are you trying to tell me that the genes from one individual can be combined with those of another? Do you know how completely ridiculous that is in the light of all the principles of cellular physiology?"

"It must be so," said Botax nervously under the other's pop-eyed glare. "Evolution *is* hastened. This planet is a riot of species. There are supposed to be a million and a quarter different species of creatures."

"A dozen and a quarter more likely. Don't accept too completely what you read in the native literature."

"I've seen dozens of radically different species myself in just a small area. I tell you, Captain, give these creatures a short space of time and they will mutate into intellects powerful enough to overtake us and rule the Galaxy."

"Prove that this cooperation you speak of exists, Investigator, and I shall consider your contentions. If you cannot, I shall dismiss all your fancies as ridiculous and we will move on."

"I can prove it." Botax's color-flashes turned intensely yellow-green. "The creatures of this world are unique in another way. They foresee advances they have not yet made, probably as a consequence of their belief in rapid change which, after all, they constantly witness. They therefore indulge in a type of literature involving the space-travel they have never developed. I have translated their term for the literature as 'science-fiction.' Now I have dealt in my readings almost exclusively with science-fiction, for there I thought, in their dreams and fancies, they would expose themselves and their danger to us. And it was from that science-fiction that I deduced the method of their inter-form cooperation."

"How did you do that?"

"There is a periodical on this world which sometimes publishes science-fiction which is, however, devoted almost entirely to the various aspects of the cooperation. It does not speak entirely freely, which is annoying, but persists in merely hinting. Its name as nearly as I can put it into flashes is 'Recreationlad.' The creature in charge, I deduce, is interested in nothing but inter-form cooperation and searches for it everywhere with a systematic and scientific intensity that has roused my awe. He has found instances of cooperation described in science-fiction and I let material in his periodical guide me. From the stories he instanced I have learned how to bring it about.

"And, Captain, I beg of you, when the cooperation is accomplished and the young are brought forth before your eyes, give orders not to leave an atom of this world in existence."

"Well," said Captain Garm, wearily, "bring them into full consciousness and do what you must do quickly."

Marge Skidmore was suddenly completely aware of her surroundings. She remembered very clearly the elevated station at the beginning of twilight. It had been almost empty, one man standing near her, another at the other end of the platform. The approaching train had just made itself known as a faint rumble in the distance.

There had then come the flash, a sense of turning inside out, the half-seen vision of a spindly creature, dripping mucus, a rushing upward, and now—

"Oh, God," she said, shuddering. "It's still here. And there's another one, too."

She felt a sick revulsion, but no fear. She was almost proud of herself for feeling no fear. The man next to her, standing quietly as she herself was, but still wearing a battered fedora, was the one that had been near her on the platform.

"They got you, too?" she asked. "Who else?"

Charlie Grimwold, feeling flabby and paunchy, tried to lift his hand to remove his hat and smooth the thin hair that broke up but did not entirely cover the skin of his scalp and found that it moved only with difficulty against a rubbery but hardening resistance. He let his hand drop and looked morosely at the thin-faced woman facing him. She was in her middle thirties, he decided, and her hair was nice and her dress fit well, but at the moment, he just wanted to be somewhere else and it did him no good at all that he had company, even female company.

He said, "I don't know, lady. I was just standing on the station platform."

"Me, too."

"And then I see a flash. Didn't hear nothing. Now here I am. Must be little men from Mars or Venus or one of them places."

Marge nodded vigorously, "That's what I figure. A flying saucer? You scared?"

"No. That's funny, you know. I think maybe I'm going nuts or I *would* be scared."

"Funny thing. I ain't scared, either. Oh, God, here comes one of them now. If he touches me, I'm going to scream. Look at those wiggly hands. And that wrinkled skin, all slimy; makes me nauseous."

Botax approached gingerly and said, in a voice at once rasping and screechy, this being the closest he could come to imitating the native timbre, "Creatures! We will not hurt you. But we must ask you if you would do us the favor of cooperating."

"Hey, it talks!" said Charlie. "What do you mean, cooperate."

"Both of you. With each other," said Botax.

"Oh?" He looked at Marge. "You know what he means, lady?"

"Ain't got no idea whatsoever," she answered loftily.

Botax said, "What I mean—" and he used the short term he had once heard employed as a synonym for the process.

Marge turned red and said, "What!" in the loudest scream she could manage. Both Botax and Captain Garm put their hands over their mid-regions to cover the auditory patches that trembled painfully with the decibels.

Marge went on rapidly, and nearly incoherently. "Of all things. I'm a married woman, you. If my Ed was here, you'd hear from *him*. And you, wise guy," she twisted toward Charlie against rubbery resistance, "whoever you are, if you think—"

"Lady, lady," said Charlie in uncomfortable desperation. "It ain't my idea. I mean, far be it from me, you know, to turn down some lady, you know; but me, I'm married, too. I got three kids. Listen—"

Captain Garm said, "What's happening, Investigator Botax? These cacophonous sounds are awful."

"Well," Botax flashed a short purple patch of embarrassment. "This forms a complicated ritual. They are supposed to be reluctant at first. It heightens the subsequent result. After that initial stage, the skins must be removed."

"They have to be *skinned?*"

"Not really skinned. Those are artificial skins that can be removed painlessly, and must be. Particularly in the smaller form."

"All right, then. Tell it to remove the skins. Really, Botax, I don't find this pleasant."

"I don't think I had better tell the smaller form to remove the skins. I think we had better follow the ritual closely. I have here sections of those space-travel tales which the man from the 'Recreationlad' periodical spoke highly of. In those tales the skins are removed forcibly. Here is a description of an accident, for instance, 'which played havoc with the girl's dress, ripping it nearly off her slim body. For a second, he felt the warm firmness of her half-bared bosom against his cheek—' It goes on that way. You see, the ripping, the forcible removal, acts as a stimulus."

"Bosom?" said the Captain. "I don't recognize the flash."

"I invented that to cover the meaning. It refers to the bulges on the upper dorsal region of the smaller form."

"I see. Well, tell the larger one to rip the skins off the smaller one. What a dismal thing this is."

Botax turned to Charlie. "Sir," he said, "rip the girl's dress nearly off her slim body, will you? I will release you for the purpose."

Marge's eyes widened and she twisted toward Charlie in instant outrage. "Don't you dare do that, you. Don't you *dast* touch me, you sex maniac."

"Me?" said Charlie plaintively. "It ain't my idea. You think I go around ripping dresses? Listen," he turned to Botax, "I got a wife and three kids. She finds out I go around ripping dresses, I get clobbered. You know what my wife does when I just look at some dame? *Listen—*"

"Is he still reluctant?" said the Captain, impatiently.

"Apparently," said Botax. "The strange surroundings, you know, may be extending that stage of the cooperation. Since I know this is unpleasant for you, I will perform this stage of the ritual myself. It is frequently written in the space-travel tales that an outer-world species performs the task. For instance, here," and he riffled through his notes finding the one he wanted, "they describe a very awful such species. The creatures on the planet have foolish notions, you understand. It never occurs to them to imagine handsome individuals such as ourselves, with a fine mucous cover."

"Go on! Go on! Don't take all day," said the Captain.

"Yes, Captain. It says here that the extraterrestrial 'came forward to where the girl stood. Shrieking hysterically, she was cradled in the monster's embrace. Talons ripped blindly at her body, tearing the kirtle away in rags.' You see, the native creature is shrieking with stimulation as her skins are removed."

"Then go ahead, Botax, remove it. But please, allow no shrieking. I'm trembling all over with the sound waves."

Botax said politely to Marge, "If you don't mind—"

One spatulate finger made as though to hook on to the neck of the dress.

Marge wiggled desperately. "Don't touch. Don't touch! You'll get slime on it. Listen, this dress cost $25.95 at Ohrbach's. Stay away, you monster. Look at those eyes on him." She was panting in her desperate efforts to dodge the groping, extraterrestrial hand. "A slimy, bug-eyed monster, that's what he is. Listen, I'll take it off myself. Just don't touch it with slime, for God's sake."

She fumbled at the zipper, and said in a hot aside to Charlie, "Don't you dast look."

Charlie closed his eyes and shrugged in resignation.

She stepped out of the dress. "All right? You satisfied?"

Captain Garm's fingers twitched with unhappiness. "Is that the bosom? Why does the other creature keep its head turned away?"

"Reluctance. Reluctance," said Botax. "Besides, the bosom

is still covered. Other skins must be removed. When bared, the bosom is a very strong stimulus. It is constantly described as ivory globes, or white spheres, or otherwise after that fashion. I have here drawings, visual picturizations, that come from the outer covers of the space-travel magazines. If you will inspect them, you will see that upon every one of them, a creature is present with a bosom more or less exposed."

The Captain looked thoughtfully from the illustrations to Marge and back. "What is ivory?"

"That is another made-up flash of my own. It represents the tusky material of one of the large sub-intelligent creatures on the planet."

"Ah," and Captain Garm went into a pastel green of satisfaction. "That explains it. This small creature is one of a warrior sect and those are tusks with which to smash the enemy."

"No, no. They are quite soft, I understand." Botax's small brown hand flicked outward in the general direction of the objects under discussion and Marge screamed and shrank away.

"Then what other purpose do they have?"

"I think," said Botax with considerable hesitation, "that they are used to feed the young."

"The young eat them?" asked the Captain with every evidence of deep distress.

"Not exactly. The objects produce a fluid which the young consume."

"Consume a fluid from a living body? Yech-h-h." The Captain covered his head with all three of his arms, calling the central supernumerary into use for the purpose, slipping it out of its sheath so rapidly as almost to knock Botax over.

"A three-armed, slimy, bug-eyed monster," said Marge.

"Yeah," said Charlie.

"All right you, just watch those eyes. Keep them to yourself."

"Listen, lady. I'm trying not to look."

Botax approached again. "Madam, would you remove the rest?"

Marge drew herself up as well as she could against the pinioning field. "Never!"

"I'll remove it, if you wish."

"Don't touch! For God's sake, don't touch. Look at the slime on him, will you? All right, I'll take it off." She was muttering under her breath and looking hotly in Charlie's direction as she did so.

"Nothing is happening," said the Captain, in deep dissatisfaction, "and this seems an imperfect specimen."

Botax felt the slur on his own efficiency. "I brought you two perfect specimens. What's wrong with the creature?"

"The bosom does not consist of globes or spheres. I know what globes or spheres are and in these pictures you have shown me, they are so depicted. Those are large globes. On this creature, though, what we have are nothing but small flaps of dry tissue. And they're discolored, too, partly."

"Nonsense," said Botax. "You must allow room for natural variation. I will put it to the creature herself."

He turned to Marge, "Madame, is your bosom imperfect?"

Marge's eyes opened wide and she struggled vainly for moments without doing anything more than gasp loudly. "*Really!*" she finally managed. "Maybe I'm no Gina Lollobrigida or Anita Ekberg, but I'm perfectly all right, thank you. Oh boy, if my Ed were only here." She turned to Charlie. "Listen, you, you tell this bug-eyed slimy thing here, there ain't nothing wrong with my development."

"Lady," said Charlie, softly, "I ain't looking, remember?"

"Oh, sure, you ain't looking. You been peeking enough, so you might as well just open your crummy eyes and stick up for a lady, if you're the least bit of a gentleman, which you probably ain't."

"Well," said Charlie, looking sideways at Marge, who seized the opportunity to inhale and throw her shoulders back, "I don't like to get mixed up in a kind of delicate matter like this, but you're all right—I guess."

"You *guess?* You blind or something? I was once runner-up for Miss Brooklyn, in case you don't happen to know, and where I missed out was on waistline, *not* on—"

Charlie said, "All right, all right. They're fine. Honest." He nodded vigorously in Botax's direction. "They're okay. I ain't that much of an expert, you understand, but they're okay by me."

Marge relaxed.

Botax felt relieved. He turned to Garm. "The bigger form expresses interest, Captain. The stimulus is working. Now for the final step."

"And what is that?"

"There is no flash for it, Captain. Essentially, it consists of placing the speaking-and-eating apparatus of one against the equivalent apparatus of the other. I have made up a flash for the process, thus: kiss."

"Will nausea never cease?" groaned the Captain.

"It is the climax. In all the tales, after the skins are removed by force, they clasp each other with limbs and indulge madly in burning kisses, to translate as nearly as possible the phrase most frequently used. Here is one example, just one, taken at random: 'He held the girl, his mouth avid on her lips.' "

"Maybe one creature was devouring the other," said the Captain.

"Not at all," said Botax impatiently. "Those were burning kisses."

"How do you mean, burning? Combustion takes place?"

"I don't think literally so. I imagine it is a way of expressing the fact that the temperature goes up. The higher the temperature, I suppose, the more successful the production of young. Now that the big form is properly stimulated, he need only place his mouth against her to produce young. The young will not be produced without that step. It is the cooperation I have been speaking of."

"That's all? Just this—" The Captain's hands made motions of coming together, but he could not bear to put the thought into flash form.

"That's all," said Botax. "In none of the tales, not even in 'Recreationlad,' have I found a description of any further physical activity in connection with young-bearing. Sometimes after the kissing, they write a line of symbols like little stars, but I suppose that merely means more kissing; one kiss for each star, when they wish to produce a multitude of young."

"Just one, please, right now."

"Certainly, Captain."

Botax said with grave distinctness, "Sir, would you kiss the lady?"

Charlie said, "Listen, I can't move."

"I will free you, of course."

"The lady might not like it."

Marge glowered. "You bet your damn boots I won't like it. You just stay away."

"I would like to, lady, but what do they do if I don't? Look, I don't want to get them mad. We can just—you know—make like a little peck."

She hesitated, seeing the justice of the caution. "All right. No funny stuff, though. I ain't in the habit of standing around like this in front of every Tom, Dick and Harry, you know."

"I know that, lady. It was none of my doing. You got to admit that."

Marge muttered angrily, "Regular slimy monsters. Must think they're some kind of gods or something, the way they order people around. Slime gods is what they are!"

Charlie approached her. "If it's okay now, lady." He made a vague motion as though to tip his hat. Then he put his hands awkwardly on her bare shoulders and leaned over in a gingerly pucker.

Marge's head stiffened so that lines appeared in her neck. Their lips met.

Captain Garm flashed fretfully. "I sense no rise in temperature." His heat-detecting tendril had risen to full extension at the top of his head and remained quivering there.

"I don't either," said Botax, rather at a loss, "but we're doing it just as the space travel stories tell us to. I think his limbs should be more extended— Ah, like that. See, it's working."

Almost absently, Charlie's arm had slid around Marge's soft, nude torso. For a moment, Marge seemed to yield against him and then she suddenly writhed hard against the pinioning field that still held her with fair firmness.

"Let go." The words were muffled against the pressure of Charlie's lips. She bit suddenly, and Charlie leaped away with a wild cry, holding his lower lip, then looking at his fingers for blood.

"What's the idea, lady?" he demanded plaintively.

She said, "We agreed just a peck, is all. What were you starting there? You some kind of playboy or something? What am I surrounded with here? Playboy and the slime gods?"

Captain Garm flashed rapid alternations of blue and yellow. "Is it done? How long do we wait now?"

"It seems to me it must happen at once. Throughout all the universe, when you have to bud, you bud, you know. There's no waiting."

"Yes? After thinking of the foul habits you have been describing, I don't think I'll ever bud again. Please get this over with."

"Just a moment, Captain."

But the moments passed and the Captain's flashes turned slowly to a brooding orange, while Botax's nearly dimmed out altogether.

Botax finally asked hesitantly, "Pardon me, madam, but when will you bud?"

"When will I *what?*"

"Bear young?"

"I've got a kid."

"I mean bear young now."

"I should say not. I ain't ready for another kid yet."

"What? What?" demanded the Captain. "What's she saying?"

"It seems," said Botax, "she does not intend to have young at the moment."

The Captain's color patch blazed brightly. "Do you know what I think, Investigator? I think you have a sick, perverted mind. Nothing's happening to these creatures. There is no cooperation between them, and no young to be borne. I think they're two different species and that you're playing some kind of foolish game with me."

"But, Captain—" said Botax.

"Don't but Captain me," said Garm. "I've had enough. You've upset me, turned my stomach, nauseated me, disgusted me with the whole notion of budding and wasted my time. You're just looking for headlines and personal glory and I'll see to it that you don't get them. Get rid of these creatures now. Give that one its skins back and put them back where you found them. I ought to take the expense of maintaining Time-stasis all this time out of your salary."

"But, Captain—"

"Back, I say. Put them back in the same place and at the same instant of time. I want this planet untouched, and I'll see to it that it stays untouched." He cast one more furious glance at Botax. "One species, two forms, bosoms, kisses, cooperation. BAH— You are a fool, Investigator, a dolt as well and, most of all, a sick, sick, sick creature."

There was no arguing. Botax, limbs trembling, set about returning the creatures.

\*     \*     \*

They stood there in the elevated station, looking around wildly. It was twilight over them, and the approaching train was just making itself known as a faint rumble in the distance.

Marge said, hesitantly, "Mister, did it really happen?"

Charlie nodded. "I remember it."

Marge said, "We can't tell anybody."

"Sure not. They'd say we was nuts. Know what I mean?"

"Uh-huh. Well." She edged away.

Charlie said, "Listen. I'm sorry you was embarrassed. It was none of my doing."

"That's all right. I know." Marge's eyes considered the wooden platform at her feet. The sound of the train was louder.

"I mean, you know, lady, you wasn't really bad. In fact, you looked good, but I was kind of embarrassed to say that."

Suddenly, she smiled. "It's all right."

"You want maybe to have a cup of coffee with me just to relax you? My wife, she's not really expecting me for a while."

"Oh? Well, Ed's out of town for the weekend so I got only an empty apartment to go home to. My little boy is visiting at my mother's," she explained.

"Come on, then. We been kind of introduced."

"I'll say." She laughed.

The train pulled in, but they turned away, walking down the narrow stairway to the street.

They had a couple of cocktails actually, and then Charlie couldn't let her go home in the dark alone, so he saw her to her door. Marge was bound to invite him in for a few moments, naturally.

Meanwhile, back in the spaceship, the crushed Botax was making a final effort to prove his case. While Garm prepared the ship for departure Botax hastily set up the tight-beam visiscreen for a last look at his specimens. He focused in on Charlie and Marge in her apartment. His tendril stiffened and he began flashing in a coruscating rainbow of colors.

"Captain Garm! Captain! Look what they're doing now!"

But at that very instant the ship winked out of Time-stasis.

*Algis Budrys has been an author, editor, critic, and college instructor, with a record of over 100 science fiction stories and ten books to his credit. Perhaps his most famous work is* Rogue Moon *(1960), a multileveled story of teleportational exploration, but he has also won the Mystery Writers' Edgar Award for the best short crime story of 1966. One of his greatest strengths is an ability to create believable people such as the farmer who is faced with a terrible choice in the following story.*

# PAGAN

## By Algis Budrys

The big thing howled out of the sky, burst the tops of the oaks into flame, and thundered into the south range of Colpaugh's farm with a sound like a dynamited vault. The oaks tore themselves out of the heaving ground and toppled on their sides, ripping through the underbrush, smoking with the aftermath of fires that had been blown out an eye-blink after they started. The range feedshed, buttressed by the hundred-pound sacks of mash that filled it from wall to wall, resisted being swept away in a body. It flew into a thousand discontinuous fragments of wood that flaked away into the air as though the feedbags had shucked off a tattered overcoat. The bags held out a fraction longer. Then they burst, and a spume of yellow-white dust erupted away from the impact locus and boiled out across the farm.

There had been four chicken shelters spotted on the range. One of them was smashed into the ground ahead of the big thing. The other three were flipped into the air, caught like sails, and hurled away, streaming the singed bodies of leg-horn pullets out behind them. There was one brief wail from the thousands of laying hens in their lines of coops. Then the radiating wave tore against the basically flimsy structures and eddied them away like rows of horrified fubbish mounting a beach.

The main house was two hundred yards away. In order to reach it, the compression wave had to first demolish the tool shed and the garage with the three-quarter-ton pickup truck in it, the main feedhouse, and the battery house where the newly hatched chicks were developing in their electrically warmed brooders. The two-and-one-half-ton truck, loaded, stood in the yard. That, the battery house, and the feedhouse deflected much of the blast.

The lights went out, and Colpaugh was showered with broken glass. Pipes snapped, and there was a gush of water before the tank upstairs was ripped away from the rest of the plumbing. There was a splintering chop, and the house slewed on its foundations and fell out of plumb. Upstairs, where a wall had been removed to make one large bedroom out of two, the roof first rose, then caved in. All the beams were cracked. The first-floor ceilings bulged downward.

Silence.

Colpaugh gulped air down his dry mouth. He got one foot under himself, threw the weight of something off his shoulders, and stood up.

"Mary?"

"George . . . George, I—"

He lurched awkwardly into the parlor, fighting the slope of the floor, the darkness, and the debris. His wife was a groping shape in front of him. He struck a match, and her eyes reflected blankly. "Are the children all right?"

He looked around, then turned and made his way into the living room. The TV set lay on its side, its face in shards. He flipped the match away from his scorching fingertips and struck another. The two children were huddled on the floor. As he bent over and touched them urgently, the boy began to cry. The girl threw her arms around her brother and clutched him.

"You kids O.K.? Come on now, it's all over—you both all right?"

The children clasped each other, both of them sobbing now. Colpaugh heard his wife behind him. He got back to his feet and turned to her. "I guess they're all right. Take care of 'em. And get 'em out of the house. Might collapse."

"Where are you going?"

"Outside. Got to see what that was."

"George, stay here!"

"Mary, you take your hand off my arm. I dunno what that was, but I gotta find out. Wasn't any explosion. Might have been a plane. Now take care of the kids and wait for me in the yard."

He pushed his way through the tangle of furniture in the dining room, got through the kitchen, and yanked open the door of the closet on the enclosed back porch. He took down his big flashlight, turned away, and turned back.

No, he thought. No, that wasn't any plane. It was too big. Even a B-36 wouldn't do something like this. How did he know? Had he ever been near a B-36 crash? No.

But it wasn't right. It wasn't right, and that's all there was to it.

He picked up his shotgun, loaded it, and dropped some extra shells in his pocket. He felt a little silly, and that made him hold the gun even more aggressively. He found an opening in the tangle of boards that had become the wall of the porch, cut himself climbing through a nest of window glass, and realized he was bleeding from a dozen superficial cuts. He let them be.

The yard had been scoured clean. He noticed that—the absolutely hard-packed clay without its cover of looser sand—before he really registered the change in what had been a familiar scene. He was not ready to believe he could look out to the south range from his back stoop. There was a hump and tangle in front of him where the main feedhouse had been, but he could see over that, now.

He could see into the center of the south range, where something that was big and glowing thrust out of the crater its nose had splashed out of the soil. There was a circle of darkness in the glow, and then there was a beam of violet light probing up out of that circle, which was a doorway. Something gray and lumpy moved in the doorway.

Colpaugh felt a tugging at the skin of his jaw. It was a corner of his mouth, moving down into an ugly snarl.

Inside the big thing, there was a mechanical humming. A metal spar telescoped into the air through the doorway and silhouetted itself against the stars. The violet beam, twitching from side to side, touched it briefly. Colpaugh saw a subsidiary arm on the spar begin to revolve, glinting with a blue-white cat's-eye glowing of its own. A high-pitched, pinging sound came from it at regular intervals. There were other things, like leaves and thorns, sprouting from the metal stalk.

A steady, thrumming undertone of vibration began to mutter against Colpaugh's eardrums. He flipped the safety catch on the shotgun and moved forward.

The gray, lumpy thing that had moved in the doorway's mouth now lowered itself to the ground. It looked like a nine-foot man who had been attacked by some fungoid disease which had thickened his limbs and torso unevenly, and made a puffy lump of his head. It moved stiffly and slowly, advancing with ponderous hesitation, like a diver underwater. It was walking toward Colpaugh.

Colpaugh scurried across the yard and behind the twisted wreck of the big truck. He crouched, brought the gun up to his shoulder, and waited. He realized he was breathing in convulsive, nervous gasps, but that hardly seemed important.

It took the thing about five minutes to get abreast of the wrecked feedhouse. Colpaugh waited, motionless, listening to the sound it was making. It was something like a wheeze, or a grunt of extreme effort. It came at intervals, a "*huh* . . . hoh . . . *huh!*" of exhalation.

Mary and the children climbed out through the broken timbers of the back porch. Mary looked around, failed to see anything in the shadows, and called: "George! George, where are you?"

Colpaugh's throat froze. He strangled on a shout, producing nothing more than a husky croak. The thing was suddenly moving very fast, laboring with what was obviously supreme effort, but closing in on Mary and the children.

Colpaugh finally got it out, like a man in a nightmare: "*Mary!* Mary, look *out!*" and he jumped from behind the truck, into the thing's path.

There was no more than a yard between them. He fired

both barrels into the monster's stomach, stumbling backward from the recoil.

The monster grunted, "*Hunh!*" Then it swung one arm out like a clumsy club that crashed against the side of Colpaugh's head with an impact that was not spongy at all.

As he fell, the shotgun flying away from him, he heard Mary screaming behind him, but he was losing consciousness.

"Hey! Hey, mister!"

Colpaugh sobbed a breath into his lungs, thrashed over on his back, and looked up. A man with a steel helmet on his head was squatted down beside him. The barrel of a carbine stuck up over one shoulder, and there were other men behind him, but it was too dark to make out many details.

"Wha—?"

"Keep it low, Mac." A hand covered his mouth momentarily. "My name's Dugan. Lieutenant, National Guard. What's out in that field?"

"It's a range."

"Huh?"

"A range. You keep pullets on it during the summer."

He sat up suddenly, throwing the lieutenant off balance and sprawling him out. "*Where's my wife?*"

"Huh? Wife? Your wife out here with you?"

Colpaugh was looking around urgently. "The kids, too." He realized what had happened and jumped to his feet. "The thing got 'em!"

The lieutenant scrambled up. "*Keep it low!*" he whispered urgently.

Colpaugh shook him off and searched for his shotgun. He remembered where it must have fallen and, on his hands and knees, began feeling the ground. The lieutenant stopped him only by grabbing his shoulder and refusing to let go.

"Now, look here, Mac, maybe you know what you're doing, but nobody else does. So suppose you hold off for a minute and fill me in. Whatever's happened to your wife and kids will get fixed that much faster if we can help you."

Colpaugh touched the gun's stock, lunged forward against the restraint of the lieutenant's hand, and clutched it. He sat down, broke it, extracted the empty shells, and reloaded. Between motions, he grunted out his explanation.

The lieutenant whistled. "You put two loads of buckshot in his middle and he just grunted?"

Colpaugh stopped short and looked down at his shotgun. "That's right," he said wonderingly, "I did, didn't I?" He let the gun slide off his lap.

"Look, about your wife and kids—"

"What?"

"We didn't know what to expect here," the lieutenant pressed on, patiently. "All we knew was a . . . call it a flying saucer . . . came down and crashed. It was tracked for about a half hour before it hit, and we were heading here without waiting for any more news. So when we pulled into your yard, and I saw you lying there, I ran over. Right away. For all we know, your wife and kids might have run away from the thing—or maybe it's lying around here somewhere, dead. Could be, you know. I'll check. You stay right here."

Colpaugh looked at him woodenly. "How come you believed me, if you didn't find them?"

The lieutenant grunted. "Take a look over into the field— the range."

Colpaugh turned his head that way for the first time since he'd been shaken awake.

The big thing still loomed up against the stars. The doorway was closed. At any rate, it looked closed. There was no longer any circle of darkness, because the big thing wasn't glowing any more. The metal spar was gone. But there was a row of lights, like portholes, and the lights dimmed occasionally, as though something was moving back and forth just behind the portholes.

"Lieutenant . . . Lieutenant, sir!"

The lieutenant cursed and whispered hoarsely back into the darkness. "Keep it down! I'm over here."

A soldier trotted up. "Sorry, sir. We found something."

A shower of ice fell into Colpaugh's stomach.

"Well?" the lieutenant asked.

"Sir, Lewicki's down by the field the thing's in, with the camera. He's been followin' these drag marks—you know, sir, like somethin' got dragged—like a cloth bag, maybe. Anyway, sir, he just passed the word back he's found a woman's shoe."

"Smoke?"

Colpaugh shook his head. He sat twisted in the jeep's seat, his head rigid, except for the one, brief, emphatic, numb motion.

"Look—it might not be the best thing in the world for you to keep watching that screen."

Colpaugh ignored him.

The soldier had moved his camera in beside the big thing, and pointed it at what seemed to be the main porthole. Inside, the big thing was full of metal fixtures that glittered oddly in the violet-tinged light. There were machines and controls of all kinds that meant nothing to Colpaugh.

This was the only camera feeding in to this screen. There were others handling the traffic into Gustafsen's farmhouse, back across the road, where the big brass had set up headquarters. The lieutenant now only had charge of this small part of what had become a full-fledged perimeter. There was a helicopter patrol over the big thing, and a flight of jet fighter-bombers up above them. Colpaugh realized he was probably the only unevacuated civilian in the whole county.

None of it was doing any good, though. The big thing just lay out in the range, without doing anything.

If the brass back in Gustafsen's house had seen anything of Mary and the kids through their cameras, they hadn't passed word down to Colpaugh, and they hadn't showed up in the compartment covered by the jeep's camera.

Colpaugh realized he was shivering. It was pretty cold.

The monster had moved in and out of camera range several times. At least, everybody figured it was the same one, because they'd seen only one, and it was definite, now, that Colpaugh's shots hadn't kept it from getting back to its ship.

Ship, Colpaugh reminded himself. They're calling it a ship, now. From *where?*

The monster was back on the screen. Dimly, Colpaugh felt the ache in his teeth as his jaws closed down.

It didn't act hurt. That was pretty much taken for granted now. Colpaugh tried to figure out what could stand up to two barrels of buckshot at a range of one yard, but you couldn't get very far with that kind of question. You just let it lay.

It moved a lot easier inside its ship. There didn't seem to be anything like the slowness it had out in the open. It was moving back and forth across the compartment, fiddling with things. It looked like it was setting up some kind of machine.

Colpaugh heard the lieutenant speaking into a microphone, and there were creaks and clicks all around him as the soldiers got set in case something new happened. Colpaugh didn't take his eyes off the screen.

The monster went out of the compartment and brought in the boy, who looked sleepy and dazed. The monster was holding him by one arm. A table unfolded out of the wall, and the monster laid the boy down on it. He swung a projector out from a stand, focused it on the boy, and moved a broad, splay-fingered hand over its controls. A beam of red light, sparkling with an internal stream of silvery motes, struck the boy in the face.

Colpaugh was vaguely aware that there was blood running down his fingers. The lieutenant took an instant to punch his hand loose from its death-grip on the sharp angle of the seat brace before he began barking orders into his microphone. Presumably, he'd gotten orders of his own through the earphones on his head.

The boy began to change.

A spotlight hit the ship's air lock, and a dozen soldiers sprang up from the soil below it and began attacking it with power tools. Other lights cut in, until the big thing was clearly lighted throughout its exposed length, gleaming harshly in the shadowless illumination.

The soldiers rebounded, the tools flying out of their hands. The men sprawled briefly in the air, then fell bonelessly.

A hell of small-arms' fire concentrated on the air lock, and a grenade bounced up against the hull. The streams of tracer arced over the ship, and the grenade failed to explode. The light faded down through yellow and died. Technicians began yelling to each other, but the lights did not come on again. All the guns jammed.

Colpaugh got one last look at the television screen before it, too, contracted to a vanishing pinpoint and went out.

He began to scream and kick the splintering panel.

"All right, now?"

The lieutenant was bending over him. A medical corpsman withdrew his hypodermic and closed Colpaugh's unresisting fingers over a dab of cotton. "Hold that there for a minute, please," he said. Colpaugh let it slip out from under his fingers, and the corpsman pressed a new one over the puncture. "Now, *hold* it there, Mac," he said, but it didn't do any good. The corpsman, instead of getting annoyed, nodded to himself, refilled his syringe, and gave Colpaugh another shot.

"Funny," Colpaugh muttered. "You take a kid . . . good-lookin' kid . . . raised him . . . gave him the best I could . . . and just like that, you squirt him with a little red light and he changes into a monster." He scratched his head fuzzily, looked at his fingers, saw his palm was bandaged, grinned apologetically at the lieutenant, and shrugged. "Must be a pretty smart monster . . . I mean the first one, not the new one . . . to do a thing like that. Just a little red light, and it's like bread dough standing on the radiator with the yeast working."

"Yeah," the lieutenant said shortly. He looked quickly at the corpsman, and the corpsman shrugged.

"Look, Colpaugh," the lieutenant went on, "we're pulling out. Nobody knows what's going on any more. None of the equipment works. We're losing men, too—they're fighting each other with their bayonets. Everybody's seeing monsters in the shadows. I just got word from a runner. They're going to drop a pony bomb. We're all pulling back on foot—they're giving us an hour to get back and dig in. So come on. Think you can walk?"

Colpaugh sighed. "I don't know," he said. "I mean, I guess so. I mean, if you can't ride, well, I guess you have to walk, don't you?"

"I guess so," the lieutenant agreed uncomfortably. He and the corpsman lifted Colpaugh out of the jeep and stood him on his feet. Colpaugh twisted his head uneasily. "It's still dark."

"It's only about midnight, or maybe one," the lieutenant explained.

"Funny."

"Uh-huh. Now, come on, Colpaugh, we've got to get clear before that bomb comes down. They're not going to hold it up for any stragglers."

"Well, well, sure, lieutenant, that makes sense." He began to walk along between the officer and the corpsman. "I guess we kind of have to give up on Mary and the girl, don't we?"

The lieutenant nodded dimly in the darkness.

Colpaugh nodded too, in affirmation. "It's O.K., lieutenant. I mean, you can't expect to . . . to—" He began to gulp for air as the tears ran down his cheeks. "It just doesn't balance. A chance of maybe doin' something—well, you've *got* to drop the bomb, that's all!"

Very dimly, through the night between him and the completely darkened ship, he heard a voice calling him.

"George! George, are you still out there?"

He stopped convulsively, the lieutenant spinning around with him. "Who is that?"

Colpaugh strained. "I . . . sounds like . . . like Mary."

"George!" The voice was a little louder.

The corpsman had stopped with them. "Might be one of the men, checking for his buddy," he pointed out. "George isn't an uncommon name."

Colpaugh shook his head. "No. Shut up."

"George! I'm over behind the feedhouse. I've got to talk to you."

The lieutenant clamped his hand around his arm. "Easy, Colpaugh. Easy. Very easy. Might be a booby trap."

"That's Mary!" Colpaugh whispered harshly.

"You don't know that."

"Think I don't know my wife's voice?"

"Yes, but—"

"George, *please!*"


Colpaugh rammed his hand into the lieutenant's face, twisted away, and ran toward the ruined feedhouse. He wasn't sure whether the lieutenant was following him or not.

He was grunting as he ran, and he realized that what he was mumbling was, "Mary, Mary, Mary, Mary," over and over again. As he got to the feedhouse, he shouted it aloud: "Mary! Where're you at?"

"Stay there a minute, George," she said. "I'm over here on the other side."

"Well, I'm coming over there!" What was she playing around for?

"No, George—not yet. You shouldn't."

He knew his wife. When she said it like that, she had a very good reason.

Maybe the monster was holding her there?

"You all right, Mary?"

"*Yes,* George. Yes, I'm fine. Now, George, I want you to just listen to what I've got to say. Promise me that?"

"Sure."

"And you won't try to come over here before I'm finished?"

"Not if you don't want me to." He twisted his lips in discomfort. There was something wrong that he couldn't figure out. Something he ought to be smart enough to know. He tried to pick at it, but he couldn't. He was too mixed up. Somebody else, now, might be able to. But he wasn't somebody else. He was George Colpaugh, and this was his wife, and he didn't know what to do.

What about their daughter?

"How's Peggy?"

"Peggy's fine," Mary said impatiently. "She's with me. Now, listen, George, please. We're short for time."

So the girl was all right. At least it sounded like she was all right. He tried to see into the shadows, but the broken feedhouse was too complex a shape of darkness for anything else to show up against it.

"George, you're all wrong about the Ond."

"The who?"

"The Ond. The . . . monster, I guess you're calling him. The soldiers are all wrong too, not just you."

"Wrong? What d'you mean, wrong? We all saw what he did to Jimmy. He dragged him into that ship thing of his and he— Don't you know what he did?"

Mary didn't say anything for a minute. "Yes, I know, George," she answered finally. "But there's no use talking about that now. There's something more important."

"What's more important than that?" he demanded loudly.

"*George!* He's my son, too. I didn't answer you lightly. There *is* something more important than that. Why do you think the Ond came here at all? He can't even stay outside his ship very long in our air, and he doesn't have much chance of ever getting back to where he lives. And he knew all that before he came here."

Colpaugh took a deep, angry breath. "I'm not much on knowing what makes monsters tick."

"No, George," Mary agreed sadly. "I don't guess anybody is. But he's good, George. He was willing to come here because he believed in what he was doing—because he knew that his people had something every living person has a right to—because he felt it was his duty. It takes somebody pretty special to do a thing like that."

"Yeah, it takes somebody pretty special to do what he did to Jim, all right."

"Stop that, George!"

"Colpaugh!" It was the lieutenant, shouting from behind the overturned two-and-one-half-ton truck. "You've got to get out of here—if you're still able."

Colpaugh jerked his head toward the sound.

"Don't listen to him, George. You don't have the time."

"Mary! We're *all* running out of time!" Colpaugh shouted, suddenly remembering. "They're going to drop an atom bomb."

Mary sighed. "It won't go off. Things like that don't work if you've got what the Ond's got."

"What's that?" Colpaugh growled.

"It's a . . . well, it's like being tuned in. There's a power . . . a . . . a something that's all around us, wherever we are, and if you know the right ways to get to it, it'll protect you and do things for you—George, I can't describe it in the words we're used to. But if you know how to get to it, you never die, and you're never hungry or thirsty or sleepy. You're never tired, and—George, I *can't* really tell you about it. But will you trust me? Will you have faith in me and come with me and Peggy and share it? The Ond's going to show everybody in the world how to get to the power. It would be nice if our whole family was the first."

What did she mean "our *whole* family"? What about Jim?

"Mary, I've had about as much of this mysterious stuff as I'm going to take. Now I'm coming over to where you are."

"*No*, George! There's still one thing, about me—"

Colpaugh moved forward. He rounded the heap of timber, peering into the shadows.

There was a big one, and a little one beside it, standing there, waiting for him. Peggy said, "Please come with us, Daddy."

He stumbled back, realizing that he should have known— that this was where he'd been stupid.

He'd let Mary get too close.

"George . . . George, will you come with us?"

He kicked the big one where its knee should have been, because the little one was close, too. The big one stumbled a little, but the little one got its hands around his upper right arm.

"Please, Daddy—we don't *want* to make you!"

He screamed hoarsely and twisted, frantic and gasping, away from its touch. At that moment he felt the bone snap.

"Hang on, Colpaugh!" the lieutenant yelled, and jumped the big one from behind. Mary whirled and tried to knock him away, and her talons caught him across the eyes. The lieutenant fell back, his hands over his face.

But that was Colpaugh's chance. He flung himself at the

big one's midsection and toppled it off balance. He grabbed the lieutenant's forearm. "Come on!" he grunted. "Come on, run!"

Colpaugh and the lieutenant stumbled up the road, helping each other along. Colpaugh kept his left hand under his right elbow, and it wasn't too bad, except that the lieutenant couldn't help jostling him once in a while.

"How's the eye?" Colpaugh asked.

"I don't know. Think they're still chasing us? They're pretty fast. I guess they're a special brand—adapted to Earth."

Colpaugh shook his head. "I guess they figure if I won't join 'em of my own free will, they'll wait until they get me in a roundup."

"You figure they can do that? Just have drives and herd people up in bunches?"

"They'll catch a few here and there to begin with, I guess. When there's enough of them, they'll set up a system for doing it in big bunches. Doesn't take a lot of help to drive chickens where you want them."

"Maybe she was lying about that power?" the lieutenant said.

"Maybe. But I put two loads of buckshot in that first one. And all the lights and guns wouldn't work. I don't think that bomb's going to go off."

"Then what're we bothering to run for?"

Colpaugh shook his head. "I don't know," he said dully. "If Mary was telling the truth, there's nothing to stop them from doing anything they please."

They moved on silently for a few minutes. Then the lieutenant said hesitantly: "Look—I'm out of line, saying this, but allowing she was telling the truth, that doesn't really sound like too bad a deal. If tuning in on that power gives you all of those things . . . well, to tell you the truth, Colpaugh, you're in rotten shape. A few hours ago, you had a farm, a wife, two kids, and a future. Now you've got nothing—you've got the clothes on your back, and nothing else. You need hospitalization, but you probably won't get it. And a month, or six months, from now, you'll be one of them anyway. Man, I'm a hundred times better off than you are, and I can feel the temptation myself.

"They're your wife and kids, Colpaugh."

"They've been changed," Colpaugh mumbled.

"Well, even so, what I'm trying to say," the lieutenant went on uncomfortably, "I don't suppose it's bad, once you're like them. There's probably good sense to the way they're built. If they don't eat or drink, maybe that skin of theirs is designed to soak up energy, or something. And they're going to get us all in the end, anyway. And, let's face it—isn't what they're offering what everybody's always wanted? Think about it, Colpaugh—here you are, half-dead from one shock reaction after another, nothing to look forward to—all you have to do to fix everything, even get your family back—is turn around and walk back to the ship."

Colpaugh stopped, turned his head painfully, and looked back down the road through his haggard eyes.

"Makes sense, doesn't it?" he mumbled. "Back there's security, rest, and I guess you could call it food and drink. Back there's my wife, my kids, and my home. If I keep going, I'll be alone—no friends, no love, and maybe gangrene. Gangrene's no way to die."

He looked at the lieutenant. "What about you? How come you're willing for me to go back, but you want to keep going—and if we both expect a mess big enough so an ordinary compound fracture can't get tended to, what's the say about your eye?"

The lieutenant looked down at the road.

"No, tell me," Colpaugh said. "Don't duck it. How come you can be sensible about me, but not you? Why won't you go back?"

The lieutenant licked his lips and slowly raised his head. "They'd change me."

Colpaugh managed a dry, crooked grin. "Uh-huh."

They went on in the direction they'd been going.

A. Bertram Chandler was born in Britain and spent many years at sea in the merchant navies of England, New Zealand, and Australia. Now an Australian citizen, he has written over 150 stories and 20 books of science fiction. He is most noted for his interstellar stories of the rim worlds, but in the following earthbound tale, he presents a brief history of saucer books and suggests an explanation for their differences.

# THE BEHOLDERS

## by A. BERTRAM CHANDLER

"There is *something* behind the flying saucer stories," said Manderley. "Not all of them, I grant you that. I am willing to admit the usual quota of motor car headlights reflected from low clouds met balloons and, even, Venus at her brightest. I could tell you a true story about *that*—the officers of a large transport that had got out of Singapore one jump ahead of the Japanese saw Venus during the day, at about eleven o'clock in the morning, through a break in the clouds, and assumed that it was a Japanese observation balloon or blimp. Then the panic started.

"Anyhow," Manderley started ticking off his points on the fingers of his right hand, "we know this much about the saucers. Firstly—they can be seen. Secondly—they can be photographed. Thirdly—they can be picked up by radar.

Fourthly—they've been knocking around for one helluva long time."

"And *that*," said Scrivens, "is the weak point in your arguments. They have been knocking around a long time. You've read Charles Fort, as we all have, and you know that his books are full of accounts of strange lights in the sky way back in the nineteenth century, and before. These lights in the sky have been knocking around for a long time. In the days before flying they were assumed by the credulous to be of supernatural origin. When Man first took to the air, they were assumed to be big dirigible airships on secret trials. In these days, when space travel is just around the corner, they are assumed to be spaceships manned by extraterrans. And here's a rather interesting point—some observers see them as 'saucers'—just because they are so conditioned by the word itself—others, notably airline pilots and the like—see them as fairly conventional rocket ships. But it all boils down to this. Somebody—he may be a country bumpkin, he may be a 'trained observer'—sees a light in the sky that he cannot account for. His imagination goes to work. If he knows nothing of astronautics he sees a huge, spinning disc. If he has read a few articles on rocketry he sees a rocket."

"That BOAC airliner captain didn't see either," Manderley pointed out. "Too—he saw his saucers by daylight. And they were neither flying discs nor rockets—they were changing shape the whole time."

"Clouds," said Scrivens. "Or some sort of mirage—a distorted reflection, possibly, of his own aircraft."

"Your trouble," said Manderley, "is that you can't forget that you're a past president of the Astronautics Society, that you've made your name (and your living) writing books—and good ones, I admit—on rocketry. You've got to the stage where you neither would nor could believe in a spaceship unless (a) it were a rocket and (b) had been designed by the bright boys of the Society . . ."

"*Your* trouble, Bill," replied Scrivens, "is that you aren't a *real* science fiction writer. You've always tended towards fantasy. You've always hankered after the rich and strange—and when science gets in the way . . . well, it's just too bad for science."

"Fantasy *does* become science eventually," said Manderley. "What about Rhine, and psionics?"

"Psionics is not a science—yet. But you're very silent, Susan. What are your views on the flying saucers?"

His hostess smiled.

"Am I supposed to have any, Arthur? You and Bill are the science fiction writers—and if I hadn't met Bill I'd never have known that such a thing as science fiction existed."

"If you'd never met Bill you'd still have read about flying saucers," said Scrivens. "For the purposes of this argument you're the intelligent laywoman. Bill and I both have a certain bias. You haven't. What *are* your views?"

"Well," she said, "I've read Adamski's first book, and I've read Allingham's book . . ."

"Bill," cried Scrivens, "don't you supervise this woman's reading?"

"Bill got the books," said Susan Manderley.

"From the library," said her husband. "I had no intention of buying them. I wanted to read 'em myself—out of curiosity."

"All right, you read 'em," said Scrivens. "It can't be helped now. What did you make of them?"

"This is going to hurt," said Susan. "Bill's not the only writer in the family—I've done my share, you know. I can recognize sincerity when I see it, when I read it. I'm quite convinced that both Adamski and Allingham *did* meet the men from the flying saucers."

"Susan!" cried Manderley. "You can't say that!"

"Can't I?" she asked sweetly. "I am saying it."

"But the absurdity of it all. Just consider the facts—the biological facts. Life on this world has evolved to suit Earthly conditions. Allingham's saucermen were, according to Allingham, Martians—yet they were, according to Allingham, human. Just consider the inferior mass of Mars, the thin atmosphere, the aridity. Intelligent life *may* have evolved—but it'd be something suited to those conditions. Adamski's saucermen—and women—came from Venus. We don't know much about conditions there—but they will, certainly, be wildly dissimilar from those on Earth. Life will have evolved to suit *those* conditions."

"There was that other crank in the U.S.A.," said Scrivens, "who started the story about the little men—but *men*, mark you—three feet tall who were found in a crashed saucer."

"All right," said the girl. "You write about Martians and Venusians, don't you? All right, Arthur—I'll let *you* off. The only Martians and Venusians in *your* stories are the descendants of the original Earth colonists. But you, Bill, have a decided fancy for Venusians built on the same lines as Disney's almost-human frogs. And I seem to remember that you peopled Mars with an intelligent plant. Don't argue—you did. Are your frogmen any more probable than Adamski's Venusians? Is your thinking Virginia creeper any more likely than Allingham's Martians?" She was warming up nicely. "The whole damn trouble with you science fiction writers (I didn't know the breed until I married one) is that you think that you *know*. Oh, you read reference books—I admit that. You read Hoyle's latest book on astronomy, and you're very impressed by his theories, especially those about Venus. I remember that you bored me with a long dissertation about the—according to Hoyle—seas of mineral oil and clouds of oily smog. Yet you still make Venus a lush, watery, jungly sort of world in your stories—and you will do so until you get round to writing a story about a line of interplanetary oil tankers. The same with Mars—you just *love* the canals. It doesn't matter if they were dug by that highly improbable intelligent plant of yours, or by some long-dead race who left all sorts of intriguing artifacts and ruins behind 'em—but canals you must have. Yet, when somebody like Adamski or Allingham flouts *your* conventions you're up in arms against him."

"You'll be saying that you believe *Worlds in Collision* next," sneered Manderley.

"And why shouldn't I if I want to?"

"Why not, darling? You read it in *The Reader's Digest,* so it must be true." He turned to Scrivens. "How any intelligent woman can read that rag just beats me."

"I could make a few remarks about *your* reading habits," said Susan. "The magazines that you bring home with half-undressed females sprawled all over the front cover and at least half the inside pages!"

"Research," said her husband. "Research."

"Research be damned. You're just a dirty old man before your time. If you took as much interest . . ." She broke off suddenly. "I don't know what you think of us, Arthur."

"And it all started with flying saucers," he grinned. "It's a good job we're drinking sherry and not tea—otherwise there might be some *real* flying saucers!"

It was a feeble joke, but it eased the tension. Scrivens looked at his watch.

"We said we'd be out at Keith's by seven-thirty," he said. "We'd better get moving."

Susan sat in the front seat with Scrivens. Manderley, sitting by himself at the back, was inclined to sulk. This, he thought, is a habit of which I shall have to cure myself. Yet—let us face the facts—things aren't what they were between Susan and myself. Not in any way. We've gone off the rails somewhere. Our dreams just haven't come true. Tonight's silly quarrel was symptomatic of what is happening—this flaring up over an absurd thing like a discussion of flying saucers. . . .

He stared out of the window at the countryside through which they were passing. He forced his thoughts away from the morbidly subjective channel that they had been following. He thought, There is not much traffic out tonight.

The evening was fine and clear. Low in the west hung a crescent moon with, just above it, the shimmering point of light that was Venus. The trees were black silhouettes against the pale, but darkening, blue of the sky.

But Venus is a morning star at this time of the year, thought Manderley. That's not Venus. And it's moving. . . . An airplane? No, it can't be. . . .

"Arthur," he said suddenly, "you're in the know. *Has* anybody put up an artificial satellite yet?"

"No, although we don't really know what's going on behind the Iron Curtain. Why?"

"What's that thing in the sky, then? Above the new moon and a little to the right . . . coming this way . . ."

Scrivens stopped the car suddenly.

"This," he said tensely, "we must see. God, what I'd give for a camera! But note every detail, both of you! Every detail!"

"I can hear it now," said Manderley. "A humming noise, like a giant bee . . ."

"No," Scrivens contradicted him. "That's rocket drive. You could never mistake that peculiar, screaming roar for anything else."

"I can't hear anything," said the girl.

The thing was approaching fast. Manderley strained his eyes, began to make out details. He saw the gleaming, lenticulate hull, rimmed with pale fire, and, as it tilted for the descent, the dome on top of it that must house the control room. The thing was flying low, and it was huge, and as it swept directly overhead it blotted out the sky. Silently it landed behind the car, blocking the road and crushing the hedges on either side of it.

"What do we do now?" asked Manderley. "Drive like hell to the nearest town, make our report and get ourselves laughed at by the whole world, and especially by those in the same trade as ourselves?"

"I'm getting out of the car," said Scrivens. "I want to meet whoever—or whatever—is piloting this thing."

"Is this wise?" asked Susan.

"As wise as running away would be—wiser perhaps."

"I'm coming with you," said Manderley. To his wife he said, "Stay in the car. If any sort of hell starts popping—get out of here fast!"

"What do you take me for?" she demanded. There was a flash of shapely legs as she eased herself from the seat, then she was standing on the road with the two men.

Manderley didn't see any door open in the side of the saucer—yet, suddenly, standing on the road and facing them was a being. He could not be sure of its actual shape—it was encased in a dull-gleaming armor with an opaque, featureless helmet that must be, Manderley decided, a spacesuit. It stood, as it were, on a tripod—was the third limb another leg, or a tail like that of a kangaroo?

Inside his head a voice was speaking.

*We come in peace. We are from the fourth planet of the sun that you call Antares. We have been seeking for a suitable ambassador, one of your species, who can represent us on this planet.*

"But I'm not qualified," said Manderley aloud.

*You are. You are not a scientist—yet you know something of science. And you have imagination.*

Manderley glanced at the others.

Scrivens, he saw to his amazement, was talking too. He listened to the incredible words.

"Of course I shall do my best to have the fault in your rocket motors repaired—I'm not without influence, you know. Payment? Well—if you insist . . . a trip to the Moon and back . . ."

The voice in Manderley's mind, the voice that had been speaking with such clarity, died to a mumble. He looked at his wife. She was not speaking, but her lips were parted, and there was a look on her face that he had not seen for a long time, for too long a time. He saw her step forward, her arms open to embrace the being in the spacesuit.

Manderley shouted. He caught the girl with his left hand, flung her behind him. With his right fist he swung a blow at the helmeted head. But he met no resistance, and the impetus of his action sent him sprawling on to the roadway. Dimly he was aware that his wife was kneeling beside him, dimly he was aware that the saucer had lifted, was hanging above them. He tensed his body for the killing impact of whatever sort of weapon the aliens might use.

They were helping him to his feet then—Scrivens and Susan. Scrivens was furious. He pointed a shaking hand to where the strange visitant was now no more than a fainter star among the faint stars, a tiny, drifting speck of light vanishing in the vast reaches of the darkling sky.

"What did you think you were doing?" he shouted. "So much we might have learned! The secrets of space travel within our grasp—and you had to attack an inoffensive being half your size and frighten him away!"

"Not so fast," said Manderley. "Tell me—what did you see? What did *you* hear?"

"A rocket, of course. A big rocket. An airlock door on its side opened, and a man—I'll call him that—came out. He was about three feet tall, and heavily furred (I don't think it was clothing). He had a face rather like that of a wise cat. He seemed to be feeling the heat rather badly and was having trouble with his breathing. He communicated by some form of telepathy, and told me that he was the captain of the first rocket from Mars to Earth, and that he had not intended to make a landing but that the rocket motors were giving trouble. He asked our help in repairing them."

"A rocket . . ." said Manderley. "Then why weren't we incinerated when it took off? Look at the asphalt of the road—unmarked!"

"You're right. What did *you* see?"

"A saucer. A huge, lenticulate disc, of metal construction. I *thought* that it crushed the hedges on either side of the road when it landed—but the hedges look untouched. And the thing that came out of it was in a spacesuit, and it either had three legs or two legs and a tail. It was a telepath. It told me that it came from Antares IV and that it was looking for some suitable Earthman to act as the agent for its race here on Earth. Then I saw Susan walking into its arms, and . . ."

"But what do you make of it, Bill?"

"You know the old saying—Beauty is in the eye of the beholder. It's the same with flying saucers. Adamski's was manned—and I use the word deliberately—by Venusians. I suppose that he had some sort of fancy for the planet Venus—but not the scientific education to realize that a Venusian could not possibly be human. Allingham's saucer was manned by Martians—and the same applied to him. That BOAC captain probably saw the saucers as they really are—things of changing shape."

"But why should *my* saucer—even though it was a rocket—have been manned by Martians?" asked Scrivens.

"Because Mars—and not the Moon—is really *the* goal of all you rocketry people. Look at von Braun's *very* detailed plans for the voyage, the landing and the exploration. But let me finish what I was going to say—it's been an idea of mine for some time, but I haven't gotten around to using it yet—which is that the saucers aren't spaceships, but living beings and intelligent ones. Just imagine intelligent creatures living on the floor of the ocean deeps! What would they, what could they, know about us? An occasional wreck might come drifting down, giving rise to all sorts of wild conjectures about *something* living in what would be, to them, a hard vacuum. Well—suppose that there are beings, as much natives of this world as we are, living at stratospheric levels but with the power of making descents to what is, to them, the ocean floor. They might not be life as we know it, they might be mere swirls of energy drawing their life force direct from the sun. They'll have been getting curious about us of late—our high-altitude aircraft, balloons and rockets must have got them rather worried. They may—assuming that they are masters of hypnotic technique—have devised a method of finding out just what makes us tick. They come down in some lonely place—and the person to whom they show themselves sees what he expects to see, what he wants to see. No two persons will see the same."

Manderley sat down on the grass verge of the road, pulled his pipe out of his pocket, filled it and lit it.

"What did *you* see, Susan?" he asked quietly.

"It was small," she said quietly. "It was a gleaming, golden bowl rather than a saucer. I don't know how it was propelled or where it came from. And there was a man. He wasn't wearing a spacesuit, and he hadn't got fur—just a man. And he wanted me to come with him to to wherever it was that he had come from—west of the moon, perhaps . . . I don't know."

"And you were going with him," said Manderley.

"Yes, I was going with him. Because . . . because . . . can't you see? Won't you see? Because he was you, as you used to be. . . ."

Manderley relit his pipe. He said nothing.

"And then you—the real you—came between us. (I didn't know, then, that it was some horrible monster you thought you were saving me from.) But it was the real you—and I realized then how much I should lose by flying off with an ideal that never existed, never could exist. . . ."

"I'm going to walk back along the road to that pub we passed," said Scrivens. "I want to use their telephone. You can sit in the car if you like."

They never heard him.

*A. Bertram Chandler's most famous character is John Grimes, a sort of interstellar Horatio Hornblower, who plies his trade next to the big dark of interjacent space at the edge of our galaxy. How does Chandler continuously keep his enthusiasm for such a series protagonist, so that each new adventure will be fresh and exciting? As the story below suggests, it isn't easy.*

# SENSE OF WONDER

## by A. Bertram Chandler

"Science fiction isn't what it was," said Crowell.

"Was it ever?" asked Samuels.

"Not very funny," said Whiting. "I agree with Bill. Science fiction isn't what it was—and for that I blame the authors and publishers of factual books on astronautics and the like. If those books had to be written, their sale should have been restricted to science fiction writers only. Our predecessors in the field had it easy. Their bold heroes could leap aboard their spaceships, press a couple of buttons and whiffle off to Proxima Centauri at fourteen times the speed of light. They didn't have to worry about escape velocity, mass ratio and all the rest of it. The Lorenz-Fitzgerald equations meant nothing in their lives—or the lives of their readers. They could populate Mars with beautiful, oviparous princesses. (I've often wondered why John Carter's girlfriends had such well-developed mammary glands) and get away with it." He lifted his glass. "Here's to the good old days, when the likes of us didn't have to beat their brains out trying to satisfy a public of potential Ph. D.s!"

"All very well said, George," admitted Crowell, "but it wasn't quite what I meant. After all, I'm an editor and, as such, I read far more sf than either you or John. My growl is this—so very little of the stuff written today has even the slightest touch of the old sense of wonder. You were sneering at Burroughs' Martian romances just now, weren't you? I agree with you that they're far from scientific. But if you're honest, you'll agree with me that Burroughs' Mars was a far more wonderful place than, say, Clarke's. Barsoom was *real*, in a way that the planet reached by orthodox rocketry, populated, or otherwise, according to sound scientific principles, never has been . . ."

"You started this," said Samuels. "You're an editor—you decide whether to buy our stories or to add to our fine collections of rejection slips. Therefore—kindly define this sense of wonder. If we knew what it was we could *saturate* our work with it."

"If I knew just what it was," said Crowell thoughtfully, "I told you blighters just what I wanted . . ."

"Perhaps," said Whiting, "it all ties up with what I was saying. Look at it this way. You're a writer way back in the good old days. You're even, for the sake of the argument, old H. G. Wells himself. You've gone to all the trouble to invent the Cavorite that the modern rocket boys are always sneering at. But it works for you. And then—*Why, I'm the First Man on the Moon!* you think. Everything's so brand, spanking new. You feel a sense of wonder—and you put it across to your readers. But write a Moon story these days—and where does it get you? Wells has been there before, and Heinlein, and Clarke, and Campbell, and . . . well, just tell me the name of anybody who *hasn't* written a first men in the Moon story—*if* you can! It's the same with Mars, and Venus, and the whole damned Solar System. It's the same with the interstellar voyages."

"Time travel's as bad," said Samuels. "Wells' *The Time Machine* was good, and had the sense of wonder that Bill's been bellyaching about. The only thing that you can do with

Time Travel *now* is to give one of the tired old paradoxes a new twist."

"And there's no sense of wonder in *that*," objected Crowell.

"There's a sense of wonder at the author's ingenuity," said Whiting.

"Not the same, George. Not the same. What I'm after, and what nobody will give me, is something on the lines of Keats' magic casements fronting perilous seas . . .' Why, *why* can't any of you stare at the Martian desert with as wild a surmise as stout Cortez stared at the Pacific?"

"I wish I could," replied Whiting. "I wish we could."

"The trouble," murmured Whiting, "is that we're all too blasé . . ."

"I *beg* your pardon," said the stout lady seated next to him in the carriage.

"I'm sorry," said Whiting. "I was talking to myself. A bad habit of mine."

"It is a bad habit," said his fellow passenger severely. She looked at the magazine on Whiting's lap, raised her eyebrows at the picture of the rather more than half undressed blonde being menaced by something that no self-respecting dinosaur would claim as a close relation.

"What sort of impression does this cover make on you?" asked Whiting.

The stout lady hesitated—it was obvious that she was debating with herself whether or not to appeal to the other passengers for help. She swallowed.

She said, "I think it's rather indecent. I think that trashy publications like that are one of the causes of juvenile delinquency."

"There I don't agree," replied Whiting. "But we'll skip that. What I want to ask you is this—does it arouse any sense of wonder in your br—bosom?"

"Yes," she said with conviction. "A strong sense of wonder that a grown man should read such rubbish."

"I not only read it," he admitted, "I write it."

"That," she said, "is worse."

"But it's useful."

"*Useful?*"

"Yes. After all, it's all propaganda. Sooner or later the taxpayer is going to have to foot a really big bill—the cost of sending the first manned rocket to the Moon. Science fiction is, as it were, softening up the public, selling them the idea."

"But why send a rocket to the Moon?"

"Why climb Everest?"

"Yes—why?"

"Well," said Whiting carefully, "I suppose it all boils down to this. There will always be people to whom Everest, and the North and South Poles, and the Moon and the planets, will be a challenge. But we're drifting away from the point. I had a talk half an hour or so ago with the editor of this magazine. He was complaining that modern science fiction just doesn't have the same sense of wonder as the old stuff. We couldn't quite decide what the reason for this is. Frankly, I hoped that a new approach to the problem—yours—might be of value."

"*Is* there such a thing as old science fiction?" asked the stout lady. "I thought that it had sprung up in the years after the war. So I'm afraid that I can't help you. The only advice I can give to you, young man, is to read and write *clean* stuff, something of some moral value."

"Stories by, for and about Boy Scouts," said Whiting.

"Precisely. You will be doing something useful then, helping to combat juvenile delinquency."

"I'll think about it," he said. "Thank you very much, Madam. I get off at this station. Goodnight, and thank you again."

"It was a pleasure," she said, smiling.

The old trout! thought Whiting, as he walked from the station. Still, there was just a chance that she might have been able to bring a fresh viewpoint to the problem. So she didn't. So what?

He looked up at the sky. There's all the wonder you want, Whiting, he thought. Star beyond star, every one of them a sun, and almost every one, if Hoyle is to be believed, with its family of planets. And practically every planet of every star already reached, explored and colonized by some writer—inertialess drives, space warps, and big ships that are almost self-contained worlds making the trip at relatively slow speeds with all hands breeding like rabbits so that their great-great-great-grandchildren can make the landing . . .

Oh, the wonder's there—but how, *how* to bring it out? As I said in the train—we're all too blasé. Readers and writers both. It used to be said that there was nothing new under the sun—now, in our racket, it's got to the stage where there's nothing new under *any* sun. Take myself—in all the years that I've been writing science fiction I've only come up with one new idea—the mutated rats taking over the spaceship, and then some people said that the story was all too reminiscent of Heinlein's *Universe*.

He thought, I don't feel like going home just yet. I'll walk on the Heath for a bit, and try to think things out. This sense-of-wonder business has me a little worried; more than a little, perhaps. How did Kipling put it? *The lamp of our youth shall be utterly out, yet we shall subsist on the smell of it.* . . .

It was dark on the Heath, and the wind was cold. Whiting walked slowly along the path, sucking his pipe. Every few minutes he would pause and look up in the dark sky and the glory of the bright stars. He watched an airliner coming in to the airport—winking colored lights against the night—and remembered the fascination of Jules Verne's *The Clipper of the Clouds*.

That's the trouble, he thought. Just as flying has become commonplace, in actuality, so has space travel because of all that has been written about it. . . . Hello, what's that? An airplane without navigation lights? I suppose they know what they're doing—it must be the RAF playing, silly beggars. Funny sort of noise their engines have—too quiet for jets, certainly not propellers . . .

The thing was coming down. Whiting felt the first stirrings of fear. He could not estimate just where the huge, dark shape was going to land—and did not fancy the idea of being underneath it when it did land. He decided that his best policy would be to stand still—if he had to he could always fling himself flat on the ground the last moment. He wished that there was sufficient light for him to be able to make out some details of the strange aircraft—it had not, he was almost sure, conventional wings. Furthermore, it was coming in far too slowly for anything other than a helicopter—and a helicopter it was not.

The thing was down, about fifty yards from where Whiting was standing. It was big—he could make out that much. Metal gleamed faintly in the starlight. Something tinkled faintly, and something else whirred intermittently, and something clanged loudly. Abruptly there was a circle of light against the darkness—an opening door?

Whiting walked towards it. Who would emerge from that door, he wondered. Englishmen? Americans? Russians? He supposed that by having witnessed the landing of this obviously experimental craft he would run afoul of Security. . . . Well, it was up to Security to give the captain of the thing a sharp rap over the knuckles for setting his ship down on public parkland.

There was somebody standing inside the door, his body silhouetted against the blue light. He raised his hand—and from the top of the aircraft a spotlight stabbed out, wavered briefly and then found and held Whiting. With half-shut eyes Whiting kept on walking. He would, he decided, make a complaint about the bad manners of those who had shone a searchlight into his eyes.

"Will you come aboard?" asked the man who was standing in the doorway.

What was the accent, wondered Whiting. It was hard to place. It was, he realized, more of an *absence* of accent than anything else.

The doorway was a few feet above the rough ground, but there was a short ramp leading up to it. Whiting mounted it cautiously—and, in spite of his caution, slipped on the smooth metal. The man put out his hand to steady Whiting.

The writer looked at the stranger—at his uniform first, to try to discover his nationality.

But the clothing—a sort of coverall of silvery-gray material, with three little golden stars over the left breast—told him nothing.

"Who are you?" asked Whiting, looking at the stranger's face. "Where are you from?"

And you're not from Russia, he thought, or from America. That pageboy bob of yours would never be tolerated in the Air Force of either country—to say nothing of the RAF. . . . Odd eyes you have, too—and those pointed ears are rather outré.

"We have returned," said the man. "We left this world at the time of the Catastrophe."

"But where are you *from?*"

The man pulled Whiting gently towards the open doorway, pointed to the sky, to Procyon.

"From the fourth planet circling that star," he said. "But forgive me—I must ask *you* questions. We learned your languages on the way here—it is lucky that you have advanced sufficiently to have rediscovered radio. We know, too, that you have flight inside the atmosphere—but have you space flight yet?"

"No," said Whiting.

The man led Whiting inside the ship, to a room that could almost have been a well-appointed lounge in the surface ship on Earth's seas. There were others of the crew there—long-haired men, and women with their hair clipped short. There were bottles and glasses, and a wine that had almost the potency and the flavor of whisky that Whiting found much to his liking.

At some stage in the proceedings the ship lifted. Whiting was conducted from the wardroom, along a maze of curving alleyways, to what was obviously the control room. He looked with polite interest at the instruments, at the various pieces of apparatus doing odd things in odd corners. He displayed still more polite interest when the Captain—the man with the three golden stars on the breast of his uniform—touched a switch and the deck of the control room became transparent. Earth lay below them— Earth as he had seen it so many times as illustrations to stories, as colored plates in factual works on astronautics, in science fiction films.

"Interesting," he said.

"And you say that your race does not have space travel!" cried the Captain. "You're looking at something that no man of your time has ever seen—and all you say is, 'Interesting'!"

"The trouble," said Whiting, "is that I've lost my sense of wonder."

*Arthur C. Clarke is a Britisher who originated the idea for communication satellites. One of our genre's most famous writers, he now resides in Sri Lanka and has produced approximately 125 stories and 30 books of science fiction, including what may be the world's best-loved science fiction novel:* Childhood's End *(1953). Besides winning the International Fantasy Award, the Hugo, and the Nebula, he has also been awarded the Kalinga Award by UNESCO for popularizing science through his many works of nonfiction. So perhaps it's apt, then, that the theme of this droll little story is how difficult it is to communicate.*

# TROUBLE WITH THE NATIVES

## by ARTHUR C. CLARKE

The flying saucer came down vertically through the clouds, braked to a halt about fifty feet from the ground, and settled with a considerable bump on a patch of heather-strewn moorland.

"That," said Captain Wyxtpthll, "was a lousy landing." He did not, of course, use precisely these words. To human ears his remarks would have sounded rather like the clucking of an angry hen. Master Pilot Krtclugg unwound three of his tentacles from the control panel, stretched all four of his legs, and relaxed comfortably.

"Not my fault the automatics have packed up again," he grumbled. "But what do you expect with a ship that should have been scrapped five thousand years ago? If those cheese-paring form-fillers back at Base Planet—"

"Oh, all right! We're down in one piece, which is more than I expected. Tell Crysteel and Danstor to come in here. I want a word with them before they go."

Crysteel and Danstor were, very obviously, of a different species from the rest of the crew. They had only one pair of legs and arms, no eyes at the back of the head, and other physical deficiencies which their colleagues did their best to overlook. These very defects, however, had made them the obvious choice for this particular mission, for it had needed only a minimum of disguise to let them pass as human beings under all but the closest scrutiny.

"Now you're perfectly sure," said the Captain, "that you understand your instructions?"

"Of course," said Crysteel, slightly huffed. "This isn't the first time I've made contact with a primitive race. My training in anthropology—"

"Good. And the language?"

"Well, that's Danstor's business, but I can speak it reasonably fluently now. It's a very simple language, and after all we've been studying their radio programs for a couple of years."

"Any other points before you go?"

"Er—there's just one matter." Crysteel hesitated slightly. "It's quite obvious from their broadcasts that the social system is very primitive, and that crime and lawlessness are widespread. Many of the wealthier citizens have to use what are called 'detectives' or 'special agents' to protect their lives and property. Now we know it's against regulations, but we were wondering . . ."

"What?"

"Well, we'd feel much safer if we could take a couple of Mark III disrupters with us."

"Not on your life! I'd be court-martialed if they heard about it at the Base. Suppose you killed some of the natives—then I'd have the Bureau of Interstellar Politics, the Aborigines Conservancy Board, and half a dozen others after me."

"There'd be just as much trouble if *we* got killed," Crysteel pointed out with considerable emotion. "After all, you're responsible for our safety. Remember that radio play I was telling you about? It described a typical household, but there were two murders in the first half hour!"

"Oh, very well. But only a Mark II—we don't want you to do too much damage if there *is* trouble."

"Thanks a lot; that's a great relief. I'll report every thirty minutes as arranged. We shouldn't be gone more than a couple of hours."

Captain Wyxtpthll watched them disappear over the brow of the hill. He sighed deeply.

"Why," he said, "of all the people in the ship did it have to be *those* two?"

"It couldn't be helped," answered the pilot. "All these primitive races are terrified of anything strange. If they saw *us* coming, there'd be general panic and before we knew where we were the bombs would be falling on top of us. You just can't rush these things."

Captain Wyxtpthll was absentmindedly making a cat's cradle out of his tentacles in the way he did when he was worried.

"Of course," he said, "if they don't come back I can always go away and report the place dangerous." He brightened considerably. "Yes, that would save a lot of trouble."

"And waste all the months we've spent studying it?" said the pilot, scandalized.

"They won't be wasted," replied the captain, unraveling himself with a flick that no human eye could have followed. "Our report will be useful for the next survey ship. I'll suggest that we make another visit in—oh, let's say five thousand years. By then the place may be civilized—though frankly, I doubt it."

Samuel Higginsbotham was settling down to a snack of cheese and cider when he saw the two figures approaching along the lane. He wiped his mouth with the back of his hand, put the bottle carefully down beside his hedge-trimming tools, and stared with mild surprise at the couple as they came into range.

"Mornin',," he said cheerfully between mouthfuls of cheese.

The strangers paused. One was surreptitiously ruffling through a small book which, if Sam only knew, was packed with such common phrases and expressions as: "Before the weather forecast, here is a gale warning," "Stick 'em up—I've got you covered!" and "Calling all cars!" Danstor, who had no needs for these aids to memory, replied promptly enough.

"Good morning, my man," he said in his best BBC accent. "Could you direct us to the nearest hamlet, village, small town or other such civilized community?"

"Eh?" said Sam. He peered suspiciously at the strangers, aware for the first time that there was something very odd about their clothes. One did not, he realized dimly, normally wear a roll-top sweater with a smart pin-striped suit of the pattern fancied by city gents. And the fellow who was still fussing with the little book was actually wearing full evening dress which would have been faultless but for the lurid green-and-red tie, the hob-nailed boots and the cloth cap. Crysteel and Danstor had done their best, but they had seen too many television plays. When one considers that they had no other source of information, their sartorial aberrations were at least understandable.

Sam scratched his head. Furriners, I suppose, he told himself. Not even the townsfolk got themselves up like this.

He pointed down the road and gave them explicit directions in an accent so broad that no one residing outside the range of the BBC's West Regional transmitter could have understood more than one word in three. Crysteel and Danstor, whose home planet was so far away that Marconi's first signal couldn't possibly have reached it yet, did even worse than this. But they managed to get the general idea and retired in good order, both wondering if their knowledge of English was as good as they had believed.

So came and passed, quite uneventfully and without record in the history books, the first meeting between humanity and beings from Outside.

"I suppose," said Danstor thoughtfully, but without much conviction, "that he wouldn't have done? It would have saved us a lot of trouble."

"I'm afraid not. Judging by his clothes, and the work he was obviously engaged upon, he could not have been a very intelligent or valuable citizen. I doubt if he could even have understood who we were."

"Here's another one!" said Danstor, pointing ahead.

"Don't make sudden movements that might cause alarm. Just walk along naturally, and let him speak first."

The man ahead strode purposefully toward them, showed not the slightest signs of recognition, and before they had recovered was already disappearing into the distance.

"Well!" said Danstor.

"It doesn't matter," replied Crysteel philosophically. "He probably wouldn't have been any use either."

"That's no excuse for bad manners!"

They gazed with some indignation at the retreating back of Professor Fitzsimmons as, wearing his oldest hiking outfit and engrossed in a difficult piece of atomic theory, he dwindled down the lane. For the first time, Crysteel began to suspect uneasily that it might not be as simple to make contact as he had optimistically believed.

Little Milton was a typical English village, nestling at the foot of the hills whose higher slopes now concealed so portentous a secret. There were very few people about on this summer morning, for the men were already at work and the womenfolk were still tidying up after the exhausting task of getting their lords and masters safely out of the way. Consequently Crysteel and Danstor had almost reached the center of the village before their first encounter, which happened to be with the village postman, cycling back to the office after completing his rounds. He was in a very bad temper, having had to deliver a penny postcard to Dodgson's farm, a couple of miles off his normal route. In addition, the weekly parcel of laundry which Gunner Evans sent home to his doting mother had been a lot heavier than usual, as well it might, since it contained four tins of bully beef pinched from the cookhouse.

"Excuse me," said Danstor politely.

"Can't stop," said the postman, in no mood for casual conversation. "Got another round to do." Then he was gone.

"This is really the limit!" protested Danstor. "Are they *all* going to be like this?"

"You've simply got to be patient," said Crysteel. "Remember their customs are quite different from ours; it may take some time to gain their confidence. I've had this sort of trouble with primitive races before. Every anthropologist has to get used to it."

"Hmm," said Danstor. "I suggest that we call at some of their houses. Then they won't be able to run away."

"Very well," agreed Crysteel doubtfully. "But avoid anything that looks like a religious shrine, otherwise we may get into trouble."

Old Widow Tomkins' council-house could hardly have been mistaken, even by the most inexperienced of explorers, for such an object. The old lady was agreeably excited to see two gentlemen standing on her doorstep, and noticed nothing at all odd about their clothes. Visions of unexpected legacies, of newspaper reporters asking about her 100th birthday (she was really only 95, but had managed to keep it dark) flashed through her mind. She picked up the slate she kept hanging by the door and went gaily forth to greet her visitors.

"You'll have to write it down," she simpered, holding out the slate. "I've been deaf this last twenty years."

Crysteel and Danstor looked at each other in dismay. This was a completely unexpected snag, for the only written characters they had ever seen were television program announcements, and they had never fully deciphered those. But Danstor, who had an almost photographic memory, rose to the occasion. Holding the chalk very awkwardly, he wrote a sentence which, he had reason to believe, was in common use during such breakdowns in communication.

As her mysterious visitors walked sadly away, old Mrs. Tomkins stared in baffled bewilderment at the marks on her slate. It was some time before she deciphered the characters—Danstor had made several mistakes—and even then she was little the wiser.

TRANSMISSIONS WILL BE RESUMED AS
SOON AS POSSIBLE.

It was the best that Danstor could do; but the old lady never did get to the bottom of it.

They were little luckier at the next house they tried. The door was answered by a young lady whose vocabulary consisted largely of giggles, and who eventually broke down completely and slammed the door in their faces. As they listened to the muffled, hysterical laughter, Crysteel and Danstor began to suspect, with sinking hearts, that their disguise as normal human beings was not as effective as they had intended.

At Number 3, on the other hand, Mrs. Smith was only too willing to talk—at 120 words to the minute in an accent as impenetrable as Sam Higginsbotham's. Danstor made his apologies as soon as he could get a word in edgeways, and moved on.

"Doesn't *anyone* talk as they do on the radio?" he lamented. "How do they understand their own programs if they all speak like this?"

"I think we must have landed in the wrong place," said Crysteel, even his optimism beginning to fail. It sagged still further when he had been mistaken, in swift succession, for a Gallup Poll investigator, the prospective Conservative candidate, a vacuum-cleaner salesman, and a dealer from the local black market.

At the sixth or seventh attempt they ran out of housewives. The door was opened by a gangling youth who clutched in one clammy paw an object which at once hypnotized the visitors. It was a magazine whose cover displayed a giant rocket climbing upward from a crater-studded planet which, whatever it might be, was obviously not the Earth. Across the background were the words: "Staggering Stories of Pseudo-Science. Price 25 cents."

Crysteel looked at Danstor with a "Do you think what I think?" expression which the other returned. Here at last, surely, was someone who could understand them. His spirits mounting, Danstor addressed the youngster.

"I think you can help us," he said politely. "We find it very difficult to make ourselves understood here. You see, we've just landed on this planet from space and we want to get in touch with your government."

"Oh," said Jimmy Williams, not yet fully returned to Earth from his vicarious adventures among the outer moons of Saturn. "Where's your spaceship?"

"It's up in the hills; we didn't want to frighten anyone."

"Is it a rocket?"

"Good gracious no. They've been obsolete for thousands of years."

"Then how does it work? Does it use atomic power?"

"I suppose so," said Danstor, who was pretty shaky on physics. "Is there any other kind of power?"

"This is getting us nowhere," said Crysteel, impatient for once. "We've got to ask *him* questions. Try and find where there are some officials we can meet."

Before Danstor could answer, a stentorian voice came from inside the house.

"Jimmy! Who's there?"

"Two . . . men," said Jimmy, a little doubtfully. "At least, they look like men. They've come from Mars. I always said that was going to happen."

There was the sound of ponderous movements, and a lady of elephantine bulk and ferocious mien appeared from the gloom. She glared at the strangers, looked at the magazine Jimmy was carrying, and summed up the situation.

"You ought to be ashamed of yourselves!" she cried, rounding on Crysteel and Danstor. "It's bad enough having a good-for-nothing son in the house who wastes all his time reading this rubbish, without grown men coming along putting more ideas into his head. Men from Mars, indeed! I suppose you've come in one of those flying saucers!"

"But I never mentioned Mars," protested Danstor feebly.

Slam! From behind the door came the sound of violent altercation, the unmistakable noise of tearing paper, and a wail of anguish. And that was that.

"Well," said Danstor at last. "What do we try next? And why did he say we came from Mars? That isn't even the nearest planet, if I remember correctly."

"I don't know," said Crysteel. "But I suppose it's natural for them to assume that we come from some close planet. They're going to have a shock when they find the truth. Mars, indeed! That's even worse than here, from the reports I've seen." He was obviously beginning to lose some of his scientific detachment.

"Let's leave the houses for a while," said Danstor. "There must be some more people outside."

This statement proved to be perfectly true, for they had not gone much further before they found themselves surrounded by small boys making incomprehensible but obviously rude remarks.

"Should we try and placate them with gifts?" said Danstor anxiously. "That usually works among more backward races."

"Well, have you brought any?"

"No, I thought you—"

Before Danstor could finish, their tormentors took to their heels and disappeared down a side street. Coming along the road was a majestic figure in a blue uniform.

Crysteel's eyes lit up.

"A policeman!" he said. "Probably going to investigate a murder somewhere. But perhaps he'll spare us a minute," he added, not very hopefully.

P. C. Hinks eyed the strangers with some astonishment, but managed to keep his feelings out of his voice.

"Hello, gents. Looking for anything?"

"As a matter of fact, yes," said Danstor in his friendliest and most soothing tone of voice. "Perhaps you can help us. You see, we've just landed on this planet and want to make contact with the authorities."

"Eh?" said P. C. Hinks startled. There was a long pause— though not too long, for P. C. Hinks was a bright young man who had no intention of remaining a village constable all his life. "So you've just landed, have you? In a spaceship, I suppose?"

"That's right," said Danstor, immensely relieved at the absence of the incredulity, or even violence, which such announcements all too often provoked on the more primitive planets.

"Well, well!" said P. C. Hinks, in tones which he hoped would inspire confidence and feelings of amity. (Not that it mattered much if they both became violent—they seemed a pretty skinny pair.) "Just tell me what you want, and I'll see what we can do about it."

"I'm so glad," said Danstor. "You see, we've landed in this rather remote spot because we don't want to create a panic. It would be best to keep our presence known to as few people as possible until we have contacted your government."

"I quite understand," replied P. C. Hinks, glancing round hastily to see if there was anyone through whom he could send a message to his sergeant. "And what do you propose to do then?"

"I'm afraid I can't discuss our long-term policy with regard to Earth," said Danstor cagily. "All I can say is that this section of the Universe is being surveyed and opened up for development, and we're quite sure we can help you in many ways."

"That's very nice of you," said P. C. Hinks heartily. "I think the best thing is for you to come along to the station with me so that we can put through a call to the Prime Minister."

"Thank you very much," said Danstor, full of gratitude. They walked trustingly beside P. C. Hinks, despite his slight tendency to keep behind them, until they reached the police station.

"This way, gents," said P. C. Hinks, politely ushering them into a room which was really rather poorly lit and not at all well furnished, even by the somewhat primitive standards they had expected. Before they could fully take in their surroundings, there was a "click" and they found themselves separated from their guide by a large door composed entirely of iron bars.

"Now don't worry," said P. C. Hinks. "Everything will be quite all right. I'll be back in a minute."

Crysteel and Danstor gazed at each other with a surmise that rapidly deepened to a dreadful certainty.

"We're locked in!"

"This is a prison!"

"Now what are we going to do?"

"I don't know if you chaps understand English," said a languid voice from the gloom, "but you might let a fellow sleep in peace."

For the first time, the two prisoners saw that they were not alone. Lying on a bed in the corner of the cell was a somewhat dilapidated young man, who gazed at them blearily out of one resentful eye.

"My goodness!" said Danstor nervously. "Do you suppose he's a dangerous criminal?"

"He doesn't look very dangerous at the moment," said Crysteel, with more accuracy than he guessed.

"What are *you* in for, anyway?" asked the stranger, sitting up unsteadily. "You look as if you've been to a fancy-dress party. Oh, my poor head!" He collapsed again into the prone position.

"Fancy locking up anyone as ill as this!" said Danstor, who was a kind-hearted individual. Then he continued, in English, "I don't know why we're here. We just told the policeman who we were and where we came from, and this is what's happened."

"Well, who are you?"

"We've just landed—"

"Oh, there's no point in going through all that again," interrupted Crysteel. "We'll never get anyone to believe us."

"Hey!" said the stranger, sitting up once more. "What language is that you're speaking? I know a few, but I've never heard anything like that."

"Oh, all right," Crysteel said to Danstor. "You might as well tell him. There's nothing else to do until that policeman comes back anyway."

At this moment, P. C. Hinks was engaged in earnest conversation with the superintendent of the local mental home, who insisted stoutly that all his patients were present. However, a careful check was promised and he'd call back later.

Wondering if the whole thing was a practical joke, P. C. Hinks put the receiver down and quietly made his way to the cells. The three prisoners seemed to be engaged in friendly conversation, so he tiptoed away again. It would do them all good to have a chance to cool down. He rubbed his eye tenderly as he remembered what a battle it had been to get

Mr. Graham into the cell during the small hours of the morning.

That young man was now reasonably sober after the night's celebrations, which he did not in the least regret. (It was, after all, quite an occasion when your degree came through and you found you'd got Honors when you'd barely expected a Pass.) But he began to fear that he was still under the influence as Danstor unfolded his tale and waited, not expecting to be believed.

In these circumstances, thought Graham, the best thing to do was to behave as matter-of-factly as possible until the hallucinations got fed up and went away.

"If you really have a spaceship in the hills," he remarked, "surely you can get in touch with it and ask someone to come and rescue you?"

"We want to handle this ourselves," said Crysteel with dignity. "Besides, you don't know our captain."

They sounded very convincing, thought Graham. The whole story hung together remarkably well. And yet . . .

"It's a bit hard for me to believe that you can build interstellar spaceships, but can't get out of a miserable village police station."

Danstor looked at Crysteel, who shuffled uncomfortably.

"We could get out easily enough," said the anthropologist. "But we don't want to use violent means unless it's absolutely essential. You've no idea of the trouble it causes, and the reports we might have to fill in. Besides, if we do get out, I suppose your Flying Squad would catch us before we got back to the ship."

"Not in Little Milton," grinned Graham. "Especially if we could get across to the White Hart without being stopped. My car is over there."

"Oh," said Danstor, his spirits suddenly reviving. He turned to his companion and a lively discussion followed. Then, very gingerly, he produced a small black cylinder from an inner pocket, handling it with much the same confidence as a nervous spinster holding a loaded gun for the first time. Simultaneously, Crysteel retired with some speed to the far corner of the cell.

It was at this precise moment that Graham knew, with a sudden icy certainty, that he was stone-sober and that the story he had been listening to was nothing less than the truth.

There was no fuss or bother, no flurry of electric sparks or colored rays—but a section of the wall three feet across dissolved quietly and collapsed into a little pyramid of sand. The sunlight came streaming into the cell as, with a great sigh of relief, Danstor put his mysterious weapon away.

"Well, come on," he urged Graham. "We're waiting for you."

There were no signs of pursuit, for P. C. Hinks was still arguing on the phone, and it would be some minutes yet before that bright young man returned to the cells and received the biggest shock of his official career. No one at the White Hart was particularly surprised to see Graham again; they all knew where and how he had spent the night, and expressed hope that the local Bench would deal leniently with him when his case came up.

With grave misgivings, Crysteel and Danstor climbed into the back of the incredibly ramshackle Bentley which Graham affectionately addressed as "Rose." But there was nothing wrong with the engine under the rusty bonnet, and soon they were roaring out of Little Milton at fifty miles an hour. It was a striking demonstration of the relativity of speed, for Crysteel and Danstor, who had spent the last few years traveling tranquilly through space at several million miles a second, had never been so scared in their lives. When Crysteel had recovered his breath he pulled out his little portable transmitter and called the ship.

"We're on the way back," he shouted above the roar of the wind. "We've got a fairly intelligent human being with us. Expect us in—whoops!—I'm sorry—we just went over a bridge—about ten minutes. What was that? No, of course not. We didn't have the slightest trouble. Everything went perfectly smoothly. *Good-by.*"

Graham looked back only once to see how his passengers were faring. The sight was rather unsettling, for their ears and hair (which had not been glued on very firmly) had blown away and their real selves were beginning to emerge. Graham began to suspect, with some discomfort, that his new acquaintances also lacked noses. Oh well, one could grow used to anything with practice. He was going to have plenty of that in the years ahead.

The rest, of course, you all know; but the full story of the first landing on Earth, and of the peculiar circumstances

under which Ambassador Graham became humanity's representative to the universe at large, has never before been
recounted. We extracted the main details, with a good deal of
persuasion, from Crysteel and Danstor themselves, while we
were working in the Department of Extraterrestrial Affairs.

It was understandable, in view of their success on Earth,
that they should have been selected by their superiors to
make the first contact with our mysterious and secretive
neighbors, the Martians. It is also understandable, in the
light of the above evidence, that Crysteel and Danstor were
so reluctant to embark on this later mission, and we are not
really very surprised that nothing has ever been heard of
them since.

*Edmund Cooper is an English novelist and book reviewer who has previously worked as a laborer, civil servant, merchant seaman, teacher, and journalist. He has authored more than 25 novels and 40 short stories of science fiction, including the inspirational and Wellsian post-holocaust novel* The Cloud Walker *(1973). In the following tale, however, he gives us a tasteful farce about the mating habits of Komodo dragons.*

# THE LIZARD OF WOZ

## by EdmuNd CoopeR

Ynkwysytyv dropped his flying saucer down to ten thousand feet and allowed it to amble through the sky at a thousand miles an hour. Below him lay the United States of America, which he found very boring to look at.

His telescope had revealed no signs at all of intelligent lizard life—only a host of odd-looking bipeds who lived in peculiar-shaped hives and used primitive land carriages to get from one place to another. True, they had flying machines—but of a somewhat amateurish design.

As a matter of fact, Ynkwysytyv had whiled away the last few minutes by playing leapfrog with two ridiculously flimsy jet aircraft. But when they began to pump rockets at him, he lost his temper and neatly burned off their wings with a heat ray—which made life interesting for a couple of incredulous Air Force pilots. Fortunately, their ejector seats and parachutes were in working order.

If the truth be known, Ynkwysytyv—or Ynky, as his colleagues in the United Planets Organization called him—was not only bored but definitely unhappy. He had to admit, however, that the assignment to this remote and backward area of the galaxy was largely his own doing. If he had not allowed his tail to be turned by the irresistible scales and the seductive yellow streak of the Senior Administrator's only daughter, he would still be at UPO headquarters on Woz.

He sighed nostalgically as he thought of his home planet, five hundred light-years away. He sighed as he remembered the clear green skies, the deep blue grass, the pink rain forests and the boiling crimson oceans. Then he snorted with disgust as he looked down at the miserable world he had come to survey.

The colors were wrong, the inhabitants were backward and ugly, and the whole place would probably have to be fumigated to make it fit for colonization. Possibly a few of the more intelligent natives could be retained for slave labor. But their rudimentary technology seemed to indicate that this was hardly worthwhile. Robots would be far more efficient.

However, his instructions were to survey the planet, establish friendly contact with the inhabitants, and prepare a detailed report on their culture—if any. All of which was a complete waste of time, since the report would be filed away and forgotten for a couple of centuries. Then some junior official would stumble across it and sign an order for total demolition under the slum clearance program.

Ynky had every justification for taking a cynical view of life. His journey to the Solar System had lasted more than ten years, and his hibernation clock had accidentally woken him up eighteen months before planetfall—thus giving him ample opportunity for reflection on lizard's inlizardity to lizard. It was downright vindictive of the Senior Administrator to pack him off to this hole—and all because his sexband had turned purple at the wrong moment.

Being a mere two hundred years old, Ynky regarded it as the worst possible beginning for the best century of his youth. By the time he got back to Woz all the females in his egg-group would have mated, and he would be condemned to a bachelor existence for at least another seventy-five years.

During his hibernation in the flying saucer, Ynky had naturally been programmed to fluency in all major terrestrial languages; for he was not the first Woz lizard to visit Earth. Some years previously, a blue-tailed language specialist had touched down to do research on elementary methods of communication. He had managed to beam back to Woz the basic language patterns of English, French, Russian and Chinese before being converted into a nourishing soup by the uncultured inhabitants of New Guinea.

Ynky gazed distastefully down at the planetary surface and shrugged. Might as well make a start somewhere. He reluctantly eased the saucer earthwards.

Below was a deserted highway and an equally deserted roadside café. Ynky hovered indecisively for a moment, wondering whether he should press on to a more promising location. But what was the use? The whole civilization was monotonously primitive.

He touched down about a hundred yards from the café. He got out of the saucer, sniffed the air cautiously—too much poisonous oxygen and not enough nitrogen—and began to walk along the highway. Then, realizing that he had forgotten something, he went back and rendered the saucer invisible as a precaution against any curious bipeds who happened along.

As lizards go, Ynky was an impressive specimen. Poised erect on his hindlegs, he was four feet tall, excluding an extra three feet of red-and-purple tail that waved proudly behind him like an animated battle standard. However, in accordance with what the late blue-tailed language specialist had observed of diplomatic procedure, he also wore a top hat and morning coat.

His entrance, therefore, at the *Shady Nook Café* introduced an element of novelty into the otherwise quiet existence of its proprietor, one Sam Goodwin. Sam, whose favorite relaxation was to read all about bug-eyed monsters, behaved with commendable fortitude when one actually appeared.

"Howdy," said Sam, scratching his gray hair and trying to look as if the top hat hadn't shaken him at all. "How are things in the galaxy?"

Ynky was pleasantly surprised by this first contact with *Homo sapiens*. He had anticipated some initial difficulty.

"We try to keep the constellations burning," he said modestly, "but you know how it is."

"Sure," agreed Sam confidentially. "What'll you eat? Steak, fried chicken, burger?"

Ynky shuddered, remembering the blue-tailed lizard's repeated warnings about the standard of terrestrial cooking. "I'll take fruit," he said. "A dozen apples, a dozen oranges and a dozen bananas."

"Drink?" said Sam, filling the counter with the fruit.

"Milk," decided Ynky. "About six quarts."

He disposed of the lot simultaneously, to Sam's intense interest. Ten seconds later, Ynky dexterously slipped an arm down his throat and extracted empty milk cartons, banana skins and orange peel all neatly tied up in a plastic wrapper for disposal.

"Cute trick," observed Sam. "Is that normal, or just for the benefit of the natives?"

"Normal," said Ynky. "We have somewhat delicate table manners on Woz."

"Come again?"

"Woz is my home planet. I have been given the task of reporting to the United Planets Organization on the state of your world. . . . I may add that, though I find you as a biped less repulsive than I had expected, I shall probably have to recommend fumigation."

"You have my interest," said Sam. "What is fumigation, and why?"

Ynky leaned on the counter, removed his top hat and expounded. "Fumigation is a means of rendering a planet sterile by the introduction of an interesting gas that our chemists have developed. It is a breeder gas. That is to say, if a small quanitity is introduced into any atmosphere it will quickly make the whole atmosphere lethal. . . . A fine achievement, don't you think? Well beyond your own elementary science, of course."

Sam had read about this sort of situation in the pulp magazines. He was not sure he approved of it.

"Permit me to inquire," he said courteously, "why this little old planet should be fumigated?"

Ynky smiled. "We have made the mistake of trying to civilize bipeds before. Too intractable. There were some rather promising apes on Sirius Five—intelligent enough to train as technicians, or so we thought. Unfortunately, they developed a mania for political independence and blew three of our battle squadrons out of space before we demonstrated to them the error of their ways. . . . So you see, it is not wise to educate inferior creatures beyond their natural ability. It will be rather a pity about *Homo sapiens*. In some ways you are a definite improvement on the apes of Sirius."

"Thank you," said Sam. "That's nice to know."

"Don't mention it," said Ynky. "There is the possibility of retaining a few slaves, of course. If you are interested, I'll gladly recommend you."

"Thank you," repeated Sam. "That's real considerate. . . . I guess you must have a pretty big team investigating Earth right now."

Ynky gave him a patronizing smile. "No," he said. "Only me. One lizard was considered adequate for such a simple assignment."

"Interesting!" Sam removed his spectacles and polished them carefully. "Now just supposing you failed to turn in a report?"

Ynky was surprised at human stupidity. "But I *shall* turn in a report. That is what I am here for. Needless to say, it will be entirely impartial and thoroughly scientific."

"Naturally," agreed Sam. "But just assuming—for the sake of argument—that your report didn't reach headquarters?"

"A ridiculous assumption." Ynky yawned. "But in that case, someone would discover the omission eventually, and another lizard would be sent. In a couple of centuries or so. After all, from our point of view the problem is not terribly urgent."

Sam Goodwin smiled. "Excuse me a moment." He disappeared through a door at the back of the café. A few seconds later he returned. There was a double-barreled shotgun in his hands. It was pointed at Ynky.

"Nothing personal," said Sam. "But as *Homo sapiens*—of which fraternity I have the honor to be a life member—is a trifle busy just now, it occurs to me that fumigation might inconvenience us a little."

Ynky had no experience of the antique weapons of Earth. He had, however, grasped the fact that Sam Goodwin seemed a shade antisocial. At the same time that superior sixth sense, which had enabled the lizards of Woz to thrive as a species for twenty million strenuous years, rang an alarm bell in the depths of his reptilian brain. Ynky dropped on all fours just as Sam squeezed the trigger.

The first blast ventilated his top hat in a most alarming manner. And the second blast, which came as he scuttled at speed through the main doorway of the Shady Nook Café, gave him the doubtful distinction of being the first lizard of Woz to sport a perforated tail complete with ornamental lead inlay. But he did not stop to admire the result. For Sam had followed him on to the highway, and was inserting fresh shells in his shotgun.

Ynky scuttled back to his saucer in nothing flat. He rendered it visible once more, and jumped in as Sam's third blast rattled harmlessly against the hull. Ynky kicked the controls. With a great whoosh, the saucer did a vertical takeoff and shot up to fifty thousand feet at a velocity which did not improve the digestive state of a dozen bananas, oranges and apples: also six quarts of milk. They seemed to be conspiring towards a minor rebellion in his third stomach.

Presently, the hiccups subsided, and Ynky was able to consider the condition of his tail. Besides being somewhat painful, it was also tattered, the red and purple hues assuming a distinctly unhealthy tonal value. He wiggled it experimentally. A new stab of pain leapfrogged along his spinal cord, but the tail responded. No permanent damage: merely a few embedded souvenirs of American hospitality.

As an attempt to establish friendly contact with the natives, Ynky's recent experience—though yielding valuable information concerning the instability of the species—was hardly an unqualified success. He relieved his feelings by stepping savagely on the accelerator, at the same time expressing his opinion of Sam Goodwin and his Shady Nook Café in the singularly poetic lizard tongue of Woz.

By the time he had run out of suitable adjectives, his flying saucer had crossed the rest of the United States, the Pacific Ocean, the Sea of Okhotsk and was already halfway across the steppes of Central Asia. Pausing for a while to inspect the somewhat different terrain, Ynky was gratified to discover vast tracts of wilderness as yet relatively unspoiled by the hand of *Homo sapiens*.

In fact, the only evidence of human stupidity was a symbolic metal snake that rippled lugubriously across the continent for hundreds of miles. Ynky realized, of course, that although mankind had partly emerged from the Stone Age, it had not yet discarded the archaic system of rail transport.

But for a lizard whose home planet had developed the more efficient methods of time travel and teleportation, the Trans-Siberian Railway was not without a certain mild historical fascination.

Somewhere between Omsk and Tomsk, Ynky—whose tail had now ceased throbbing—decided to drop down and investigate. At a point where an apparently disused road intersected the railway, there was a single stone hive, obviously the dwelling of a biped. Here would be an excellent opportunity to reestablish friendly contact for the purpose of culture analysis, while at the same time watching the trains go by.

Ynky touched his flying saucer down about fifty yards from the house of one, Ivan Sergeyevitch Poushov, who had had the honor of being a Stakhanovite Crossing Keeper of the Soviet Union ever since the 1936 purge had accounted for his predecessor. This time, Ynky did not bother to render the saucer invisible. It would be easier to locate if he should again need to depart rapidly.

Ivan Sergeyevitch had observed the saucer's arrival with some apprehension. It had not come from the direction of Moscow, but then the ways of the political police are inscrutable. Hastily he polished his shoes, combed his beard and went out to greet his visitor—at the same time mentally preparing himself to deny everything.

"Greetings, Comrade," said Ivan Sergeyevitch, gazing at Ynky and privately marveling at the lengths to which the political police will go in the matter of disguise.

"Greetings," responded Ynky cautiously. "I am Ynkwysytyv of Woz."

"And I, Excellency, am Poushov of Slobovanutsky Crossing." Ivan Sergeyevitch hesitated, then added tentatively: "I trust, Comrade, that you will do me the honor of taking a glass of vodka at my unworthy table? We will drink to the health of our heroic collective leadership."

"I have no doubt," retorted Ynky, "that your heroic collective leadership would be much improved by fumigation. Incidentally, we lizards of Woz do not approve of alcohol—except for medicinal pruposes."

At which point it began to dawn upon Ivan Sergeyevitch that Ynky might possibly not be a secret agent after all. He was forced to admit that the lizard skin looked genuine enough; and Ynky's tail possessed an independence of movement that was slightly suggestive of western decadence. But clearly, an error of judgment in this delicate matter might well prove fatal.

"Excellency," said Ivan Sergeyevitch, "pardon the stupidity of a politically enlightened though culturally confused Crossing Keeper, but where is Woz?"

"In a more select residential area of the galaxy."

"Permit me to ask," continued Ivan Sergeyevitch, surprised at his own temerity, "how one gets there."

Ynky gave him a superior lizard smile. "One turns sharp left after the Pole Star and continues straight ahead for five hundred light-years."

"It is, perhaps, a satellite?"

"Certainly not!" exclaimed Ynky with indignation. "It is a world of the first magnitude."

"No doubt recently liberated by the glorious Red Army?" pursued Ivan Sergeyevitch.

Ynky shook his head scornfully. "Your mother was an idiot, your father was an imbecile, and you are in a state of intellectual delirium. Fumigation will be an act of mercy."

By this time, Ivan Sergeyevitch had reached a definite conclusion. This strange visitor could not possibly be a member of the secret police. No M.V.D. agent would ever stoop to wearing a morning coat. His self-confidence returned.

"Woz is not, then, a Communist state?" he asked.

"Blockhead! Why should intelligent lizards descend to Communism?"

"If it is not a Communist state," reasoned Ivan Sergeyevitch grimly, "it is therefore a reactionary capitalist fascist democracy. I trust the proletariat is organized?"

"We have no proletariat."

"Impossible!" exclaimed Ivan Sergeyevitch. "You could not liquidate *all* the workers!"

"My friend," said Ynky gently, "there were no workers to liquidate. We use robots."

Ivan Sergeyevitch thrust his beard out aggressively. "Barbaric! How long have these unfortunate robots been exploited?"

"About twenty thousand years."

"What sublime endurance!" breathed Ivan Sergeyevitch in awe. "I expect the revolution will be unusually bloody."

Ynky yawned. "Poushov, you bore me. Fumigation of the planet seems to be inevitable. . . . Incidentally, when is the next train due?"

"Tomorrow, Excellency—or is it the day after? Perhaps you would care to wait. I cannot guarantee that it will stop, you understand."

"But I," said Ynky with a bland smile, "can guarantee that presently everything will stop. Meanwhile, I will pursue my investigations elsewhere. Good morning."

"One moment, Excellency. Permit me to present you with a small souvenir of this historic meeting." Ivan Sergeyevitch ran back into his cottage and returned a couple of minutes later with a small metal box to which a key was fixed. "It is a machine designed to cure fatigue and sleeplessness," he explained. "Especially for intellectuals such as yourself, Excellency. Many of our most prominent party members have given similar models to their closest friends. The results proved highly satisfactory." Ivan Sergeyevitch gave the key a few turns, then handed the box to Ynky.

The lizard examined it carefully. "A most interesting example of peasant craftsmanship," he announced. "I presume it develops psychostatic induction?"

"Undoubtedly," agreed Ivan Sergeyevitch. "I trust your honor will have a pleasant journey."

"Thank you," said Ynky. "I am almost inclined to change my mind and recommend you for slave labor."

With these expressions of mutual regard, Ivan Sergeyevitch returned to his cottage, and Ynky to his saucer. The Crossing Keeper watched Ynky's vertical takeoff with a crafty smile. The mysterious flying machine was impressive, but definitely not to be compared with the wonderful MIGs that Ivan Sergeyevitch had read about. Besides, was not the saucer the product of a capitalistic economy?

Ivan Sergeyevitch was pleased with his morning's work on three counts. First, by a process of brilliant deduction, he had eliminated the possibility of Ynky being a member of the secret police. Second, he had unmasked the visitor as a capitalist spy. Third, he had struck a blow for the martyred robots of Woz. For his present to Ynky was an ingenious relic of the scorched earth program devised by the military genius of the late Comrade Stalin. It had been originally intended for the benefit of occupation forces.

Ivan Sergeyevitch arrived at an intelligent decision. He would write a report about the incident. This, perhaps, would facilitate his promotion to the coveted post of assistant ticket collector at Tomsk.

Meanwhile, Ynky had climbed to thirty thousand feet and was proceeding southward in a leisurely fashion at three times the speed of sound. After the desolate stretches of Siberia, he was of a mind to sample terrestrial life in a tropical area. Possibly there would be a more amusing local variation.

He had crossed Sinkiang, Tibet, Burma and Siam; and was cruising slowly round the Malay Archipelago to choose an island suitable for investigation. Unfortunately, just as he was over the middle of the South China Sea, Ivan Sergeyevitch's time bomb—one of the few serviceable ones to be manufactured—blew the flying saucer's turret off in a most abrupt fashion.

For Ynky, in his confined cabin, the sound effect was like a hundred cymbals being clashed together. But eventually the vibrations died down; and he discovered much to his surprise that, although his morning coat was now reduced to a few strands of tattered fiber, he personally was intact. Except for the fact that his tail had turned white with shock.

It was then that the resourcefulness for which the lizards of Woz are justly renowned came to his aid. Ynky saw that the South China Sea was coming up towards him more rapidly than he would have wished, and that presently he would be a very wet lizard. He promptly switched on the antigravity beam and the emergency superheated steam rockets. The antigravity beam, being quite disoriented, tipped the saucer upside down; but Ynky hung on by his tail, and with the aid of the steam rockets gained a certain rudimentary control. He promptly headed for the nearest piece of land, which, as it happened, was the tiny jungle island of Komodo.

By the superb feat of saucer balancing, Ynky managed to crash-land in a grove of palm trees. By the time it had stopped raining coconuts, he had recovered from the ordeal sufficiently to wriggle out of the saucer and inspect the damage. Despondently, he concluded that the repairs would take at least three days. At the end of which, he promised himself grimly, he would return to Slobovanutsky Crossing and deal with Ivan Sergeyevitch in such a way that he would yearn for the blissful release of fumigation.

Absorbed as he was in contemplating the damage to the saucer's turret and the prospect of a just vengeance, Ynky was unaware that he was no longer alone. Finally, a discreet breathing on the back of his neck caused him to turn round.

He was confronted with the most wonderful, the most sylphlike, the most radiantly beautiful female he had ever seen. Her eyes were wide with innocence and deep with mystery. Her lovely sinuous body was a poem in plastic art. She wore a dazzling smile, and the air of one whose gentle form somehow concealed hot unquenchable fires. Which, in a way, was true, since she happened to be a carnivorous Komodo dragon.

"I—I—I . . ." began Ynky in the lizard tongue, which is conveniently universal. But then words failed him. He had never seen anything like this on Woz.

"Are you in trouble?" she asked in a voice that was at once as sweet as a siren and husky with a strange longing.

"No, dear lady," said Ynky, pulling himself together. "I am in paradise. . . . Never have I seen such perfection of form! I feel that I have journeyed five hundred light-years just for this moment."

The Komodo dragon's five-foot tail shivered slightly, and she blushed. "I bet you say that to all the lizards."

"Angel," confessed Ynky, remembering the Senior Administrator's daughter, "it is true that there were others. But they meant nothing. Until now, I have never lived. . . . Incidentally, my name is Ynkwysytyv. But you may call me Ynky."

She held out her hand, and Ynky was entranced by the razor-sharp talons. "I am a Komodo dragon," she murmured softly. "But just call me Kanna-Belle."

"Kanna-Belle!" exclaimed Ynky in rapture. "What a perfect name."

The Komodo dragon blushed once again. "It is rather unusual, isn't it?"

"So tender, so appropriate," said Ynky.

The Komodo dragon smiled, displaying rows of flawless teeth. "Oh, well, if you say so." She turned towards the flying saucer. "Tell me, dear Ynky, what is *that* peculiar thing?"

Ynky puffed out his chest and explained his mission. "Theoretically," he concluded, "I should repair the saucer and take my report back to Woz. . . . But, beloved, I can't possibly recommend fumigation of the planet where we first set eyes on each other."

"I should think not," said the Komodo dragon indignantly. "Especially as I have no desire to emigrate. I am perfectly well adjusted to my present environment, thank you."

"But there is my duty to consider," said Ynky sadly. "Although you may not be aware of it, Kanna-Belle, the lizards of Woz are the most enlightened in the galaxy. Destiny has chosen us for the creation of a galactic empire, which will be a monument to the indomitability of the lizard spirit for all time."

"How terribly aggressive you are," said the Komodo dragon demurely. "It frightens me."

Ynky, who had completely lost his heart to this adorable creature, threw himself at her feet and said: "Kanna-Belle, I cannot bear to make you unhappy. . . .If only it were possible for me to stay with you in this delicious paradise."

The Komodo dragon looked thoughtful. "Perhaps that can be arranged," she whispered. And her voice held such promise that Ynky forgot all about fumigation and galactic empires.

He leaped up exultantly. "My darling, why not? We will be inseparable."

"Forever," agreed the Komodo dragon, with a faraway look in her eyes.

"The perfect partnership," said Ynky. "My brains and your beauty."

"Indissolubly united," smiled Kanna-Belle, coiling her long and magnificent tail. "In life and also in death. . . .Forgive me for mentioning it, my love, but I am really quite famished."

Whereupon two hundred pounds of muscle uncoiled with the speed of a whiplash and the function of a blackjack. Ynky was permitted one moment of horrified disbelief before his confused brain was efficiently homogenized. He hit the ground with a reproachful sigh.

The Komodo dragon measured his corpse critically, and shook her head. Ynky was just a trifle undernourished by Komodo standards.

"Much better, my love," she soliloquized sadly, "than a broken heart. . . .And how noble to perish for an ideal!"

Then she sat down and systematically ate him.

And this, my friends, is the true reason why Earth will not be fumigated for at least a couple of centuries; why Sam

Goodwin's Shady Nook Café has been remodeled as The Flying Saucer Roadhouse; why Ivan Sergeyevitch Poushov is an assistant ticket collector at Tomsk; and why Kanna-Belle, the Komodo dragon, has a snug circular apartment in the jungle—with atomic air conditioning!

*Avram Davidson has been a soldier as well as the editor of*
The Magazine of Fantasy and Science Fiction. *He has also pro-*
*duced over 75 short stories and 20 novels and anthologies of*
*science fiction and fantasy. Considered one of the most liter-*
*ate of writers, he has written extensively in the mystery*
*field, and has won both the Hugo and Edgar awards. In the*
*following story (which is interesting to compare with the*
*prior one by Budrys), he explores the reaction of ordinary*
*people to the extraordinary.*

# THE GRANTHA SIGHTING

### by Avram Davidson

There were visitors, of course—there were visitors pretty
nearly every night nowadays. The side road had never had
such traffic. Emma Towns threw the door open and welcomed
them, beaming. Walt was there behind her, smiling in his
usual shy way.

"Hello there, Emma," Joe Trobridge said. "Won't let me
call her 'Mrs. Towns,' you know," he explained to his friends.
They went into the warm kitchen of the farmhouse. "This is
Si Haffner, this is Miss Anderson, this is Lou DelBello—all
members of the Unexplained Aerial Phenomena Coordina-
tors, too. And *this* gentleman," he added, when the other
three had finished shaking hands, "is Mr. Tom Knuble."

"Just call me Long Tom," said Long Tom.

Emma said, "Oh, not the radio man? *Really?* Well, my goodness!"

"Tom would like to make some tape recordings from here," Joe explained. "To replay on his program. If you don't mind, that is?"

Why of *course* they didn't mind. And they made the visitors sit right down and they put hot coffee on the table, and tea and home-baked bread and some of Emma's preserves and some of Walt's scuppernong wine, and sandwiches, because they were sure their visitors must be tired and hungry after that long drive.

"This is mighty nice of you," Long Tom said. "*And* very tasty." The Townses beamed, and urged him to take more. Joe cleared his throat.

"This must be at least the fifth or sixth time *I've* been up here," he said. "As well as people I've told they could come up—"

"Any time—" said Emma.

"Any friends—" said Walt.

Joe half-smiled, half-chuckled. A slight trace of what might have been embarrassment was in the sound. "Well, from what I hear, you always put out a spread like this no matter who comes, and I . . . we . . . well . . ."

Miss Anderson came to his rescue. "We talked it over coming up," she said. "And we feel and we are agreed that you are so helpful and accommodating and in every way," she floundered.

"So we want to pay for the refreshments which is the least we can do," Lou DelBello intervened. The visitors nodded and said, Absolutely. Only Right.

Walt and Emma looked at each other. Either the idea had never occurred to them or they were excellent actors. "Oh, *no!*" said Walt. "Oh, we wouldn't *think* of it," said Emma.

They were glad to, she said. It was their privilege. And nothing could induce them to take a cent.

Long Tom put down his cup. "I understand that you wouldn't take any payment for newspaper stories or posing for photographs, either," he said. The Townses shook their heads. "In short—wait a minute, let's get these tapes rolling. . . .

"Now, Mr. and Mrs. Walter F. Towns up here in Paviour's Bridge, New York," he continued after a moment, having started the recording machine, "I understand that you have both refused to commercialize in any way your experiences on the third of October, is that right? Never taken any money—AP, UP, *Life* magazine, *Journal-American*—wouldn't accept payment, is that right, Mr. and Mrs. Walter F. Towns up here in Paviour's Bridge, New York?"

Emma and Walt urged each other with nods of the head to speak first into the whizzing-rolling device, wound up saying together, "That's *No we* right *didn't*."

"I would just like to say—oh excuse me Tom—" Lou began.

"No, go right ahead—"

"I would just like—"

"This is Lou DelBello, you folks out there on the party line: Lou. Del. Bello. Who is up here in Paviour's Bridge, New York, at the Walter F. Townses', along with Miss Jo Anderson, Si Haffner, and Joe Trobridge—as well as myself, Long Tom—all members of that interesting organization you've heard of before on our five-hour conversations over Station WRO, sometimes called familiarly the Flying Saucer Club, but known officially as the Unexplained Aerial Phenomena Coordinating Corps. *Well.* Quite a mouthful. And we are up here accepting the very gracious hospitality of Walt and Emma who are going to tell us, in their own words just exactly. what. it was. that happened on the famous night of October third, known as the October Third Sighting or the Grantha Incident; go right ahead, Lou DelBello."

Still dogged and game, Lou went ahead. "I would just like to say that in speaking of that very gracious hospitality that Walt and Emma have refused to take one red cent for so much as a sandwich or a cup of coffee. To all the visitors up here, I mean. So that certainly should take care of in advance of any charges or even the mention of, ah, com*mer*cialism."

Long Tom paused with a piece of home-baked bread and apple butter halfway into his mouth and gestured to Joe Trobridge.

"Yes, Lou," Joe leaped into the breach, "the same people who didn't believe Columbus and are now so scornful of all the various and innumerable UAP sightings, well, the same *type* people, I mean—some certain individuals who shall be nameless who have been suggesting that the Grantha Incident is just a *trick*, or maybe the Townses and myself are in business together—"

Miss Anderson said, "The Clothlike Substance, you mean, Joe?"

Long Tom swallowed, wiped his mouth. "Well, I didn't know they *made* apple butter like that anymore, Emma," he said. "Yessir folks out there on the party line, the Townses up here in Paviour's Bridge, New York, are poultry farmers by profession but anytime Emma wants to go into the preserves business she can sure count on me to—"

Joe interrupted. "I'd just like to clear up one point, Tom—"

"Why sure, Joe, go right ahead. This is the Long Tom Show, you folks out there on the party line. Five hours of talk and music on Station WRO . . ."

Si Haffner for the first time spoke up:

"I understand this Clothlike Substance is still refusing or rather I should say *defying* analysis in the laboratories; is that right, Joe?"

Joe said it certainly was. This Clothlike Substance, he reminded the listeners-to-be, was left behind at the Townses after the October Third Sighting. It was soft, it was absorbent, it was noninflammable; and it resembled nothing known to our terrestrial science. He had tried to analyze it in his own lab, but, failing to do so, he had turned it over to the General Chemical Company. So far even *they*, with their vastly superior facilities, were unable to say just what it was. And while in a way he was *flattered* that some people thought well maybe he was in cahoots with an outfit like GenChem, well—

"Yessir," said Long Tom; "just let me tell you folks out there on the party line that there is *noth*ing like this chicken-salad sandwich that Mrs. Emma F. Towns puts up out here in Paviour's Bridge, New York. *Won*derful. But I would like you to tell us in your own words, Emma, just what exactly *did* happen that certain night of October third, known to some as the Grantha Incident. Tell us in your own words."

Emma said, "Well."

"Tell us what kind of a day it was. What was the first thing you did?"

Emma said, "Well . . ."

The first thing she did was to get up and heat the mash for the chicks. Not that she minded getting up that early. Some people who'd lived in the city and talked of settling down on a little poultry farm, when it actually came *to* it, they found they didn't care for it too much. But not Emma. No; it wasn't the hours she minded.

And it wasn't the work. She *liked* work. The house was well-built, it was easy to keep warm, it had a lovely view. But it was so far away from everybody. Even the mailman left his deliveries way down at the bottom of the hill. There was the radio, there was the television, but—when you came right down to it—who came to the house? The man who delivered the feed. The man who collected the eggs. And that was all.

The day passed like every other day. Scatter cracked corn. Regular feeding. Scatter sawdust. Clean out from under the wiring. Mix the oats and the clarified buttermilk. Sardine oil. Collect the eggs. Wash them. Pack them. And, of course, while the chickens had to eat, so did the Townses.

No, there was nothing unusual about the day. Until about—

"—about five o'clock, I think it was," Emma said.

"*Nothing* unusual had happened previous to this?" Long Tom asked. "You had *no* warning?"

Emma said No, none.

"I would just like to say—" Joe Trobridge began.

"Well, now just a min—" Tom cut in.

"I just want to clear up one point," Joe said. "Now, prior to the time I arrived at your doorstep that night, had you ever seen or heard of me before, Emma?"

"No, never."

"That's all I wanted to say. I just wanted to clear up that point."

"You got that, did you, all you folks out there on the party line?" inquired Long Tom. "They. had. never. seen, *or* heard. of each other. before. And then, Emma, you were about to say, about five o'clock?"

About five o'clock, when the dark was falling, Emma first noticed the cloud. She called it to Tom's attention. It was a funny-looking cloud. For a long time it didn't move, although the other clouds did. And then—as the bright reds of the sunset turned maroon, magenta, purple—the cloud slowly came down from the sky and hovered about ten feet over the Townses' front yard.

"Walt, there is something *very* funny about that cloud," said Emma.

"I don't believe it's no cloud," Walt declared. "Listen to that noise, would you." It came from the . . . cloud—thing—

whatever it was: a rattling muffled sort of noise, and an angry barking sort of noise. The air grew very dark.

"Do you think we should put on the lights?" Emma said. Walt grunted. And the—whatever it was—came down with a lurching motion and hit the sod with a clonk. It was suddenly lit up by a ring of lights, which went out again almost at once, went on, went out. Then there was a long silence.

A clatter. A rattle. And again, the barking sound.

"Sounds like someone's cussing, almost. Somehow," Walt said.

"*I* am going to put on the *light*," said Emma. And she did. The noise stopped. Emma put on her sweater. "Come out on the porch with me," she said. They opened the door and stepped out on the porch. They looked over at the . . . thing. It sat on the ground about fifty feet away.

"Is anything *wrong?*" Emma called. "Yoo-hoo! Anything wrong?"

There was a slither and a clatter. The lights went on again in the thing and there was now an opening in it and two figures in the opening. One of them started forward, the other reached out a—was that an *arm?* but the first figure barked angrily and it drew back. And there was another sound now, a sort of yelping noise, as the first figure walked towards the house and the second figure followed it.

"A man and his wife," said Emma. Walt observed they were dressed light, considering the time of year.

"That's really nothing but what you might call, well, bloomers, that they got on, though they *are* long and they *do* reach up high."

"Sssshh! Hello, there. My name is Mrs. Towns and this is my husband, Mr. Towns. You folks in any trouble?"

The folks halted some distance away. Even at that distance it was possible to see that they were much shorter and broader than the Townses.

"Why you'll catch your *death* out there with no coats on!" Emma exclaimed. "You're all *blue!*" Actually, it was sort of blue-*green*, but she didn't want to embarrass them. "Come in, come on in," she gestured. They came on in. The yelping noise began again. "There. Now isn't it warmer?" Emma closed the door.

From the crook of her—*was* it an arm? It couldn't be anything else—one of the figures lifted up the source of the yelping. Emma peered at it.

"Well, my *goodness!*" Emma said. She and Walt exchanged glances. "Isn't it just the picture of its father!" she said. An expression which might have been a smile passed over the faces of the two figures.

The first figure reached into its garment and produced an oval container, offered it, withdrew it as a petulant yelp was heard. The figure looked at Emma, barked diffidently.

"Why, don't you *know* what she's saying, Walt?" Emma asked.

Walt squirmed. "It seems like I do, but I know I couldn't hardly," he said.

Emma was half-indignant. "Why, you can, too. She's saying: 'The car broke down and I wonder if I might warm the baby's bottle?' *That's* what she's saying.—Of *course* you may. You just come along into the kitchen."

Walt scratched his ear, looked at the second figure. It looked at him.

"Why, I guess I'd better go along back with you," Walt said, "and take a look at your engine. That was a bad rattle you got there."

It was perhaps half an hour later that they returned. "Got it fixed all right now," Walt said. "Loose umpus on the hootenanny. . . .Baby OK?"

"Sshh . . . it's asleep. All it wanted was a warm bottle and a clean diaper."

There was a silence. Then everyone was talking (or barking) at once—of course, in low tones. "Oh, glad to do it, glad to be of help," said Emma. "Any time . . . and whenever you happen to be around this way, why just you drop in and see us. Sorry you can't stay."

"Sure thing," Walt seconded. "That's right."

Emma said, "It's so lonely up here. We hardly ever have any visitors at all. . . . Goodby! Goodby, now!" And finally the visitors closed the opening in their vehicle.

"Hope the umpus stays fixed in the hootenanny . . ." There was a burst of pyrotechnic colors, a rattling noise, and a volley of muffled barks. "It didn't," Walt said. "*Hear* him cussing!" The rattling ceased, the colors faded into a white mist. "Got it now . . . look at those lights go round and round . . . there they go. Wherever it is they're going," he concluded, uncertainly. They closed the door. Emma sighed.

"It *was* nice having someone to visit with," she said.

"Heaven only knows how long it will be before anyone else comes here."

It was exactly three hours and five minutes. Two automobiles came tearing up the road and screamed to a stop. People got out, ran pounding up the path, knocked at the door. Walt answered.

At first they all talked at once, then all fell silent. Finally, one man said, "I'm Joe Trobridge of the U.A.P.C.C.—the Unexplained Aerial—listen, a *sighting* was reported in this vicinity! Did you see it? A flying saucer? Huh?"

Walt nodded slowly. "So *that's* what it was," he said. "I thought it was some kind of a airship."

Trobridge's face lit up. Everyone began to babble again. Then Trobridge said, "You *saw* it? Was it close? What? SHUT UP, EVERYBODY! On your front lawn? What'd they look like? What—?"

Walt pursed his mouth. "I'll tell ya," he began. "They were blue."

"*Blue?*" exclaimed Trobridge.

"Well . . ." Walt's tone was that of a man willing to stretch a point. "Maybe it was green."

"*Green?*"

"Well, which was it?" someone demanded. "Blue or green?"

Walt said, in the same live-and-let-live tone, "Bluish-green." Joe Trobridge opened his mouth. "Or, greenish-blue," Walt continued, cutting him off. The visitors milled around, noisily.

"How were they dressed?"

Walt pursed his mouth. "I'll tell ya," he said. "They were wearing what ya might call like bloomers . . ."

"*Bloomers?*"

Emma glanced around nervously. The visitors didn't seem to like what Walt was telling them. Not at all.

Joe Trobridge pressed close. "Did they say what their purpose was, in visiting the Earth?" he asked, eagerness restored somewhat—but only somewhat.

Walt nodded. "Oh, sure. Told us right away. Come to see if they could warm the baby's bottle." Someone in the crowd made a scornful noise. "That was it, y'see . . ." his voice trailed off uncertainly.

The man named Joe Trobridge looked at him, his mouth twisted. "Now, *wait* a minute," he said. "Just wait a *min*ute . . ."

Emma took in the scene at a glance. No one would believe them. They'd all go away and never come back and no one would ever visit them again—except the man who delivered the feed and the man who collected the eggs. She looked at the disappointed faces around her, some beginning to show anger, and she got up.

"My husband is joking," she said, loudly and clearly. "Of *course* it wasn't like that."

Joe turned to her. "Did you see it, too, lady? What happened, then? I mean, *really* happened? Tell us in your own words. What did they look like?"

Emma considered for a moment. "They were very tall," she said. "And they had on spacesuits. And their leader spoke to us. He looked just like us only maybe his head was a bit bigger. He didn't have no hair. He didn't really speak English— it was more like telepathy—"

The people gathered around her closely, their eyes aglow, their faces eager. "Go on," they said; "go on—"

"His name was . . . Grantha—"

"*Grantha,*" the people breathed.

"And he said we shouldn't be afraid, because he came in peace. 'Earth people,' he said, 'we have observed you for a long time and now we feel the time has come to make ourselves known to you. . . .'"

Long Tom nodded. "So that's the way it was."

"That's the way it was," she said. "More coffee, anybody?"

"You brew a mighty fine cup of coffee, Mrs. Emma Towns up here in Paviour's Bridge, New York, let me tell the folks on the party line," Long Tom said. "No sugar, thanks, just cream. . . . Well, say, about this piece of Clothlike Substance. It's absorbent—it's soft—it doesn't burn—and it can't be analyzed. Now, about how big is this wonderful item which Grantha and his people left behind as a sample of their superior technicology and peaceful intentions and which continues to baffle scientists? And how big is it? Just tell us in your own words. . . ."

Emma considered. Joe pursed his lips.

Lou DelBello smiled. "Well, I've had the good fortune to see it," he said, "and—speaking as the father of three—the, uh, best comparison of its size which I could give you, I'd say it's just about as big as a diaper!"

He guffawed. Joe burst out laughing, as did Si Haffner.

Miss Anderson giggled. Long Tom chuckled. Emma and Walt looked nervously at each other, looked anxiously at their oh, so very welcome guests—but only for a moment. Then, reassured, they leaned back and joined in the merriment.

*Larry Eisenberg has written one book and approximately 40 short stories of science fiction. Perhaps his quintessential creation is wacky Emmett Duckworth, research biochemist extraordinary whose madcap adventures, including "The Saga of DMM," can be found in* The Best Laid Schemes *(1971). Most of his works are satires, and many touch upon scientific research and psychology. However, in the story below, the focus is on politicians, paranoia, and peace.*

# THE MERCHANT

## by Larry Eisenberg

I was in the President's office trying to steady his nerves and dispel his sense of persecution when a phone call was put through directly to his desk. He listened for a while, unusually silent, eyes darting about. Then he barked a few short questions into the phone before handing it over to me.

"What's this all about, Mr. President?" I asked.

His mouth twitched.

"I'm not sure," he said. His brow was damp with cold sweat. "He claims to be General Mackay."

I took the phone and listened.

It was General Mackay, all right. I recognized the voice. He was calling from the Ice River Air Base in Montana and he swore an extraterrestrial spaceship had landed.

I began to snicker. "Is this a practical joke?"

The President grabbed hold of my shirt collar. "I won't be laughed at," he muttered into my ear.

Between the President complaining and this Air brass spouting about creatures from outer space I nearly slipped my moorings.

"For God's sake, General, what do they look like?"

"Well, I not only saw one," he said, "I've talked to it. It has a kind of luminescent glow but no body that I can see."

At this point the President snatched the phone from my hand and slammed it back on the cradle.

"What do you make of all this?" he asked, eyes big as silver dollars.

"I think the general's brains have boiled over. The Air Force has been under a terrible strain lately, what with not being able to drop nuclear bombs. The general must have broken under the tension."

"I'm frightened," said the President. "Maybe that was the general calling and maybe it was a Sovcom agent trying to make me panic. I want you to go to Ice River and find out. Then come right back here and report in person."

Hearing the edge to his voice I didn't wait for further instructions.

Three hours later I reached the Air Force base at Ice River. General Mackay was waiting there for me, creases missing from his trousers, cap awry, eyes numb with excitement.

On our way to the landing site he outlined what had happened.

"At 0300 this morning a fireball was observed about fifty miles from here near Pioneer Falls. The local sheriff, after he'd received a dozen phone calls, decided to investigate. He drove his station wagon all over the terrain for an hour before he sighted this glowing oval disk in a frozen cow pasture."

"How big a disk?"

"About five, maybe six feet high," said the general. "The sheriff approached it warily, sniffing fire and brimstone, he says, and holding on to a small pocket Bible that he keeps in his breast pocket. He keeps it there so it will be over his heart. Bibles have been known to stop bullets, you see—"

"Goddamn it, General," I snapped, "can't you cut out all the details and get down to the raw meat?"

The general flushed and resumed his story.

"The sheriff heard what sounded like a human voice coming from inside the disk and decided that he'd gone as far as he was going to. He hustled back to his car, radioed the State Police. They notified the Air Force at Ice River. I was roused out of bed, pretty damn sore and ready to bust the idiot who had concocted this insane story."

"And then you found out it wasn't insane?"

"Come see for yourself," said the general. "I've got a jeep ready to take you to the landing site."

"What about the spaceship?"

"There's a guard surrounding it. Our visitor is now waiting patiently to talk to you. I got word to him that you're the personal representative of the President." That was all Mackay would tell me. "I want your impressions to be unbiased," he said.

I was still annoyed and skeptical when we pulled up to the cow pasture where the alleged space vehicle had landed. There was a peculiar odor in the air and there was something sitting in the pasture. It was barely visible in the moonlight, just an amorphous grayish-white mass. The military guard parted and we drove up slowly, right to the edge of the ship. General Mackay stepped outside and called a greeting. Just ahead of us a flickering glow appeared.

"That's our guest," whispered the general.

"My name is Wade Holcomb," I called out to no one in particular, feeling like an idiot. "I represent our President and I wish to talk to you in his name."

The glow seemed to hover and then moved closer to me. My eye caught a flash of metal; I stepped back. The general dropped his hand reassuringly to my shoulder.

"What the hell is that?" I asked.

"Just a box," said the general. "Don't panic."

"I have come in peace," said the soft voice. "This box harbors a transducer which enables me to communicate with you. By profession I am a Merchant and my four colleagues within the vessel are sales assistants. We have come from a planet of the star which you call Mekta in the constellation Ursa Major. Our sole purpose is commercial in nature. We wish to exchange goods."

I began to laugh. Tension, I guess.

"Maybe they expect to buy America for beads and trinkets," I muttered to General Mackay.

He simply shrugged.

Turning back to the box, I said, "I'm not certain we have anything in our country to interest you, but I know one thing for sure. You may be the answer to our prayers."

After more talk we agreed to arrange a meeting with the President and perhaps his Secretary of Commerce. Then I flew right back to the White House.

The President jumped out of his seat when he saw me.

"Are they for real?" he asked.

His fingernails seemed to have edged down to the skin line. I grinned at him.

"I have something to tell you that should please you, sir. It occurs to me that with the help of our outer-space friends we may have the answer to the nuclear stalemate. What a great stroke of luck that they landed on our side of the world and not the other! It puts us in position to leapfrog over the entire balance of power."

The President's eyes, normally oysterlike in appearance, gleamed for the first time in months.

"Maybe," he said softly, his throat muscles working as though a savory dinner were being heaped in front of him. "But before I raise my hopes let me eyeball this planetary freak."

"He may be freaklike in aspect," I warned, "but he makes a lot of sense. We'd better proceed cautiously in our dealings with him. In my opinion he and his buddies really have come for purposes of trade. I'm just wondering what we can offer them in return."

"I'm on my toes," said the President. "Whatever they try, I won't lower my guard."

The arrival of the space visitors was kept absolutely secret. Rumors did float about the country and all were denied vigorously by authoritative spokesmen. One persistent newspaper columnist found himself in protective custody, unable to draw bail, which seemed to have a salutary effect on other journalists.

In the meantime I was grappling with the problem of how to smuggle the Merchant of Mekta into the White House. After much discussion it was finally decided, instead, to take the President to the spaceship in Pioneer Falls. He was in knots all through the flight and required constant reassurance that the Merchant would not be a threat to his life. As he repeated the same questions over and over again my good humor wore thin.

But when we landed the President seemed to pull himself together. He said nothing at all as we drove to the cow pasture and when the spaceship finally materialized before his eyes he nodded confidently as though all his preconceptions had been confirmed.

"I want Wade, General Mackay and myself, nobody else, to talk to this creature," he said. "But see that we're closely guarded."

There was some grumbling among the military staff members but no one was willing to buck the President on the issue. The introduction to the Merchant went off well. The President flashed all of his city-lawyer charm, even forcing his dew-laps back into a semblance of a smile. He welcomed the Merchant and his aides with a flowery speech filled with brilliant phrases like "our hearts brim over" and "it is a rare pleasure indeed."

"And now," he concluded, "we must come down to the mundane matters that concern our little world. What did you have in mind when you talked about trading?"

"It is somewhat difficult to say," answered the Merchant. "We are an advanced people. We can fabricate objects and machinery of the greatest complexity. Our community has no material needs. What we are looking for is that which is unique—one-of-a-kind art objects, animals or even handmade jewelry. In other words, we seek what we cannot duplicate. We are most inquisitive, always thirsting for novelties."

"So are we," said the President. "We're pretty clever ourselves and I'm sure we make some unusual gadgets that you'd want to take home with you. But what can you give us in return?"

"As an example," said the Merchant, "let me show you a unique material."

A long glistening tube seemed to emerge from nowhere and flowed toward us.

"Pick it up, Mr. Holcomb," said the Merchant.

I did. It was a transparent material, hard to the touch and light as a feather. I passed it over to the President, who seemed quite unimpressed.

"We can supply you with unlimited quantities of this material in any desired shape," said the Merchant. "It has some quite desirable properties. It resists impact well, is chemically nonreactive and absolutely leakproof. You may find it ideal for construction purposes."

"Don't you have any weapons?" asked the President.

There was a pronounced silence from the Merchant. Then: "We will not deal in weapons under any circumstances."

"Why not?" asked the President.

I tugged at his sleeve. "Mr. President, let me talk to you a minute."

"Not just yet," he said. "I want to pursue this weapons question."

I ignored protocol and whispered into his ear. "Don't you see? This material he's showing us may be bomb-resistant. Suppose it's impervious to nuclear weapons? It would break the nuclear deadlock!"

"Too iffy," said the President. "Let's try it my way first."

"Please," I begged. "Give it a chance."

The President pondered a moment and then, though reluctantly, he acceded.

I turned to the Merchant. "Would you object if we suspended our talks for a few days? We'd like to conduct some engineering tests on this material you've shown us."

"By all means," said the Merchant, and after some formal expressions of goodwill we parted.

The test results were exciting beyond belief. The material was impervious even to nuclear explosions. When I brought this information to the President he finally got my point.

"If we build above-ground shelters of this stuff," he mused, "we would be on the verge of permanent peace for the first time in the history of mankind. I could go on the air and issue an ultimatum to our enemies without fear of retaliation. By God, Wade, you were absolutely right! This stuff may be better than any weapon he could have given us."

"I don't like to be a wet blanket, Mr. President," I said, "but we've got to handle this point with great delicacy. If the Merchant gets wind of what we plan to do, he may not go along with us."

"None of that," said the President peevishly. "Either he'll go along with us or his ship will never leave the ground. I'll make sure of that."

"I don't see how," I started to say, but knowing the President I kept my mouth shut.

When I returned to the cow pasture to tell the Merchant of

Mekta that we were delighted with his material, I brought along plans for an above-ground structure capable of housing ventilating machinery and a large population.

The Merchant seemed to be giving considerable thought to the plans. I had to wait fifteen minutes for a response.

"What do you plan to do with these structures?"

"Alleviate our severe housing shortage," I said. "Much of our population is still inadequately housed."

"What you say is probably true," said the Merchant. "And yet I know enough about your society to suspect that what you seek from these structures is some military advantage."

I sighed. "Such advantage would be purely coincidental."

"We are a pacific people," said the Merchant. "Even in self-defense we never resort to violence. Perhaps that makes us unduly suspicious of you. What is needed is a gesture of trust in one another. Therefore if you solemnly promise that your application will be solely peaceful, our bargain can be completed."

"A sacred promise," I said, knowing full well that the ends we sought were peaceful.

The President was elated at the news and rubbed his hands joyfully.

"Time is the important factor here," he said. "We've got to get one of these shelters fully equipped. We must find out for sure if people can live in it."

Which was exactly what we did. The Merchant furnished us with a nearly weightless, translucent tunnel section capable of housing twenty thousand people. He even provided an ingenious, atomically fueled pump mechanism to circulate and at the same time purify the atmosphere within the chamber. We gathered up four hundred volunteers to stay in the structure for a two-week period. The test proved a smashing success.

We placed an order with the Merchant for ten thousand units, in return giving him credits for an equivalent value in American goods. He and his assistants set to work at once. Week after week, fifty fully equipped units issued from his vessel and were immediately towed by plane to different parts of the country. Our entire administrative machinery was put into high gear, and food, clothing, recreational supplies, everything we could think of, went into the shelters.

Apparently this flurry of activity went unnoticed by our

enemies—a tribute to the effectiveness of our superlative counterespionage services. From time to time, a vehicle would "lose" itself in the vicinity of one of our new installations, but always an alert guard would direct it out of the neighborhood.

At the end of eight months, each of the new units was fully operational and a full session of the National Security Council was called. After more than three days of discussion the Council decided to publicize our new posture. Both the national and international press were alerted. All diplomats of the United Nations and all accredited ambassadors were sent engraved invitations to the unusual dedication ceremony to be held at Pioneer Falls.

Just before the ceremony, the President flew out to thank the Merchant and give him a list of items from which repayment would be made. I started to tell the Merchant, in terms as diplomatic as I could muster, what was now afoot. But the President brushed me aside. He detailed exactly what he now planned to do and then waited for the Merchant's reply. It was not long in coming.

"As I feared," said the Merchant. "You never meant to keep your promise."

"But that's not true," said the President. "You, sir, seem to have missed my point. We don't seek a nuclear war. We want a peaceful world for all of us. And now we're in a position to enforce that peace."

"On what terms?"

"Let me say something," I blurted. "Our neighbors across the sea are unreliable, untrustworthy. They understand only the force of arms. We, on the other hand, are good people. We are not malicious or vindictive. We covet no territory, we threaten no lives. In fact we want everyone to have a full life, a free life. Our hands and our hearts are clean. Would you give the Sovcoms the advantage over us?"

"We never intended to change a balance of power," said the Merchant. "It is completely foreign to our code of ethics. And I am seriously disturbed that you should have used us in this way."

"I don't mean to be cynical or crassly commercial," I said, "but you still have a considerable payment coming from us. Do you remember?"

"I haven't forgotten," said the Merchant.

\*   \*   \*

The President was now in his dress rehearsal. The preliminary reading of his speech was delivered with earnestness and in a room chilled to forty degrees Fahrenheit to slow down his continual facial sweating. The room itself was in our new shelter, the one to be dedicated to peace.

One by one our military men marched in, resplendent in full dress uniform with all battle ribbons neatly displayed. A chaplain of each religion including Islam was also present. At the hand signal of the communications director, the breathtaking ceremony began. Before the entire nation and the rest of the world the President acknowledged the presence of extraterrestrial visitors. There was a good deal of agitation outside the shelter where the diplomatic corps was gathered.

The President then described in measured words the nature of the shelters the Merchant had built for us. When the President was finished he accepted a bottle of chilled champagne from one of his aides and smashed it against a wall. A ribbon was cut, and then the President, at the head of a beaming array of military figures and cabinet members, led them on a tour of the shelter. He pointed out every detail of the living quarters, the library that included all the current best sellers, the immaculate washrooms . . .

When the tour was completed, the presidential party turned to leave—and found the outer doors could not be opened.

I heard nervous chuckles as I approached the doors myself and activated each of the electrical fail-safe interlocks. None responded. There was a scuffling outside and a flurry of shots, then silence. At that point, over the community speakers in the shelter came the soothing voice of the Merchant.

"Don't be alarmed," he said. "There is no danger to anyone."

Three of the military aides began to batter at the doors.

General Mackay stopped them, yelling, "The shelter is in motion!"

"General Mackay is right," confirmed the Merchant's voice. "You are now being towed by my vessel. Rest assured that when we reach Mekta you will enjoy unending ease and comfort."

There was a last desperate chance and the President took it.

"What about fair play?" he cried. "You say you don't want us to have a military advantage over the other side. But now you strip our country of its President and military leaders."

A hush followed. It was as if the Merchant were marshaling his thoughts.

"The self-deception of your culture is absolutely staggering," said the Merchant. "At the very moment we landed in your nation our sister ship came down in the icy wastes of the other hemisphere. The measures taken there to keep our landing secret were apparently as effective as your own. And of course, the leaders of that region claimed to be eager for housing, as you did. It should come as no surprise to you, then, to learn that they now have an equal number of shelters and that at this very moment a good-sized contingent of their own military leaders, and their Premier, are also en route to Mekta."

General Mackay took off his braided cap and wiped his forehead.

"God help us, we're his prisoners."

"Prisoners?" said the Merchant. "None of you are prisoners. You will live in habitats as much like your own as possible. And your freedom to roam those habitats will be unlimited. Our acquisitions are always treated in this way."

"Acquisitions?" I yelped. "For what?"

"For the Mekta Zoo," said the Merchant softly.

I would not care to repeat what the President said.

*Howard Fast has won the Breadloaf Literature Award, the Schomburg Award for Race Relations, the Newspaper Guild Award, and the Screen Writers' Annual Award. His major efforts have been devoted to screenplays and best-selling novels such as* Spartacus *(1951) and the "Immigrant" series. However, he produced his first science fiction story more than 50 years ago and has subsequently published 30 additional works, many of which, like the one below, are cautionary in nature.*

# THE MOUSE

### by Howard Fast

Only the mouse watched the flying saucer descend to earth. The mouse crouched apprehensively in a mole's hole, its tiny nose twitching, its every nerve quivering in fear and attention as the beautiful golden thing made a landing.

The flying saucer—or circular spaceship, shaped roughly like a flattened, wide-brimmed hat—slid past the roof of the split-level suburban house, swam across the back yard, and then settled into a tangle of ramblers, nestling down among the branches and leaves so that it was covered entirely. And since the flying saucer was only about thirty inches in diameter and no more than seven inches in height, the camouflage was accomplished rather easily.

It was just past three o'clock in the morning. The inhabitants of this house and of all the other houses in this particular suburban development slept or tossed in their beds and struggled with insomnia. The passage of the flying saucer was soundless and without odor, so no dog barked; only the mouse watched—and he watched without comprehension, even as he always watched, even as his existence was—without comprehension.

What had just happened became vague and meaningless in the memory of the mouse—for he hardly had a memory at all. It might never have happened. Time went by, seconds, minutes, almost an hour, and then a light appeared in the tangle of briars and leaves where the saucer lay. The mouse fixed on the light, and then he saw two men appear, stepping out of the light, which was an opening into the saucer, and onto the ground.

Or at least they appeared to be vaguely like creatures the mouse had seen that actually were men—except that they were only three inches tall and enclosed in spacesuits. If the mouse could have distinguished between the suit and what it contained and if the mouse's vision had been selective, he might have seen that under the transparent covering the men from the saucer differed only in size from the men on earth—at least in general appearance. Yet in other ways they differed a great deal. They did not speak vocally, nor did their suits contain any sort of radio equipment; they were telepaths, and after they had stood in silence for about five minutes they exchanged thoughts.

"The thing to keep in mind," said the first man, "is that while our weight is so much less here than at home, we are still very, very heavy. And this ground is not very dense."

"No, it isn't is it? Are they all asleep?"

The first reached out. His mind became an electronic network that touched the minds of every living creature within a mile or so.

"Almost all of the people are asleep. Most of the animals appear to be nocturnal."

"Curious."

"No—not really. Most of the animals are undomesticated—small, wild creatures. Great fear—hunger and fear."

"Poor things."

"Yes—poor things, yet they manage to survive. That's quite a feat, under the noses of the people. Interesting people. Probe a bit."

The second man reached out with his mind and probed. His reaction might be translated as "Ugh!"

"Yes—yes, indeed. They think some horrible thoughts, don't they? I'm afraid I prefer the animals. There's one right up ahead of us. Wide awake and with nothing else in that tiny brain of his but fear. In fact, fear and hunger seem to add up to his total mental baggage. Not hate, no aggression."

"He's also quite small as things go on this planet," the second spaceman observed. "No larger than we are. You know, he might just do for us."

"He might," the first agreed.

With that, the two tiny men approached the mouse, who still crouched defensively in the mole hole, only the tip of its whiskered nose showing. The two men moved very slowly and carefully, choosing their steps with great deliberation. One of them suddenly sank almost to his knees in a little bit of earth, and after they they attempted to find footing on stones, pebbles, bits of wood. Evidently their great weight made the hard, dry earth too soft for safety. Meanwhile the mouse watched them, and when their direction became evident, the mouse attempted the convulsive action of escape.

But his muscles would not respond, and as panic seared his small brain, the first spaceman reached into the mouse's mind, soothing him, finding the fear center and blocking it off with his own thoughts and then electronically shifting the mouse's neuron paths to the pleasure centers of the tiny animal's brain. All this the spacemen did effortlessly and almost instantaneously, and the mouse relaxed, made squeaks of joy, and gave up any attempt to escape. The second spaceman then broke the dirt away from the tunnel mouth, lifted the mouse with ease, holding him in his arms, and carried him back to the saucer. And the mouse lay there, relaxed and cooing with delight.

Two others, both women, were waiting in the saucer as the men came through the air lock, carrying the mouse. The women—evidently in tune with the men's thoughts—did not have to be told what had happened. They had prepared what could only be an operating table, a flat panel of bright light overhead and a board of instruments alongside. The light made a square of brilliance in the darkened interior of the spaceship.

"I am sterile," the first woman informed the men, holding

up hands encased in thin, transparent gloves, "so we can proceed immediately."

Like the men's, the women's skin was yellow, not sallow but a bright, glowing lemon yellow, the hair rich orange. Out of the spacesuits, they would all be dressed more or less alike, barefoot and in shorts in the warm interior of the ship; nor did the women cover their well-formed breasts.

"I reached out," the second woman told them. "They're all asleep, but their minds!"

"We know," the men agreed.

"I rooted around—like a journey through a sewer. But I picked up a good deal. The animal is called a mouse. It is symbolically the smallest and most harmless of creatures, vegetarian, and hunted by practically everything else on this curious planet. Only its size accounts for its survival, and its only skill is in concealment."

Meanwhile the two men had laid the mouse on the operating table, where it sprawled relaxed and squeaking contentment. While the men went to change out of their spacesuits, the second woman filled a hypodermic instrument, inserted the needle near the base of the mouse's tail, and gently forced the fluid in. The mouse relaxed and became unconscious. Then the two women changed the mouse's position, handling the—to them huge—animal with ease and dispatch, as if it had almost no weight; and actually in terms of the gravitation they were built to contend with, it had almost no weight at all.

When the two men returned, they were dressed as were the women, in shorts, and barefoot, with the same transparent gloves. The four of them then began to work together, quickly, expertly—evidently a team who had worked in this manner many times in the past. The mouse now lay upon its stomach, its feet spread. One man put a cone-shaped mask over its head and began the feeding of oxygen. The other man shaved the top of its head with an electric razor, while the two women began an operation which would remove the entire top of the mouse's skull. Working with great speed and skill, they incised the skin, and then using trephines that were armed with a sort of laser beam rather than a saw, they cut through the top of the skull, removed it, and handed it to one of the men who placed it in a pan that was filled with a glowing solution. The brain of the mouse was thus exposed. The two women then wheeled over a machine with a turret

top on a universal joint, lowered the top close to the exposed
brain, and pressed a button. About a hundred tiny wires
emerged from the turret top, and very fast, the women began
to attach these wires to parts of the mouse's brain. The man
who had been controlling the oxygen flow now brought over
another machine, drew tubes out of it, and began a process of
feeding fluid into the mouse's circulatory system, while the
second man began to work on the skull section that was in
the glowing solution.

The four of them worked steadily and apparently without
fatigue. Outside, the night ended and the sun rose, and still
the four space people worked on. At about noon they finished
the first part of their work and stood back from the table to
observe and admire what they had done. The tiny brain of the
mouse had been increased fivefold in size, and in shape and
folds resembled a miniature human brain. Each of the four
shared a feeling of great accomplishment, and they mingled
their thoughts and praised each other and then proceeded to
complete the operation. The shape of the skull section that
had been removed was now compatible with the changed
brain, and when they replaced it on the mouse's head, the
only noticeable difference in the creature's appearance was a
strange, high lump above his eyes. They sealed the breaks
and joined the flesh with some sort of plastic, removed the
tubes, inserted new tubes, and changed the deep uncon-
sciousness of the mouse to a deep sleep.

For the next five days the mouse slept—but from motionless sleep, its condition changed gradually, until on the fifth
day it began to stir and move restlessly, and then on the sixth
day it awakened. During these five days it was fed intrave-
nously, massaged constantly, and probed constantly and telepathically. The four space people took turns at entering its
mind and feeding it information, and neuron by neuron,
section by section, they programmed its newly enlarged
brain. They were very skilled at this. They gave the mouse
background knowledge, understanding, language, and self-
comprehension. They fed it a vast amount of information,
balanced the information with a philosophical comprehension of the universe and its meaning, left it as it had been
emotionally, without aggression or hostility, but also without
fear. When the mouse finally awakened, it knew what it was
and how it had become what it was. It still remained a mouse,
but in the enchanting wonder and majesty of its mind, it

was like no other mouse that had ever lived on the planet Earth.

The four space people stood around the mouse as it awakened and watched it. They were pleased, and since much in their nature, especially in their emotional responses, was childlike and direct, they could not help showing their pleasure and smiling at the mouse. Their thoughts were in the nature of a welcome, and all that the mind of the mouse could express was gratitude. The mouse came to its feet, stood on the floor where it had lain, faced each of them in turn, and then wept inwardly at the fact of its existence. Then the mouse was hungry and they gave it food. After that the mouse asked the basic, inevitable question:

"Why?"

"Because we need your help."

"How can I help you when your own wisdom and power are apparently without measure?"

The first spaceman explained. They were explorers, cartographers, surveyors—and behind them, light-years away, was their home planet, a gigantic ball the size of our planet Jupiter. Thus their small size, their incredible density. Weighing on earth only a fraction of what they weighed at home, they nevertheless weighed more than any earth creature their size—so much more that they walked on earth in dire peril of sinking out of sight. It was quite true that they could go anywhere in their spacecraft, but to get all the information they required, they would have to leave it—they would have to venture forth on foot. Thus the mouse would be their eyes and their feet.

"And for this a mouse!" the mouse exclaimed. "Why? I am the smallest, the most defenseless of creatures."

"Not any longer," they assured him. "We ourselves carry no weapons, because we have our minds, and in that way your mind is like ours. You can enter the mind of any creature, a cat, a dog—even a man—stop the neuron paths to his hate and aggression centers, and you can do it with the speed of thought. You have the strongest of all weapons—the ability to make any living thing love you, and having that, you need nothing else."

Thus the mouse became a part of the little group of space people who measured, charted, and examined the planet Earth. The mouse raced through the streets of a hundred cities, slipped in and out of hundreds of buildings, crouched

in corners where he was privy to the discussions of people of
power who ruled this part or that part of the planet Earth,
and the space people listened with his ears, smelled with his
sensitive nostrils, and saw with his soft brown eyes. The
mouse journeyed thousands of miles, across the seas and
continents whose existence he had never dreamed about. He
listened to professors lecturing to auditoriums of college
students, and he listened to the great symphony orchestras,
the fine violinists and pianists. He watched mothers give
birth to children and he listened to wars being planned and
murders plotted. He saw weeping mourners watch the dead
interred in the earth, and he trembled to the crashing sounds
of huge assembly lines in monstrous factories. He hugged the
earth as bullets whistled overhead, and he saw men slaugh-
ter each other for reasons so obscure that in their own minds
there was only hate and fear.

As much as the space people, he was a stranger to the
curious ways of mankind, and he listened to them speculate
on the mindless, haphazard mixture of joy and horror that
was mankind's civilization on the planet Earth.

Then, when their mission was almost completed, the mouse
chose to ask them about their own place. He was able to
weigh facts now and to measure possibilities and to grapple
with uncertainties and to create his own abstractions; and so
he thought, on one of those evenings when the warmth of the
five little creatures filled the spaceship, when they sat and
mingled thoughts and reactions in an interlocking of body
and mind of which the mouse was a part, about the place
where they had been born.

"Is it very beautiful?" the mouse asked.

"It's a good place. Beautiful—and filled with music."

"You have no wars?"

"No."

"And no one kills for the pleasure of killing?"

"No."

"And your animals—things like myself?"

"They exist in their own ecology. We don't disturb it, and
we don't kill them. We grow and we make the food we eat."

"And are there crimes like here—murder and assault and
robbery?"

"Almost never."

And so it went, question and answer, while the mouse lay
there in front of them, his strangely shaped head between his

paws, his eyes fixed on the two men and the two women with worship and love; and then it came as he asked them:

"Will I be allowed to live with you—with the four of you? Perhaps to go on other missions with you? Your people are never cruel. You won't place me with the animals. You'll let me be with the people, won't you?"

They didn't answer. The mouse tried to reach into their minds, but he was still like a little child when it came to the game of telepathy, and their minds were shielded.

"Why?"

Still no response.

"Why?" he pleaded.

Then, from one of the women. "We were going to tell you. Not tonight, but soon. Now we must tell you. You can't come with us."

"Why?"

"For the plainest of reasons, dear friend. We are going home."

"Then let me go home with you. It's my home too—the beginning of all my thoughts and dreams and hope."

"We can't."

"Why?" the mouse pleaded. "Why?"

"Don't you understand? Our planet is the size of your planet Jupiter here in the solar system. That is why we were so small in earth terms—because our very atomic structure is different from yours. By the measure of weight they use here on earth, I weigh almost a hundred kilograms, and you weigh less than an eighth of a kilogram, and yet we are almost the same size. If we were to bring you to our planet, you would die the moment we reached its gravitational pull. You would be crushed so completely that all semblance of form in you would disappear. You can't ask us to destroy you."

"But you're so wise," the mouse protested. "You can do almost anything. Change me. Make me like yourselves."

"By your standards we're wise—" The space people were full of sadness. It permeated the room, and the mouse felt its desolation. "By our own standards we have precious little wisdom. We can't make you like us. That is beyond any power we might dream of. We can't even undo what we have done, and now we realize what we have done."

"And what will you do with me?"

"The only thing we can do. Leave you here."

"Oh, no." The thought was a cry of agony.

"What else can we do?"

"Don't leave me here," the mouse begged them. "Anything—but don't leave me here. Let me make the journey with you, and then if I have to die I will die."

"There is no journey as you see it," they explained. "Space is not an area for us. We can't make it comprehensible to you, only tell you that it is an illusion. When we rise out of the earth's atmosphere, we slip into a fold of space and emerge in our own planetary system. So it would not be a journey that you would make with us—only a step to your death."

"Then let me die with you," the mouse pleaded.

"No—you ask us to kill you. We can't."

"Yet you made me."

"We changed you. We made you grow in a certain way."

"Did I ask you to? Did you ask me whether I wanted to be like this?"

"God help us, we didn't."

"Then what am I to do?"

"Live. That's all we can say. You must live."

"How? How can I live? A mouse hides in the grass and knows only two things—fear and hunger. It doesn't even know that it is, and of the vast lunatic world that surrounds it, it knows nothing. But you gave me the knowledge—"

"And we also gave you the means to defend yourself, so that you can live without fear."

"Why? Why should I live? Don't you understand that?"

"Because life is good and beautiful—and in itself the answer to all things."

"For me?" The mouse looked at them and begged them to look at him. "What do you see? I am a mouse. In all this world there is no other creature like myself. Shall I go back to the mice?"

"Perhaps."

"And discuss philosophy with them? And open my mind to them? Or should I have intercourse with those poor, damned mindless creatures? What am I to do? You are wise. Tell me. Shall I be the stallion of the mouse world? Shall I store up riches in roots and bulbs? Tell me, tell me," he pleaded.

"We will talk about it again," the space people said. "Be with yourself for a while, and don't be afraid."

Then the mouse lay with his head between his paws and he thought about the way things were. And when the space people asked him where he wanted to be, he told them:

"Where you found me."

So once again the saucer settled by night into the back yard of the surburban split-level house. Once again the air lock opened, and this time a mouse emerged. The mouse stood there, and the saucer rose out of the swirling dead leaves and spun away, a fleck of gold losing itself in the night. And the mouse stood there, facing its own eternity.

A cat, awakened by the movement among the leaves, came toward the mouse and then halted a few inches away when the tiny animal did not flee. The cat reached out a paw, and then the paw stopped. The cat struggled for control of its own body and then it fled, and still the mouse stood motionless. Then the mouse smelled the air, oriented himself, and moved to the mouth of an old mole tunnel. From down below, from deep in the tunnel, came the warm, musky odor of mice. The mouse went down through the tunnel to the nest, where a male and a female mouse crouched, and the mouse probed into their minds and found fear and hunger.

The mouse ran from the tunnel up to the open air and stood there, sobbing and panting. He turned his head up to the sky and reached out with his mind—but what he tried to reach was already a hundred light-years away.

"Why? Why?" the mouse sobbed to himself. "They are so good, so wise—why did they do it to me?"

He then moved toward the house. He had become an adept at entering houses, and only a steel vault would have defied him. He found his point of entry and slipped into the cellar of the house. His night vision was good, and this combined with his keen sense of smell enabled him to move swiftly and at will.

Moving through the shifting web of strong odors that marked any habitation of people, he isolated the sharp smell of old cheese, and he moved across the floor and under a staircase to where a mousetrap had been set. It was a primitive thing, a stirrup of hard wire bent back against the tension of a coil spring and held with a tiny latch. The bit of cheese was on the latch, and the lightest touch on the cheese would spring the trap.

Filled with pity for his own kind, their gentleness, their helplessness, their mindless hunger that led them into a trap so simple and unconcealed, the mouse felt a sudden sense of triumph, of ultimate knowledge. He knew now what the space people had known from the very beginning, that they had given him the ultimate gift of the universe—consciousness of his own being—and in a flash of that knowledge the mouse knew all things and knew that all things were encompassed in consciousness. He saw the wholeness of the world and of all the worlds that ever were or would be, and he was without fear or loneliness.

In the morning, the man of the split-level suburban house went down into his cellar and let out a whoop of delight.

"Got it," he yelled up to his family. "I got the little bastard now."

But the man never really looked at anything, not at his wife, not at his kids, not at the world; and while he knew that the trap contained a dead mouse, he never even noticed that this mouse was somewhat different from the other mice. Instead, he went out to the back yard, swung the dead mouse by his tail, and sent it flying into his neighbor's back yard.

"That'll give him something to think about," the man said, grinning.

*Donald Franson is a type of science fiction writer who drives anthologists wild. Though much of what he does is interesting, he is so involved in fannish activities (coauthor of* A History of the Hugo, Nebula and International Fantasy Award, Listing Nominees and Winners and Science Fiction Title Changes, *1980) that he has produced only approximately 15 science fiction short stories in 25 years. In any case, you can enjoy his following story of cultists, and how they tend to assimilate seemingly incompatible information, while we prod him for more work.*

# THE TIME FOR DELUSION

## by Donald Franson

The phone rang, just when I was in the middle of classifying slides, steles, and rock strata, an occupation, believe me, requiring much concentration. It rang and rang. It didn't go away as I hoped—it kept on, ten, eleven, twelve times.

Dropping a precious diffraction grating, shattering it to bits, I stumbled over to the phone. I thought, Who could be calling at this hour? Who would be up at four in the morning but cops, drunks, night watchmen and mad college professors?

I glanced at my frizzled hound, who was snoring undisturbed, and grabbed at the phone. I gave my four-A.M. version of "Professor Potts speaking," which was "Mmmp."

The voice sounded far away, but I heard no long-distance operator. A pleasant voice it was, which I could not identify positively as male or female, saying, "Professor Potts?"

"Yes."

"This is Sacaj calling, from Venus. Don't be surprised."

I wasn't surprised, and told him, her, it, so. I was irritated at the practical joker who was bothering me in the middle of the night.

"What do you mean by ringing my phone in the middle of the night?" I screamed. "Wake up my dog and he barks all night and I can't shut him up."

"Your dog didn't wake up, did he?"

"Well, no, but he usually does. He usually does, when the phone rings at night." I don't know why I was keeping up this idiotic conversation, except that I couldn't get any madder than I was already.

"I can explain why your dog didn't wake up this time," said the voice, smugly.

"He just missed it, luckily." I was about to hang up.

"No, the reason is that the phone didn't ring."

"What kind of nonsense? Who the hell are you, anyway? If I wasn't a patient man and didn't have to watch my blood pressure—oh, what's the use? What do you want? Speak up."

"Ah, ah! Don't change the subject. I said the phone didn't ring."

I decided to give him an argument, as long as he was asking for one. "Ah, but it did ring. Twelve times. I counted them."

"Ah, but it didn't," said the sugary voice. "No times. I didn't have to count them."

"Now see here—!" My blood pressure started to rocket.

"Hold it, Professor. Blood pressure—remember? You're a man of science. You never turn down a hypothesis, however unbelievable, without giving it a trial? Make a scientific test. I'll hang up and call you back in two minutes. Leave the phone off the hook if you want. It can't ring then, can it?" He, it, she, clicked off.

I said something unprintable, and hung up the phone, then took it off the base again and laid it on the table. I looked at my wrist watch.

When two minutes were up, I heard the phone ring again. Grinning my satisfaction, I reached to pick it up.

But it was not there, not where it ought to be in order to ring. It was lying on the table, where I had left it.

And ringing like mad.

And the dog was barking—no he wasn't. He wasn't barking at all. He was snoring.

I twisted my finger in my ear, shook my head, but the ringing persisted.

I picked up the phone and it stopped ringing.

"Satisfied?" said the honeyed voice in my ear.

I said, "Mmmf." It was the nearest thing to an admission I could manage at the moment.

"Now that you've had a convincing demonstration," the voice went on, "we may proceed. I find that facts presented too early seldom sink in, so I will repeat. I am Sacaj. I am calling from Venus. I am using the telephone only as a fortune-teller uses a crystal ball—to solidify the thought that really needs no medium of transmission. The voice you hear, the bells you heard—they are all in your mind. But I have perfected no other way to reach anyone on Earth—and I have contacted few."

I couldn't think of a thing to say, except a stupefied "Venus?"

"Yes," said the person called Sacaj, amused. "Isn't it fortunate that I really don't use the telephone system? The tolls would be tremendous. Just now I am 84,369,220-odd miles away from you. But now I think that's enough for one time. The wonders must be parceled out little by little, to the uninitiated. I'll call you again tomorrow, that is, when Venus has rotated once—in forty-nine hours and thirteen minutes. Goodbye, Sacaj off and clear."

I slowly replaced the phone, stood there pondering. Venus? Forty-nine hours? Why, nobody knew that. Venus' rotation time was still unknown, far as I knew, because of the clouds. It could be a guess, of course—no one could flatly deny it.

The phone rang again, while I was standing there. *Now what?* I thought, picking it up. "Hello?" I said.

"Ish thish Margie?" said a different voice.

"No, this is Professor—"

"You *shound* like Margie. Whayou doing in Margie's room, anyhow? You're drunk, thatsh what."

"Goodbye!" I said, and slammed the phone down.

Then I heard another sound.

The dog was barking.

"Say, that's a dilly," said Bronker. He put down the manuscript and turned to Denworth. "Why don't you write it as fiction, instead of pretending it really happened? You'd do a lot better, I think."

"Oh, no I wouldn't," said Denworth, shaking his head. "I'm not such a good writer, really, on those terms. What I'm trying to prove is that any kind of writer who says what he says is fact, fact, fact, sets the world on its ear. That's the magic word. Fact. If I said it was fiction, they would say it was too unbelievable."

"But," sputtered Bronker, "this is *too* full of nonsense. Diffraction gratings and steles—what kind of scientist is this professor? And human beings on Venus with phone etiquette— did you ever hear of oxygen being necessary for life?"

"How far did you get—let's see—the end of the first chapter, eh? You missed one. I planted a good one there, and you missed it." Denworth chuckled.

"Planted? You *planted* stuff here? Er—what did I miss?"

"Sacaj," said Denworth. "Sacaj is 'jackass' backwards."

Bronker read some more of the book manuscript. Then he handed it back to Denworth. "Just answer me one question. What's the purpose of this book? It doesn't make sense to me, you, of all people, putting out this thing. I suppose you're going to get it published somehow, and pass it out to your friends. But I always thought you were the one person in the world who didn't believe in any of these pseudoscientific revelations. Didn't you once say, 'Anyone that saw saucers much have been in his cups'?"

"Listen to this one," said Denworth. " 'I thought I saw a disc fly up, but I had only flipped my lid.' "

"Well, I see you're still the same old Denworth. But you've got more nerve, then, to put out this—this *hoax*."

"That's the idea. Now don't get me wrong—it *is* a hoax. *I* haven't flipped my lid, yet. It's a test. I want to puncture a balloon—but I've got to blow it up first. A controlled experiment. You see, *people believe too much, nowadays*."

"People believe too much—I agree with you there," said Bronker, who was a science fiction writer. "It used to be 'I do not expect anyone to believe me'—that's how the old-time writers used to start out. 'You will think me mad, but I am not mad.' Now they'd think him boring—get on with the impossible."

"Isn't that really the big difference, Bronker, between fifty years ago and today? Then, if anyone came up with a crazy idea, they could expect opposition. But now! Any statement made seriously, not in a story but in the newspapers or in a book as bald fact, is bound to be taken seriously, by some section of the people. This is the Age of Credulity. Why?"

Bronker frowned. "Oh, I suppose it's because they're afraid to doubt any more. So many funny things have come true lately, they don't know what to *not* believe. I suppose it's the fault of us s-f writers."

"No, it isn't. They still think straight science fiction is bunk. It's these *other* dreamers—these rank amateurs mostly—that captivate them. Because they say what they say is *fact*. Not only that. If you don't believe—"

"You're a square."

"Exactly," said Denworth. " 'They laughed at Columbus. They laughed at the Wright Brothers, the Smith Brothers, and the Marx Brothers. Now they've got the nerve to laugh at me,' they say. And it's been pounded into the public mind so long that science can do *anything,* that seemingly nothing is impossible to the unscientific layman. So therefore it follows that this latest moonshine is also not impossible. Just because a few ideas contrary to apparent common sense were proven right, that doesn't mean that *every* idea contrary to reason must be automatically accepted until it's proven wrong."

"Oh, why fight it?" said Bronker. "It doesn't matter what people believe. The truth is the truth. Let them be nitwits—"

"Yes, it matters!" said Denworth. "Every unscientific idea in the mass mind crowds out a scientific one. I've been fighting these things as fast as they come up. And it's like weeds—two spring up in the place of every one I root out—and I'm beginning to doubt that I've really rooted out any. You see, I'm handicapped. *I* don't have all the facts either, mainly because there *aren't* any facts. How can you disprove a nonexistent fact? It's just like a rumor—the only way you can get to the bottom of a rumor is to find out how it started in the first place. Then you can show just how the fact was distorted or misinterpreted to grow into the full-fledged rumor.

"But if you can do that—then you may have done more than just scotch the one rumor. You may have helped show up *all* rumors. You've shaken people's faith in rumors, especially if the one explained is an important one. But—suppose it's impossible to even track down one rumor, in order to undermine them all by its exposure? Then you'd have to start a rumor yourself.

"If you do that, and if you're careful to document it, put it down in writing, seal it, date it, and so forth—then when it blooms into a big thing, all you have to do to puncture it is bring forth your documents. That's what I propose to do here. I can't do anything about the saucers, now. But I can start my own legend. I can't just say I saw another saucer, or transported my mind to the past century. It has to be something new. Something that I can identify as my own, when it finally pops up somewhere else. It has to be, ah, patentable. It has to have my trademark on it."

"I think you overdid it, with all this questionable science in it."

"Oh, no. That was intentional. You see, I *want* the scientific men to debunk it. That gets 'em every time. The 'authorities' are against it. The publicity this'll get ought to be tremendous, because it's so unusual. Anything out of the ordinary, on an interesting subject like pseudoscience, should command more free space than the original saucer did." Denworth put the manuscript back in his desk drawer.

"I'm going to get this published and help distribute it myself, and here's how it will go: Seventy-five percent will think it's a joke, ten percent will be open minded about it, ten percent will believe it, and five percent will have *also* got phone calls from Venus, or Mars, or somewhere."

"Where did you get those percentages?" asked Bronker.

"I made them up," said Denworth. "That's what they all do. Why can't I make up scientific facts? The more concrete they are, the more believable they are. You should know, verisimilitude. Like the bookkeeper who made up the figure of $3,456.02. The world will come to an end at 3:45 P.M., October 1, 1981. I saw seven saucers, green with orange spots, triangular in shape. The Martians have attacked Pine Ridge, Arkansas, but nobody is allowed to release anything yet."

"I see your point. You've certainly put plenty of it in here. One thing I like. They're always talking Martians, and Mars. There's nothing mysterious about Mars. Venus is the real planet of mystery. Forty-nine hours—you almost had me believing it myself."

"Well, what *is* the rotation period?"

"I don't know, you joker. Anywhere from a day to a few months, or none at all."

"Then what I say must be *fact*, and you dassen't contradict me."

Bronker groaned. "What title are you going to use?"

Denworth paused. "I've been thinking of *Dial Planet 3-2000,* but that's kind of complicated. It doesn't have to be too original. Just startling, like *Saucers Are Flying,* or *I Was My Own Grandfather.*"

"How about *Venus on the Phone?* But do you really think this is going to do any good?"

"The hoaxers have gone too far, Bronker. Something must be done to show them up. I don't mean the people who honestly think they saw flying discs, or those who actually saw them for all I know, or those who believe in the general principle. I mean the ones who take advantage of that belief, and come up with some story about Mercurians coming out of the gopher hole in their back yard, or three saucers they saw in a bar, and then get onto a television program or in the newspaper and sell a book on the strength of the publicity."

"Maybe that's their purpose—to sell books."

"Certainly, and think of the psychology in it," said Denworth. *"Have you read all the books on saucers? If not, you can't have an open mind about them."*

"I admit *I* haven't," said Bronker. "I can't afford it. Everytime someone comes out with a new angle, I'd have to buy their book—a crafty way to sell books, at that."

"People have a natural desire to not be considered backward or narrow-minded. They give every new idea a break if possible. So the result is, they buy anything new, and these characters have accomplished their purpose—they've sold you a book, and you can't sell it back to them."

"Well, you're going to do the same thing."

"In a good cause. It's like a war to end wars," said Denworth.

The man looked doubtful. "Book dealers are supposed to be neutral, Mr. Denworth. On everything. Better that way. We'd rather not say anything about this flying saucer controversy except 'Go ahead and fight, and I'll sell tickets.'"

"Then you can't object to featuring my book, even when I admit it's a hoax?"

"I don't know if it's honest—well, publishers *do* protect pen names, there's nothing unethical about that—but it seems kind of unfair, to fool the public like this. Why don't you call it straight fiction? You've got a crackerjack book here. I read some of it last night—as much as I read any book, you know." He indicated the walls of books surrounding him, as if to say, *How could anyone read all the books?*

"Well, what if I hadn't told you anything?" asked Denworth, stubbornly. "What if I had walked in here and said this was my book, that my name is Potts, and—what would you have done?"

"You've got me there," admitted the bookseller. "All right, I'll take the book—whether you're Potts or not, makes no difference. It's all crazy stuff anyway—but it ought to attract customers. Tell you what—leave the book here, and a few extra copies, and we'll find out how it goes. That's what you said you wanted anyway, wasn't it?"

"Do me another favor, will you?" asked Denworth, as he brought in half a dozen copies and piled them on the counter. "Let me stand around here and watch the customers, and see what their reactions are when they pick up the book."

"It's your time," said the book man. "You won't be in our way—just don't go to sleep in here. We have a strict no-bother-the-browser rule. We'll just treat you like another browser—dust you off once in a while."

The book dealer grew expansive. "I could write a book"—he winced at the thought—"about the people who come in here to buy books. You know how they pick out a book? They open it in the middle, read a few lines; and if it isn't absolute nonsense, or maybe if it *is*, in the case of this kind of book, they might decide to buy it. That's something for the writer to know. You've got to catch 'em, not by the opening paragraph, like they always say, or by the ending, but by the *middle* paragraph. You've got to make your middle paragraph interesting, wherever it may be, wherever the book falls open. That means almost anywhere. They flip and skip.

"That's one kind of browser. Then there's the 'whole-book' type. I often wonder why they buy the book after they have read it in here from cover to cover, but some do. Then some people prowl the whole store. End up buying nothing. But I don't resent them. I used to do the same thing when I was a kid. Got almost my entire education in bookstores."

He arranged the books, putting three of them on the science-fiction shelf, while storing the other three away. "You sure you don't want to put a little comment in the front—a little sticker on the first page, maybe, or around the dust jacket, saying, 'I decided to publish this as fiction, because it's not'?"

"No," said Denworth, smiling.

"Okay. I'm putting it on this end with the other stuff that's supposed to be true. Right in between *The Earth Is a Cube* and *I Was a Disc Jockey for the Martians*."

Denworth looked up furtively, then down to the book he was holding. *"Dawnan addressed the pterodactyl, mockingly, but with a hint of aggressiveness in his voice,"* he was reading. *" 'Ptery, both of us can't share this ledge.' To Dawnan's surprise, the pterodactyl flapped his leathery wings, opened his sharp-toothed mouth, and buzzed—"*

"Do you think all this really happened?"

Denworth jumped a bit, looked up and faced the sharp-toothed woman who had addressed him. She was holding a copy of his Venus book in her hand.

"Why, I don't know," he said, flustered. "I'm a stranger here myself. I mean, I don't have any opinions on the subject."

"I think it did," she said positively, not listening anyway, going through the middle of the book. "This is too accurate to be a story." She put the book under her arm, fumbled in her purse. She waggled a finger at Denworth.

"You know what's the matter with all these other books?" she said, nodding at the science-fiction shelf. "They don't tell the truth."

But Denworth stood by fictitious science fiction, rereading *The Skylark of Space, Twenty Thousand Leagues under the Sea*, etc., watching and listening for the reactions of readers of his book. It was just as he had expected. The customers who came in almost always glanced at the book—the cover was certainly eye-catching. Most of the readers were silent, of course, being alone, and not likely to talk to such a forbidding-looking stranger as himself; but when they came in pairs, he caught their conversation. It sometimes ran like this:

"Just a minute, Barb, I want to look at this."

"Some more of that Marty Ann stuff?"

"No, Venus. Look at this—'*Venus on the Phone*. The true-fact story that actually happened.' Look here. 'I didn't realize I was face to face with the real power behind Earth's wars, treaties, fads, hit songs, ideologies—' "

Or it went thus:

"Here's a whopper—this guy's got a direct phone connection to Venus."

"Don't laugh—there's more to that than meets the eye. You

can't judge a book by its cover. They can't always print what they want in the regular scientific circles—they have to tell people this way. Seems I've heard of this Professor Potts somewhere."

"Isn't he the guy who discovered you could make stuff out of atoms?"

"No, something to do with electronic brains or something. The government clamped down on it, whatever it was."

"How come they let him get on the phone to Venus? Seems like they would wiretap, or something."

"You can't put it past these scientists. They know all the answers."

"Maybe the reason they know all the answers is *they ask all the questions.* Now if *I* was asking questions—"

"What would you ask?"

"Why are death and taxes so doggone certain?"

Denworth had to go out and get more books. He took the opportunity to distribute more to other booksellers, guessing right that their stock had also been depleted. He went back to the first bookstore, to wait another hour or so.

The next customer he saw come in was Bronker, his friend. Bronker had not appeared to notice him, so Denworth hid behind Stapledon and watched.

With satisfaction he saw Bronker come over to the science-fiction shelf, look it over carefully. Denworth tensed in anticipation. Now he would observe the reactions of an intelligent critic.

To Denworth's disgust, Bronker did not pick up *Venus on the Phone,* but one of his own new works.

Denworth sidled up to him. "Don't buy that—it's a direct plagiarism of Verne's *Five Weeks in a Balloon.*"

Bronker looked up, annoyance changing to friendly recognition. "How's the book going? What do the people say about it?"

"I wish I had a tape recorder," said Denworth. He recounted his experiences. "That book sells *too* fast. I feel guilty every time someone buys one. It isn't the money I'm making—and believe it or not, I think I'm already selling enough to pay expenses—I can always turn it over to some worthy charity and salve my conscience. But the thought of people believing this stuff—"

Bronker said, "What difference does it make, as long as it makes them think?"

"It doesn't make them think. It makes them stop thinking. That's just the trouble—my point originally. It's the kind of thing that I want to stop—people believing everything that someone says with a straight face. We will never get a science-based civilization until every citizen has a minimum understanding of science—that the earth goes around the sun, that astrology is the bunk, that luck is only cause and effect—not a deep knowledge, but as much as people know about automobiles, or politics, or baseball, or gardening. You don't have to know Bernoulli's principle to understand a curve ball. And you don't have to be a scientist to know simple scientific facts—if only other people would stop contradicting them all the time."

"It's the scientists' own fault, isn't it?" said Bronker, looking up from his book. "They act so mysterious about their magical profession that the common people can't help but think that Secrets Are Being Withheld. Then they turn to these guys—who give them what they want to hear, right or wrong."

Denworth nodded. "My point exactly. The scientists stay up in their ivory tower, most of them, content to discuss Planck's Constant, or something else obscure, when the people want to know, *What makes the world go round?* Does anyone ever tell them? Are they expected to dig into physics texts for the facts? They ought to teach science in every magazine, every newspaper, and not just for the kiddies. No wonder they think scientists are a race apart. Every man should be his own scientist, which means *thinker*. Every man should be able to open one of these books and see for himself what's wrong with it. The beginning of scientific thought is *skepticism*—not uncritical belief because someone says it's so."

"And how will you foster skepticism with this book?"

"Not with this book—with its exposure. How do you teach skepticism? How do you teach anything so it'll stick? By letting them get burned; then they'll sure find out the fire's hot. I can't go around contradicting everything that people read—it's impossible. But this way, it's going to make them a little leery of the next book that comes along."

"You're going to a lot of trouble, when the whole thing'll blow over in a few years. Remember the pyramid club? That blew over."

"Sure it did—it was an inverted pyramid. But this stuff is taking too long to blow over. If I can get people to be skeptical, I may be able to put a stop to it, once and for all. Then when something really new or strange is discovered, people will discuss it calmly and scientifically, not jump at once to controversy and prejudices. It's got me the way they jumped at this Venus thing. Do you know there's even a Friends of Venus club formed already? I'm getting kind of worried—maybe it's getting out of hand. The book's selling unnaturally fast."

Bronker said, "Maybe they're just buying the book because it's controversial."

"No. I'm getting letters denouncing me, as Denworth. I criticized the book, in the papers. Then I pick up letters at the bookstores addressed to Potts. *They* are full of praise."

Denworth pulled himself together. "Well, I mustn't get jittery. This is working out just the way I planned. They're grabbing at the hook just as I wanted them to—though I didn't expect them to jerk the pole right out of my hand. Bronker, I wouldn't mind if it was just the uninformed layman that believed this, but the thing has been given favorable reviews."

"Not in science-fiction magazines, though. They panned heck out of it."

"A few of them praised it, Bronker, ones apparently you don't read—and I don't blame you. Seems like some screwballs praised it, for fear someone would knock their pet ideas in retaliation, I guess. Get your book and let's go—I'm through with this part of the experiment. It's gone far enough. Now I'm going to puncture my little balloon."


"Now to continue with our TV discussion, 'Forum-Against-um.' We have received just scores of phone calls since this program went on the air." The moderator laughed with pleasure. "You know, there's an old saying, 'Publish a volume of verse, and it's like dropping a rose petal down into the Grand Canyon and listening for the echo.' But publish a controversial book and—*stand back!* I think there will be time for the panel to answer a few of the questions. If not, our sponsor has agreed to extend the program another half hour. So you gentlemen can go ahead with your closing arguments, and I won't ring the bell on you, too soon, that is. Mr. Denworth?"

"If you don't mind, I'd like to wait till later."

"All right. Mr. Hatfield?"

"My point is this. I wouldn't mind if they said there *may* be saucers, or water-witching, or clairvoyancy, and just gave arguments as to why they may be so. And stop there. Oh, no. You must be a moron if you don't believe, you are a closed-minded old fuddy-duddy, because they are *so* and I *know*, because I didn't read it in a scientific journal, I read it in a picture magazine, and they are so *much* more reliable. As for this Venus book. I can't swallow any of it. It's just a fairy tale, from start to finish."

"Mr. Madigan."

"Did you ever consider, Mr. Hatfield, that some fairy tales have turned out to be true? That Nostradamus' predictions are coming about, one by one? That there is even something in alchemy, after all these years, because you can now transmute metals one into the other by nuclear fission? That old witches' potions are now found to have had medically proven ingredients? Don't sell fairy tales short, Mr. Hatfield. There's something in them, or they never would have started. Take this book now. Mr. Potts, whoever he is—and I'm sure this is a pen name for some distinguished scientist—didn't invent this out of whole cloth. The character Sacaj rings so true—and it's not proven that Venus is uninhabited."

"Mr. Moderator," interrupted Denworth.

"Mr. Denworth, I thought you said you wanted to wait till last. However, if you want to go ahead of Mr. Pontus—"

"No, I'm sorry."

"Go ahead, Mr. Pontus," said the moderator.

"Thank you. There is no scientific proof there are flying saucers, moon people, ancestral memories, and whatnot. *But,* I maintain, there is no scientific proof that they do not exist either. Therefore it is our duty to be neutral. We must open our minds to whatever comes up, and take no opinion on it, until we have definite proof on one side or the other. On this Venus question, I, for one, have not received a phone call from our Venusian friend. But do I say *there is no such person*, because I personally have not been so honored? No. I keep an open mind about it. I lean to the positive, until the negative has been proved. I take the word of authorities such as Professor Potts, whom I greatly respect."

"Mr. Moderator."

"All right, now, Mr. Denworth."

Denworth looked around at all of them. "Would you accept a negative proof if I gave you one? Would you really?"

"Yes." "Of course." "Sure." "Certainly."

"This is a definite negative proof. You won't be able to contradict it. I couldn't find any evidence about saucers or reincarnation that would convince you, but this one thing I *do* have. I want to show you that you are wrong in believing indiscriminately in everything that appears in print, that at least one of the things you so uncritically accept is false. I am going to give you a specific example of *one* pseudoscientific book that is an out-and-out hoax."

"One exception doesn't prove anything," said Madigan. "Disprove something important, like, say, *Venus on the Phone*."

"That's exactly what I intend to do. *Venus on the Phone* is a hoax."

"What?" "I knew it!" "Preposterous!" "Order!"

"Did you ever hear of *The Moon Hoax,* the *Balloon Hoax* of Poe's?" went on Denworth. "Did you ever hear the story of the newspaper editor who, suspecting a rival paper was copying his scoops, inserted a hidden phrase in the material, which came out in the copying newspaper as 'We pilfer the news'?"

"Get to the point," said Madigan.

"That *is* the point. There are phrases in *Venus on the Phone* which disprove the main premise, in fact the whole phony story."

The moderator rang the little bell. "Now just a minute, Mr. Denworth. I think you're going too far. It's all right to criticize the book, that's what were here for. But you can't accuse the author of fraud. Mr. Potts is not here to defend himself, unfortunately."

"Mr. Potts *is* here," said Denworth. "I am Potts. *I* wrote *Venus on the Phone.*"

Nothing could be heard for ten seconds but a general babble, broken by insistent pings on the bell. Finally the moderator said, with an uneasy laugh, "I don't know whether to laugh, or protest. You took advantage of us. I admit I half-believed your story." He paused uncertainly. "I don't know whether to adjourn for lack of a subject or continue the discussion on another tack. I would be interested to know your reasons—first for the hoax, then the exposure. Just a minute. No, Mr. Madigan, I think it is more important to hear what Mr. Denworth has to say."

Denworth began, "First I want to explain why I am against

all these things. It isn't the fantastic and wild ideas involved—no, there are some scientific facts much more fantastic and unbelievable than these. It's the idea of extra-scientific belief, outside of science, defiant of science, scornful of science, contemptuous of science, but in reality *afraid* of science. For 'science' is only *the careful examination of evidence in search of facts*—scientists don't take sides, they're only seeking for the truth from the evidence at hand. If any evidence doesn't stand up in the court of open examination, does it do any good to say, 'The examiners are not fair'? But that's exactly what they do say, over and over again. These pseudoscientist authors are continually complaining about scientists' being afraid to investigate their theories, even when they *have* been investigated over and over again, and most of them rejected. But the cry goes on, 'They don't give this a chance.' It reminds me of Russian propaganda. They ignore it when someone does prove them wrong, so must the scientists continue to review and review? Prove that they are wrong? How can you prove anything to these people? They are far more narrow-minded than the scientists they accuse, who will not accept their stories as fact. I say it is *their* duty to furnish positive proof. I stand on the statement that there are no poltergeists, espers or flying saucers—now prove that there are."

"What are they then?" said Madigan.

"What are *what*? I still haven't seen any convincing proof that they are anything."

The bell rang. "Now let's not get off on saucers. We're still talking about the Venus book, and why you wrote it."

"I was coming to that," said Denworth. "I wanted to explain how hard it is to convince anyone on these matters, once they make up their minds. So I thought why not start a *new* story and see how many of these same people instantly take it in? I always had an ambition to do this, ever since the first saucer stories appeared in the newspapers and were so readily accepted. I almost decided one time to call up a paper and tell them I've seen a flying disc, just to see how quickly it would be printed. But then I realized it would only bolster the opinions of the believers, not disillusion them, because it is easier to start a rumor or story than to stop one.

"Then I eventually developed my elaborate plan. Now you may think I went to a lot of trouble to do this, and I did. You see, in one way I am just as fanatic as the saucerers. When I see people believing such miserable nonsense I get mad, not at them but at those who are supposedly responsible for education in this world. We scientists are responsible, really. It's our fault that astrology is flourishing, that other misleading philosophies abound. I wanted to do something about it. So I wrote *Venus on the Phone*. It was a test, a trap. It was to find out how far people would go in their quick acceptance of every new crackpot statement. And I tell you, I was astounded. I didn't expect people to be detectives and find the buried clues hidden in the book, proving its fallacies. But I did half expect people not to swallow the utter nonsense I literally *packed* into the book. So I am both satisfied and disappointed. Satisfied because I hope I've done something to slow down the future book fakers, who will find it tougher sledding from now on. Disappointed because so few really saw through this hoax."

"If I may interrupt," said the moderator, "you've been talking about proofs, within the book, I believe you said. I'm curious to know what these proofs are."

"All right," said Denworth. "Everybody got a book? Turn to page 202, the ninth chapter, last sentence on the page. 'No other nation since Egypt noticed such enigmas.' The first letter of each word spells 'nonsense.' See page 95, at the very top, and elsewhere. The name 'Poncipomon' is an anagram of another word, scrambled—nincompoop. On some of these I didn't expect anyone to find the clue until after I pointed it out, of course.

"But they ought to have got this one: page 211—Sacaj is explaining that 45 percent of his people are students, 35 percent are teachers, and only 25 percent are production workers. Add up those percentages. On the last page is a Nostradamus-type cryptic and prophetic poem, which is left as a parting message by Sacaj; Potts has tried to fit it in with the future war situation, being hard put to account for all the allusions (as Nostradamus quatrains are always vague, too). I'll repeat it for the benefit of our listeners, and see if they can get it before I tell you what it means:

> " '*The first success goes to the Reds,*
> *Brings Yankee blows upon their heads;*
> *In the strike to target whistles;*
> *Out go the ballistic missiles.*

*While the battle rolls and roars,*
*Oft the heavy bomber scores;*
*All day long, to hill, from pen,*
*Sounds the tramp of marching men.*

*Long it seesaws, long in doubt,*
*Ere it turns into a rout;*
*When the path's cleared all is done,*
*Another American victory won.'*

"If you see it as a description of the last World Series, it makes more sense, doesn't it?" Denworth looked around at the panel. "Had enough? There are hundreds of them—so many they make the book uneven. I thought you *read* this book, but apparently it was over your heads. I'm not sorry for you. I caught you in my trap, and now I'm going to stamp on you. Stop believing all this nonsense!"

Denworth finished, wished he could walk out dramatically at this point, but the show must needs go on. After a few bitter remarks from the others, they came to the question period. The moderator was in confusion trying to decide to whom each question should be addressed, since those that defended or attacked *Venus on the Phone* could not be satisfactorily answered by its author, who was at the same time its chief critic.

To solve a perplexing problem, the moderator laid these aside, and finished out the program lamely with irrelevant questions like "Are there people on Mars as well as Venus?" and "Who will win the next election?" The panel shook hands with Denworth as they left, but he didn't see any of them again for years.

The hall was packed, Denworth could see from his chair on the platform. The chairman rapped for order. Denworth fidgeted, prepared to listen to much criticism of himself, in the course of the debate or whatever it turned out to be, before, during and after his speech.

"The fifteenth meeting of the Friends of Venus Club will come to order. We will dispense with the reading of the minutes and all such hogwash, to save time for the very important business we have on hand, and our distinguished guest speaker." This was echoed by applause.

"First we will hear a statement by John Everett, founder of the club, in a summary of recent developments."

Mr. Everett rose, to generous applause. "Much has happened since the last meeting. When I founded this club, along with others, I based my belief not only on personal experiences and thoughts, but on a book which has come to be, in effect, our 'bible.' Since our last meeting, there has been some doubt cast on this book, to the effect that some parts of it are inaccurate and misleading. Now if this book, great as it is, were all I had to stand on, I would be indignant and try to defend it, or perhaps have some doubts myself.

"But no book written by human hand is perfect. There may be some errors, or even downright falsehoods, in *Venus on the Phone;* but that doesn't destroy my faith in its general principles. The fact that it was not a critic but the author himself who pointed out these mistakes testifies to his honesty, and to the underlying truth of the book.

"Tonight we will hear Mr. Denworth, who has revealed himself as the author of this epoch-making volume, in his first appearance before this club, the first that it has been possible for him to make, due to his previous anonymity. He appears at his own request. I'm sure you will all make him welcome." (Applause.) "First, however, before he speaks, we'll have our usual interlude of democracy in action. We'll hear members' experiences and greet recent converts. I leave the floor to you, with the assurance that I, personally, would require more than one television program, nay, a thousand such programs, to shake my faith in our noble Sacaj!"

The audience cheered, and Denworth put his finger under his collar, stretching it. He'd have to make his speech much stronger than he had intended.

The chairman was recognizing someone, and a man in the back of the hall stood up.

"I got a *television* call from Venice. I *saw* it. There was pictures right in the middle of the phone dial, where the numbers is."

"What did you see?" said a woman. Discussion was very informal here.

"A big city, scenery like it is on Venice."

"Did you see any *canals* in *Venice?*" said a heckler.

The first man said indignantly, "There ain't no canals on Venice. There's canals on *Mars.*"

"I saw canals in Venice," persisted the other. "In a painting. There was gondoolas." Laughter. "Did you see any gondoolas?"

The first man refused to answer, and sat down. After some more disturbances, the hall quieted.

Another man got up. "Mr. Chairman, our opinions have been challenged. I move we take a vote."

"A vote?" said the chairman.

"Yes, a vote. We ought to find out whether we still have the same opinion of the communication with Venus as we had a few weeks ago."

A man answered, "Don't you think the very fact that we are *here,* even after this so-called exposé, proves anything?"

"Not necessarily," said the first man. "Maybe some of us are here in curiosity, or to hear Mr. Denworth's explanation."

The jeers about him seemed to show this idea was not shared by the rest of the audience.

The chairman rose to the occasion with an action to stop the argument. "All right. All right. Suppose we take a voice vote. How many of us still believe in Sacaj, regardless of what has been said? Say aye."

A roar shook the hall, and with it Denworth.

"We won't need a negative vote," said the chairman. This relieved Denworth, who feared he would be the only one. This was getting uncomfortable. What a shock they would have when he convinced them!

The next half hour was taken up by short speeches of members telling about their experiences, conversion of other members, then speeches by the converts themselves.

Finally the chairman introduced Denworth glowingly, and he got up and made his way to the microphone, amid polite applause. He felt as he had the first time he'd gone up on the high diving board. But they could do no more than murder him. Well, here's where that long-forgotten public-speaking course would pay off. He hoped.

He began in the best political tradition, with a bit of humor. "First I want to say I don't know whether there are any canals on Venice."

After a comfortable laugh, audiences were more responsive. He must remember to keep them in this good humor.

"When I wrote the book *Venus on the Phone,* I had no intention of duping any of you. It was an experiment, and no harm was intended, I assure you. It seems to have gone wrong, somehow. When I came here tonight I had only intended to amplify my previous statement on the television program, and to apologize to anyone whose sensibilities I had hurt. But it seems, judging from your rafter-shaking vote of confidence, that you still believe in the book, and don't take any stock in the television program that denounced it.

"For this I don't blame you. I always said that a book was more convincing than a television program. And many of you, of course, only heard of the program at second hand. So, if I may, I will repeat the statements I made on that television show." Denworth paused dramatically, spoke slowly. "I am the author of *Venus on the Phone,* using the pen name of Potts. The story is fiction, from start to finish. There were *no* phone calls from Venus. Sacaj is purely an imaginary character. I don't know anything about the planet Venus, except what the astronomers do, which is very little."

He expected a shocked silence, but instead almost felt a tolerant attitude, waiting for him to go ahead and say some more ridiculous things. Denworth sighed and went on.

"I never intended to fix belief in this story. I mistakenly thought everyone would assume it was fiction." Here he lied, and he knew it, but he felt he wouldn't get anywhere by making them out like absolute fools. The rule is, *Don't call a fool a fool, he may quit being a fool, but you can call a mule a mule, he won't change.* Denworth wondered fleetingly if he was dealing with fools or mules.

"I must however make plain to you that if you still believe in the book, you are relying on a very shaky foundation; this book, like almost every other pseudoscientific book, flying saucers and the rest, is fiction, not fact. It is only words in print, and words are only words, not proofs. The word 'fact' does not *make* a fact."

A man called out, "That's all right what you say about flying saucers, but don't knock Venusian civilization."

"I think I have a perfect right to," said Denworth sarcastically. "I created it with my own two little typing fingers."

In the hubbub that followed, Denworth pulled himself together. He mustn't, mustn't be sarcastic. The gavel brought silence.

"Please don't misunderstand me," continued Denworth. "I am not deriding you for believing the book. I am not making fun of you for doing the natural thing. If I were in your place I would believe it too, not knowing all the facts. But I am *telling* you that it is a work of fiction. I put a lot of effort into making it as plausible as possible, as believable as possible, to make it a more interesting work of fiction. However, in case anyone *did* take it seriously, I deliberately put some defects into the story.

"And I'm going to tell you why. If the worst came to worst, and the story became an accepted fact, just as these other stories have, I wanted to be able to point out that it was only fiction, after all. And as even the word of the author may sometimes be doubted, I wished to have proof within the story that I could point to.

"To be perfectly honest, I welcomed the first indications of belief in this story. It was following in the course of the other books which have pretended to be fact, which, I'll admit, was also inadvertently done in this case. It was my mistake not to make the book as fiction in the first place. But due to this unfortunate mischance, I now had an opportunity to do that which I had always wanted to do, which was to expose one of these pseudoscientific books, even if it had to be my own.

"I decided to make it an example. A perfect example of all the books that are constantly coming out, claiming to be true stories about some amazing event, it doesn't matter what, which the author says he has experienced, and has written up as fact instead of fiction. This book differs only in detail from such other books.

"I thought, having written such a book, by then exposing it as false, I would pull the rug out from all the other books, bring the whole house of cards and saucers tumbling down. For people will say, 'This book is a hoax, it's admitted by the author—what about the other ones? What about the worlds in collision, the landing parties, the lunar messages? Are they hoaxes too, only the authors aren't honest enough to admit it?'

"When I wrote this—never seriously believing it would be so seriously believed—I planted certain evidence within the story, evidence that when exposed to light would cause people to say, 'Why didn't I see that?' But of course this evidence is not so easy to discover until pointed out. Those of you who are students of the book may have some inkling of what I am talking about. There are certain self-revealing inconsistencies—"

A hand shot up. Denworth nodded and the chairman recognized a young man with glasses, who stood up.

"Mr. Denworth," he said in an apologetic tone, "I'm the

librarian of the club, and I believe I'm the most thorough student of this book and its commentaries." (*Were there commentaries?* though Denworth.)

"I know," went on the young man, more confidently, "there are inconsistencies in *Venus on the Phone*. I could name at least six. But they are very minor ones, for example the mathematical problem on page 61 which is incorrect. But if you are talking about major falsehoods, or that the whole story is a hoax, I beg to differ with you. You may think that what has been revealed to you is the work of a practical joker, maybe, but—"

The chairman came to Denworth's rescue. "Benny, don't make a speech. We get your drift, and so does Mr. Denworth, so let him go on."

After Benny subsided, miffed, Denworth resumed, changed his tack. "This is the age of belief. A century ago any new invention, any new idea, was scoffed at. But in the intervening century so many crazy things have come true, so many new inventions have been realized, that the picture has changed. Now the pendulum has swung the other way. We are now all too willing to believe any new amazing story, knowing that miracles have been accomplished, that this is the age of science fiction coming true.

"But I say we have gone too far. Because of the atom bomb, which few knew about until its appearance as an accomplished fact, and other military secrets which are no doubt being perfected even now, we are prone to believe that *anything* is possible, that the Air Force is stockpiling saucers, that they have the Little Green Men locked up in Alcatraz, that the Pentagon is working on a plan to split the world like a melon and give half to the Russians. Due to the vacuum of actual information, something has to fill it, because nature abhors a vacuum, on the surface of the earth, that is.

"Because of this belief in the unlimited powers of science and the military to produce things fantastic, people have gotten away completely from the old habit of skepticism, and have acquired instead the habit of credulity—unquestioning belief—in anything that is said with a straight face, or written with a statement proclaiming it is fact.

"That is what has sustained this flood of pseudoscientific books, each one more strange than its predecessor. No matter what it is, no matter how ridiculous it sounds, someone will think there is a grain of truth in it. Some of these are unsalable failures, others are best-sellers. It is these *successful* books that I am afraid of. Yes, afraid for you, the reader. Afraid they will destroy your common sense, your ability to distinguish right from wrong, black from white. *You* are the backbone of the future. On you is the responsibility to improve the world. But you can't improve it if you are as gullible as the people of the Middle Ages. Only when the great thinkers of the reawakening made light of medieval notions, and substituted scientific method, and scientific doubt, only then did the world progress." Denworth paused for a drink of water.

"Galileo doubted. He read the works of Aristotle, then the accepted philosopher and authority on all things scientific, who said that heavy objects fall faster than light ones. It was right there in print, Aristotle said so. But Galileo doubted. And he experimented himself, dropping a heavy object and a light object from the leaning tower of Pisa. And he *proved* Aristotle was wrong. The falling objects both reached the ground at the same time, regardless of weight. This developed into the mathematical theory of falling bodies. Galileo had advanced science a great deal. But he couldn't have done anything if he hadn't been skeptical. I would like to see more skepticism today."

"What about Charles Fort?" someone shouted.

Denworth was annoyed. "Yes, what about him? Charles Fort fostered skepticism, and all that is very admirable. But after doubting everybody else's explanations, he goes on to explanations of his own which are open to question."

Another man stood up, was recognized. "Just what is there that's wrong with *Venus?* I want to hear it." A chorus of seconds arose.

Denworth looked toward the chairman. "Do you have a copy of the book handy?"

It was brought to him reverently. It was the first one he had ever seen with a *gold* cover. He flipped the pages.

"I'll quote a passage or two." He'd have to use his best ones. And simplest.

"At the start of Chapter Two, page 29: 'That evening, just after the sun went down, I saw Venus rising in the east, and was thrilled . . . Venus is never more than forty-seven degrees from the sun; it can't be in the opposite section of the sky."

Benny interrupted. "*I* noticed that—I figured it was a

printer's error, and I still think so. It should say *west* instead of *east*."

"Rising?" said Denworth, his eyebrows also rising.

"Here's another," he continued. "One afternoon, Poncipomon calls up Professor Potts and says, 'Please take down this message, quickly. Every second counts.' The message goes: 'This planet's entire construction work now is concentrated all on a thousand-story transmitter. Don't want you to believe that a telephone line is of importance. It isn't. Now you will hear, you will see, by the television's light.'

"Every second counts, he said. Every second word. Taking every other word of the message, you get: 'This entire work is all a story. Don't you believe a line of it. Now will you see the light.'

"I put that sort of thing in about ten different places, mostly in messages from Sacaj or Poncipomon, so you would notice them more easily.

"There is a statement somewhere in the book to the effect that Venus and Earth are then in opposition, that is, on opposite sides of the sun. This is not opposition but superior conjunction. It is exactly the opposite of opposition, if you get what I mean.

"But if you don't want to stick to astronomy, let's turn to other sciences that are defied in these pages. One page 238, Sacaj explains some of the marvels of his world. One is that they need no flying machines, because they have discovered a gas ten thousand times lighter than hydrogen, which they force under high pressure into a harness that they wear around their shoulders. Thus they flit about without the necessity of airplanes. This is a scientific impossibility. There is no gas lighter than hydrogen, none possible, and compressing any gas would only lessen its lifting power.

"There is also nothing colder than absolute zero, the absence of all molecular motion. Yet Poncipomon uses a temperature lower than this to freeze ideas for reuse.

"Believe me, these deliberate fakes are no worse than things I have read in some of these recent best-sellers.

"Then, Sacaj has films of all past events on Earth, which they had taken from Venus through the centuries, and he describes to Potts such events as George Washington chopping down the cherry tree, Nero fiddling while Rome burns, and the midnight ride of Paul Revere. Now the first two events are fictitious, and the last happened at midnight, so therefore wouldn't be visible from Venus, which is on the sunny side of Earth. Sacaj claimed they used nothing but strong infrared telescopes to record the films, penetrating clouds but not solid rock.

"I don't think I need to go on. I think you must realize by now the whole thing is a hoax. Maybe I overdid it, in the number of proofs—I've only quoted a small fraction so far. I only want to convince you, I don't want to bury you. I'm sure you'll go home tonight, read over the book, and see that I am right. Then I hope you'll forgive me for leading you astray. I hope you'll understand that I had only your own interests at heart.

"Don't be too disappointed. I think you will realize that you have learned a valuable lesson from this. In the future, I think you won't embrace any new book that comes along without examining its validity.

"How will you do this? First wait. Wait for the expert and considered opinions of the scientists, the educators, the reputable journalists. I'm sure the alien benefactors or universe explainers can wait around for a few months. Then, when these opinions have been expressed, weigh them. Don't necessarily go by majority rule. Ten doctors may tell you how to fix your automobile, but you would sooner take the word of one automobile mechanic. See what they all have to say, then decide for yourself. Accept the new philosophy, if that's what you've been convinced of, after careful consideration. But keep an open mind still. If someone later has a critical suggestion, don't instantly reject it because it comes after you have already made up your mind.

"Remember also that *facts are not swayed by majority opinion*. Majority opinion may be swayed by facts, but not the other way around. Does the fact that everyone is for it make it so? No. Does the fact that everyone is *against* it make it so? No. Decide the question on its own merits. Choose in your own mind. And when you have chosen at last what *you* think is the truth, then don't let yourself be swayed by anything *but* a sound, reasoning argument, based on facts.

"It may be then that you will find yourself having to say, 'I can't find anyone to share my opinion with me.' Don't worry about that. Have the courage to say, like Copernicus, Galileo and Columbus, '*I am right, and the whole world is wrong*.'

"I suggest you go home and think about this book, *Venus on the Phone*. Take your time—there's no rush. The planet

Venus will still be around for a while. Ask yourself, for instance, why should they be calling up only a chosen few? It's almost the same question as why are saucers only seen by a few people at a time, if there are so many of them? And ponder the other questions—the ones I brought up, and others that you will discover yourself.

"I hope you don't immediately disband this club, but keep it active for a while, so you can debate all these questions in an open forum, until all of you are convinced of the book's fallacies. You may call on me at any time, and I will explain any points not clear, or answer any of your questions by letter. Now if you will excuse me, I will end my speech, again with an apology, and with good wishes to all of you, hoping you have no hard feelings toward me. Thank you."

He turned and walked back toward his chair. There was a silence, then a few scattered handclaps, dying away, and a buzz of talk. This didn't quiet down as he expected, but increased to a rumble, and he stopped and went back to the microphone, fearing but facing an expected barrage of questions.

Hardly audible through the noise came the first one: "How do you know all this stuff?"

Denworth just had a chance to open his mouth to answer this when someone else shouted, "How do we know you *are* the author?" This was greeted by a chorus of approval, then some booing started. He looked around, saw the boy named Benny on his feet, pointed to him, hoping for a sensible argument from him at least. Benny was shouting something at him, which he could not hear. Denworth appealed mutely to the chairman, who gaveled and gaveled, ineffectually. Maybe it was for the best Denworth could not be heard. If he opened his mouth, he would put his foot in it for sure.

Benny was shouting something, but he could only catch a few words here and there, as two other people also had taken the floor. "The *real* Potts," Benny was saying. "Ancestors—generations—I have genealogy going back to—impostor." Another man close to the speaker's platform shouted something which was clearer, and also enlightening to Denworth. "How can we believe you, when you say you lied before?"

Denworth screamed, "What about the proofs?"

A roar went up. "Faked," was the general sound of it, though Denworth couldn't be sure.

He was wondering how he could get out of this, when he was saved from an unforeseen direction.

One of the men on the platform, one of the officers of the club, came up beside Denworth and started shouting into the microphone.

"Order, please," was what he put into it. Denworth doubted if anything was coming out of it or being understood. But the audience, seeing him there, quieted down somewhat, although the more raucous ones were now shouting at the man instead of at Denworth, the words most frequently used being "out," "kick," and "throw." But the man's appeal of upraised, downward-waving arms was slowly heeded, and comparative quiet came.

Then the man, whose name was Collins, he remembered, the club's secretary, surprisingly put his arm around Denworth's neck and shoulder. This was a gesture to impress the audience, Denworth figured, and did not resist. The arm soon left his shoulder to do its important job of helping the other arm quiet the audience again.

"Please don't be angry with him," said Collins, as soon as he could be heard. "I think he has had a hard enough time, recanting—when you and I know he has been *ordered to recant.*"

This produced a sensation, and when it was over, the secretary continued. (Denworth was too bewildered to open his mouth.)

"I'm glad he reminded us of Galileo," Collins went on. "Like Galileo, who when facing the Inquisition, could only say to himself in an undertone, 'but the earth *does* move, all the same,' he has shown us that he really doesn't mean what he says. He *knows* that this book is still the real truth. Look at him. Did you ever see such a downcast expression?" (Denworth straightened his face.) "Does he look like a man who is satisfied that he has said what he wanted to? If he were exposing a hoax, he would be laughing at us." (Denworth wished he could laugh.) "Instead he is almost sad."

Collins turned dramatically to face Denworth. "We respect your statements, Mr. Denworth, but we *refuse to accept them.*" (Applause.) "We sympathize with you, we understand your reasons for trying to deceive us now, but we don't believe what you say, and we don't think anyone can make us." As Denworth opened his mouth to speak, Collins quickly stopped him. "*Now don't say anything!* We don't want you to get into trouble! We know your responsibilities to the Authorities. We only want to tell you that *we* understand." He turned again to the audience. "Let us show Mr. Denworth that we don't condemn him for this. Rather we—uh—*forgive* him."

This got a big cheer. In two minutes the audience had changed from hostile to sympathetic. Denworth's admiration flashed for this man, who would be a credit to any political party. The audience was now singing "For He's a Jolly Good Fellow" and they were standing in the aisles. Collins took his hand and led him down the steps to the side aisle, where Denworth was immediately hoisted upon shoulders and carried around the hall.

In a whirl, he saw the chairman was apparently adjourning the meeting, as he moved his gavel up and down silently, shouted a few words inaudibly and started putting papers into a folder. The parading audience carried Denworth up and down the aisles, and those who were standing up in their seats, unable to get to the aisles, called to him such gems as: "I know they made you recount," and "I get phone calls from Venus every day."

Denworth wanted to pinch himself to see if he was dreaming, but he couldn't get his arms loose.

The parade led outside, and somehow in the traffic of the sidewalk, Denworth got down and made his getaway. He sneaked around the corner, then ran at top speed for a dark alley, which he ducked into.

Alone in the alley, he brushed himself off. There was a tear in his sleeve and a few of his coat buttons were ripped off, and he felt a scratch on his ankle. Strangely, he still had the gold-covered book under his arm. With an expression of disgust, he hurled it from him, over a fence.

A crash of glass startled him. Cursing, he ran out of the alley, and emerged into another busy street. He took it as an omen that this book would continue to do untold damage, as long as it remained in existence.

He hailed a taxi and went home in defeat.

Bronker said, "People believe what they want to believe. But my gosh, don't let it get you down. *You* don't have to believe it, do you? You made it up."

"I don't know what to believe any more. Talk about brainwash. After listening to those people I feel like a flash flood has just gone through my head."

"Why do you keep going to those meetings? You're just asking for it. Concentrate on the *sane* people in the world."

"Yeah. I have," said Denworth. "I've been going around trying to get my hands on all the unsold copies of the book so I could destroy them. I even asked friends for their copies back, no matter how nutty it made me look. Some of them wouldn't give them to me, just promised not to believe the book. I told them I knew they wouldn't anyway, but didn't want the book around. I didn't want the blasted thing doing any more harm. I felt like the repentant scientist destroying his invention, in the old stories.

"I went to all the bookstores and tried to pick up the remainders, but there weren't many. Some of them were all sold out.

"And you know what's happened, dammit? Vanity Press went ahead and published another edition. I told them not to, but it was too late. Seems it's automatic—they did it as soon as the first edition was nearly sold out. Oh, it's hopeless.

"I've been thinking of publishing another book explaining the first one. *An Answer to the Venus Phone* or something. But it's a dismal prospect, the thought of one book chasing another down the corridors of time, never quite catching up. As in politics, the denial never catches up with the accusation."

Bronker said, "What are all those letters you're throwing in the wastebasket—aren't any of them any good?"

"No. Yes—here's one. It's the only sensible one I've received, from a science writer, 'O'Limpus.' You'd hardly call it good, though. I'm accused of fostering pseudoscience. He says I've succeeded only in adding another myth to the unanswerable. And he's *so* right. It's ironic. I'm castigated for doing the very thing I tried to stop."

"What are some of the others?" asked Bronker in curiosity, picking a few out of the wastebasket.

"Go ahead, read them. Throw them back in the wastebasket when you're through. Don't read too many of them—they'll come out in your bad dreams, or your science-fiction stories."

" 'You have no right to deny the truth of this classic,' " muttered Bronker, reading. " 'You're only the messenger, you have no right to question the message.' Wastebasket." He picked out another. " 'I'm sure you put all those mistakes in the book to protect it. Camouflage against serious investigation—' Hmm. They're all like this?"

Denworth nodded. "They refuse to be disillusioned. I've created a Frankenstein's monster that I can't control." He put his foot in the wastebasket, packing it down to make room for more, and spent a little time getting his foot out again.

After a few moments of silence, Bronker said, "I just happened to remember a case something like this. It was a man who was asked to write an article for a cheap encyclopedia. In a mischievous moment he put some phony fact in that didn't belong there. I wish I could remember what it was—it would have made this story more interesting. Anyway, nobody noticed, and years later this guy picked up a *different* encyclopedia, and his fake information was in it too—it had been copied out of the first one. The moral is: Don't start anything."

"*Now* he tells me," said Denworth bitterly.

"Aw, cheer up," said Bronker. "Here's a new twist on an old saying: 'If you can't convince 'em, amuse 'em.' *Capitalize* on your ability as myth-maker. Become a science-fiction writer."

"Oh no, not that," snickered Denworth. "Nothing so low."

"Cheer up anyway," said Bronker. "Let's have a drink."

They stopped for refreshment.

Bronker offered a toast. "To fact," he said.

"To fiction," said Denworth.

The phone rang.

Denworth dropped his glass and swore nervously.

Bronker put his glass down. "Is that one of your crank friends calling you up?"

"No, it can't be," said Denworth. "I had the phone number changed—it's unlisted now." He picked up the phone, answered it.

He didn't speak for several minutes, getting whiter and whiter. Bronker fidgeted, wondering who he could be talking to. Who would be calling an unlisted phone? Finally Denworth took the phone from his ear, without having said a word. He looked at Bronker with a wooden expression, holding the phone limply.

"Sacaj?" whispered Bronker.

Denworth stared at him. "No, you idiot. It's Hollywood. They got the number from my lawyer. They're making a movie of the book and want me to come and be technical adviser."

*Randall Garrett has been so prolific a writer during his peak periods, over ten books and 200 stories, that he has not been taken as seriously as he should be for his is a great talent. Perhaps his most famous works are a series of longish stories about Lord D'Arcy, a detective living in a magical parallel world where Plantagenets still rule England. However, Garrett is also a master of the vignette, as the following story of gigantic misunderstandings illustrates.*

# SMALL MIRACLE

## by Randall Garrett

Major August Cantrell, USAF, was by no means a nervous man. You don't get very far in the Air Force if you're nervous, and certainly you wouldn't be allowed to pilot a jet plane that cost upwards of a million dollars, which is just what Major Cantrell was doing in the Air Force.

But, nerves or no, the major felt just a little queer when he heard the voice in his left ear.

"Major Cantrell," said the voice, "I'd like a word with you."

Now, let it be said at the outset that Major Cantrell was not unused to hearing voices in his ears. Indeed, he heard them frequently. A jet pilot wearing a helmet with earphones gets used to the phenomenon rather quickly. But there was something about this voice—something the major couldn't quite place—that worried him.

He turned on his throat mike. "Who's calling? This is Major Cantrell"—he gave his identification—"over Omaha, Nebraska. Who's calling?"

"My name," said the voice, "is Quadgop. There's no need to use your microphone. I can hear you quite well without it."

"This is a U. S. Air Force wavelength," Cantrell snapped. "Get the hell off the air and quit playing tricks."

"Please, Major," said the voice, "if you'll just lend me your ear for a moment, I'll explain."

"It better be good," said the major. If there was anything he hated, it was practical jokers—the kind that fiddle around on telephones and radios, trying to be funny.

"All right, then," said the voice that had identified itself as Quadgop, "shut off your throat mike."

The major thought it over and shrugged. What could he lose? He took a look around to see if there were any other aircraft near him, but the thin air was clean for miles around. He shut off the throat mike.

After all, it just might be some sort of Air Force test. He doubted it, but it was still possible.

"But if it's a joke," he said aloud, "somebody's going to be in trouble."

"It's no joke, I assure you, Major," said Quadgop.

"Whup!" The major checked his throat mike again. It was definitely off. "How did you hear me?"

"Oh, we have our ways," said Quadgop, chuckling.

"We? Who's 'we'?" Cantrell asked suspiciously.

"I'll explain in a moment. First, I want to make sure that my identification is correct. You *are* Major August Cantrell, USAF, Serial Number 0-633919?"

"That's right," said Cantrell.

"You wrote the book entitled *The Air Force and the Unidentified Flying Objects?*" Quadgop persisted.

"That's right," Cantrell repeated. "So?"

"You made the statement in that book that you don't believe that any extraterrestrial visitors would necessarily be warlike or bent on conquest, but should be treated with wary respect and a show of friendliness until and unless they prove themselves hostile."

It was an almost perfect quotation from his book.

"Do you," asked Quadgop, "still believe that?"

"Certainly," said Cantrell. Then he laughed. "I get it now," he said; "I'm being ribbed. Next you'll tell me that you are an extraterrestrial—from Venus, I suppose."

"No," said Quadgop, sounding a little irritated, "we are not from Venus. We are from Merca, a planet some four hundred light-years from here—a good deal farther away than Venus."

"Oh, come off it," said Cantrell, forcing a chuckle. But there was something about that voice that was oddly convincing, even to him.

"Major Cantrell," said Quadgop, becoming even more irritated, "we picked you for our first contact because we felt that you would be more understanding, more receptive to us. We do not want to fight Earthmen; we want to be received as friends. We feel that you would be in an excellent position to open negotiations for us. Please don't act as though this were a hoax."

"All right," Cantrell agreed. "Just for the sake of argument, we'll assume that you're on the level. But I won't completely believe it until I see you."

"That's fair enough," agreed Quadgop.

"I suppose that when I see you, I'll know you're not Earthmen, eh?" the major asked. "I mean, according to reports, you're little green men, two and a half or three feet high."

Quadgop laughed sardonically. "You have an entirely erroneous idea of our size, Major, and I assure you, we are *not* green. As to our physical shape, we are bilaterally symmetrical mammalian bipeds. Frankly, we look exactly like Earthmen."

"Oh, sure," said the major sarcastically, "just like us, except that you wear a Flash Gordon uniform and carry a Buck Rogers ray pistol."

"Believe me, Major," said Quadgop, "if you saw me, you would know instantly that I am not an Earthman."

"Look, Quadgop," Cantrell said patiently, "I'd like to believe this isn't just a gag; I really would. But I've seen too many of the boys being razzed because they fell for some practical joke like this. If you could just prove—"

"Major," Quadgop interrupted, "can I trust you?"

"What do you mean?"

"I mean, you wouldn't try to kill me would you?"

"Hell, no! Why should I?"

"Very well, then. I'll trust you. I *must* trust you. It's the only way."

"What are you talking about?" Cantrell asked. "Are you going to bring your saucer down here or what?"

"Oh, nothing as complicated as all that," said Quadgop. "Just take off your helmet, that's all."

"Take off my helm— But, *why?*"

"Because I'm sitting in your left earphone," said Quadgop.

*Joe Haldeman is a Vietnam veteran who began publishing Heinlein-like technological science fiction during the mid-60's and has subsequently won the Hugo and Nebula awards. The Forever War (1975) may be his most famous work, but he has also produced five other books and approximately 35 short stories, including (would you believe?) the following account of a close encounter of the fifth kind.*

# ALL THE UNIVERSE IN A MASON JAR

## by Joe Haldeman

New Homestead, Florida: 1990.

John Taylor Taylor, retired professor of mathematics, lived just over two kilometers out of town, in a three-room efficiency module tucked in an isolated corner of a citrus grove. Books and old furniture and no neighbors, which was the way John liked it. He only had a few years left on this Earth, and he preferred to spend them with his oldest and most valued friend: himself.

But this story isn't about John Taylor Taylor. It's about his moonshiner, Lester Gilbert. And some five billion others.

This day the weather was fine, so the professor took his stick and walked into town to pick up the week's mail. A thick cylinder of journals and letters was wedged into his box; he had to ask the clerk to remove them from the other side. He tucked the mail under his arm without looking at it, and wandered next door to the bar.

"Howdy, Professor."

"Good afternoon, Leroy." He and the bartender were the only ones in the place, not unusual this late in the month. "I'll take a boilermaker today, please." He threaded his way through a maze of flypaper strips and eased himself into a booth of chipped, weathered plastic.

He sorted his mail into four piles: junk, bills, letters, and journals. Quite a bit of junk; two bills, a letter that turned out to be another bill, and three journals—*Nature, Communications* of the American Society of Mathematics, and a collection of papers delivered at an ASM symposium on topology. He scanned the contributors lists and, as usual, saw none of his old colleagues represented.

"Here y'go." Leroy sat a cold beer and a shot glass of whiskey between *Communications* and the phone bill. John paid him with a five and lit his pipe carefully before taking a sip. He folded *Nature* back at the letters column and began reading.

The screen door slapped shut loudly behind a burly man in wrinkled clean work clothes. John recognized him with a nod; he returned a left-handed V-sign and mounted a bar stool.

"How 'bout a red-eye, Leroy?" Mixture of beer and tomato juice with a dash of Louisiana, hangover cure.

Leroy mixed it. "Rough night, Isaac?"

"Shoo. You don' know." He downed half the concoction in a gulp, and shuddered. He turned to John. "Hey, Professor. What you know about them flyin' saucers?"

"Lot of them around a few years ago," he said tactfully. "Never saw one myself."

"Me neither. Wouldn't give you a nickel for one. Not until last night." He slurped the red-eye and wiped his mouth.

"What," the bartender said, "you saw one?"

"*Saw* one. Shoo." He slid the two-thirds-empty glass across the bar. "You wanta put some beer on top that? Thanks.

"We was down the country road seven-eight klicks. You know Eric Olsen's new place?"

"Don't think so."

"New boy, took over Jarmin's plat."

"Oh yeah. Never comes in here; know of him, though."

"You wouldn't hang around no bar neither if you had a

pretty little . . . well. Point is, he was puttin' up one of them new stasis barns, you know?"

"Yeah, no bugs. Keeps stuff forever, my daddy-in-law has one."

"Well, he picked up one big enough for his whole avocado crop. Hold on to it till the price is right, up north, like January? No profit till next year, help his 'mortization."

"Yeah, but what's that got to do with the flying—"

"I'm gettin' to it." John settled back to listen. Some tall tale was on the way.

"Anyhow, we was gonna have an old-fashion barn raisin' . . . Miz Olsen got a boar and set up a pit barbecue, the other ladies they brought the trimmin's. Eric, he made two big washtubs of spiced wine, set 'em on ice till we get the barn up. Five, six hours, it turned out (the directions wasn't right), *hot* afternoon, and we just headed for that wine like you never saw.

"I guess we was all pretty loaded, finished off that wine before the pig was ready. Eric, he called in to Samson's and had 'em send out two kegs of Bud."

"Got to get to know that boy," Leroy said.

"Tell me about it. Well, we tore into that pig and had him down to bones an' gristle in twenty minutes. Best god-dern pig *I* ever had, anyhow.

"So's not to let the fire permit go to waste, we went out an' rounded up a bunch of scrap, couple of good-size logs. Finish off that beer around a bonfire. Jommy Parker went off to pick up his fiddle and he took along Midnight Jackson, pick up his banjo. Miz Olsen had this Swedish guitar, one too many strings but by God could she play it.

"We cracked that second keg 'bout sundown and Lester Gilbert—you know Lester?"

Leroy laughed. "Don't I just. He was 'fraid the beer wouldn't hold out, went to get some corn?"

John made a mental note to be home by four o'clock. It was Wednesday; Lester would be by with his weekly quart.

"We get along all right," the bartender was saying. "Figure our clientele don't overlap that much."

"Shoo," Isaac said. "Some of Lester's clientele overlaps on a regular basis.

"Anyhow, it got dark quick, you know how clear it was last night. Say, let me have another, just beer."

Leroy filled the glass and cut the foam off. "Clear enough to see a flyin' saucer, eh?"

"I'm gettin' to it. Thanks." He sipped it and concentrated for a few seconds on tapping tobacco into a cigarette paper. "Like I say, it got dark fast. We was sittin' around the fire, singin' if we knew the words, drinkin' if we didn't—"

" 'Speck you didn't know many of the songs, yourself."

"Never could keep the words in my head. Anyhow, the fire was gettin' a mite hot on me, so I turned this deck chair around and settled down lookin' east, fire to my back, watchin' the moon rise over the government forest there—"

"Hold on now. Moon ain't comin' up until after midnight."

"You-God-damn-*right* it ain't!" John felt a chill even though he'd seen it coming. Isaac had a certain fame as a storyteller. "That wan't *nobody's* moon."

"Did anybody else see it?" John asked.

"Ev'rybody. Ev'rybody who was there—and one that wasn't. I'll get to that.

"I saw that thing and spilled my beer gettin' up, damn near trip and fall in the pit. Hollered 'Lookit that goddamn thing!' and pointed, jumpin' up an' down, and like I say, they all did see it.

"It was a little bigger than the moon and not quite so round, egg-shaped. Whiter than the moon, an' if you looked close you could see little green and blue flashes around the edge. It didn't make no noise we could hear, and was movin' real slow. We saw it for at least a minute. Then it went down behind the trees."

"What could it of been?" the bartender said. "Sure you wan't all drunk and seein' things?"

"No way in hell. You know me, Leroy, I can tie one on ev'y now and again, but I just plain don't get that drunk. Sure thing I don't get that drunk on beer an' *wine!*"

"And Lester wasn't back with the 'shine yet?"

"No . . . an' that's the other part of the story." Isaac took his time lighting the cigarette and drank off some beer.

"I'm here to tell you, we was all feelin' sorta spooky over that. Hunkered up around the fire, lookin' over our shoulders. Eric went in to call the sheriff, but he didn't get no answer.

"Sat there for a long time, speculatin'. Forgot all about Lester, suppose to be back with the corn.

"Suddenly we hear this somethin' crashin' through the

woods. Jommy sprints to his pickup and gets out his over-and-under. But it's just Lester. Runnin' like the hounds of Hell is right behind him.

"He's got a plywood box with a half-dozen mason jars in her, and from ten feet away he smells like Saturday night. He don't say a word; sets that box down, not too gentle, jumps over to Jommy and grabs that gun away from him and aims it at the government woods, and pulls both triggers, just *boom-crack* 20-gauge buckshot and a .30-caliber rifle slug right behind.

"Now Jommy is understandable pissed off. He takes the gun back from Lester and shoves him on the shoulder, follows him and shoves him again; all the time askin' him, just not too politely, don't he know he's too drunk to handle a firearm? and don't he know we could all get busted, him shootin' into federal land? and just in general, what the Sam Hill's goin' on, Lester?"

He paused to relight the cigarette and take a drink. "Now Lester's just takin' it and not sayin' a thing. How 'bout *that?*"

"Peculiar," Leroy admitted.

Isaac nodded. "Lester, he's a good boy but he does have one hell of a temper. Anyhow, Lester finally sits down by his box and unscrews the top off a full jar—they's one with no top but it looks to be empty—and just gulps down one whole hell of a lot. He coughs once and starts talkin'."

"Surprised he could talk at all," John agreed. He always mixed Lester's corn with a lot of something else.

"And listen—that boy is sober like a parson. And he says, talkin' real low and steady, that he seen the same thing we did. He describes it, just exactly like I tole you. But he sees it on the ground. Not in the air."

Isaac passed the glass over and Leroy filled it without a word. "He was takin' a long-cut through the government land so's to stay away from the road. Also he had a call of Nature and it always felt more satisfyin' on government land.

"He stopped to take care of that and have a little drink and then suddenly saw this light. Which was the saucer droppin' down into a clearing, but he don't know that. He figures it's the sheriff's copter with its night lights on, which don't bother him much, 'cause the sheriff's one of his best customers."

"That a fact?"

"Don't let on I tole you. Anyways, he thought the sheriff might want a little some, so he walks on toward the light. It's on the other side of a little rise; no underbresh but it takes him a few minutes to get there.

"He tops the rise and there's this saucer—bigger'n a private 'copter, he says. He's stupefied. Takes a drink and studies it for a while. Thinks it's probably some secret government thing. He's leanin' against a tree, studying . . . and then it dawns on him that he ain't alone."

Isaac blew on the end of his cigarette and shook his head. "I 'spect you ain't gonna believe this—not sure I do myself—but I can't help that, it's straight from Lester's mouth.

"He hears something on the other side of the tree where he's leanin'. Peeks around the tree and—there's this *thing*.

"He says it's got eyes like a big cat, like a lion's, only bigger. And it's a big animal otherwise, about the size of a lion, but no fur, just wrinkled hide like a rhino. It's got big shiny claws that it's usin' on the tree, and a mouthful of big teeth, which it displays at Lester and growls.

"Now Lester, he got nothin' for a weapon but about a quart of Dade County's finest—so he splashes that at the monster's face, hopin' to blind it, and takes off like a bat.

"He gets back to his box of booze, and stops for a second and looks back. He can see the critter against the light from the saucer. It's on its hind legs, weavin' back and forth with its paws out, just roarin'. Looks like the booze works, so Lester picks up the box, ammunition. But just then that saucer light goes out.

"Lester knows good and God damn well that that damn thing can see in the dark, with them big eyes. But Les can see our bonfire, a klick or so west, so he starts runnin' holdin' on to that box of corn for dear life.

"So he comes in on Eric's land and grabs the gun and all that happens. We pass the corn around a while and wash it down with good cold beer. Finally we got up enough Dutch courage to go out after the thing.

"We got a bunch of flashlights, but the only guns were Jommy's over-and-under and a pair of antique flintlock pistols that Eric got from his dad. Eric loaded 'em and give one to me, one to Midnight. Midnight, he was a sergeant in the Asia war, you know, and he was gonna lead us. Eric himself didn't think he could shoot a animal. Dirt farmer (good boy, though)."

"Still couldn't get the sheriff? What about the Guard?"

"Well, no. Truth to tell, everybody—even Lester—was halfway convinced we ain't seen nothin', nothin' real. Eric had got to tellin' us what went into that punch, pretty weird, and the general theory was that he'd whipped up a kind of halla, hallo—"

"Hallucinogen," John supplied.

"That's right. Like that windowpane the old folks take. No offense, Professor."

"Never touch the stuff."

"Anyhow, we figured that we was probably seein' things, but we'd go out an' check, just in case. Got a bunch of kitchen knives and farm tools, took the ladies along too.

"Got Midnight an' Lester up in the front, the rest of us stragglin' along behind, and we followed Lester's trail back to where he seen the thing."

Isaac took a long drink and was silent for a moment, brow furrowed in thought. "Well, hell. He took us straight to that tree and I'm a blind man if there weren't big ol' gouges all along the bark. And the place did smell like Lester's corn.

"Midnight, he shined a light down to where Lester'd said the saucer was, and sure enough, the bresh was all flat there. He walked down to take a closer look—all of us gettin' a little jumpy now—and God damn if he didn't bump right into it. That saucer was there but you flat couldn't see it.

"He let out one hell of a yelp and fired that ol' flintlock down at it, pointblank. Bounced off, you could hear the ball sing away. He come back up the rise just like a cat on fire; when he was clear I took a pot shot at the damn thing, and then Jommy he shot it four, six times. Then there was this kind of wind, and it was gone."

There was a long silence. "You ain't bullshittin' me," Leroy said. "This ain't no story."

"No." John saw that the big man was pale under his heavy tan. "This ain't no story."

"Let me fix you a stiff one."

"No, I gotta stay straight. They got some newspaper boys comin' down this afternoon. How's your coffee today?"

"Cleaned the pot."

John stayed for one more beer and then started walking home. It was hot, and he stopped halfway to rest under a big willow, reading a few of the *Nature* articles. The one on the Ceres probe was fascinating; he reread it as he ambled the rest of the way home.

So his mind was a couple of hundred million miles away

when he walked up the path to his door and saw that it was slightly ajar.

First it startled him, and then he remembered that it was Lester's delivery day. He always left the place unlocked (there were ridge-runners but they weren't interested in old books), and the moonshiner probably just left his wares inside.

He checked his watch as he walked through the door: it was not quite three. Funny. Lester was usually late.

No mason jar in sight. And from his library, a snuffling noise.

The year before, some kind of animal—the sheriff had said it was probably a bear—had gotten into his house and made a shambles of it. He eased open the end-table drawer and took out the Walther P-38 he had taken from a dead German officer, half a century before. And as he edged toward the library, the thought occurred to him that the 50-year-old ammunition might not fire.

It was about the size of a bear, a big bear.

Its skin was pebbly gray, with tufts of bristle. It had two arms, two legs, and a stiff tail to balance back on.

The tail had a serrated edge on top, that looked razor-sharp. The feet and hands terminated in pointed black claws. The head was vaguely saurian; too many teeth and too large.

As he watched, the creature tore a page out of Fadeeva's *Computational Methods of Linear Algebra*, stuffed it in his mouth and chewed. Spat it out. Turned to see John standing at the door.

It's probably safe to say that any other resident of New Homestead, faced with this situation, would either have started blazing away at the apparition, or would have fainted. But John Taylor Taylor was nothing if not a cool and rational man, and had besides suffered a lifelong addiction to fantastic literature. So he measured what was left of his life against the possibility that this fearsome monster might be intelligent and humane.

He laid the gun on a writing desk and presented empty hands to the creature, palms out.

The thing regarded him for a minute. It opened its mouth, teeth beyond counting, and closed it. Translucent eyelids nictated up over huge yellow eyes, and slid back. Then it replaced the Fadeeva book and duplicated John's gesture.

In several of the stories John had read, humans had communicated with alien races through the medium of mathematics, a pure and supposedly universal language. Fortunately, his library sported a blackboard.

"Allow me to demonstrate," he said with a slightly quavering voice as he crossed to the board, "the Theorem of Pythagorus." The creature's eyes followed him, blinking. "A logical starting place. Perhaps. As good as any," he trailed off apologetically.

He drew a right triangle on the board, and then drew squares out from the sides that embraced the right angle. He held the chalk out to the alien.

The creature made a huffing sound, vaguely affirmative, and swayed over to the blackboard. It retracted the claws on one hand and took the chalk from John.

It bit off one end of the chalk experimentally, and spit it out.

Then it reached over and casually sketched in the box representing the square of the hypotenuse. In the middle of the triangle it drew what was obviously an equals sign: ~

John was ecstatic. He took the chalk from the alien and repeated the curly line. He pointed at the alien and then at himself: equals.

The alien nodded enthusiastically and took the chalk. It put a slanted little line through John's equals sign.

Not equals. —

It stared at the blackboard, tapping it with the chalk; one universal gesture. Then, squeaking with every line, it rapidly wrote down:

$$1$$
$$\sim$$
$$- - -1$$
$$\sim$$
$$1 \sim 1 - 1 \sim 1$$
$$\sim$$
$$1 \sim 1 - 1 \sim 1$$
$$\sim$$
$$1$$

John studied the message. Some sort of tree diagram? Perhaps a counting system. Or maybe not mathematical at all. He shrugged at the creature. It flinched at the sudden motion, and backed away growling.

"No, no." John held his palms out again. "Friends."

The alien shuffled slowly back to the blackboard and pointed to what it had just written down. Then it opened its terrible mouth and pointed at that. It repeated the pair of gestures twice.

"Oh." Eating the Fadeeva and the chalk. "Are you hungry?" It repeated the action more emphatically.

John motioned for it to follow him and walked toward the kitchen. The alien waddled slowly, its tail a swaying counterweight.

He opened the refrigerator and took out a cabbage, a package of catfish, an avocado, some cheese, an egg, and a chafing dish of leftover green beans, slightly dried out. He lined them up on the counter and demonstrated that they were food by elaborately eating a piece of cheese.

The alien sniffed at each item. When it got to the egg, it stared at John for a long time. It tasted a green bean but spat it out. It walked around the kitchen in a circle, then stopped and growled a couple of times.

It sighed and walked into the living room. John followed. It went out the front door and walked around behind the module. Sighed again and disappeared, from the feet up.

John noted that where the creature had disappeared, the grass was crushed in a large circle. That was consistent with Isaac's testimony: it had entered its invisible flying saucer.

The alien came back out with a garish medallion around its neck. It looked like it was made of rhinestones and bright magenta plastic.

It growled and a voice whispered inside his brain: "Hello? Hello? Can you hear me?"

"Uh, yes. I can hear you."

"Very well. This will cause trouble." It sighed. "One is not to use the translator with a Class 6 culture except under the most dire of emergency. But I am starve. If I do not eat soon the fires inside me will go out. Will have to fill out many forms, may they reek."

"Well . . . anything I can do to help . . ."

"Yes." It walked by him, back toward the front door. "A simple chemical is the basis for all my food. I have diagrammed it." He followed the alien back into the library.

"This is hard." He studied his diagram. "To translator is hard outside of basic words. This top mark is the number 'one.' It means a gas that burns in air."

"Hydrogen?"

"Perhaps. Yes, I think. Third mark is the number 'eight,' which means a black rock that also burns, but harder. The mark between means that in very small they are joined together."

"A hydrogen-carbon bond?"

"This is only noise to me." Faint sound of a car door slamming, out on the dirt road.

"Oh, oh," John said. "Company coming. You wait here." He opened the door a crack and watched Lester stroll up the path.

"Hey, Perfesser! You ain't gonna believe what—"

"I know, Les. Isaac told me about it down at Leroy's." He had the door open about twelve centimeters.

Lester stood on the doormat, tried to look inside. "Somethin' goin' on in there?"

"Hard to explain, uh, I've got company."

Lester closed his mouth and gave John a broad wink. "Knew you had it in you, Doc." He passed the mason jar to John. "Look, I come back later. Really do want yer 'pinion."

"Fine, we'll do that. I'll fix you a—"

A taloned hand snatched the mason jar from John.

Lester turned white and staggered back. "Don't move a muscle, Doc. I'll git my gun."

"No, wait! It's friendly!"

"Food," the creature growled. "Yes, friend." The screw-top was unfamiliar but only presented a momentary difficulty. The alien snapped it off, glass and all, with a flick of the wrist. It dashed the quart of raw 'shine down its throat.

"Ah, fine. So good. Three parts food, one part water. Strange flavor, so good." It pushed John aside and waddled out the door.

"You have more good food?"

Lester backed away. "You talkin' to me?"

"Yes, yes. You have more of this what your mind calls 'corn'?"

"I be damned." Lester shook his head in wonder. "You are the ugliest sumbitch I ever did see."

"This is humor, yes. On my world, egg-eater, you would be in cage. To frighten children to their amusement." It looked left and right and pointed at Lester's beat-up old Pinto station wagon. "More corn in that animal?"

"Sure." He squinted at the creature. "You got somethin' to pay with?"

"Pay? What is this noise?"

Lester looked up at John. "Did he say what I thought he said?"

John laughed. "I'll get my checkbook. You let him have all he wants."

When John came back out, Lester was leaning on his station wagon, sipping from a jar, talking to the alien. The creature was resting back on its tail, consuming food at a rate of about a quart every thirty seconds. Lester had showed it how to unscrew the jars.

"I do not lie," it said. "This is the best food I have ever tasted."

Lester beamed. "That's what I tell ev'ybody. You can't *git* that in no store."

"I tasted only little last night. But could tell from even that. Have been seeking you."

It was obvious that the alien was going to drink all three cases. Twenty-five dollars per jar, John calculated, thirty-six jars. "Uh, Les, I'm going to have to owe you part of the money."

"That's okay, Doc. He just tickles the hell outa me."

The alien paused in mid-jar. "Now I am to understand, I think. You own this food. The Doc gives to you a writing of equal value."

"That's right," John said.

"You, the Les, think of things you value. I must be symmetry . . . I must have a thing you value."

Lester's face wrinkled up in thought. "Ah, there is one thing, yes. I go." The alien waddled back to his ship.

"Gad," Lester said. "If this don't beat all."

(Traveling with the alien is his pet treblig. He carries it because it always emanates happiness. It is also a radioactive creature that can excrete any element. The alien gives it a telepathic command. With an effort that scrambles television reception for fifty miles, it produces a gold nugget weighing slightly less than one kilogram.)

The alien came back and handed the nugget to Lester. "I would take some of your corn back to my home world, yes? Is this sufficient?"

\*       \*       \*

The alien had to wait a few days while Lester brewed up enough 'shine to fill up his auxiliary food tanks. He declined an invitation to go to Washington, but didn't mind talking to reporters.

Humankind learned that the universe was teeming with intelligent life. In this part of the Galaxy there was an organization called the Commonality—not really a government; more like a club. Club members were given such useful tools as faster-than-light travel and immortality.

All races were invited to join the Commonality once they had evolved morally above a certain level. Humankind, of course was only a Class 6. Certain individuals went as high as 5 or as low as 7 (equivalent to the moral state of an inanimate object), but it was the average that counted.

After a rather grim period of transition, the denizens of Earth settled down to concentrating on being good, trying to reach Class 3, the magic level.

It would take surprisingly few generations. Because humankind had a constant reminder of the heaven on Earth that awaited them, as ship after ship drifted down from the sky to settle by a still outside a little farm near New Homestead, Florida: for several races, the gourmet center of Sirius Sector.

*Raymond F. Jones began publishing in* Astounding *during the 1940s and has, so far, completed over 15 books and 75 stories of science fiction. His most popular works are adventure stories, such as* Renaissance *(1951), considered by some to be the greatest space opera ever written, and* This Island Earth *(1952), which was the basis for the similarly titled film of 1955. Here, however, he presents a gentle little tale, much in the vein of Clifford D. Simak.*

# CORRESPONDENCE COURSE

## by Raymond F. Jones

The old lane from the farmhouse to the letter box down by the road was the same dusty trail that he remembered from eons before. The deep summer dust stirred as his feet moved slowly and haltingly. The marks of his left foot were deep and firm as when he had last walked the lane, but where his right foot moved there was a ragged, continuous line with irregular depressions and there was the sharp imprint of a cane beside the dragging footprints.

He looked up to the sky a moment as an echelon of planes from the advanced trainer base fifty miles away wheeled overhead. A nostalgia seized him, an overwhelming longing for the men he had known—and for Ruth.

He was home; he had come back alive, but with so many gone who would never come back, what good was it?

With Ruth gone it was no good at all. For an instant his mind burned with pain and his eyes ached as if a bomb-burst had blinded him as he remembered that day in the little field hospital where he had watched her die and heard the enemy planes overhead.

Afterwards, he had gone up alone, against orders, determined to die with her, but take along as many Nazis as he could.

But he hadn't died. He had come out of it with a bullet-shattered leg and sent home to rust and die slowly over many years.

He shook his head and tried to fling the thoughts out of his mind. It was wrong. The doctors had warned him—

He resumed his slow march, half dragging the all but useless leg behind him. This was the same lane down which he had run so fast those summer days so long ago. There was a swimming hole and a fishing pond a quarter of a mile away. He tried to dim his vision with half-shut eyes and remember those pleasant days and wipe out all fear and bitterness from his mind.

It was ten o'clock in the morning and Mr. McAfee, the rural postman, was late, but Jim Ward could see his struggling, antique Ford raising a low cloud of dust a mile down the road.

Jim leaned heavily upon the stout cedar post that supported the mailbox and when Mr. McAfee rattled up he managed to wave and smile cheerily.

Mr. McAfee adjusted his spectacles on the bridge of his nose with a rapid trombone manipulation.

"Bless me, Jim, it's good to see you up and around!"

"Pretty good to be up." Jim managed to force enthusiasm into his voice. But he knew he couldn't stand talking very long to old Charles McAfee as if everything had not changed since the last time.

"Any mail for the Wards, today?"

The postman shuffled the fistful of mail. "Only one."

Jim glanced at the return address block and shrugged. "I'm on the sucker lists already. They don't lose any time when they find out there's still bones left to pick on. You keep it."

He turned painfully and faced toward the house. "I've got to be getting back. Glad to have seen you, Mr. McAfee."

"Yeah, sure, Jim. Glad to have seen you. But I . . . er . . . got to deliver the mail—" He held the letter out hopefully.

"O.K." Jim laughed sharply and grasped the circular.

He went only as far as the giant oak whose branches extended far enough to overshadow the mailbox. He sat down in the shade with his back against the great bole and tried to watch the echelon still soaring above the valley through the rifts in the leaf coverage above him. After a time he glanced down at the circular letter from which his fingers were peeling little fragments of paper. Idly, he ripped open the envelope and glanced at the contents. In cheap, garish typograph with splatterings of red and purple ink the words seemed to be trying to jump at him.

## SERVICEMAN—WHAT OF THE FUTURE?

You have come back from the wars. You have found life different than you knew it before, and much that was familiar is gone. But new things have come, new things that are here to stay and are a part of the world you are going to live in.

Have you thought of the place you will occupy? Are you prepared to resume life in the ways of peace?

## WE CAN HELP YOU

Have you heard of the POWER CO-ORDINATOR? No, of course you haven't because it has been a hush-hush secret source of power that has been turning the wheels of war industries for many months. But now the secret of this vast source of new power can be told, and the need for hundreds, yes, thousands of trained technicians—such as you, yourself, may become—will be tremendous in the next decade.

## LET US PROVE TO YOU

Let us prove to you that we know what we are talking about. We are so certain that you, as a soldier trained in intricate operations of the machines of war, will be interested in this almost miraculous new source of power and the technique of handling it that we are willing to send you absolutely FREE the first three lessons of our twenty-five-lesson course that will train you to be a POWER CO-ORDINATOR technician.

Let us prove it to you. Fill out the enclosed coupon and mail it today!

Don't just shrug and throw this circular away as just another advertisement. MAIL THE COUPON NOW!

Jim Ward smiled reminiscently at the style of the circular. It reminded him of Billy Hensley and the time when they were thirteen. They sent in all the clipped and filled-out coupons they could find in magazines. They had samples of soap and magic tricks and catalogues and even a live bird came as the result of one. They kept all the stuff in the Hensleys' attic until Billy's dad finally threw it all out.

Impulsively, in whimsical tribute to the gone-forever happiness of those days, Jim Ward scratched his name and address in pencil and told the power co-ordinators to send him their three free lessons.

Mr. McAfee had only another mile to go up the road before he came to the end and returned past the Ward farm to Kramer's Forks. Jim waited and hailed him.

"Want to take another letter?"

The postman halted the clattering Ford and jumped down. "What's that?"

Jim repeated his request and held up the stamped reply card. "Take this with you?"

Mr. McAfee turned it over and read every word on the back of the card. "Good thing," he grunted. "So you're going to take a correspondence course in this new power what-is-it? I think that's mighty fine, Jim. Give you new interests—sort of take your mind off things."

"Yeah, sure." Jim struggled up with the aid of his cane and the bole of the oak tree. "Better see if I can make it back to the house now."

All the whimsy and humor had suddenly gone out of the situation.

It was a fantastically short time—three days later—that Mr. McAfee stopped again at the Ward farm. He glanced at the thick envelope in his pack and the return address block it bore. He could see Jim Ward on the farmhouse porch and turned the Ford up the lane. Its rattle made Jim turn his head and open his eyes from the thoughtless blankness into which he had been trying to sink. He removed the pipe from his mouth and watched the car approach.

"Here's your course," shouted Mr. McAfee. "Here's your first lesson!"

"What lesson?"

"The correspondence course you sent for. The power what-is-it? Don't you remember?"

"No," said Jim. "I'd forgotten all about it. Take the thing away. I don't want it. It was just a silly joke."

"You hadn't ought to feel that way, Jim. After all, your leg is going to be all right. I heard the Doc say so down in the drugstore last night. And everything is going to be all right. There's no use of letting it get you down. Besides—I got to deliver the mail."

He tossed the brown envelope on the porch beside Jim. "Brought it up special because I thought you'd be in hurry to get it."

Jim smiled in apology. "I'm sorry, Mac. Didn't mean to take it out on you. Thanks for bringing it up. I'll study it good and hard this morning right here on the porch."

Mr. McAfee beamed and nodded and rattled away. Jim closed his eyes again, but he couldn't find the pleasing blankness he'd found before. Now the screen of his mind showed only the sky with thundering, plummeting engines— and the face of a girl lying still and white with closed eyes.

Jim opened his eyes and his hands slipped to his sides and touched the envelope. He ripped it open and scanned the pages. It was the sort of stuff he had collected as a boy, all right. He glanced at the paragraph headings and tossed the first lesson aside. A lot of obvious stuff about comparisons between steam power and waterfalls and electricity. It seemed all jumbled up like a high school student's essay on the development of power from the time of Archimedes.

The mimeographed pages were poorly done. They looked as if the stencils had been cut on a typewriter that had been hit on the type faces with a hammer.

He tossed the second lesson aside and glanced at the top sheet of the third. His hands arrested itself midway in the act of tossing this lesson beside the other two. He caught a glimpse of the calculations on an inside page and opened up the booklet.

There was no high school stuff there. His brain struggled to remember the long-unused methods of the integral calculus and the manipulation of partial differential equations.

There were pages of the stuff. It was like a sort of beacon light, dim and far off, but pointing a sure pathway to his mind and getting brighter as he progressed. One by one, he followed the intricate steps of the math and the short paragraphs of description between. When at last he reached the final page and turned the book over and scowled heavily the sun was halfway down the afternoon sky.

He looked away over the fields and pondered. This was no elementary stuff. Such math as this didn't belong in a home study correspondence course. He picked up the envelope and concentrated on the return address block.

All it said was: M. H. Quilcon Schools, Henderson, Iowa. The lessons were signed at the bottom with the mimeographed reproductions of M. H. Quilcon's ponderous signature.

Jim picked up lesson one again and began reading slowly and carefully, as if hidden between the lines he might find some mystic message.

By the end of July his leg was strong enough for him to walk without the cane. He walked slowly and with a limp and once in a while the leg gave way as if he had a trick knee. But he learned quickly to catch himself before he fell and he reveled in the thrill of walking again.

By the end of July the tenth lesson of the correspondence course had arrived and Jim knew that he had gone as far as he could alone. He was lost in amazement as he moved in the new scientific wonderland that opened up before him. He had known that great strides had been made in techniques and production, but it seemed incredible that such a basic discovery as power co-ordination had been producing war machines these many months. He wondered why the principle had not been applied more directly as a weapon itself—but he didn't understand enough about it to know whether it could or not. He didn't even understand yet from where the basic energy of the system was derived.

The tenth lesson was as poorly produced as the rest of them had been, but it was practically a book in its thickness. When he had finished it Jim knew that he had to know more of the background of the new science. He had to talk to someone who knew something about it. But he knew of no one who had ever heard of it. He had seen no advertisements of the M. H. Quilcon Schools. Only that first circular and these lessons.

As soon as he had finished the homework on lesson ten and had given it into Mr. McAfee's care, Jim Ward made up his mind to go down to Henderson, Iowa, and visit the Quilcon School.

He wished he had retained the lesson material because he could have taken it there faster than it would arrive via the local mail channels.

*     *     *

The streamliner barely stopped at Henderson, Iowa, long enough to allow him to disembark. Then it was gone and Jim Ward stared about him.

The sleepy-looking ticket seller, dispatcher, and janitor eyed him wonderingly and spat a huge amber stream across his desk and out the window.

"Looking for somebody, mister?"

"I'm looking for Henderson, Iowa. Is this it?" Jim asked dubiously.

"You're here, mister. But don't walk too fast or you'll be out of it. The city limits only go a block past Smith's Drugstore."

Jim noticed the sign over the door and glanced at the inscription that he had not seen before: Henderson, Iowa, Pop. 806.

"I'm looking for a Mr. M. H. Quilcon. He runs a correspondence school here somewhere. Do you know of him?"

The depot staff shifted its cud again and spat thoughtfully. "Been here twenty-nine years next October. Never heard a name like that around here, and I know 'em all."

"Are there any correspondence schools here?"

"Miss Marybell Anne Simmons gives beauty operator lessons once in a while, but that's all the school of that kind that I know of."

Disconcerted, Jim Ward murmured his thanks and moved slowly out of the station. The sight before him was dismaying. He wondered if the population hadn't declined since the estimate on the sign in the station was made.

A small mercantile store that sagged in the middle faced him from across the street. Farther along was a tiny frame building labeled Sheriff's Office. On his side Jim saw Smith's Drugstore a couple of hundred feet down from the station with a riding saddle and a patented fertilizer displayed in the window. In the other direction was the combined post office, bank and what was advertised as a newspaper and printing office.

Jim strode toward this last building while curious watchers on the porch of the mercantile store stared at him trudging through the dust.

The postmistress glanced up from the armful of mail that she was sorting into boxes as Jim entered. She offered a cheery hello that seemed to tinkle from the buxom figure.

"I'm looking for a man named Quilcon. I thought you might be able to give me some information concerning him."

"*Kweelcon?*" She furrowed her brow. "There's no one here by that name. How do you spell it?"

Before he could answer, the woman dropped a handful of letters on the floor. Jim was certain that he saw the one he had mailed to the school before he left.

As the woman stooped to recover the letters a dark brown shadow streaked across the floor. Jim got the momentary impression of an enormous brown slug moving with lightning speed.

The postmistress gave a scream of anger and scuffled her feet to the door. She returned in a moment.

"Armadillo," she explained. "Darn thing's been hanging around here for months and nobody seems to be able to kill it." She resumed putting the mail in the boxes.

"I think you missed one," said Jim. She did not have the one that he recognized as the one he'd mailed.

The woman looked about her on the floor. "I got them all, thank you. Now what did you say this man's name was?"

Jim leaned over the counter and looked at the floor. He was sure— But there was obviously no other letter in sight and there was no place it could have gone.

"Quilcon," said Jim slowly. "I'm not sure of the pronunciation myself, but that's the way it seemed it should be."

"There's no one in Henderson by that name. Wait a minute now. That's a funny thing—you know it was about a month ago that I saw an envelope going out here with a name something like that in the upper left corner. I thought at the time it was a funny name and wondered who put it in, but I never did find out and I thought I'd been dreaming. How'd you know to come here looking for him?"

"I guess I must have received the mail you saw."

"Well, you might ask Mr. Herald. He's in the newspaper office next door. But I'm sure there's no one in this town by that name."

"You publish a newspaper here?"

The woman laughed. "We call it that. Mr. Herald owns the bank and a big farm and puts this out free as a hobby. It's not much, but everybody in town reads it. On Saturday he puts out a regular printed edition. This is the daily."

She held up a small mimeographed sheet that was moderately legible. Jim glanced at it and moved towards the door. "Thanks, anyway."

As he went out into the summer sun there was something gnawing at his brain, an intense you-forgot-something-in-there sort of feeling. He couldn't place it and tried to ignore it.

Then as he stepped across the threshold of the printing office he got it. That mimeographed newssheet he had seen—it bore a startling resemblance to the lessons he had received from M. H. Quilcon. The same purple ink. Slightly crooked sheets. But that was foolish to try to make a connection there. All mimeographed jobs looked about alike.

Mr. Herald was a portly little man with a fringe around his baldness. Jim repeated his inquiry.

"Quilcon?" Mr. Herald pinched his lips thoughtfully. "No, can't say as I ever heard the name. Odd name—I'm sure I'd know it if I'd ever heard it."

Jim Ward knew that further investigation here would be a waste of time. There was something wrong somewhere. The information in his correspondence course could not be coming out of this half-dead little town.

He glanced at a copy of the newssheet lying on the man's littered desk beside an ancient Woodstock. "Nice little sheet you put out there," said Jim.

Mr. Herald laughed. "Well, it's not much, but I get a kick out of it, and the people enjoy reading about Mrs. Kelly's lost hogs and the Dorius kid's whooping cough. It livens things up."

"Ever do any work for anybody else—printing or mimeographing?"

"If anybody wants it, but I haven't had an outside customer in three years."

Jim glanced about searchingly. The old Woodstock seemed to be the only typewriter in the room.

"I might as well go on," he said. "But I wonder if you'd mind letting me use your typewriter to write a note to leave in the post office for Quilcon if he ever shows up."

"Sure, go ahead. Help yourself."

Jim sat down before the clanking machine and hammered out a brief paragraph while Mr. Herald wandered to the back of the shop. Then Jim rose and shoved the paper in his pocket. He wished he had brought a sheet from one of the lessons with him.

"Thanks," he called to Mr. Herald. He picked up a copy of the latest edition of the newspaper and shoved it in his pocket with the typed sheet.

On the trip homeward he studied the mimeographed sheet until he had memorized every line, but he withheld conclusions until he reached home.

From the station he called the farm and Hank, the hired man, came to pick him up. The ten miles out to the farm seemed like a hundred. But at last in his own room Jim spread out the two sheets of paper he'd brought with him and opened up lesson one of the correspondence course.

There was no mistake. The stencils of the course manuals had been cut on Mr. Herald's ancient machine. There was the same nick out of the side of the o, and the b was flattened on the bulge. The r was minus half its base.

Mr. Herald had prepared the course.

Mr. Herald must then be M. H. Quilcon. But why had he denied any knowledge of the name? Why had he refused to see Jim and admit his authorship of the course?

At ten o'clock that night Mr. McAfee arrived with a special delivery letter for Jim.

"I don't ordinarily deliver these way out here this time of night," he said. "But I thought you might like to have it. Might be something important. A job or something, maybe. It's from Mr. Quilcon."

"Thanks. Thanks for bringing it, Mac."

Jim hurried into his room and ripped open the letter. It read:

Dear Mr. Ward:

Your progress in understanding the principles of power co-ordination are exceptional and I am very pleased to note your progress in connection with the tenth lesson which I have just received from you.

An unusual opportunity has arisen which I am moved to offer you. There is a large installation of a power co-ordination engine in need of vital repairs some distance from here. I believe that you are fully qualified to work on this machine under supervision which will be provided and you would gain some valuable experience.

The installation is located some distance from the city of Henderson. It is about two miles out on the Balmer Road. You will find there the Hortan Machine Works at which the installation is located. Repairs are urgently needed and you are the closest qualified student able to take advantage of this opportunity which might lead to a valuable permanent connection. Therefore, I request that you come at once. I will meet you there.

Sincerely,
M. H. Quilcon

For a long time Jim Ward sat on the bed with the letter and the sheets of paper spread out before him. What had begun as a simple quest for information was rapidly becoming an intricate puzzle.

Who was M. H. Quilcon?

It seemed obvious that Mr. Herald, the banker and part-time newspaper publisher, must be Quilcon. The correspondence course manuals had certainly been produced on his typewriter. The chances of any two typewriters having exactly the same four or five disfigurements in type approached the infinitesimal.

And Herald—if he was Quilcon—must have written this letter just before or shortly after Jim's visit. The letter was certainly a product of the ancient Woodstock.

There was a fascination in the puzzle and a sense of something sinister, Jim thought. Then he laughed aloud at his own melodrama and began repacking the suitcase. There was a midnight train he could get back to Henderson.

It was hot afternoon again when he arrived in the town for the second time. The station staff looked up in surprise as he got off the train.

"Back again? I thought you'd given up."

"I've found out where Mr. Quilcon is. He's at the Hortan Machine Works. Can you tell me exactly where that is?"

"Never heard of it."

"It's supposed to be about two miles out of town on Balmer Road."

"That's just the main street of town going on down through the Willow Creek district. There's no machine works out there. You must be in the wrong state, mister. Or somebody's kidding you."

"Do you think Mr. Herald could tell me anything about

such a machine shop? I mean, does he know anything about machinery or things related to it?"

"Man, no! Old man Herald don't care about nothing but money and that little fool paper of his. Machinery! He can't hook up anything more complicated than his suspenders."

Jim started down the main street toward the Willow Creek district. Balmer Road rapidly narrowed and turned, leaving the town out of sight behind a low rise. Willow Creek was a glistening thread in the midst of meadowland.

There was no more unlikely spot in the world for a machine works of any kind, Jim thought. Someone must be playing an utterly fantastic joke on him. But how or why they had picked on him was mystifying.

At the same time he knew within him that it was no joke. There was a deadly seriousness about it all. The principles of power co-ordination were right. He had slaved and dug through them enough to be sure of that. He felt that he could almost build a power co-ordinating engine now with the proper means—except that he didn't understand from where the power was derived!

In the timelessness of the bright air about him, with the only sound coming from the brook and the leaves on the willow trees beside it, Jim found it impossible to judge time or distance.

He paced his steps and counted until he was certain that at least two miles had been covered. He halted and looked about almost determined to go back and reexamine the way he had come.

He glanced ahead, his eyes scanning every minute detail of the meadowland. And then he saw it.

The sunlight glistened as if on a metal surface. And above the bright spot in the distance was a faintly readable legend:

HORTAN MACHINE WORKS

Thrusting aside all judgment concerning the incredibility of a machine shop in such a locale, he crossed the stream and made his way over the meadow toward the small rise.

As he approached, the machine works appeared to be merely a dome-shaped structure about thirty feet in diameter and with an open door in one side. He came up to it with a mind ready for anything. The crudely painted sign above the door looked as if it had been drawn by an inexpert barn painter in a state of intoxication.

Jim entered the dimly lit interior of the shop and set his case upon the floor beside a narrow bench that extended about the room.

Tools and instruments of unfamiliar design were upon the bench and upon the walls. But no one appeared.

Then he noticed an open door and a steep, spiral ramp that led down to a basement room. He stepped through and half slid, half walked down to the next level.

There was artificial lighting by fluorescent tubes of unusual construction, Jim noticed. But still no sign of anyone. And there was not an object in the room that appeared familiar to him. Articles that vaguely resembled furniture were against the walls.

He felt uneasy amid the strangeness of the room and he was about to go back up the steep ramp when a voice came to him.

"This is Mr. Quilcon. Is that you, Mr. Ward?"

"Yes. Where are you?"

"I am in the next room, unable to come out until I finish a bit of work I have started. Will you please go on down to the room below? You will find the damaged machinery there. Please go right to work on it. I'm sure that you have a complete understanding of what is necessary. I will join you in a moment."

Hesitantly, Jim turned to the other side of the room, where he saw a second ramp leading down to a brilliantly lighted room. He glanced about once more, then moved down the ramp.

The room was high-ceilinged and somewhat larger in diameter than the others he had seen, and it was almost completely occupied by the machine.

A series of close-fitting towers with regular bulbous swellings on their columns formed the main structure of the engine. These were grouped in a solid circle with narrow walkways at right angles to each other passing through them.

Jim Ward stood for a long time examining their surfaces that rose twenty feet from the floor. All that he had learned from the curious correspondence course seemed to fall into place. Diagrams and drawings of such machines had seemed incomprehensible. Now he knew exactly what each part was for and how the machine operated.

He squeezed his body into the narrow walkway between the towers and wormed his way to the center of the engine. His bad leg made it difficult, but he at last came to the damaged structure.

One of the tubes had cracked open under some tremendous strain, and through the slit he could see the marvelously intricate wiring with which it was filled. Wiring that was burned now and fused to a mass. It was in a control circuit that rendered the whole machine functionless, but its repair would not be difficult, Jim knew.

He went back to the periphery of the engine and found the controls of a cranelike device, which he lowered, and seized the cracked sleeve and drew off the damaged part.

From the drawers and bins in the walls he selected parts and tools and returned to the damaged spot.

In the cramped space he began tearing away the fused parts and wiring. He was lost and utterly unconscious of anything but the fascination of the mighty engine. Here within this room was machine capacity to power a great city.

Its basic function rested upon the principle of magnetic currents in contrast to electric currents. The discovery of magnetic currents had been announced only a few months before he came home from the war. The application of the discovery had been swift.

And he began to glimpse the fundamental source of the energy supplying the machine. It was in the great currents of gravitational and magnetic force flowing between the planets and the suns of the universe. As great as atomic energy and as boundless in its resources, this required no fantastically dangerous machinery to harness. The principle of the power co-ordinator was simple.

The pain of his cramped position forced Jim to move out to rest his leg. As he stood beside the engine he resumed his pondering on the purpose it had in this strange location. Why was it built there and what use was made of its power?

He moved about to restore the circulation in his legs and sought to trace the flow of energy through the engine, determine where and what kind of a load was placed upon it.

His search led him below into a third sub-basement of the building, and there he found the thing he was searching for, the load into which the tremendous drive of the engine was coupled.

But here he was unable to comprehend fully, for the load was itself a machine of strange design, and none of its features had been covered in the correspondence course.

The machine upstairs seized upon the magnetic currents of space and selected and concentrated those flowing in a given direction.

The force of these currents was then fed into the machines in this room, but there was no point of reaction against which the energy could be applied.

Unless—

The logical, inevitable conclusion forced itself upon his mind. There was only one conceivable point of reaction.

He stood very still and a tremor went through him. He looked up at the smooth walls about him. Metal, all of them. And this room—it was narrower than the one above—as if the entire building was tapered from the dome protruding out of the earth to the basement floor.

The only possible point of reaction was the building itself.

But it wasn't a building. It was a vessel.

Jim clawed and stumbled his way up the incline into the engine room, then beyond into the chamber above. He was halfway up the top ramp when he heard the voice again.

"Is that you, Mr. Ward? I have almost finished and will be with you in a moment. Have you completed the repairs? Was it very difficult?"

He hesitated, but didn't answer. Something about the quality of that voice gave him a chill. He hadn't noticed it before because of his curiosity and his interest in the place. Now he detected its unearthly, inhuman quality.

He detected the fact that it wasn't a voice at all, but that the words had been formed in his brain as if he himself had spoken them.

He was nearly at the top of the ramp and drew himself on hands and knees to the floor level when he saw the shadow of the closing door sweep across the room and heard the metallic clang of the door. It was sealed tight. Only the small windows—or ports—admitted light.

He rose and straightened and calmed himself with the thought that the vessel could not fly. It could not rise with the remainder of the repair task unfinished—and he was not going to finish it; that much was certain.

"Quilcon!" he called. "Show yourself! Who are you and what do you want of me?"

"I want you to finish the repair job and do it quickly," the voice replied instantly. "And quickly—it must be finished quickly."

There was a note of desperation and despair that seemed to cut into Jim. Then he caught sight of the slight motion against the wall beside him.

In a small, transparent hemisphere that was fastened to the side of the wall lay the slug that Jim had seen at the post office, the thing the woman had called an "armadillo." He had not even noticed it when he had first entered the room. The thing was moving now with slow pulsations that swelled its surface and great welts like dark veins stood out upon it.

From the golden-hued hemisphere a maze of cable ran to instruments and junction boxes around the room and a hundred tiny pseudopods grasped terminals inside the hemisphere.

It was a vessel—and this slug within the hemisphere was its alien, incredible pilot. Jim knew it with startling cold reality that came to him in waves of thought that emanated from the slug called Quilcon and broke over Jim's mind. It was a ship and a pilot from beyond Earth—from out of the reaches of space.

"What do you want of me? Who are you?" said Jim Ward.

"I am Quilcon. You are a good student. You learn well."

"What do you want?"

"I want you to repair the damaged engine."

There was something wrong with the creature. Intangibly, Jim sensed it. An aura of sickness, a desperate urgency, came to his mind.

But something else was in the foreground of Jim's mind. The horror of the alien creature diminished and Jim contemplated the miracle that had come to mankind.

"I'll bargain with you," he said quietly. "Tell me how to build a ship like this for my people and I will fix the engines for you."

"No! No—there is no time for that. I must hurry—"

"Then I shall leave without any repairs."

He moved toward the door and instantly a paralyzing wave

took hold of him as if he had seized a pair of charged electrodes. It relaxed only as he stumbled back from the door.

"My power is weak," said Quilcon, "but it is strong enough for many days yet—many of your days. Too many for you to live without food and water. Repair the engine and then I shall let you go."

"Is what I ask too much to pay for my help?"

"You have had pay enough. You can teach your people to build power co-ordinator machines. Is that not enough?"

"My people want to build ships like this one and move through space."

"I cannot teach you that. I do not know—I did not build this ship."

There were surging waves of troubled thought that washed over his mind, but Jim Ward's tenseness eased. The first fear of totally alien life drifted from his mind and he felt a strange affinity for the creature. It was injured and sick, he knew, but he could not believe that it did not know how the ship was built.

"Those who built this ship come often to trade upon my world," said Quilcon. "But we have no such ships of our own. Most of us have no desire to see anything but the damp caves and sunny shores of our own world. But I longed to see the worlds from which these ships came.

"When this one landed near my cave I crept in and hid myself. The ship took off then and we traveled an endless time. Then an accident to the engine killed all three of those who manned the ship and I was left alone.

"I was injured, too, but I was not killed. Only the other of me died."

Jim did not understand the queer phrase, but he did not break into Quilcon's story.

"I was able to arrange means to control the flight of the ship, to prevent its destruction as it landed upon this planet, but I could not repair it because of the nature of my body."

Jim saw then that the creature's story must be true. It was obvious that the ship had been built to be manned by beings utterly unlike Quilcon.

"I investigated the city of yours nearby and learned of your ways and customs. I needed the help of one of you to repair the ship. By force I could persuade one of you to do simple tasks, but none so complex as this requires.

"Then I discovered the peculiar customs of learning among

you. I forced the man Herald to prepare the materials and send them to you. I received them before the person at the post office could see them. I got your name from the newspapers along with several others who were unsatisfactory.

"I had to teach you to understand the power co-ordinator because only by voluntary operation of your highest faculties will you be able to understand and repair the machine. I can assist but not force you to do that."

The creature began pleading again. "And now will you repair the engine quickly. I am dying—but shall live longer than you—it is a long journey to my home planet, but I must get there and I need every instant of time that is left to me."

Jim caught a glimpse of the dream vision that was the creature's home world. It was a place of security and peace—in Quilcon's terms. But even its alienness did not block out the sense of quiet beauty that Quilcon's mind transmitted to Jim's. They were a species of high intelligence. Exceptionally developed in the laws of mathematics and theory of logic, they were handicapped in bodily development from inquiring into other fields of science whose existence was demonstrated by their logic and their mathematics. The more intellectual among them were frustrated creatures whose lives were made tolerable only by infinite capacity for stoicism and adaptation.

But of them all, Quilcon was among the most restless and rebellious and ambitious. No one of them had ever dared such a journey as he had taken. A swelling pity and understanding came over Jim Ward.

"I'll bargain with you," he said desperately. "I'll repair the engine if you'll let me have its principles. If you don't have them, you can get them to me with little trouble. My people must have such a ship as this."

He tried to visualize what it would mean to Earth to have space flight a century or perhaps five centuries before the slow plodding of science and research might reveal it.

But the creature was silent.

"Quilcon—" Jim repeated. He hoped it hadn't died.

"I'll bargain with you," said Quilcon at last. "Let me be the other of you, and I'll give you what you want."

"The other of me? What are you talking about?"

"It is hard for you to understand. It is union—such as we make upon our world. When two or more of us want to be together we go together in the same brain, the same body. I am alone now, and it is an unendurable existence because I have known what it is to have another of me.

"Let me come into your brain, into your mind, and live there with you. We will teach your people and mine. We will take this ship to all the universes of which living creatures can dream. It is either this or we both die together, for too much time has gone for me to return. This body dies."

Stunned by Quilcon's ultimatum, Jim Ward stared at the ugly slug on the wall. Its brown body was heaving with violent pulsations of pain, and a sense of delirium and terror came from it to Jim.

"Hurry! Let me come!" it pleaded.

He could feel sensations as if fingers were probing his cranium looking, pleading for entrance. It turned him cold.

He looked into the years and thought of an existance with this alien mind in his. Would they battle for eventual possession of his body and he perhaps be subjected to slavery in his own living corpse?

He tried to probe Quilcon's thoughts, but he could find no sense or intent of conquest. There were almost human amenities intermingled with a world of new science and thought.

He knew Quilcon would keep his promise to give the secrets of the ship to the men of Earth. That alone would be worth the price of his sacrifice—if it should be sacrifice.

"Come!" he said quietly.

It was as if a torrent of liquid light were flowing into his brain. It was blinding and excruciating in its flaming intensity. He thought he sensed rather than saw the brown husk of Quilcon quiver in the hemisphere and shrivel like a brown nut.

But in his mind there was union and he paused and trembled with the sudden great reality of what he knew. He knew what Quilcon was and gladness flowed into him like light. A thought soared through his brain: Is sex only in the difference of bodily function and the texture of skin and the tone of voice?

He thought of another day when there was death in the sky and on the Earth below, and in a little field hospital. A figure on a white cot had murmured, "You'll be all right, Jim. I'm going on, I guess, but you'll be all right. I know it. Don't miss me too much."

He had known there would be no peace for him ever, but

now there was peace and the voice of Quilcon was like that voice from long ago, for as the creature probed into his thoughts its inherent adaptability matched its feelings and thought to his and said, "Everything is all right, isn't it, Jim Ward?"

"Yes . . . yes it is." The intensity of his feelings almost blinded him. "And I want to call you Ruth, after another Ruth—"

"I like that name." There was shyness and appreciation in the tones, and it was not strange to Jim that he could not see the speaker, for there was a vision in his mind far lovelier than any Earthly vision could have been.

"We'll have everything," he said. "Everything that your world and mine can offer. We'll see them all."

But like the other Ruth who had been so practical, this one was, too. "First we have to repair the engine. Shall we do it, now?"

The solitary figure of Jim Ward moved toward the ramp and disappeared into the depths of the ship.

*Unlike most science fiction writers, Leo P. Kelley's career started in 1954 with a one-page biographical sketch. He had placed third in If's $2,000 college science fiction contest (andrew j. offut won). Since then he has written approximately ten books and 20 stories as well as editing two very good anthologies for classroom use:* Themes in Science Fiction *(1972) and* Fantasy: The Literature of the Marvelous *(1973). In the following story, which might have been called "The Missionary Position," he examines Catholicism, confession, and catharsis.*

# SAM

## by Leo P. Kelley

Yawning, Father Matthew Ryan began to put on his vestments for the first Mass of the morning. The alb. The cincture— *Lord, bind my loins* . . . Ah, no need, Lord, he thought. Not these lean sixty-year-old loins of mine. Some years ago, yes. But now my juices have dried up and the volcano of my blood is sound asleep. For me a pretty girl is merely a delight to look at now—no temptation at all.

A firm but genteel knock on the sacristy door. And then another.

"Yes? Who is it?"

The unmarried Malone sisters, shriveled from the heat of their imagined sins, sidled into the sacristy, all lacy and sly. "Good morning, Father, and God bless you," they bleated together, a two-toned choir.

"What is it, ladies?" Couldn't they wait until after Mass? Was their spiritual crisis so severe that it must be dealt with before six o'clock on a chilly Sunday morning?

"It's that Sam Bailey," said Miss Marlene.

"That reprobate," added Miss Aileen.

"What's old Sam been up to now?" Father Ryan asked, slipping his chasuble over his bald head. He smelled fire and brimstone. Sam may well be Saint Gabriel's sacristan, he thought, but these witches will burn him if they can.

"He's a devil," said Miss Aileen.

"From outer space," said Miss Marlene. "You remember, Father, the night he suddenly showed up in Little Falls last year? The same night the flying saucer landed out on Carter's Meadow?"

"There was no saucer," Father Ryan said, calmly covering his chalice.

"It was in the paper," protested Miss Aileen.

"Big as life," added her sister. "Pictures and all."

"Saint Elmo's Fire," Father Ryan said. "Aurora borealis."

"And he's not even a Catholic," said Miss Marlene.

Father Ryan frowned. "Sam's a good man. He just won't act his age, that's his only trouble. He thinks he's twenty years old instead of fifty."

"Lena Carlisle," said Miss Aileen with a superior sniff. "We saw him take her home from Beau's Bar and Grill last night."

"You two were there?" Father Ryan exclaimed, raising his gray eyebrows and pretending profound shock.

"Oh, no!" Miss Aileen replied. "We were out taking the late-night air. But we saw what we saw!" She folded her hands and demanded Sam's dismissal. "Saint Gabriel's," she went on, "should have one of its own to look after it."

Miss Marlene said, "Pat Fahey and his wife Mary—lovely couple—chased him right out of their house night before last. And only last week, Denny Maclean threw him out of the firehouse for interfering in the poker game."

"Sam does seem to get himself in a peck of trouble," Father Ryan said, knowing it was true. Ever since Sam had appeared in Little Falls last year, he had managed to get himself in the middle of almost every brawl and brouhaha staged by the good citizens of the small town. "You can't condemn a man for that, though. It may not be his fault."

"Well!" exclaimed Miss Marlene, giving Father Ryan the look she usually reserved for tardy Sunday School children.

"Well, I never!" exclaimed Miss Aileen.

Father Ryan called out to Pete Casello, the altar boy, as the ladies left the sacristy in a righteous huff, convinced that their pastor must have signed a pact with Satan (their private name for Sam Bailey).

"Let's go, Pete," Father Ryan said. "We can't keep God waiting."

Pete stepped in front of the priest, folded his hands, bowed his head, and out they went into the sanctuary where the two tapers flickered and peace was a fact.

Father Ryan mounted the altar steps, placed his chalice in front of the tabernacle, and opened the huge Missal to the proper page. As he started down the steps again, the sound of Sam's rough voice singing outside the church shattered the candlelit silence.

"*Roll me over in the clover, roll me over, lay me down and do it again!*"

Father Ryan caught the I-told-you-so looks on the faces of the Malone sisters seated in the first pew. When they were sure that he had seen their icy indictment (of himself, of Sam, of sin—all in one glance), they piously lowered their eyes to their prayer books.

"*Oh, roll me over in the clover . . . !*"

Father Ryan bowed his head at the foot of the steps. "Et introibo ad altare Dei." The bishop's order, after all, had said the use of the vernacular was optional. And Father Ryan considered himself too old a dog to learn new tricks.

Pete responded, "Ad Deum qui laetificat juventutem meum."

Father Ryan would go unto the altar of God.

"To God who giveth joy to my youth," in Pete's words.

"*. . . roll me over, lay me down and do it again!*"

At last Sam fell silent. The Mass proceeded.

"Credo in unum Deum . . ."

And, "Pater noster qui es in coeli . . ."

And finally, as always, "Ite missa est."

The Malone sisters closed their prayer books—*snap, snick*—and swooped up to the altar railing to light votive candles to guard them against flying saucer invasions and shamelessly sinful sacristans. Father Ryan, proceeded by Pete, made his way out of the sanctuary and back to the dim sacristy.

Sam Bailey was there, vigorously polishing a brass doorknob and singing softly to himself. *"How you going to keep 'em down on the farm after they've seen Parreeeee!"*

Father Ryan suppressed a grin and tried to look stern. "That hymn you were singing outside a little while ago, Sam. Hardly suitable for morning Mass."

"Now, Matt, don't take on so. You know you can drown me out with all that Latin mumbo jumbo of yours any day in the week. Besides, which, I didn't think you could hear me."

Father Ryan dismissed Pete and began to remove his vestments.

Sam said, "Well, how'd it go this morning? Did you help those Malone girls sneak through the pearly gates?"

"They came to see me this morning," Father Ryan said. "They want you to get back in your flying saucer and go back wherever it is you came from. Or else."

Sam stopped his polishing, straightened, and glanced speculatively at Father Ryan. And then he smiled. "Well, if they can believe in angels and devils, I guess they can believe in flying saucers."

"Don't blaspheme," Father Ryan said without anger. Was it blasphemy? He wasn't sure.

Sam went back to his polishing.

"They also accused you of Lena Carlisle, Sam."

"Lena's a fine port in a storm, Matt. Getting on in years a bit, she is, but still fine."

"The weather was fair and clear last night. Not a storm in sight."

Sam winked. "Now, Matt, is it that you don't know the heart has its own weather? Its own uneasy climate?"

"I know," Father Ryan said somewhat sadly. "Every priest does." He looked up at his friend. "What's this I hear about Pat and Mary Fahey chasing you out of their house night before last?"

"The Misses Malone again?"

Father Ryan nodded, grinned.

"I just happened to be passing by the Fahey house and heard them hollering and hooting inside, so I just stepped in to see if I could referee. Before long, they were after me instead of each other. Pat came at me with a butcher knife, he did."

"And the poker game at the firehouse?"

Sam sighed. "Denny Maclean had an extra ace stuck in his anklet. Harry Bolinsky spotted it and they started at each other hot and heavy. I agreed with Harry about Denny being a cheat. Then Mac Maguire accused me of maligning the name of a good God-fearing man. Mac claimed Denny Maclean was as honest as the day was long and as good a man as God ever put down here in this vale of tears. Before I knew what had happened, Mac and Harry had thrown me out on my—right on my ear. After which they all went back to being bosom buddies and me to being *persona non grata* at the firehouse."

"A word of advice, Sam—"

"Save it for the Malone sisters, Matt."

Father Ryan persisted. "It's about Lena Carlisle. Her husband—her common-law husband, Zack—got out of Keane County prison last week. Before you came to Little Falls last year, Zack Carlisle attacked a man he thought was paying too close attention to Lena. That's what landed him in the county prison on a charge of aggravated assault. Now he'll be coming back and—"

"Lena told me about Zack. 'Mean as they make 'em,' was the way she put it." He paused and chuckled. "I never did tumble a woman who talked as much as that Lena does, I swear."

Father Ryan breathed a quick prayer. "Sam, I don't know why you and I get along so well. I don't know why I like you as much as I do."

"It's simple," Sam said. "You have an alliance with the Devil, same as I do."

"I do not have—"

"If Beelzebub didn't exist, you'd be out of a job, Matt, and you know it. At least out of the one you've got. You'd probably be managing a supermarket somewhere with a pencil stuck behind your ear and your fingers smelling of pinched fruit." Sam put an arm around his friend and walked him to the sacristy door. "Better get something to eat, Matt. Drinking wine on an empty stomach is a bad habit. It'll ruin your liver for sure."

As Father Ryan made his slow way to the rectory, Sam's laughter followed him. To Father Ryan it sounded less like profane merriment at his expense than just plain down-home humor.

That night, as snow dashed down from the dark January sky, Father Ryan sat reading his office in the rectory parlor.

The phone rang twice before he heard it. When he did, he got up and answered it. He listened in shocked silence to Lena Carlisle's anguished voice on the other end of the line.

". . . and Zack came home an hour ago, Father, and he grabbed Sam and . . ."

"Sam Bailey? Sam was there with you?"

Her voice lowered. "Well, we were having us a little talk, Father. And a couple of beers. But—about Zack. He's got a knife!"

"Where are you calling from, Lena?"

"I slipped out the back door and came over here to Mrs. Aberswift's to call you. You could talk to him, Father. He'd listen to you, Zack would."

Father Ryan wasn't so sure. Every Saturday afternoon when he sat in the hot darkness of the confessional booth, it seemed to him that sin was getting worse, if anything. It seemed to him that he could preach every Sunday for the next million years and people would go on—well, go on being people. It seemed to him that nobody listened to him, hadn't for years.

"Father, are you there? Will you come over and talk to Zack?"

"I'll come, Lena. Now, don't you go back there. You know what happened last time."

"Father, I feel terrible about this. Besides, you see—" She drew a dry breath.

"Lena? Are you all right?"

"You see, Father, it's me that Zack wants to cut with that knife of his. It's me he hates. It's not really my gentlemen friends at all. It's *me!*"

Father Ryan tried to talk over the sad sound of her sobbing, and at last succeeded. She promised him she wouldn't move from the safety of Mrs. Aberswift's house.

He hung up, started out, remembered his overcoat, came back and struggled into it, went out and got into his dusty old Dodge and drove off under the eyes of the stars. He drove for fifteen minutes, made a wrong turn on Spruce Street, doubled back, and at last pulled up in front of the Carlisle house on New Hope Street. He got out, crossed himself while cursing his lack of courage, and made his way up the path to the front door. He pounded on it in what he hoped was a commanding manner.

At first, there was only silence inside the lighted house.

And then Zack's voice yelled, "If you think you can take me back to that hellhole of a prison—well, you'll have to plug me full of holes first, you fuzz bastards!"

Father Ryan shuddered, perhaps because of the coldness of the night. "Zack Carlisle! Open the door! It's Father Ryan from Saint Gabriel's."

More silence. More shivering. And then the door opened an inch. Zack's heavy face with several days' growth of beard maning it peered out. His eyes were wild and his lips were wet. An animal, Father Ryan thought and then promptly chastised himself for his lack of charity. It wasn't an animal. It was Zack Carlisle. "Zack, let me in. I want to talk to you."

"Go to hell," came the blunt response. Zack started to shut the door, but Father Ryan stuck his foot in it as he had learned to do when he was selling magazine subscriptions door to door before entering the seminary.

"Where's Sam Bailey?" he asked Zack, once he had managed to shoulder his way inside.

"Well, he ain't dead yet if that's what you mean. But he will be pretty soon." A snicker. "You come to say the holy words over his corpse?" Zack had been drinking. The whiskey fired his cheeks and reeked on his breath.

"Sam!" Father Ryan yelled, feeling real fear for the first time in his life.

"In here, Matt!" Sam yelled from the kitchen. "He's got me tied to the sink!"

"Get out of my way, Zack," Father Ryan ordered and strode forward. To his surprise and genuine relief, Zack grinned and stepped out of his way. Father Ryan found Sam with his back against the sink and his hands pulled up behind him and tied tightly to the two faucets. He went over to him, reached out . . .

"Don't touch him!" It was Zack, standing in the doorway.

As Father Ryan turned around, Zack took the switchblade knife out of his pocket. He sprung the blade and gestured at Father Ryan with it. "This'll all be over pretty quick. Sit yourself down, Father, and start practicing your weasel words." He moved menacingly toward Sam, who glared at him.

Father Ryan sat down. What good now were all his years in the seminary, the countless rosaries told, the Masses said, the solitary penances performed? Nothing in his life had prepared him for this moment, for this confrontation with a man who might soon become a murderer.

Zack touched Sam's throat with the tip of his blade. "This here old fox can't stay away from the chicken coop when the farmer's away. Now I admit that Lena is a plump and tasty hen to find among the straw and eggs, sure enough. But the way I figure it, you got to kill foxes to save your chickens."

At that moment, the kitchen door flew open and a flurry of flannel robe and blue mules burst into the kitchen. "You leave him be, Zack!" Lena yelled and began to pummel Zack's chest.

He flung her aside easily and she fell against Father Ryan, who helped her sit down. "Father!" she cried. "*Help* him!"

Father Ryan didn't know whether she referred to Sam or to Zack. But he did know it didn't matter. They both needed help. "Zack, let's be reasonable. I'm sure no harm was done. Sam was just—"

"You bet your ass he was!"

"Matt," Sam muttered, "get Lena out of here."

Lena shook her head. She looked at Zack. "Don't hurt him, please. Just because he was nice to me, you don't have to hurt him."

Zack shouted an obscenity and spun around again to face Sam. Perhaps he hadn't meant to do it. Perhaps he had lost his balance. But the blade of his knife plunged into Sam's chest, and Sam's blood soaked through his clothes within seconds. He fell forward gasping, his head hanging down, his hands straining at the lengths of clothesline with which Zack had bound him to the faucets.

"Father!" Lena screamed.

Zack was standing with his back to them, staring at Sam in surprise.

Father Ryan turned to find that Lena had gotten to her feet and seized the iron handle used to lift the heavy lids from the coal stove. She was holding it out to him. He took it from her, raised it, and brought it down against the back of Zack's skull. The terrible sound of the iron smashing flesh and then bone caused Father Ryan's spine to sag. Zack fell to the floor and lay there motionless.

"Jesus, Mary and Joseph!" Father Ryan whispered, looking down at the bloody weapon in his hand. He dropped it beside Zack's unconscious body.

"Call the police," he told Lena in a weak voice. Why hadn't he told her to do that when she had first called him? Had he felt a certain pride that she had turned to him instead, believing him to be a wise and clever man, a man who would surely know how to handle the enraged Zack? As Lena ran for the phone in the living room, he hurried over to Sam. He reached out with one hand to support his friend. With the other he began to untie the cords that bound his hands. Minutes later, he eased Sam to the floor and then noticed that his own hands were red with Sam's blood. He stared helplessly at them and then at Sam as Lena came back and announced that the police were on their way.

He spent the night waiting for word of the results of the emergency surgery they were performing on Sam. At last the doctor appeared and said they would just have to wait and see. It was touch and go. He went back to Saint Gabriel's, said Mass, and then returned in the afternoon to the hospital to see Sam, who had regained consciousness. He talked to the doctor again. The doctor said that a man Sam's age—well, if he were a few years younger ... Younger. Father Ryan knew that the doctor had no cure for the disease of inevitably advancing age, complicated in Sam's case by two inches of steel that had violated his heart.

Later, as he sat beside Sam's bed in the intensive-care room, he said, "They've got Zack locked up in the jail in the basement of the courthouse pending trial. Lena's doing fine, considering."

The briefest of smiles from Sam.

"I had to open the church myself this morning. Couldn't find the keys for the longest time. I'll be glad when you're back to do all the dirty work, Sam."

"How's everything in town now that I'm out of circulation?" Sam asked.

"Well, there are the usual problems."

"Problems, Matt?" Sam eased himself up on his pillow.

"It seems that Pat Fahey blacked Mary's eyes—both of them—and then she broke his nose with their cuckoo clock. Pete Casello got in a fight with one of the other altar boys after Mass this morning. Denny Maclean pushed Mac Maguire down the steps of the firehouse last night because Mac had accused him of cheating during their poker game. The same old story." Father Ryan frowned thoughtfully. No, it wasn't the same old story at all. It was a slightly different story. Now what—? He thought about it for a moment. Always before, it had been Sam who had been the one in all the trouble. Sam was the one who had been thrown out of the firehouse. Sam was the one who had been attacked by both Pat and Mary Fahey. Sam was the one who had taken the knife wound from Zack Carlisle instead of Lena. *Instead of Lena!*

Sam said, "Well, Matt, judging by the expression on your face, I'd say that you've got it all figured out finally."

Father Ryan started to speak, but the idea he was going to voice was ridiculous, impossible!

"No," Sam said, as if Father Ryan had actually spoken, "it's true. I was a sort of lightning rod, you might say. For the Faheys, the boys at the firehouse—all of them."

Father Ryan stared at the man he thought he knew but now began to suspect he didn't really know at all. "Sam, the Malone sisters said—"

"They were right. I landed in Carter's Meadow, just like they said."

"Then there really *was* a flying saucer?"

"There was—it was mine. I came and did what I had been trained to do."

"Sam—" The name suddenly tasted strange to Father Ryan. "What—why—?"

A flicker of an indulgent smile momentarily erased the pain on Sam's face. "Where I come from, we have—well, castes. Or orders, as you'd call them. We do good works. Some of us like me are members of a penitent order. We are assigned as missionaries to minister to some of the more backward—" He cleared his throat with some difficulty. "What we do is, we draw other people's anger to ourselves to keep—we sort of defuse them, you could say, to keep them from hurting one another."

"A missionary," Father Ryan murmured, thinking of martyrs. "But Sam—the whiskey, the women—*Lena!*"

Sam laughed, a wet bubbly sound. "Sin changes from time to time, Matt. And from place to place. Now bedding a girl or draining a bottle now and then has nothing at all to do with sin where I come from."

"Where you come from?" Father Ryan repeated, dazed.

"Don't you worry about Saint Gabriel's, Matt," Sam said. "Somebody'll be along to help you out."

"Oh, you'll be back in a week, Sam," Father Ryan said quickly. "Any day now. The doctor told me—"

"Mendacity, Matt, is a sin for you."

Father Ryan lowered his eyes.

"Like I said, somebody'll be along, Matt. Listen, give me your hand. It's time to say—give me your hand, Matt."

They shook hands gently and Father Ryan quickly excused himself and hurried from the room, away from—away.

He was reading his office in the rectory parlor that night when the hospital called to say that Sam had died suddenly. He put down the phone and stood there for a long moment feeling terribly alone. Well, he told himself, life had to go on. He would remember Sam tomorrow morning at Mass.

The phone rang again.

It was Miss Marlene Malone. "There's been another saucer sighting, Father!" she yelped. "An hour ago—out in Carter's Meadow, just like the last time when that awful Sam—"

On the Malone extension, Miss Aileen cried, "Father, you'd best come out right this minute and exorcise the area so that—!"

Father Ryan hung up on the Malone sisters and sat down to wait, knowing quite well what he was waiting for, believing in miracles as he always had.

Less than fifteen minutes later, there was a knock on the front door of the rectory. He got up and opened it to confront the young man standing on the porch and smiling at him.

"I heard you were in need of a sacristan," the young man said.

"Experience?" Father Ryan inquired.

"Some."

"References?"

"Sam Bailey."

"What's your name?"

"Sam," the young man answered. "Sam Ralston."

And then it struck Father Ryan. *Sam.* Perhaps it was a title—a designation translated into English. Like *Father.* Or *Monsignor.* "Come in," he said, taking the young man by the arm and leading him into the rectory. "I'm very glad you're—uh, here. I sure can use some help, God knows. Oh, by the way, my name is Father Matthew Ryan."

"I know," the young man said. "Sam told me before he died."

"Call me Matt," Father Ryan said. "We might just as well be informal since we'll be working together from now on."

He said a silent prayer for the Misses Malone in the days to come as he shook hands with Sam.

*One of Frank Belknap Long's ancestors came over on the* Mayflower, *while another was involved in constructing the Statue of Liberty. Long himself was H. P. Lovecraft's closest friend and began writing fantasy over 55 years ago. So far, he has produced more than 25 books and 150 short stories of fantasy and science fiction. Here he presents a charming account of a young boy's adventures which could easily have been called "Bayou Leave."*

# THE MISSISSIPPI SAUCER

## by FRANK BELKNAP LONG

Jimmy watched the *Natchez Belle* draw near, a shining eagerness in his stare. He stood on the deck of the shantyboat, his toes sticking out of his socks, his heart knocking against his ribs. Straight down the river the big packet boat came, purpling the water with its shadow, its smokestacks belching soot.

Jimmy had a wild talent for collecting things. He knew exactly how to infuriate the captains without sticking out his neck. Up and down the river, from the bayous of Louisiana to the Great Sandy, other little shantyboat boys envied Jimmy and tried hard to imitate him.

But Jimmy had a very special gift, a genius for pantomime. He'd wait until there was a glimmer of red flame on the river and small objects stood out with a startling clarity. Then he'd go into his act.

Nothing upset the captains quite so much as Jimmy's habit of holding a big, croaking bullfrog up by its legs as the riverboats went steaming past. It was a surefire way of reminding the captains that men and frogs were brothers under the skin. The puffed-out throat of the frog told the captains exactly what Jimmy thought of their cheek.

Jimmy refrained from making faces, or sticking out his tongue at the grinning roustabouts. It was the frog that did the trick.

In the still dawn things came sailing Jimmy's way, hurled by captains with a twinkle of repressed merriment dancing in eyes that were kindlier and more tolerant than Jimmy dreamed.

Just because shantyboat folk had no right to insult the riverboats Jimmy had collected forty empty tobacco tins, a down-at-heels shoe, a Sears Roebuck catalogue and—more rolled-up newspapers than Jimmy could ever read.

Jimmy could read, of course. No matter how badly Uncle Al needed a new pair of shoes, Jimmy's education came first. So Jimmy had spent six winters ashore in a first-class grammar school, his books paid for out of Uncle Al's "New Orleans" money.

Uncle Al, blowing on a vinegar jug and making sweet music, the holes in his socks much bigger than the holes in Jimmy's socks. Uncle Al shaking his head and saying sadly, "Some day, young fella, I ain't gonna sit here harmonizing. No siree! I'm gonna buy myself a brand new store suit, trade in this here jig jug for a big round banjo, and hie myself off to the Mardi Gras. Ain't too old thataway to git a little fun out of life, young fella!"

Poor old Uncle Al. The money he'd saved up for the Mardi Gras never seemed to stretch far enough. There was enough kindness in him to stretch like a rainbow over the bayous and the river forests of sweet, rustling pine for as far as the eye could see. Enough kindness to wrap all of Jimmy's life in a glow, and the life of Jimmy's sister as well.

Jimmy's parents had died of winter pneumonia too soon to appreciate Uncle Al. But up and down the river everyone knew that Uncle Al was a great man.

Enemies? Well, sure, all great men made enemies, didn't they?

The Harmon brothers were downright sinful about carrying their feuding meanness right up to the doorstep of Uncle Al, if it could be said that a man living in a shantyboat had a doorstep.

Uncle Al made big catches and the Harmon brothers never seemed to have any luck. So, long before Jimmy was old enough to understand how corrosive envy could be, the Harmon brothers had started feuding with Uncle Al.

"Jimmy, here comes the *Natchez Belle!* Uncle Al says for you to get him a newspaper. The newspaper you got him yesterday he couldn't read no-ways. It was soaking wet!"

Jimmy turned to glower at his sister. Up and down the river Pigtail Anne was known as a tomboy, but she wasn't—no-ways. She was Jimmy's little sister. That meant Jimmy was the man in the family, and wore the pants, and nothing Pigtail said or did could change that for one minute.

"Don't yell at me!" Jimmy complained. "How can I get Captain Simmons mad if you get me mad first? Have a heart, will you?"

But Pigtail Anne refused to budge. Even when the *Natchez Belle* loomed so close to the shantyboat that it blotted out the sky she continued to crowd her brother, preventing him from holding up the frog and making Captain Simmons squirm.

But Jimmy got the newspaper anyway. Captain Simmons had a keen insight into tomboy psychology, and from the bridge of the *Natchez Belle* he could see that Pigtail was making life miserable for Jimmy.

True—Jimmy had no respect for packet boats and deserved a good trouncing. But what a scrapper the lad was! Never let it be said that in a struggle between the sexes the men of the river did not stand shoulder to shoulder.

The paper came sailing over the shining brown water like a white-bellied buffalo cat shot from a sling.

Pigtail grabbed it before Jimmy could give her a shove. Calmly she unwrapped it, her chin tilted in bellicose defiance.

As the *Natchez Belle* dwindled around a lazy, cypress-shadowed bend Pigtail Anne became a superior being, wrapped in a cosmopolitan aura. A wide-eyed little girl on a swaying deck, the great outside world rushing straight toward her from all directions.

Pigtail could take that world in her stride. She liked the fashion page best, but she was not above clicking her tongue at everything in the paper.

"Kidnap plot linked to airliner crash killing fifty," she read. "Red Sox blank Yanks! Congress sits today, vowing vengeance! Million-dollar heiress elopes with a clerk! Court lets dog pick owner! Girl of eight kills her brother in accidental shooting!"

"I ought to push your face right down in the mud," Jimmy muttered.

"Don't you dare! I've a right to see what's going on in the world!"

"You said the paper was for Uncle Al!"

"It is—when I get finished with it."

Jimmy started to take hold of his sister's wrist and pry the paper from her clasp. Only started—for as Pigtail wriggled back sunlight fell on a shadowed part of the paper which drew Jimmy's gaze as sunlight draws dew.

*Exciting* wasn't the word for the headline. It seemed to blaze out of the page at Jimmy as he stared, his chin nudging Pigtail's shoulder.

NEW FLYING MONSTER REPORTED
BLAZING GULF STATE SKIES

Jimmy snatched the paper and backed away from Pigtail, his eyes glued to the headline.

He was kind to his sister, however. He read the news item aloud, if an account so startling could be called an item. To Jimmy, it seemed more like a dazzling burst of light in the sky.

"A New Orleans resident reported today that he saw a big bright object 'roundish like a disk' flying north, against the wind. 'It was all lighted up from inside!' the observer stated. 'As far as I could tell there were no signs of life aboard the thing. It was much bigger than any of the flying saucers previously reported!' "

"People keep seeing them!" Jimmy muttered, after a pause. "Nobody knows where they come from! Saucers flying through the sky, high up at night. In the daytime, too! Maybe we're being *watched*, Pigtail!"

"Watched? Jimmy, what do you mean? What you talking about?"

Jimmy stared at his sister, the paper jiggling in his clasp. "It's way over your head, Pigtail!" he said sympathetically. "I'll prove it! What's a planet?"

"A star in the sky, you dope!" Pigtail almost screamed. "Wait'll Uncle Al hears what a meanie you are. If I wasn't your sister you wouldn't dare grab a paper that doesn't belong to you."

Jimmy refused to be enraged. "A planet's not a star, Pigtail," he said patiently. "A star's a big ball of fire like the sun. A planet is small and cool, like the Earth. Some of the planets may even have people on them. Not people like us, but people all the same. Maybe we're just frogs to them!"

"You're crazy, Jimmy! Crazy, crazy, you hear?"

Jimmy started to reply, then shut his mouth tight. Big waves were nothing new in the wake of steamboats, but the shantyboat wasn't just riding a swell. It was swaying and rocking like a floating barrel in the kind of blow shantyboaters dreaded worse than the thought of dying.

Jimmy knew that a big blow could come up fast. Straight down from the sky in gusts, from all directions, banging against the boat like a drunken roustabout, slamming doors, tearing away mooring planks.

The river could rise fast too. Under the lashing of a hurricane blowing up from the gulf the river could lift a shantyboat right out of the water, and smash it to smithereens against a tree.

But now the blow was coming from just one part of the sky. A funnel of wind was churning the river into a white froth and raising big swells directly offshore. But the river wasn't rising and the sun was shining in a clear sky.

Jimmy knew a dangerous floodwater storm when he saw one. The sky had to be dark with rain, and you had to feel scared, in fear of drowning.

Jimmy was scared, all right. That part of it rang true. But a hollow, sick feeling in his chest couldn't mean anything by itself, he told himself fiercely.

Pigtail Anne saw the disk before Jimmy did. She screamed and pointed skyward, her twin braids standing straight out in the wind like the ropes on a bale of cotton, when smokestacks collapse and a savage howling sends the river ghosts scurrying for cover.

Straight down out of the sky the disk swooped, a huge, spinning shape as flat as a buckwheat cake swimming in a golden haze of butterfat.

But the disk didn't remind Jimmy of a buckwheat cake. It made him think instead of a slowly turning wheel in the pilot house of a rotting old riverboat, a big, ghostly wheel manned by a steersman a century dead, his eyesockets filled with flickering swamp lights.

It made Jimmy want to run and hide. Almost it made him want to cling to his sister, content to let her wear the pants if only he could be spared the horror.

For there was something so chilling about the down-sweeping disk that Jimmy's heart began leaping like a vinegar jug bobbing about in the wake of a capsizing fishboat.

Lower and lower the disk swept, trailing plumes of white smoke, lashing the water with a fearful blow. Straight down over the cypress wilderness that fringed the opposite bank, and then out across the river with a long-drawn whistling sound, louder than the air-sucking death gasps of a thousand buffalo cats.

Jimmy didn't see the disk strike the shining broad shoulders of the Father of Waters, for the bend around which the *Natchez Belle* had steamed so proudly hid the sky monster from view. But Jimmy did see the waterspout, spiraling skyward like the atom bomb explosion he'd goggled at in the pages of an old *Life* magazine, all smudged now with oily thumbprints.

Just a roaring for an instant—and a big white mushroom shooting straight up into the sky. Then, slowly, the mushroom decayed and fell back, and an awful stillness settled down over the river.

The stillness was broken by a shrill cry from Pigtail Anne. "It was a flying saucer! Jimmy, we've seen one! We've seen one! We've—"

"Shut your mouth, Pigtail!"

Jimmy shaded his eyes and stared out across the river, his chest a throbbing ache.

He was still staring when a door creaked behind him.

Jimmy trembled. A tingling fear went through him, for he found it hard to realize that the disk had swept around the bend out of sight. To his overheated imagination it continued to fill all of the sky above him, overshadowing the shantyboat, making every sound a threat.

Sucking the still air deep into his lungs, Jimmy swung about.

Uncle Al was standing on the deck in a little pool of sunlight, his gaunt, hollow-cheeked face set in harsh lines.

Uncle Al was shading his eyes too. But he was staring up the river, not down.

"Trouble, young fella," he grunted. "Sure as I'm a-standin' here. A barrelful o' trouble—headin' straight for us!"

Jimmy gulped and gestured wildly toward the bend. "It came down *over there,* Uncle Al!" he got out. "Pigtail saw it, too! A big, flying—"

"The Harmons are a-comin', young fella," Uncle Al drawled, silencing Jimmy with a wave of his hand. "Yesterday I rowed over a Harmon jug line without meanin' to. Now Jed Harmon's tellin' everybody I stole his fish!"

Very calmly Uncle Al cut himself a slice of the strongest tobacco on the river and packed it carefully in his pipe, wadding it down with his thumb.

He started to put the pipe between his teeth, then thought better of it.

"I can bone-feel the Harmon boat a-comin', young fella," he said, using the pipe to gesture with. "Smooth and quiet over the river like a moccasin snake."

Jimmy turned pale. He forgot about the disk and the mushrooming water spout. When he shut his eyes he saw only a red haze overhanging the river, and a shantyboat nosing out of the cypresses, its windows spitting death.

Jimmy knew that the Harmons had waited a long time for an excuse. The Harmons were law-respecting river rats with sharp teeth. Feuding wasn't lawful, but murder could be made lawful by whittling down a lie until it looked as sharp as the truth.

The Harmon brothers would do their whittling down with double-barreled shotguns. It was easy enough to make murder look like a lawful crime if you could point to a body covered by a blanket and say, "We caught him stealing our fish! He was a-goin' to kill us—so we got him first."

No one would think of lifting the blanket and asking Uncle Al about it. A man lying stiff and still under a blanket could no more make himself heard than a river cat frozen in the ice.

"Git inside, young 'uns. *Here they come!*"

Jimmy's heart skipped a beat. Down the river in the sunlight a shantyboat was drifting. Jimmy could see the Harmon brothers crouching on the deck, their faces livid with hate, sunlight glinting on their arm-cradled shotguns.

The Harmon brothers were not in the least alike. Jed Harmon was tall and gaunt, his right cheek puckered by a knife scar, his cruel, thin-lipped mouth snagged by his teeth. Joe Harmon was small and stout, a little round man with bushy eyebrows and the flabby face of a cottonmouth snake.

"Go inside, Pigtail," Jimmy said, calmly. "I'm a-going to stay and fight!"

Uncle Al grabbed Jimmy's arm and swung him around. "You heard what I said, young fella. Now git!"

"I want to stay here and fight with you, Uncle Al," Jimmy said.

"Have you got a gun? Do you want to be blown apart, young fella?"

"I'm not scared, Uncle Al," Jimmy pleaded. "You might get wounded. I know how to shoot straight, Uncle Al. If you get hurt I'll go right on fighting!"

"No you won't, young fella! Take Pigtail inside. You hear me? You want me to take you across my knee and beat the livin' stuffings out of you?"

Silence.

Deep in his uncle's face Jimmy saw an anger he couldn't buck. Grabbing Pigtail Anne by the arm, he propelled her across the deck and into the dismal front room of the shantyboat.

The instant he released her she glared at him and stamped her foot. "If Uncle Al gets shot it'll be your fault," she said cruelly. Then Pigtail's anger really flared up.

"The Harmons wouldn't dare shoot us 'cause we're children!"

For an instant brief as a dropped heartbeat Jimmy stared at his sister with unconcealed admiration.

"You can be right smart when you've got nothing else on your mind, Pigtail," he said. "If they kill me they'll hang sure as shooting!"

Jimmy was out in the sunlight again before Pigtail could make a grab for him.

Out on the deck and running along the deck toward Uncle Al. He was still running when the first blast came.

It didn't sound like a shotgun blast. The deck shook and a big swirl of smoke floated straight toward Jimmy, half blinding him and blotting Uncle Al from view.

When the smoke cleared Jimmy could see the Harmon shantyboat. It was less than thirty feet away now, drifting straight past and rocking with the tide like a topheavy flatbarge.

On the deck Jed Harmon was crouching down, his gaunt

face split in a triumphant smirk. Beside him Joe Harmon stood quivering like a mound of jelly, a stick of dynamite in his hand, his flabby face looking almost gentle in the slanting sunlight.

There was a little square box at Jed Harmon's feet. As Joe pitched Jed reached into the box for another dynamite stick. Jed was passing the sticks along to his brother, depending on wad dynamite to silence Uncle Al forever.

Wildly Jimmy told himself that the guns had been just a trick to mix Uncle Al up, and keep him from shooting until they had him where they wanted him.

Uncle Al was shooting now, his face as grim as death. His big heavy gun was leaping about like mad, almost hurling him to the deck.

Jimmy saw the second dynamite stick spinning through the air, but he never saw it come down. All he could see was the smoke and the shantyboat rocking, and another terrible splintering crash as he went plunging into the river from the end of a rising plank, a sob strangling in his throat.

Jimmy struggled up from the river with the long, leg-thrusts of a terrified bullfrog, his head a throbbing ache. As he swam shoreward he could see the cypresses on the opposite bank, dark against the sun, and something that looked like the roof of a house with water washing over it.

Then, with mud sucking at his heels, Jimmy was clinging to a slippery bank and staring out across the river, shading his eyes against the glare.

Jimmy thought, "I'm dreaming! I'll wake up and see Uncle Joe blowing on a vinegar jug. I'll see Pigtail, too. Uncle Al will be sitting on the deck, taking it easy!"

But Uncle Al wasn't sitting on the deck. There was no deck for Uncle Al to sit upon. Just the top of the shantyboat, sinking lower and lower, and Uncle Al swimming.

Uncle Al had his arm around Pigtail, and Jimmy could see Pigtail's white face bobbing up and down as Uncle Al breasted the tide with his strong right arm.

Closer to the bend was the Harmon shantyboat. The Harmons were using their shotguns now, blasting fiercely away at Uncle Al and Pigtail. Jimmy could see the smoke curling up from the leaping guns and the water jumping up and down in little spurts all about Uncle Al.

There was an awful hollow agony in Jimmy's chest as he stared, a fear that was partly a soundless screaming and partly a vision of Uncle Al sinking down through the dark water and turning it red.

It was strange, though. Something was happening to Jimmy, nibbling away at the outer edges of the fear like a big, hungry river cat. Making the fear seem less swollen and awful, shredding it away in little flakes.

There was a white core of anger in Jimmy which seemed suddenly to blaze up.

He shut his eyes tight.

In his mind's gaze Jimmy saw himself holding the Harmon brothers up by their long, mottled legs. The Harmon brothers were frogs. Not friendly, good-natured frogs like Uncle Al, but snake frogs. Cottonmouth frogs.

All flannel red were their mouths, and they had long evil fangs which dripped poison in the sunlight. But Jimmy wasn't afraid of them no-ways. Not any more. He had too firm a grip on their legs.

"Don't let anything happen to Uncle Al and Pigtail!" Jimmy whispered, as though he were talking to himself. No—not exactly to himself. To someone like himself, only larger. Very close to Jimmy, but larger, more powerful.

"Catch them before they harm Uncle Al! Hurry! *Hurry!*"

There was a strange lifting sensation in Jimmy's chest now. As though he could shake the river if he tried hard enough, tilt it, send it swirling in great thunderous white surges clear down to Lake Pontchartrain.

But Jimmy didn't want to tilt the river. Not with Uncle Al on it and Pigtail, and all those people in New Orleans who would disappear right off the streets. They were frogs too, maybe, but good frogs. Not like the Harmon brothers.

Jimmy had a funny picture of himself much younger than he was. Jimmy saw himself as a great husky baby, standing in the middle of the river and blowing on it with all his might. The waves rose and rose, and Jimmy's cheeks swelled out and the river kept getting angrier.

No—he must fight that.

"Save Uncle Al!" he whispered fiercely. "Just save him—and Pigtail!"

It began to happen the instant Jimmy opened his eyes. Around the bend in the sunlight came a great spinning disk, wrapped in a fiery glow.

Straight toward the Harmon shantyboat the disk swept, water spurting up all about it, its bottom fifty feet wide.

There was no collision. Only a brightness for one awful instant where the shantyboat was twisting and turning in the current, a brightness that outshone the rising sun.

Just like a camera flashbulb going off, but bigger, brighter. So big and bright that Jimmy could see the faces of the Harmon brothers fifty times as large as life, shriveling and disappearing in a magnifying burst of flame high above the cypress trees. Just as though a giant in the sky had trained a big burning glass on the Harmon brothers and whipped it back quick.

Whipped it straight up, so that the faces would grow huge before dissolving as a warning to all snakes. There was an evil anguish in the dissolving faces which made Jimmy's blood run cold. Then the disk was alone in the middle of the river spinning around and around, the shantyboat swallowed up.

And Uncle Al was still swimming, fearfully close to it.

The net came swirling out of the disk over Uncle Al like a great, dew-drenched gossamer web. It enmeshed him as he swam, so gently that he hardly seemed to struggle or even to be aware of what was happening to him.

Pigtail didn't resist, either. She simply stopped thrashing in Uncle Al's arms, as though a great wonder had come upon her.

Slowly Uncle Al and Pigtail were drawn into the disk. Jimmy could see Uncle Al reclining in the web, with Pigtail in the crook of his arm, his long, angular body as quiet as a butterfly in its deep winter sleep inside a swaying glass cocoon.

Uncle Al and Pigtail, being drawn together into the disk as Jimmy stared, a dull pounding in his chest. After a moment the pounding subsided and a silence settled down over the river.

Jimmy sucked in his breath. The voices began quietly, as though they had been waiting for a long time to speak to Jimmy deep inside his head, and didn't want to frighten him in any way.

"Take it easy, Jimmy! Stay where you are. We're just going to have a friendly little talk with Uncle Al."

"A t-talk?" Jimmy heard himself stammering.

"We knew we'd find you where life flows simply and serenely, Jimmy. Your parents took care of that before they left you with Uncle Al.

"You see, Jimmy, we wanted you to study the Earth people on a great, wide flowing river, far from the cruel, twisted places. To grow up with them, Jimmy—and to understand them. Especially the Uncle Als. For Uncle Al is unspoiled, Jimmy. If there's any hope at all for Earth as we guide and watch it, that hope burns most brightly in the Uncle Als!"

The voice paused, then went on quickly. "You see, Jimmy, you're not human in the same way that your sister is human— or Uncle Al. But you're still young enough to feel human, and we want you to feel human, Jimmy."

"W-Who are you?" Jimmy gasped.

"We are the Shining Ones, Jimmy! For wide wastes of years we have cruised Earth's skies, almost unnoticed by the Earth people. When darkness wraps the Earth in a great, spinning shroud we hide our ships close to the cities, and glide through the silent streets in search of our young. You see, Jimmy, we must watch and protect the young of our race until sturdiness comes upon them, and they are ready for the Great Change."

For an instant there was a strange, humming sound deep inside Jimmy's head, like the drowsy murmur of bees in a dew-drenched clover patch. Then the voice droned on. "The Earth people are frightened by our ships now, for their cruel wars have put a great fear of death in their hearts. They watch the skies with sharper eyes, and their minds have groped closer to the truth.

"To the Earth people our ships are no longer the fireballs of mysterious legend, haunted will-o'-the-wisps, marsh flickerings and the even more illusive distortions of the sick in mind. It is a long bold step from fireballs to flying saucers, Jimmy. A day will come when the Earth people will be wise enough to put aside fear. Then we can show ourselves to them as we really are, and help them openly."

The voice seemed to take more complete possession of Jimmy's thoughts then, growing louder and more eager, echoing through his mind with the persuasiveness of muted chimes.

"Jimmy, close your eyes tight. We're going to take you across wide gulfs of space to the bright and shining land of your birth."

Jimmy obeyed.

It was a city, and yet it wasn't like New York or Chicago or any of the other cities Jimmy had seen illustrations of in the newspapers and picture magazines.

The buildings were white and domed and shining, and they seemed to tower straight up into the sky. There were streets, too, weaving in and out between the domes like rainbow-colored spider webs in a forest of mushrooms.

There were no people in the city, but down the aerial streets shining objects swirled with the swift easy gliding of flat stones skimming an edge of running water.

Then as Jimmy stared into the depths of the strange glow behind his eyelids the city dwindled and fell away, and he saw a huge circular disk looming in a wilderness of shadows. Straight toward the disk a shining object moved, bearing aloft on filaments of flame a much smaller object that struggled and mewed and reached out little white arms.

Closer and closer the shining object came, until Jimmy could see that it was carrying a human infant that stared straight at Jimmy out of wide, dark eyes. But before he could get a really good look at the shining object it pierced the shadows and passed into the disk.

There was a sudden, blinding burst of light, and the disk was gone.

Jimmy opened his eyes.

"You were once like that baby, Jimmy!" the voice said. "You were carried by your parents into a waiting ship, and then out across wide gulfs of space to Earth.

"You see, Jimmy, our race was once entirely human. But as we grew to maturity we left the warm little worlds where our infancy was spent, and boldly sought the stars, shedding our humanness as sunlight sheds the dew, or a bright, soaring moth of the night its ugly pupa case.

"We grew great and wise, Jimmy, but not quite wise enough to shed our human heritage of love and joy and heartbreak. In our childhood we must return to the scenes of our past, to take root again in familiar soil, to grow in power and wisdom slowly and sturdily, like a seed dropped back into the loam which nourished the great flowering mother plant.

"Or like the eel of Earth's seas, Jimmy, that must be spawned in the depths of the great cold ocean, and swim slowly back to the bright highlands and the shining rivers of Earth. Young eels do not resemble their parents, Jimmy.

They're white and thin and transparent and have to struggle hard to survive and grow up.

"Jimmy, you were planted here by your parents to grow wise and strong. Deep in your mind you knew that we had come to seek you out, for we are all born human, and are bound one to another by that knowledge, and that secret trust.

"You knew that we would watch over you and see that no harm would come to you. You called out to us, Jimmy, with all the strength of your mind and heart. Your Uncle Al was in danger and you sensed our nearness.

"It was partly your knowledge that save him, Jimmy. But it took courage too, and a willingness to believe that you were more than human, and armed with the great proud strength and wisdom of the Shining Ones."

The voice grew suddenly gentle, like a caressing wind.

"You're not old enough yet to go home, Jimmy! Or wise enough. We'll take you home when the time comes. Now we just want to have a talk with Uncle Al, to find out how you're getting along."

Jimmy looked down into the river and then up into the sky. Deep down under the dark, swirling water he could see life taking shape in a thousand forms. Caddis flies building bright, shining new nests, and dragonfly nymphs crawling up toward the sunlight, and pollywogs growing sturdy hind limbs to conquer the land.

But there were cottonmouths down there too, with death behind their fangs, and no love for the life that was crawling upward. When Jimmy looked up into the sky he could see all the blazing stars of space, with cottonmouths on every planet of every sun.

Uncle Al was like a bright caddis fly building a fine new nest, thatched with kindness, denying himself bright little Mardi Gras pleasures so that Jimmy could go to school and grow wiser than Uncle Al.

"That's right, Jimmy. You're growing up—we can see that! Uncle Al says he told you to hide from the cottonmouths. But you were ready to give your life for your sister and Uncle Al."

"Shucks, it was nothing!" Jimmy heard himself protesting.

"Uncle Al doesn't think so. And neither do we!"

A long silence while the river mists seemed to weave a bright cocoon of radiance about Jimmy clinging to the bank, and the great circular disk that had swallowed up Uncle Al.

Then the voices began again. "No reason why Uncle Al shouldn't have a little fun out of life, Jimmy. Gold's easy to make and we'll make some right now. A big lump of gold in Uncle Al's hand won't hurt him in any way."

"Whenever he gets any spending money he gives it away!" Jimmy gulped.

"I know, Jimmy. But he'll listen to you. Tell him you want to go to New Orleans, too!"

Jimmy looked up quickly then. In his heart was something of the wonder he'd felt when he'd seen his first riverboat and waited for he knew not what. Something of the wonder that must have come to men seeking magic in the sky, the rainmakers of ancient tribes and of days long vanished.

Only to Jimmy the wonder came now with a white burst of remembrance and recognition.

It was as though he could sense something of himself in the two towering spheres that rose straight up out of the water behind the disk. Still and white and beautiful they were, like bubbles floating on a rainbow sea with all the stars of space behind them.

Staring at them, Jimmy saw himself as he would be, and knew himself for what he was. It was not a glory to be long endured.

"Now you must forget again, Jimmy! Forget as Uncle Al will forget—until we come for you. Be a little shantyboat boy! You are safe on the wide bosom of the Father of Waters. Your parents planted you in a rich and kindly loam, and in all the finite universes you will find no cosier nook, for life flows here with a diversity that is infinite and—*Pigtail!* She gets on your nerves at times, doesn't she, Jimmy?"

"She sure does," Jimmy admitted.

"Be patient with her, Jimmy. She's the only human sister you'll ever have on Earth."

"I—I'll try!" Jimmy muttered.

Uncle Al and Pigtail came out of the disk in an amazingly simple way. They just seemed to float out, in the glimmering web. Then, suddenly, there wasn't any disk on the river at all—just a dull flickering where the sky had opened like a great, blazing furnace to swallow it up.

"I was just swimmin' along with Pigtail, not worryin' too much, 'cause there's no sense in worryin' when death is starin' you in the face," Uncle Al muttered, a few minutes later.

Uncle Al sat on the riverbank beside Jimmy, staring down at his palm, his vision misted a little by a furious blinking.

"It's gold, Uncle Al!" Pigtail shrilled. "A big lump of solid gold—"

"I just felt my hand get heavy and there it was, young fella, nestling there in my palm!"

Jimmy didn't seem to be able to say anything.

"High school books don't cost no more than grammar school books, young fella," Uncle Al said, his face a sudden shining. "Next winter you'll be a-goin' to high school, sure as I'm sittin' here!"

For a moment the sunlight seemed to blaze so brightly about Uncle Al that Jimmy couldn't even see the holes in his socks.

Then Uncle Al made a wry face. "Someday, young fella, when your books are all paid for, I'm gonna buy myself a brand new store suit, and hie myself off to the Mardi Gras. Ain't too old thataway to git a little fun out of life, young fella!"

*Mack Reynolds has worked as a newspaper editor, supervisor for IBM, lecturer for the Socialist Labor Party, and foreign correspondent for* Rogue. *He has written over 40 books and 150 short stories of science fiction, many of which make serious attempts at socioeconomic extrapolation. Although not known as a stylist, his ideas are so interesting that at one time the readers of* If *and* Galaxy *voted him their favorite author. In the following vignette, he suggests a reason why, in spite of all the supposed sightings, aliens from flying saucers have not yet conquered the world.*

# POSTED

## by Mack Reynolds

The alien took only moderate pains to keep his ship from being spotted. He landed in a hilly wooded area and immediately set his scanners for a routine check of the planet's development. It had been but ten years since the last check of Terra but the planet was progressing nicely and undoubtedly soon would be ripe for conquest.

He let the scanner run over several of the larger cities, probed here, there, followed for a time an aircraft, checked the railroads for estimated tonnage.

They were coming along very nicely indeed.

He was somewhat surprised when a human figure detached itself from the shadows of the trees and approached his craft casually. But, if necessary, he could destroy the other; meanwhile a bit of personal prying into the human's brain might be rewarding in results.

The human said, telepathically, "You're too late, you know. You should have taken over after your last check. Now you will never succeed."

The alien looked at him for long shocked moments.

This was unbelievable. But there was no immediate need for violence and there was great need for information.

"I don't know what you mean," he replied.

The human smiled wryly. "I mean you are from Deneb. Following a policy your race has continued for literally millions of our Earth years, you left a few score humanoid slaves on this planet long, long ago. Slowly through the ages they developed, slowly they multiplied and conquered the Earth. Now you plan to return and again assert authority over them." The human shook its head. "This time you fail."

A yellowish flush suffused the alien's face. "How do you know all this?"

The other shook his head in denial of answer.

The alien said, "Ten years ago this planet had barely discovered atomic power; now you speak as though you were my equal." He sneered.

"More, much more than your equal, Denebian," the human said softly. "I have no desire to destroy you, but if you make the move toward your weapon which you are now planning, it will be necessary."

"Slave!" the alien hissed and his tentacle darted for the weapon.

Only seconds later there were but smoldering, twisted bits of metal where the space scout had squatted.

The human looked thoughtfully at the wreckage. "They waited too long, this time," he murmured. "It possibly never occurred to their leaders that if man ever developed time travel he would return and police his space-time continuum. We of a thousand years in the future have no desire to have Denebians take over Earth and humanity in the year 1956."

*C. C. Rössel-Waugh has worked as a janitor in a woman's dormitory, sewing instructor, doll artist, college professor, and free-lance writer. The author of three books and co-editor of 40 anthologies, Rössel-Waugh has also produced approximately 80 shorter articles, and currently resides in a nineteenth-century lakefront house in central Maine. However, Melvin, the tormented protagonist of the following story, is not so lucky; he succeeds in getting away with murder only to be tongue-tied.*

# SPEAK UP, MELVIN!

## by C. C. Rössel-Waugh

From his armchair, Melvin's newspaper crackled in angry counterpoint to the fire. A barely perceptible groan escaped his lips. There was Gloria's wedding picture splashed across page twelve.

"Melvin, speak up! Must you always mumble when you're excited? Besides, it's not polite."

The young man leaped up, glanced wildly about, then stalked to the fireplace to attack the burning logs with a poker.

"Melvin!"

He swung about. "All right, Mama. This time I will speak up! All these years I've done what you wanted. Only what *you* wanted. Now Gloria is married and you've ruined my life.

214

You didn't like the competition so you shut out my ray of happiness."

Contemplating the poker's ash-covered tip, he twisted it around to target his chest. "If I can't have her, I don't want to live." But before he could stab himself, his mother lunged from her nearby rocker to clutch the weapon.

"Don't do it, Melvin! You're too young to die. Be a good boy and put this silly thing away. You'll soon forget her. The little tramp!"

He wrenched the poker away. Brown eyes narrowing with resolution, he swung wildly at the dainty, gray-haired woman.

"Maybe I'm too young to die, but you're not!"

It was over in a moment. The stylishly coiffed head broke open with a crunch. Mama slumped to the floor in an aristocratic swoon, ladylike to the end.

Melvin dropped the poker and sank back into his chair to think. He rubbed his chin. How lucky he was they lived on the Maine coast. If he was careful, he could get away with murder. His mother loved to walk along the rock-strewn beach. Her friends often expressed concern.

"One of these days, Martha," they would cluck, "you'll slip and fall with nobody there to save you."

Now all he had to do was wait until the full moon rose. He'd plop her over an appropriately nasty boulder by the crashing waves and poor Martha would have finally met her doom.

An hour later Melvin had sweated his grisly burden down to a likely spot. The night was ideal: thick and heavy with moist concealing fog. He arranged the body and was confident of success as he slowly picked his way back along the beach. But the pain-filled moan froze him.

"She's dead," he thought. "I know she's dead. It's not her! It's not."

Another hideous moan. Melvin located its direction. From the right. That meant someone else. Someone who might have seen him. Someone who might need help. Whatever the case, he knew he couldn't let it rest. He had to know. So he scrambled toward the cries. And between two seaweed-slicked rocks at ocean's edge, he found a greenish-bronze man pinned by a metal beam. The man was obviously an alien, but Melvin thought of him only as someone in need. There was a sturdy piece of driftwood near by, Melvin used it as a lever.

"Maybe God is giving me a second chance," he thought. "If

I took a life, maybe I can make amends by saving one. C'mon, starman. Don't give out on me."

He dabbed at the alien's face with a handkerchief he had swirled through a tidal pool.

Almond-shaped eyes opened tentatively.

Mevin extended a hand. "Come on, starman. You come home with me."

The next two weeks flew by. Melvin juggled roles of grief-stricken son and nurse. He mouthed platitudes and administered chicken soup. Eventually, Mama's friends stopped dropping by to confirm their told-you-so's and he was able to concentrate on the alien. Sign language was replaced by words and phrases.

"Roaun" rapidly assimilated English, encountering problems only when Melvin occasionally lapsed into excited mumbling.

Melvin, himself, almost wallowed in happiness, often singing lustily as he shuttled to and from the electronics store. He had freedom, a new friend, and a purpose in life—to help Roaun build a rescue beacon. Still, the pain over Gloria remained. He even framed her wedding picture, placing it on the mantel next to the glaring countenance of Mama, destined to be soon discarded.

Finally, the communicator was completed and activated. A few evenings later a luminous saucer-shaped craft swooped down feather-light to the lawn outside the patio window. A bronze being emerged, saw Roaun, and signaled heartily.

"It's my father," cried Roaun. Then, turning to Melvin, "Good friend, I have life only because of you. Is there anything I can do for you before I go?"

Melvin shook his head. Gloria. There was only Gloria and there could be no duplicate of her. But wait a minute! Maybe there could be. Maybe there could be. Dare he dream? Dare he ask?

Red with embarrassment, he mumbled: "Does your society have machines that can duplicate matter?"

"No," said Roaun. "But I imagine our scientists could invent one for you easily enough."

Indeed, it was only ten days later that Roaun returned with a large refrigeratorlike machine. The noise of uncrating it awoke Melvin, who dashed into the living room.

"Roaun," he cried. "How does it work? What do I do?"

Roaun smiled and pointed. "Just press that power button. I have already constructed a master tape of your loved one."

Melvin jabbed the button. "Gloria, Gloria, come to me." He flung out his arms in beseechment, accidentally knocking the quantity dial to 85. "Oh, no! What have I done? Eighty-five Glorias! But oh, what heaven!"

Green lights flared.

"Ping!"

The first of the duplicates was done. He yanked open the door and there she was—blood-caked hair and all—Mother!

"Melvin! How could you try to murder me, your mother, after all I've done for you?"

"Ping!"

Mother number 2 said, "We're not going to forget this, Melvin!"

"No! No!" he cried. "Something's wrong!"

"Ping!"

Now there was a chorus, demanding, imploring. "Melvin, that hussy poisoned you against us, didn't she? Speak up, boy! Speak up!"

"Roaun!" he shouted desperately. "What happened? What's wrong with my matter duplicator?"

"Ping!"

"Matter duplicator? Matter duplicator? My gosh!" came the crushing reply. "I thought you said *mother* duplicator."

*Eric Frank Russell was an English science fiction writer often referred to as* Astounding/Analog's *resident humorist. But "Stellar Kipling" would have been better, since many of his approximately 15 books and 100 short stories of science fiction dealt with quick-thinking earthmen outfoxing doltish aliens. A Hugo Award winner, his most famous work is ". . . And Then There Were None," a humorous exemplification of Gandhistic principles of nonviolence. Below he demonstrates how easy it would be for Earth to defend itself against unsuitable aliens.*

# EXPOSURE

## by Eric Frank Russell

The Rigelian ship came surreptitiously, in the deep of the night. Choosing a heavily forested area, it burned down a ring of trees, settled in the ash, sent out a powerful spray of liquid to kill the fires still creeping outward through the undergrowth.

Thin coils of smoke ascended from dying flames. Now adequately concealed from all directions but immediately above, the ship squatted amid towering conifers while its tubes cooled and contracted with metallic squeaks. There were strong smells of wood smoke, pine resin, acrid flamekiller and superheated metal.

Within the vessel there was a conference of aliens. They had two eyes apiece. That was their only positive feature: two eyes. Otherwise they had the formlessness, the almost liquid sloppiness of the completely malleable. When the three in the chart room consulted a planetary photograph they gestured with anything movable, a tentacle, pseudopod, a long, stump-ended arm, a mere digit, anything that struck their fancy at any given moment.

Just now all three were globular, shuffled around on wide, flat feet and were coated with fine, smooth fur resembling green velvet. This similarity was due to politeness rather than desire. During conversation it is conventional to assume the shape of one's superior and, if he changes, to change with him.

So two were spherical and furry solely because Captain Id-Wan saw fit to be spherical and furry. Sometimes Id-Wan was awkward. He'd give himself time to do a difficult shape such as that of reticulated molobater then watch them strain-ing their innards in an effort to catch up.

Id-Wan said: "We've recorded this world from far out on its light side and not a spaceship came near to challenge our presence. They have no spaceships." He sniffed expressively and went on, "The blown-up pictures are plenty good enough for our purpose. We've got the lay of the land and that's as much as we need."

"There appears to be a lot of sea," remarked Chief Naviga-tor Bi-Nak, peering at a picture. "Too much sea. More than half of it is sea."

"Are you again belittling my conquests?" demanded Id-Wan, producing a striped tail.

"Not at all, captain," assured Bi-Nak, dutifully imitating the tail. "I was simply pointing out—"

"You point too much," snapped Id-Wan. He turned to the third Rigelian. "Doesn't he, Po-Duk?"

Pilot Po-Duk played safe by remarking, "There are times and there are times."

"That is truly profound," commented Id-Wan, who had a robust contempt for neutrals. "One points while the other functions as a fount of wisdom. It would be a pleasant change if for once you did the pointing and let Bi-Nak be the oracle. I could stand that. It would make for variety."

"Yes, captain," agreed Po-Duk.

"Certainly, captain," endorsed Bi-Nak.

"All right." Id-Wan, turning irritably to the photographs, said: "There are many cities. That means intelligent life. But we have seen no spaceships and we know they've not yet reached even their own satellite. Hence, their intelligence is not of high order." He forced out a pair of mock hands so that he could rub them together. "In other words, just the sort of creatures we want—ripe for the plucking."

"You said that on the last planet," informed Bi-Nak, whose strong point was not tact.

Id-Wan pulled in his tail and bawled, "That was relative to worlds previously visited. Up to that point they were the best. These are better."

"We haven't seen them yet."

"We shall. They will give us no trouble." Id-Wan cooled down, mused aloud, "Nothing gives us trouble and I doubt whether anything is capable of it. We have fooled half a hundred successive life forms, all utterly different from any known in our home system. I anticipate no difficulties with another. Sometimes I think we must be unique in creation. On every world we've explored the creatures were fixed in form, unchangeable. It would appear that we alone are not the slaves of rigidity."

"Fixedness of form has its advantages," denied Bi-Nak, a glutton for punishment. "When my mother first met my father in the mating-field she thought he was a long-horned nodus, and—"

"There you go again," shouted Id-Wan, "criticizing the self-evident." Sourly, Id-Wan turned back to the photographs, indicated an area toward the north of a great landmass. "We are located there, well off the beaten tracks, yet within individual flying distance of four medium-sized centers. The big cities which hold potential dangers—though I doubt any real dangers—are a good way off. Nearer villages are too small to be worth investigating. The medium-sized places are best for our purpose and, as I've said, there are four within easy reach."

"Which we'll proceed to inspect?" suggested Po-Duk, mostly to show that he was paying attention.

"Of course. The usual tactics—two scouts in each. One day's mixing among the natives and they'll get us all we need to know, while the natives themselves learn nothing. After that—"

"A demonstration of power?" asked Po-Duk.

"Most certainly." Id-Wan extended something like a hair-thin tentacle, used it to mark one of the four near towns. "That place is as good as any other. We'll scrape it clean off

Earth's surface, then sit in space and see what they do about it. A major blow is the most effective way of persuading a world to reveal how highly it is organized."

"If the last six planets are anything to go by," ventured Po-Duk, "we won't see much organization here. They'll panic or pray or both."

"Much as we did when the Great Spot flared in the year of—" began Bi-Nak. His voice trailed off as he noted the gleam in Id-Wan's eyes.

Id-Wan turned to Po-Duk: "Summon the chief of the scouts and tell him to hurry. I want action." Staring hard at Bi-Nak, he added, "Action—not talk!"

The fat man whose name was Ollie Kampenfeldt waddled slowly through the dark toward the log hut whence came the thrum of a guitar and the sound of many voices. He was frowning as he progressed, and mopping his forehead at regular intervals.

There were other log huts scattered around in the vicinity, a few showing lights, but most in darkness. A yellow moon hung only a little above the big stockade of logs which ran right around the encampment; it stretched the shadows of the huts across neatly trimmed lawns and grassy borders.

Kampenfeldt lumbered into the noisy hut and yelped in shrill tones. The guitar ceased its twanging. The talking stopped. Presently the lights went out. He emerged accompanied by a small group of men, most of whom dispersed.

Two stayed with him as he made toward the building nearest the only gate in the heavy stockade. One of them was expostulating mildly.

"All right. So guys need sleep. How were we to know it was that late? Why don'tcha put a clock in the place?"

"The last one got snitched. It cost me fifty."

"Hah!" said the grumbler. "So time doesn't matter. What do I care about it? There's plenty of it and I'm going noplace. Make less noise and get to bed. We've got no clock because the place is full of thieves. You'd think I was back in the jug."

His companion on the other side of Kampenfeldt perked up with sudden interest. "Hey, I didn't know you'd been in clink."

"After ten years on the night beat for a big sheet you've been everywhere," said the first. "Even in a crackpotorium— even in a cemetery, for that matter." Then he stopped his forward pacing, raised himself on his toes, stared northward. "What was *that?*"

"What was what?" inquired Kampenfeldt, mopping his brow and breathing heavily.

"Sort of ring of brilliant red light. It floated down into the forest."

"Meteor," suggested Kampenfeldt, not interested.

"Imagination," said the third, having seen nothing.

"Too slow for a meteor," denied the observer, still peering on tiptoe at the distant darkness. "It floated down, like I said. Besides, I've never heard of one that shape or color. More like a plane in flames. Maybe it was a plane in flames."

"We'll know in an hour," promised Kampenfeldt, a little disgruntled at the thought of further night-time disturbances.

"How?"

"The forest will be ablaze on a ten-mile front. It's drier than I've ever known it, and ripe for the kindling." He made a clumsy gesture with a fat hand. "No fire, no plane."

"Well, what else might it be?"

Kampenfeldt said wearily: "I neither know nor care. I have to get up in the morning."

He waddled into his hut, yawning widely. The others stood outside a short time and stared northward. Nothing extraordinary was visible.

"Imagination," repeated one.

"I saw something queer. Dunno what could be out there in all that timber, but I saw something—and I've got good eyes." He removed his gaze, shrugged. "Anyway, the heck with it!"

They went to bed.

Captain Id-Wan gave his orders to the chief of the scouts. "Bring in some local life forms. The nearest and handiest will do providing they're assorted, small and large. We want to test them."

"Yes, captain."

"Collect them only from the immediate neighborhood. There is a camp to the south which undoubtedly holds superior forms. Keep away from it. Orders concerning that camp will be given you after the more primitive forms have been tested."

"I see, captain."

"You do not see," reproved Id-Wan. "Otherwise you would have noted that I have created flexible digits upon my feet."

"I beg your pardon, captain," said the chief, hastening to create similar extensions.

"The discourtesy is overlooked, but do not repeat it. Send in the head radio technician, then get on with your task."

To the radio officer, who made toes promptly, he said: "What have you to report?"

"The same as we noted upon our approach—they fill the air."

"What?" Id-Wan pulled surprisedly at an ear which he had not possessed a moment before. The ear stretched like soft rubber. "I was not informed of that during the approach."

"I regret, I forgot to—" commenced Bi-Nak, then ceased and strained himself before Id-Wan's eyes could catch him without a rubber ear.

"They fill the air," repeated the radio technician, also dutifully eared. "We've picked up their noises from one extreme to the other. There seem to be at least ten different speech patterns."

"No common language," Bi-Nak mourned. "That complicates matters."

"That simplifies matters," Id-Wan flatly contradicted. "The scouts can masquerade as foreigners and thus avoid speech troubles. The Great Green God could hardly have arranged it better."

"There are also other impulse streams," added the technician. "We suspect them of being pictorial transmissions."

"Suspect? Don't you *know?*"

"Our receivers cannot handle them, captain."

"Why not?"

The radio officer said patiently: "Their methods do not accord with ours. The differences are technical. To explain them would take me a week. In brief, our receivers are not suitable for their transmitted pictures. Eventually, by trial-and-error methods, we could make them suitable, but it would take a long time."

"But you do receive their speech?"

"Yes—that is relatively easy."

"Well, it tells us something. They've got as far as radio. Also, they're vocal and therefore unlikely to be telepathic. I would cross the cosmos for such bait." Dismissing the radio officer, he went to the lock, looked into the night-wrapped forest to see how his scouts were doing.

His strange Rigelian life-sense enabled him to detect their

quarry almost at a glance, for life burned in the dark like a tiny flame. There was just such a flame up a nearby tree. He saw it come tumbling down when the paralyzing dart from a scout's gun struck home. The flame flickered on landing but did not die out. The hunter picked it up, brought it into the light. It was a tiny animal with prick ears, coarse, reddish fur and a long, bushy tail.

Soon eight scouts struggled in bearing a huge, thickly furred form of ferocious aspect. It was big-pawed, clawed, and had no tail. It stank like molobater blood mixed with aged cheese. Half a dozen other forms were brought in, two of them winged. All were stiffened by darts, had their eyes closed, were incapable of movement. All were taken to the examiners.

One of the experts came to Id-Wan in due course. He was red-smeared and had an acrid smell.

"Nonmalleable. Every one of them."

"Bhingho!" exclaimed Id-Wan. "As are the lower forms, so will be the higher."

"Not necessarily, but very probably," said the expert, dodging the appearance of contradiction.

"We will see. Had any of these creatures possessed the power of imitative and ultra-rapid reshaping, I should have had to modify my plans. As it is, I can go right ahead."

The other responded, "So far as can be judged from these simple types you should have little trouble with their betters."

"That's what I think," agreed Id-Wan. "We'll get ourselves a sample."

"We need more than one. Two at least. A pair of them would enable us to determine the extent to which individuals differ. If the scouts are left to draw upon their own imaginations in creating differences, they may exaggerate sufficiently to betray themselves."

"All right, we'll get two," said Id-Wan. "Call in the chief of the scouts."

To the chief of the scouts, Id-Wan said: "All your captures were of unalterable form."

"Excellent!" The chief was pleased.

"Pfah!" murmured Bi-Nak.

Id-Wan jerked around. "What was that remark?"

"Pfah, captain," admitted Bi-Nak, mentally cursing the efficiency of the rubber ear. As mildly as possible, he added,

"I was considering the paradox of rigid superiority, and the pfah popped out."

"If I were telepathic," answered Id-Wan, very deliberately, "I would know you for the liar you are."

"Now there's something," offered Bi-Nak, sidetracking the insult. "So far we've encountered not one telepathic species. On this planet there are superior forms believed to be rigid— so whence comes their superiority? Perhaps they are telepathic."

Id-Wan complained to the chief scout, "Do you hear him? He points and pops out and invents obstacles. Of all the navigators available I had to be burdened with this one."

"What could be better could also be worse," put in Po-Duk, for no reason whatsoever.

Id-Wan yelled, "And this other one hangs around mouthing evasions." His fur switched from green to blue.

They all went blue, Po-Duk being the slowest. He was almost a color-cripple, as everyone knew. Id-Wan glared at him, swiftly changed to a reticulated molobater. That caught all three flat out. Id-Wan excelled at molobaters and gained much satirical satisfaction from their mutual writhings as each strove to be first. "See," he snapped, when finally they had assumed the new shape. "You are not so good, any of you."

"No, captain, we are very bad," endorsed Bi-Nak, oozing the characteristic molobater stench.

Id-Wan eyed him as if about to challenge the self-evident, decided to let the matter drop, returned his attention to the chief of the scouts. He pointed to the photographs. "There is that encampment a little to our south. As you can see, it is connected by a long, winding path to a narrow road which ambles far over the horizon before it joins a bigger road. The place is pretty well isolated; that is why we picked it."

"Picked it?" echoed the chief.

"We chose it and purposefully landed near it," Id-Wan explained. "The lonelier the source of samples, the less likelihood of discovery at the start, and the longer before an alarm can be broadcast."

"Ah," said the chief, recovering the wits strained by sudden molobating. "It is the usual technique. We are to raid the camp for specimens?"

"Two of them," confirmed Id-Wan. "Any two you can grab without rousing premature opposition."

"That will be easy."

"It cannot be otherwise. Would we be here, doing what we are doing, if all things did not come easy to our kind?"

"No, captain."

"Very well. Go get them. Take one of the radio technicians with you. He will first examine the place for signs of a transmitter or any other mode of ultra-rapid communication which cannot be detected on this photograph. If there proves to be a message-channel, of any sort at all, it must be put out of action, preferably in a manner which would appear accidental."

"Do we go right now?" asked the chief. "Or later?"

"At once, while it remains dark. We have observed how their cities dim by night, watched their lights go out, the traffic thin down. Obviously they are not nocturnal. They are most active in the daytime. Obtain those samples now and be back here before dawn."

"Very well, captain." The chief went out, still a molobater, but not for long.

Bi-Nak yawned and remarked, "I'm not nocturnal either."

"You are on duty," Id-Wan reminded him severely, "until I see fit to say that you are not on duty. And furthermore, I am disinclined to declare you off duty so long as I remain at my post."

"Example is better than precept," approved Po-Duk, currying favor.

Id-Wan promptly turned on him and bawled, "Shut up!"

"He was only pointing out," observed Bi-Nak, picking his not-teeth with fingers that weren't.

Kampenfeldt lumbered with elephantine tread to where three men were lounging full length on the grass. He wiped his forehead as he came, but it was from sheer habit. The sun was partway up and beginning to warm. The cool of the morning was still around. Kampenfeldt wasn't sweating, nevertheless he mopped.

One of the men rolled lackadaisically onto one side, welcomed him with, "Always on the run, Ollie. Why don'tcha flop down on your fat and absorb some sun once in a while?"

"Never get the chance." Kampenfeldt mopped, looked defeated. "I'm searching for Johnson and Greer. Every morning it's the same—somebody's late for breakfast."

"Aren't they in their hut?" inquired a second man, sitting up with an effort and plucking idly at blades of grass.

"Nope. First place I looked. Must've got up mighty early because nobody saw them go. Why won't guys tell me they're going out and might be late? Am I supposed to save something for them or not?"

"Let 'em do without," suggested the second man, lying down again and shading his eyes.

"Serves them right," added the first.

"They're not anywhere around," complained Kampenfeldt, "and they didn't go out the gate."

"Probably climbed the logs," offered one. "They're both batty. Most times they climb the logs when they go moonlight fishing. Anyone who wanders around like that in the middle of the night has got a hole in his head." He glanced at the other. "Were their rods in the hut?"

"Didn't think to look," admitted Kampenfeldt.

"Don't bother to look. They like to show they're tough. Let 'em be tough. It's a free country."

"Yeah," admitted Kampenfeldt reluctantly, "but they ought to have told me about their breakfasts. Now they'll be wasted unless I eat them myself."

They watched him waddle away, still worried, and mopping himself at regular intervals.

One said: "That silhouette shows there isn't much wasted."

Another said: "Hah!" and shaded his eyes with one hand and tried to look at the sun.

An examiner appeared, red-smeared and acrid-smelling as before. "They're like all the others—fixed."

"Unalterable?" insisted Id-Wan.

"Yes, captain." Distastefully he gazed down at the lurid stains upon himself, added, "Eventually we separated them, putting them in different rooms, and revived them. We killed one, then the other. The first fought with his limbs and made noises, but displayed no exceptional powers. The other one, in the other room, was already agitated but did not become more so during this time. It was obvious that he had no notion of what was happening to his companion. We then killed him after he had resisted in the same manner. The conclusion is that they are neither hypnotic nor telepathic. They are remarkably ineffectual even at the point of death."

"Good!" exclaimed Id-Wan, with great satisfaction. "You have done well."

"That is not all, captain. We have since subjected the bodies to a thorough search and can find no organs of life-sense. Evidently they have no way of perceiving life."

"Better still," enthused Id-Wan, "no life-sense means no dynamic receivers—no way of tuning an individual life and tracing its whereabouts. So those in the camp cannot tell where these two have gone."

"They couldn't in any case, by this time," the other pointed out, "since both are dead." He tossed a couple of objects onto a table. "They had those things with them. You may wish to look at them."

Id-Wan picked up the articles as the examiner went away. They were a pair of small bags or satchels made of treated animal hide, well finished, highly polished, and attached to adjustable belts.

He tipped out their contents upon the table, pawed them over: A couple of long, flat metal cases containing white tubes stuffed with herbs. Two metal gadgets, similar but not the same, which could be made to spark and produce a light. A thin card with queer, wriggly writing on one side and a colored picture of a tall-towered city on the other. One small magnifying glass. Two writing instruments, one black, the other silvery. A crude time meter with three indicators and a loud tick. Several insectlike objects with small, sharp hooks attached. Four carefully folded squares of cloth of unknown purpose.

"Humph!" He scooped the lot back, tossed the satchels to Po-Duk. "Take them to the workshop, tell them to make six reasonably good copies complete with contents. They must be ready by next nightfall."

"Six?" queried Po-Duk. "There will be eight scouts."

"Imbecile! You are holding the other two."

"So I am," said Po-Duk, gaping fascinatedly at the objects as if they had just materialized from thin air.

"There are times and there are times," remarked Bi-Nak as Po-Duk departed.

Id-Wan let it pass. "I must have a look at these bodies. I am curious about them." He moved off to the operating room, Bi-Nak following.

The kidnapped and slaughtered creatures proved to be not as repulsive as some they'd found on other worlds. They lay side by side, long, lean, brown-skinned, with two arms, two legs, and with dark, coarse hair upon their heads. Their dead eyes were very much like Rigelian eyes. Their flesh was horribly firm despite the fact that it was full of red juice.

"Primitive types," pronounced Id-Wan, poking at one of them. "It's a marvel they've climbed as high as they have."

"Their digits are surprisingly dexterous," explained the head examiner. "And they have well-developed brains, more so than I had expected."

"They will need all their brains," promised Id-Wan. "We are too advanced to be served by idiots."

"That is true," endorsed Bi-Nak, gaining fresh heart.

"Although sometimes I wonder," added Id-Wan, staring hard at him. He shifted his attention back to the examiner: "Give these cadavers to the scouts and tell them to get in some practice. I'll pick out the eight best imitators tonight. They had better be good!"

"Yes, captain."

The sinking sun showed no more than a sliver of glowing rim on a distant hill when the chief of the scouts reported to Id-Wan. There was a coolness creeping over the land, but it was not coldness. Here, at this time, the nights were merely less warm than the days.

Id-Wan inquired: "Did you have any difficulty in obtaining those two specimens this morning?"

"No, captain. Our biggest worry was that of getting there before broad daylight. It took longer than we'd anticipated to reach the place. In fact dawn was already showing when we arrived. However, we were lucky."

"In what way?"

"Those two were already outside the camp, just as if the Great Green God had provided them for us. They bore simple apparatus for trapping water game and evidently intended an early-morning expedition. All we had to do was plant darts in them and take them away. They had no chance to utter a sound. The camp slumbered undisturbed."

"And what about the message channels?"

"The technician could find none," said the chief. "No overhead wires, no underground cables, no antenna, nothing."

"That is peculiar," remarked Bi-Nak. "Why should creatures so forward be so backward? They *are* superior types, aren't they?"

"They are relatively unimportant in this world's scheme of things," declared Id-Wan. "Doubtless they serve these trees in some way, or watch for fires. It is of little consequence."

"Sitting down on their dirt is not of little consequence," grumbled Bi-Nak to himself. "I'll be happier after we've blasted one of their towns, or ten of them, or fifty. We can then get their reaction and beat it home with the news. I am more than ready to go home even if I am chosen to return with the main fleet sometime later."

"Are the scouts ready for my inspection?" Id-Wan asked the chief.

"Waiting now, captain."

"All right, I'll look them over." Going to the rear quarters, he studied the twenty Rigelians lined up against a wall. The two corpses reposed nearby for purposes of comparison. Subjecting each scout to long and careful scrutiny, he chose eight, whereupon the remaining twelve promptly switched to his own shape. The eight were good. Four Johnsons and four Greers.

"It is a simple form to duplicate," commented the chief. "I could hold it myself for days on end."

"Me, too," agreed Id-Wan. He addressed the row of two-armed, brown-skinned bipeds who could be whatever he wanted them to be. "Remember the most stringent rule: In no circumstances will you change shape before your task is done. Until then, you will retain that precise form and appearance, even under threat of destruction."

They nodded silently.

He continued, "All your objectives have large parks into which you will be dropped shortly before dawn. You will then merge as unobtrusively as possible with the creatures appearing in each awakening town. After that, do as you've done many a time before—dig up all the useful data you can get without arousing suspicion. Details of weapons and power sources are especially needed. Enter no building until you are sure that your entry will not be challenged. Do not speak or be spoken to if it is avoidable. In the last resort, respond with imitations of a different speech pattern."

*"Fanziki moula? Sfinadacta bu!"* said Bi-Nak, concocting an example.

Id-Wan paused to scowl at him before he went on, "Above all, there are eight of you, and one may find what another has missed."

They nodded again, bipeds all of them, but with the Rigelian life-flame burning up within them.

He finished, "If absolutely imperative, give up the quest and hide yourselves until the time for return. Be at your respective dropping-points in the parks at the mid-hour of the following night. You will then be picked up." He raised his voice in emphasis. "And do not change shape before then!"

They didn't. They had not altered by as much as one hair when they filed impassively into the ship's lifeboat between the mid-hour and dawn. Id-Wan was there to give them a final lookover. Each walked precisely as the now-dead samples had walked, swinging his arms in the same manner, using the same bearing, wearing the same facial expression. Each had a satchel complete with alien contents, plus a midget dart gun.

The lifeboat rose among the trees into the dark, bore them away. A few creatures in the trees resented the brief disturbance, made squawking sounds.

"Not one other ship in the night," remarked Id-Wan, looking upward. "Not one rocket trail across the stars. They've got nothing but those big, clumsy air machines which we saw toiling through the clouds." He gave a sigh. "In due time we'll take over this planet like taking a karda-fruit from a nodus. It is all too easy, too elementary. Sometimes I feel that a little more opposition might be interesting."

Bi-Nak decided to let that point go for what it was worth, which wasn't much. Two days and nights on continual duty with the indefatigable Id-Wan had tired him beyond argument. So he yawned, gave the stars a sleepless, disinterested eye, and followed Id-Wan into the ship.

Making for the dynamic receivers, Id-Wan had a look at their recording globes, each of which had been tuned to a departing scout. Each globe held a bright spot derived from a distant life-glow. He watched the spots shrink with distance until eventually they remained still. A bit later the lifeboat came back, reported all landed. The spots continued to shine without shifing. None moved until the sun stabbed a red ray in the east.

Planting another filled glass on the tray, Ollie Kampenfeldt gloomed at a night-shrouded window and said: "It's been dark two hours. They've been gone all day. No breakfast, no dinner, no supper, nothing. A feller can't live on nothing. I don't like it."

"Me neither," approved somebody. "Maybe something's happened."

"If one had broken his leg or his neck, the other would be here to tell us," another pointed out. "Besides, if it were anyone else, I'd suggest a search for them. But you know those two coots. Isn't the first time Johnson and Greer have taken to the jungle. Reckon they've seen too many Tarzan pictures. Just a pair of overgrown, muscle-bound kids."

"Johnson's no kid," denied the first. "He's an ex-navy heavyweight who still likes to jump around."

"Aw, probably they've got lost. It's the easiest thing in the world to get lost if you wander a bit. Four times I've had to camp out all night, and—"

"I don't like it," interjected Kampenfeldt, firmly.

"O.K., you don't like it. What are you going to do about it? Phone the cops?"

"There's no phone, as you know," said Kampenfeldt. "Who'd drag a line right up here?" He thought it over, frowning fatly, and wiped his forehead. "I'll give 'em to morning. If they're not back by then, I'll send Sid on his motorcycle to tell the forest rangers. Nobody's going to say I did nothing about it."

"That's the spirit, Ollie," one of them approved. "You look after nature's children and they'll look after you."

Several laughed at that, heartily. Within half an hour Johnson and Greer were forgotten.

It was early in the afternoon when the tracer operators rushed into the main cabin and so far forgot themselves as not to match Id-Wan's shape. Remaining rotund, tentacular and pale purple, the leading one of the three gestured excitedly as he spoke.

"Two have gone, captain."

"Two what have gone where?" demanded Id-Wan, glowering at him.

"Two dynamic sparks."

"Are you certain?" Without waiting for a reply, Id-Wan ran to the receivers.

It was true enough. Six globes still held their tiny lights. Two were dull, devoid of any gleam. Even as he watched, another became extinguished. Then, in rapid succession, three more.

The chief of the scouts came in saying: "What's the matter? Is there something wrong?"

Slowly, almost ponderously, Id-Wan said, "Six scouts have surrendered life in the last few moments." He breathed heavily, seemed to have trouble in accepting the evidence of the globes. "These instruments say they are dead, and if indeed they are dead they cannot retain shape.Their bodies automatically will revert to the form of their fathers. And you know that means—"

"A complete giveaway," said the chief of the scouts, staring grimly at the globes.

Both remaining lights went out.

"Action stations!" yelled Id-Wan, electrified by the sight. "Close all ports! Trim the tubes! Prepare for takeoff!" He turned savagely upon Po-Duk. "You're the pilot. Don't squat there gaping like an ebelmint halfway out of its egg! Get into the control seat, idiot—we've no time to lose!"

Something whisked overhead. He caught a fleeting glimpse of it through the nearest observation port. Something long, shapely and glistening, but much too fast to examine. It had gone almost before it registered. Seconds later its noise followed a terrible howl.

The radio technician said: "Powerful signals nearby. Their sources seem to be—"

The ship's tubes coughed, spluttered, shot fire, coughed again. A tree began to burn. Id-Wan danced with impatience. He dashed to the control room.

"Blast, Po-Duk, blast!"

"There is not yet enough lift, captain, and until the meters show that—"

"Look!" screamed Bi-Nak, pointing for the last time.

They could see what was coming through the facing port; seven ultra-rapid dots in V-formation. The dots lengthened, sprouted wings, swept immediately overhead without a sound. Black lumps fell from their bellies, came down, struck the ship and all around the ship.

The badly lagging noise of the planes never got that far. Their leading waves were repulsed by the awful blast of the bombs.

For the final change, the Rigelians became a cloud of scattered molecules.

\*　　\*　　\*

Settling himself more comfortably in the chair, the roving video reporter griped, "I'd no sooner shown my face in the office than the area supervisor grabbed me, told me to chase up here and give the breathless world a candid close-up of mad Martians on the rampage. I'm partway here when the Air Force chips in, holds me back a couple of hours. When I do get here what do I find?" He sniffed sourly, "Some timber smoking around a whacking big crater. Nothing else. Not a pretzel."

Dragging an almost endless handkerchief from his pocket, Kampenfeldt smeared it across his brow. "We keep civilization at arm's length here. We've no radio, no video. So I don't know what you're talking about."

"It's like this," explained the reporter. "They dumped their spies in the parks during the night. They weren't around long because they got picked up with the milk. Twenty steps and Clancy had 'em."

"Eh?"

"The cops," elucidated the other. "We put the faces of the first pair on the breakfast-time videocast. Ten people phoned through in a hurry and identified them as Johnson and Greer. So we assumed that said Johnson and Greer were nuts." He gave a lugubrious laugh.

"Sometimes I've thought so myself," Kampenfeldt offered.

"Then, half an hour later, the next station on the chain infringed our copyright by also showing Johnson and Greer. Another followed suit ten minutes later still. By ten o'clock there were four pairs of them, as alike as two of you, and all grabbed in similar circumstances. It looked like the whole cockeyed world wanted to be Johnson or, alternatively, Greer."

"Not me," denied Kampenfeldt. "Neither of them."

"The news value of that was, of course, way up. We planted the entire eight of them on the midmorning boost, which is nationwide, our only thought being that we'd got something mighty queer. Military intelligence boys in Washington saw the videocast, pestered local cops for details, put two and two together and made it four, if not eight."

"And then?"

"They clamped heavy pressure on all these Johnsons and Greers. They talked all right, but nothing they said made sense. Eventually one of them tried a fast out, got killed on the run. He was still Johnson when he flopped, but a couple of minutes later his body turned to something else, something right out of this world. Boy, it would have turned your stomach!"

"In that case, I want no description," said Kampenfeldt, defensively nursing his outsize paunch.

"That was an eye-opener. Anything not of this world obviously must be of some other. The authorities bore down on the remaining seven, who acted as before until they realized that we knew what we knew. Forthwith they put death before dishonor, leaving us with eight dollops of goo and no details."

"Ugh!" said Kampenfeldt, hitching his paunch.

"Our only clue lay in Johnson and Greer. Since these creatures had copied real people, the thing to do was find the last known whereabouts of said people. Chances were good that alien invaders would be found in that vicinity. A shout went up for Johnson and Greer. Fifty friends of theirs put them here, right here. The forest rangers chipped in saying you'd just reported them missing."

"I did," admitted Kampenfeldt. "And if I'd known where they'd gone, I'd be missing myself—and still running."

"Well, the Air Force took over. They were told to look-see. If an alien ship was down, it was to stay down. You know those boys. They swoop around yipping. They overdid the job, left not a sliver of metal as big as my finger. So what do I put on the videocast? Just a crater and some smoking tree stumps."

"Which is no great pity," opined Kampenfeldt. "Who wants to see things that could climb into your bed as Uncle Willie? You wouldn't know who was who with creatures like that around."

"You would not." The reporter pondered awhile, added, "Their simulation was perfect. They had the power to lead us right up the garden path if only they'd known how to use it. Power is never much good unless you know how to use it. They made a first-class blunder when they grabbed their models." He scratched his head, eyed the other speculatively. "It sure beats me that of all places in this wide world they had to pick on a nudist camp."

"Solar health center," corrected Kampenfeldt, primly.

*Between 1951 and 1963, Will Stanton published eleven brief tales in* The Magazine of Fantasy and Science Fiction, *then simply seemed to vanish from the field. His works are well written, clever, and sometimes wistful, and include such classics as "Barney," "Dodger Fan," and the following story of a young boy's adventures with a friendly alien.*

# THE GUMDROP KING

## by Will Stanton

At first Raymond thought it was a flying saucer when it flashed over his head and disappeared behind the trees. He took a couple of steps in that direction and then he decided it probably wasn't a saucer at all—it had looked more like a cereal bowl. He turned and walked down the path to the lion trap. It was empty—it usually was. Once he had almost captured a kangaroo, but it got away.

Beyond the trap was the place where the treasure chest was buried. He dug it up to make sure it was all right and buried it in a safer place. Then he walked along the creek, looking for lucky stones. It was about half an hour before he came to the clearing where the saucer was.

The pilot was sitting back against a stump, chewing a piece of grass. He was about Raymond's size or a little smaller. He had pointed ears and was wearing a tight-fitting green suit. Raymond approached him warily.

"You a new kid?" he asked.

The other smiled. "My name is Korko," he said. "I guess I'm new—I've never been here before. As a matter of fact I don't seem to know where I am."

"You're in the woods in back of my house," Raymond said. He pointed to the spaceship. "Is that yours?"

"Uh huh," Korko said. "I'm refueling—solar energy." He grinned. "I forgot to fill the spare tanks before I left."

Raymond nodded. "Sometimes I forget things. I forgot to brush my teeth this morning."

Korko stretched out his legs. "Well, they can't expect you to remember everything. There's just too much."

"That's what I tell my sister," Raymond said. "But then I forget to put on my overshoes and she gets mad."

"You can't expect too much from sisters, can you?" Korko said. He folded his hands behind his head and looked up into the sky. "I keep mine in a cage most of the time," he added. "Haven't you ever thought of that?"

Raymond picked up a branch and started peeling the bark off it. "I guess it wouldn't be very nice—locked up in a cage all by yourself."

"I never said she was by herself," Korko pointed out. "I put some tigers in too."

"Tigers?" Raymond said. "Aren't you afraid they'll eat her up?"

Korko shook his head slowly. "No, I'm not. Not the kind of tigers you get these days."

Raymond held out his hand. "Would you like a gumdrop?"

"Thank you." Korko took one and chewed it thoughtfully. "It's delicious, I've never had anything like it."

"Take another," Raymond said.

"You're a good fellow," Korko said. "Do you have a wife?"

"No, I live with my sister Molly. But she's going to get married soon—a fellow named Walter. I don't like him."

"Ah—" Korko folded his arms. "You don't like him. What does Walter do?"

"He's a developer," Raymond said. "After they get married he's going to develop this farm."

"I see. Just how do you do that?"

"You put in a road," Raymond said. "Then you cut down all the trees and build houses."

Korko twisted around so as to see all the clearing. "I like it better with the trees," he said.

"So do I—so does Molly. But Walter says you can't fight progress."

"Aha—progress." Korko nodded his head wisely. "They tried that in my country too but I soon put a stop to it, I can tell you that."

"I don't see how you can."

"When you're king you can do any blasted thundering thing you want," Korko said. "I told you I was king, didn't I? Wait a minute—" He disappeared into the spaceship. In a moment he was back with a shiny crown that seemed badly out of shape. "I'm very fond of tin," he said, "but it does bend so. I must have sat on it." He went over it with his fingers, pressing it back into shape.

"Of course, my official crown is gold," he said; "this is a lightweight crown for traveling." He put it on the back of his head. "How does it look?"

"Just fine," Raymond said.

"I'm glad you think so. People keep telling me I'm a splendid-looking king, but then they'd say just about anything." He poked the ground moodily with a stick.

"Have a gumdrop," Raymond said.

Korko smiled. "You're a good friend, Raymond." He put the gumdrop in his mouth. "Isn't there somebody else your sister could marry—somebody you like?"

"There's Bartholomew," he said. "I think Molly likes him too. Only he doesn't have enough money to get married. He's a painter."

"How much money does it take to get married?"

"I don't know," Raymond said. "There's going to be an exhibit next month—Bartholomew says if he wins a prize then people will start to buy his pictures."

Korko waved his hand. "It's as good as done. Tell him to enter another picture. He might as well get second prize too."

"I'll tell him," Raymond said. He stepped over to the spaceship. "I don't suppose we could go for a ride?"

Korko shook his head. "Not while it's refueling. Of course if you just want to go someplace here on the planet we could use teleportation."

"Well," Raymond said, "I had a friend named Piggy—he moved away last year. I thought it might be nice to see him."

"Good old Piggy," Korko said. "Do you want to go to his house or would you rather bring him here?"

"Can you really do that?" Raymond asked. "Make a person travel all that distance?"

"Certainly," Korko said. "Put any person any place you want to. It's easy as that—" He rubbed his middle finger against his thumb. "As easy as—" He tried again.

Raymond snapped his fingers. "As that?"

"Show me how you do it," Korko said. "I never have been able to get the hang of it." Raymond showed him. "I guess I'll have to keep practicing," Korko said. "Where does your friend Piggy live?"

Raymond closed his eyes. He remembered Piggy had moved out West—all the way to Idaho. If only he could remember the name of the town!

"Moscow," he said suddenly, "that's where he lives. Can we go there?"

"We're there," Korko said.

They were standing in the center of a large table, surrounded by a circle of a dozen men, frozen in the chairs, staring at the two of them.

"Surprise!" Korko cried happily. "Which one is Piggy?"

Raymond nudged him in the ribs. "This isn't the right place."

"Excuse us please," Korko said. The room vanished and they were back in the clearing. Raymond let out his breath.

"What enormous people you know," Korko said. "They must be giants."

"I don't know them," Raymond said. "I don't even know where we were."

"Here's a souvenir I brought back." Korko handed him a small paperweight. "Notice the pretty design."

"It looks like a sickle," Raymond said, "and a hammer. But we shouldn't keep this—not without paying."

"Aha." Korko took off his crown, looked at it and put it back on. "Not without paying. What do we pay with?"

Raymond held out a nickel. "I guess this should be enough. Anyhow it's all I've got."

"I'll take it to them," Korko said. "You wait right here," and he was gone.

In a moment he was back smiling happily. "How fast they get things done," he said. "Just in the little time since we were there—the table tipped over, chairs smashed up and soldiers all around. I picked out the fattest man and gave him the money. He jumped back and threw it on the floor." He shook his head admiringly. "It's a pleasure to do business with such fine exciting people."

He walked over to the ship and looked inside. "Enough fuel for a takeoff," he announced. "Better be going."

"You have to go home?" Raymond asked.

"First I have to move closer to the sun," Korko said, "for solar energy. It will take about twelve hours to store up enough for the trip home."

Raymond picked up a stone and examined it carefully. "Then I won't be seeing you again?"

"Well, I really should be getting home," Korko said. He looked at Raymond for a moment. "I don't suppose you have any gumdrops left? I'd give anything to know how to make them."

"I have a whole sack of them back at the house," Raymond said.

"You have?" He grinned delightedly. "I could have my royal alchemist work out the formula. I'll be here first thing in the morning."

"Goodbye, Korko." Raymond turned and headed back toward his house.

Molly was in the kitchen when he got there. "You're late," she said; "what have you been doing all afternoon?"

Raymond got himself a drink of water. "I talked with a new kid," he said. "We went to see Piggy, but he wasn't there."

"Honestly, Raymond. Piggy moved to Idaho last year—you knew that. Some of the stories you make up—" she shook her head. "Wash your hands now, supper's ready."

Raymond took his place at the table. "Aren't you going to eat?"

"I'm going out to dinner with Walter," she said.

Raymond scowled. "I don't like Walter much. I wish he'd leave us alone. I wish we could keep the farm just the way it is."

"I know," Molly said, "I do too." She sat down and rested her arms on the table. "But you've got to understand, Raymond, we can't afford to keep up this big place for just the two of us."

"You could marry Bartholomew," he said. "Then he could live here and help keep the place up."

"All he can do is support himself. Nobody wants to buy his paintings."

"They will." Raymond swallowed a mouthful of potato and took a gulp of milk. "Next month his picture is going to win first prize. Then everybody will want to buy them."

Molly reached out and smoothed back a lock of his hair. "You're just like Dad always was," she said, "impractical and optimistic. I don't know—" She traced a crack in the table top. "Maybe that's the best way to be."

"Sure it is," Raymond said. "Bart's going to win first prize. Second prize too."

She smiled. "It's wonderful to have big dreams, but somebody has to be practical. The thing you want most isn't always what's best. You're doing so well in school it would be a shame if you couldn't go to college. That takes a lot of money. Now go on and finish your supper—I have to change."

Raymond was sitting on the front steps when Walter arrived. Molly came to the door. "Right on time," she said.

Walter came up the walk. He was handsomely dressed and knew it and he walked slowly enough so everybody could tell. He glanced coldly at Raymond and turned to Molly. "Look at the condition of the boy's clothes," he said. "Does he have to go around looking like a tramp?"

"I know," she said, "but after all, Walter, it's vacation and he plays hard."

"Then perhaps it's time he learned to work hard," Walter said, "instead of mooning around all day. I think maybe a good stiff military school might be the answer."

"Walter—he's only a child."

"Only a child, is he—" He reached down and picked up the paperweight Raymond had been holding. He looked at it more closely and held it out to Molly, his hand trembling with fury. "Just how do you explain this? Young man—answer me!" His voice was choked with indignation. "Where did this come from?"

Raymond looked down at the steps. "I got it from a kid I know," he said.

Walter turned to Molly, "You hear that?" he demanded. "That's the sort of trash and riff-raff you allow him to associate with."

"Walter, I'm sure it doesn't mean anything," she said. "Children collect all kinds of things."

"Do they indeed?" Walter slipped the paperweight into his

pocket. "Well, this particular thing is going to be turned over to the proper authorities first thing in the morning."

"Whatever you think best." Molly started down the steps. "Goodnight, Raymond, we won't be late."

"Okay," he said. He picked up a paper sack from the floor beside him and took out some gumdrops.

"Another thing," Walter said, "you can just stop eating that stuff—ruining your teeth—running up dental bills. You'd better not forget."

Raymond studied the candy thoughtfully.

"Raymond, where are your manners?" Molly asked. "Walter spoke to you. Say goodnight."

"Goodnight, Molly." He dropped the gumdrops back in the sack. "Goodbye, Walter," he said.

*Theodore Sturgeon has worked as trapeze artist, bulldozer operator, and hotel manager. He has won the International Fantasy Award, the Hugo, and the Nebula and is the author of over 20 books and 125 short stories of science fiction and fantasy. His two most prominent themes, love and psychology, appear in many of his works, such as the famous novel* More Than Human *(1953), and the following short story of a woman forced to live with an unwanted halo.*

# SAUCER OF LONELINESS

## by Theodore Sturgeon

If she's dead, I thought, I'll never find her in this white flood of moonlight on the white sea, with the surf seething in and over the pale, pale sand like a great shampoo. Almost always, suicides who stab themselves or shoot themselves in the heart carefully bare their chests; the same strange impulse generally makes the sea-suicide go naked.

A little earlier, I thought, or later, and there would be shadows for the dunes and the breathing toss of the foam. Now the only real shadow was mine, a tiny thing just under me, but black enough to feed the blackness of the shadow of a blimp.

A little earlier, I thought, and I might have seen her plodding up the silver shore, seeking a place lonely enough to die in. A little later and my legs would rebel against this shuffling trot through sand, the maddening sand that could not hold and would not help a hurrying man.

My legs did give way then and I knelt suddenly, sobbing— not for her; not yet—just for air. There was such a rush about me: wind, and tangled spray, and colors upon colors and shades of colors that were not colors at all but shifts of white and silver. If light like that were sound, it would sound like the sea on sand, and if my ears were eyes, they would see such a light.

I crouched there, gasping in the swirl of it, and a flood struck me, shallow and swift, turning up and outward like flower petals where it touched my knees, then soaking me to the waist in its bubble and crash. I pressed my knuckles to my eyes so they would open again. The sea was on my lips with the taste of tears and the whole white night shouted and wept aloud.

And there she was.

Her white shoulders were a taller curve in the sloping foam. She must have sensed me—perhaps I yelled—for she turned and saw me kneeling there. She put her fists to her temples and her face twisted, and she uttered a piercing wail of despair and fury, and then plunged seaward and sank.

I kicked off my shoes and ran into the breakers, shouting, hunting, grasping at flashes of white that turned to sea-salt and coldness in my fingers. I plunged right past her, and her body struck my side as a wave whipped my face and tumbled both of us. I gasped in solid water, opened my eyes beneath the surface and saw a greenish-white distorted moon hurtle as I spun. Then there was sucking sand under my feet again and my left hand was tangled in her hair.

The receding wave towed her away and for a moment she streamed out from my hand like steam from a whistle. In that moment I was sure she was dead, but as she settled to the sand, she fought and scrambled to her feet.

She hit my ear, wet, hard, and a huge pointed pain lanced into my head. She pulled, she lunged away from me, and all the while my hand was caught in her hair. I couldn't have freed her if I had wanted to. She spun to me with the next wave, battered and clawed at me, and we went into deeper water.

"Don't . . . don't . . . I can't swim!" I shouted, so she clawed me again.

"Leave me alone," she shrieked. "Oh, dear God, why can't you *leave*" (said her fingernails) "me . . ." (said her snapping teeth) *"alone!"* (said her small hard fist).

So by her hair I pulled her head down tight to her white shoulder; and with the edge of my free hand I hit her neck twice. She floated again, and I brought her ashore.

I carried her to where a dune was between us and the sea's broad noisy tongue, and the wind was above us somewhere. But the light was as bright. I rubbed her wrists and stroked her face and said, "It's all right," and, "There!" and some names I used to have for a dream I had long, long before I ever heard of her.

She lay still on her back with the breath hissing between her teeth, with her lips in a smile which her twisted-tight, wrinkle-sealed eyes made not a smile but a torture. She was well and conscious for many moments and still her breath hissed and her closed eyes twisted.

"Why couldn't you leave me alone?" she asked at last. She opened her eyes and looked at me. She had so much misery that there was no room for fear. She shut her eyes again and said, "You know who I am."

"I know," I said.

She began to cry.

I waited, and when she stopped crying, there were shadows among the dunes. A long time.

She said, "You don't know who I am. Nobody knows who I am."

I said, "It was in all the papers."

"That!" She opened her eyes slowly and her gaze traveled over my face, my shoulders, stopped at my mouth, touched my eyes for the briefest second. She curled her lips and turned away her head. "Nobody knows who I am."

I waited for her to move or speak, and finally I said, "Tell me."

"Who are you?" she asked, with her head still turned away.

"Someone who . . ."

"Well?"

"Not now," I said. "Later, maybe."

She sat up suddenly and tried to hide herself. "Where are my clothes?"

"I didn't see them."

"Oh," she said. "I remember. I put them down and kicked

sand over them, just where a dune would come and smooth them over, hide them as if they never were. . . . I hate sand. I wanted to drown in the sand, but it wouldn't let me. . . . You mustn't look at me!" she shouted. "I hate to have you looking at me!" She threw her head from side to side, seeking. "I can't stay here like this! What can I do? Where can I go?"

"Here," I said.

She let me help her up and then snatched her hand away, half-turned from me. "Don't touch me. Get away from me."

"Here," I said again, and walked down the dune where it curved in the moonlight, tipped back into the wind and down and became not dune but beach. "Here." I pointed behind the dune.

At last she followed me. She peered over the dune where it was chest-high, and again where it was knee-high. "Back there?"

I nodded.

"I didn't see them."

"So dark . . ." She stepped over the low dune and into the aching black of those moon-shadows. She moved away cautiously, feeling tenderly with her feet, back to where the dune was higher. She sank down into the blackness and disappeared there. I sat on the sand in the light. "Stay away from me," she spat.

I rose and stepped back. Invisible in the shadows, she breathed, "Don't go away." I waited, then saw her hand press out of the clean-cut shadows, "There," she said, "over there. In the dark. Just be a . . . Stay away from me now. . . . Be a—voice."

I did as she asked, and sat in the shadows perhaps six feet from her.

She told me about it. Not the way it was in the papers.

She was perhaps seventeen when it happened. She was in Central Park, in New York. It was too warm for such an early spring day, and the hammered brown slopes had a dusting of green of precisely the consistency of that morning's hoarfrost on the rocks. But the frost was gone and the grass was brave and tempted some hundreds of pairs of feet from the asphalt and concrete to tread on it.

Hers were among them. The sprouting soil was a surprise to her feet, as the air was to her lungs. Her feet ceased to be shoes as she walked, her body was consciously more than clothes. It was the only kind of day which in itself can make a city-bred person raise his eyes. She did.

For a moment she felt separated from the life she lived, in which there was no fragrance, no silence, in which nothing ever quite fit nor was quite filled. In that moment the ordered disapproval of the buildings around the pallid park could not reach her; for two, three clean breaths it no longer mattered that the whole wide world really belonged to images projected on a screen; to gently groomed goddesses in these steel-and-glass towers; that it belonged, in short, always, always to someone else.

So she raised her eyes, and there above her was the saucer.

It was beautiful. It was golden, with a dusty finish like that of an unripe Concord grape. It made a faint sound, a chord composed of two tones and a blunted hiss like the wind in tall wheat. It was darting about like a swallow, soaring and dropping. It circled and dropped and hovered like a fish, shimmering. It was like all these living things, but with that beauty it had all the loveliness of things turned and burnished, measured, machined, and metrical.

At first she felt no astonishment, for this was so different from anything she had ever seen before that it had to be a trick of the eye, a false evaluation of size and speed and distance that in a moment would resolve itself into a sunflash on an airplane or the lingering glare of a welding arc.

She looked away from it and abruptly realized that many other people saw it—saw *something*—too. People all around her had stopped moving and speaking and were craning upward. Around her was a globe of silent astonishment, and outside it she was aware of the life-noise of the city, the hard-breathing giant who never inhales.

She looked up again, and at last began to realize how large and how far away the saucer was. No: rather, how small and how very near it was. It was just the size of the largest circle she might make with her two hands, and it floated not quite eighteen inches over her head.

Fear came then. She drew back and raised a forearm, but the saucer simply hung there. She bent far sideways, twisted away, leaped forward, looked back and upward to see if she had escaped it. At first she couldn't see it; then as she looked up and up, there it was, close and gleaming, quivering and crooning, right over her head.

She bit her tongue.

From the corner of her eye, she saw a man cross himself. *He did that because he saw me standing here with a halo over my head,* she thought. And that was the greatest single thing that had ever happened to her. No one had ever looked at her and made a respectful gesture before, not once, not ever. Through terror, through panic and wonderment, the comfort of that thought nestled into her, to wait to be taken out and looked at again in lonely times.

The terror was uppermost now, however. She backed away, staring upward, stepping a ludicrous cakewalk. She should have collided with people. There were plenty of people there, gaping and craning, but she reached none. She spun around and discovered to her horror that she was the center of a pointing, pressing crowd. Its mosaic of eyes all bulged and its inner circle braced its many legs to press back and away from her.

The saucer's gentle note deepened. It tilted, dropped an inch or so. Someone screamed, and the crowd broke away from her in all directions, milled about, and settled again in a new dynamic balance, a much larger ring, as more and more people raced to thicken it against the efforts of the inner circle to escape.

The saucer hummed and tilted, tilted . . .

She opened her mouth to scream, fell to her knees, and the saucer struck.

It dropped against her forehead and clung there. It seemed almost to lift her. She came erect on her knees, made one effort to raise her hands against it, and then her arms stiffened down and back, her hands not reaching the ground. For perhaps a second and a half the saucer held her rigid, and then it passed a single ecstatic quiver to her body and dropped it. She plumped to the ground, the backs of her thighs heavy and painful on her heels and ankles.

The saucer dropped beside her, rolled once in a small circle, once just around its edge, and lay still. It lay still and dull and metallic, different and dead.

Hazily, she lay and gazed at the gray-shrouded blue of the good spring sky, and hazily she heard whistles.

And some tardy screams.

And a great stupid voice bellowing "Give her air!" which made everyone press closer.

Then there wasn't so much sky because of the blue-clad bulk with its metal buttons and its leatherette notebook. "Okay, okay, what's happened here stand back figods sake."

And the widening ripples of observation, interpretation and comment: "It knocked her down." "Some guy knocked her down." "He knocked her down." "Some guy knocked her down and—" "Right in broad daylight this guy . . ." "The park's gettin' to be . . ." onward and outward, the adulteration of fact until it was lost altogether because excitement is so much more important.

Somebody with a harder shoulder than the rest bulling close, a notebook here, too, a witnessing eye over it, ready to change ". . . a beautiful brunet . . ." to "an attractive brunet" for the afternoon editions, because "attractive" is as dowdy as any woman is allowed to get if she is a victim in the news.

The glittering shield and the florid face bending close: "You hurt bad, sister?" And the echoes, back and back through the crowd, "Hurt bad, hurt bad, badly injured, he beat the hell out of her, broad daylight . . ."

And still another man, slim and purposeful, tan gabardine, cleft chin and beard-shadow: "Flyin' saucer, hm? Okay, Officer, I'll take over here.

"And who the hell might you be, takin' over?"

The flash of a brown leather wallet, a face so close behind that its chin was pressed into the gabardine shoulder. The face said, awed: "FBI" and that rippled outward, too. The policeman nodded—the entire policeman nodded in one single bobbing genuflection.

"Get some help and clear this area," said the gabardine.

"Yes, sir!" said the policeman.

"FBI, FBI," the crowd murmured and there was more sky to look at above her.

She sat up and there was a glory in her face. "The saucer talked to me," she sang.

"You shut up," said the gabardine. "You'll have lots of chance to talk later."

"Yeah, sister," said the policeman. "My God, this mob could be full of Communists."

"You shut up, too," said the gabardine.

Someone in the crowd told someone else a Communist beat up this girl, while someone else was saying she got beat up because she was a Communist.

She started to rise, but solicitous hands forced her down again. There were thirty police there by that time.

"I can walk," she said.

"Now you just take it easy," they told her.

They put a stretcher down beside her and lifted her onto it and covered her with a big blanket.

"I can walk," she said as they carried her through the crowd.

A woman went white and turned away moaning, "Oh, my God, how awful!"

A small man with round eyes stared and stared at her and licked and licked his lips.

The ambulance. They slid her in. The gabardine was already there.

A white-coated man with very clean hands: "How did it happen, miss?"

"No questions," said the gabardine. "Security."

The hospital.

She said, "I got to get back to work."

"Take your clothes off," they told her.

She had a bedroom to herself then for the first time in her life. Whenever the door opened, she could see a policeman outside. It opened very often to admit the kind of civilians who were very polite to military people, and the kind of military people who were even more polite to certain civilians. She did not know what they all did nor what they wanted. Every single day they asked her four million five hundred thousand questions. Apparently they never talked to each other because each of them asked her the same questions over and over.

"What is your name?"

"How old are you?"

"What year were you born?"

"What is your name?"

Sometimes they would push her down strange paths with their questions.

"Now your uncle. Married a woman from Middle Europe, did he? Where in Middle Europe?"

"What clubs or fraternal organizations did you belong to? Ah! Now about that Rinkeydinks gang on 63rd Street. Who was *really* behind it?"

But over and over again, "What did you mean when you said the saucer talked to you?"

And she would say, "It talked to me."

And they would say, "And it said—"

And she would shake her head.

There would be a lot of shouting ones, and then a lot of kind ones. No one had ever been so kind to her before, but she soon learned that no one was being kind to *her*. They were just getting her to relax, to think of other things, so they could suddenly shoot that question at her: "What do you mean it talked to you?"

Pretty soon it was just like Mom's or school or any place, and she used to sit with her mouth closed and let them yell. Once they sat her on a hard chair for hours and hours with a light in her eyes and let her get thirsty. Home, there was a transom over the bedroom door and Mom used to leave the kitchen light glaring through it all night, every night, so she wouldn't get the horrors. So the light didn't bother her at all.

They took her out of the hospital and put her in jail. Some ways it was good. The food. The bed was all right, too. Through the window she could see lots of women exercising in the yard. It was explained to her that they all had much harder beds.

"You are a very important young lady, you know."

That was nice at first, but as usual it turned out they didn't mean her at all. They kept working on her. Once they brought the saucer in to her. It was inside a big wooden crate with a padlock, and a steel box inside that with a Yale lock. It only weighed a couple of pounds, the saucer, but by the time they got it packed, it took two men to carry it and four men with guns to watch them.

They made her act out the whole thing just the way it happened, with some soldiers holding the saucer over her head. It wasn't the same. They'd cut a lot of chips and pieces out of the saucer and, besides, it was that dead gray color. They asked her if she knew anything about that and for once she told them.

"It's empty now," she said.

The only one she would ever talk to was a little man with a fat belly who said to her the first time he was alone with her, "Listen, I think the way they've been treating you stinks. Now get this: I have a job to do. My job is to find out *why* you won't tell what the saucer said. I don't want to know what it

said and I'll never ask you. I don't even want you to tell me.
Let's just find out why you're keeping it a secret."

Finding out why turned out to be hours of just talking about
having pneumonia and the flower pot she made in second
grade that Mom threw down the fire escape and getting left
back in school and the dream about holding a wineglass in
both hands and peeping over it at some man.

And one day she told him why she wouldn't say about the
saucer, just the way it came to her: "Because it was talking to
*me,* and it's just nobody else's business."

She even told him about the man crossing himself that day.
It was the only other thing she had of her own.

He was nice. He was the one who warned her about the
trial. "I have no business saying this, but they're going to
give you the full dress treatment. Judge and jury and all. You
just say what you want to say, no less and no more, hear?
And don't let 'em get your goat. You have a right to own
something."

He got up and swore and left.

First a man came and talked to her for a long time about
how maybe this Earth would be attacked from outer space by
beings much stronger and cleverer than we are, and maybe
she had the key to a defense. So she owed it to the whole
world. And then even if Earth wasn't attacked, just think of
what an advantage she might give this country over its
enemies. Then he shook his finger in her face and said that
what she was doing amounted to working *for* the enemies of
her country. And he turned out to be the man that was
defending her at the trial.

The jury found her guilty of contempt of court and the
judge recited a long list of penalties he could give her. He
gave her one of them and suspended it. They put her back in
jail for a few more days, and one fine day they turned her
loose.

That was wonderful at first. She got a job in a restaurant
and a furnished room. She had been in the papers so much
that Mom didn't want her back home. Mom was drunk most
of the time and sometimes used to tear up the whole neighborhood, but all the same she had very special ideas about
being respectable, and being in the papers all the time for
spying was not her idea of being decent. So she put her
maiden name on the mailbox downstairs and told her daughter not to live there any more.

At the restaurant she met a man who asked her for a date. The first time. She spent every cent she had on a red handbag to go with her red shoes. They weren't the same shade, but anyway they were both red. They went to the movies and afterward he didn't try to kiss her or anything, he just tried to find out what the flying saucer told her. She didn't say anything. She went home and cried all night.

Then some men sat in a booth talking and they shut up and glared at her every time she came past. They spoke to the boss, and he came and told her that they were electronics engineers working for the government and they were afraid to talk shop while she was around—wasn't she some sort of spy or something? So she got fired.

Once she saw her name on a jukebox. She put in a nickel and punched that number, and the record was all about "the flyin' saucer came down one day, and taught her a brand new way to play, and what it was I will not say, but she took me out of this world." And while she was listening to it, someone in the juke joint recognized her and called her by name. Four of them followed her home and she had to block the door shut.

Sometimes she'd be all right for months on end, and then someone would ask for a date. Three times out of five, she and the date were followed. Once the man she was with arrested the man who was tailing them. Twice the man who was tailing them arrested the man she was with. Five times out of five, the date would try to find out about the saucer. Sometimes she would go out with someone and pretend that it was a real date, but she wasn't very good at it.

So she moved to the shore and got a job cleaning at night in offices and stores. There weren't many to clean, but that just meant there weren't many people to remember her face from the papers. Like clockwork, every eighteen months, some feature writer would drag it all out again in a magazine or a Sunday supplement; and every time anyone saw a headlight on a mountain or a light on a weather balloon it had to be a flying saucer, and there had to be some tired quip about the saucer wanting to tell secrets. Then for two or three weeks she'd stay off the streets in the daytime.

Once she thought she had it whipped. People didn't want her, so she began reading. The novels were all right for a while until she found out that most of them were like the movies—all about the pretty ones who really own the world. So she learned things—animals, trees. A lousy little chipmunk caught in a wire fence bit her. The animals didn't want her. The trees didn't care.

Then she hit on the idea of the bottles. She got all the bottles she could and wrote on papers which she corked into the bottles. She'd tramp miles up and down the beaches and throw the bottles out as far as she could. She knew that if the right person found one, it would give that person the only thing in the world that would help. Those bottles kept her going for three solid years. Everyone's got to have a secret little something he does.

And at last the time came when it was no use any more. You can go on trying to help someone who *maybe* exists; but soon you can't pretend there's such a person any more. And that's it. The end.

"Are you cold?" I asked when she was through telling me. The surf was quieter and the shadows longer.

"No," she answered from the shadows. Suddenly she said, "Did you think I was mad at you because you saw me without my clothes?"

"Why shouldn't you be?"

"You know, I don't care? I wouldn't have wanted ... wanted you to see me even in a ball gown or overalls. You can't cover up my carcass. It shows; it's there whatever. I just didn't want you to see me. At all."

"Me, or anyone?"

She hesitated. "You."

I got up and stretched and walked a little, thinking. "Didn't the FBI try to stop you throwing those bottles?"

"Oh, sure. They spent I don't know how much taxpayers' money gathering 'em up. They still make a spot check every once in a while. They're getting tired of it, though. All the writing in the bottles is the same." She laughed. I didn't know she could.

"What's funny?"

"All of 'em—judges, jailers, jukeboxes—people. Do you know it wouldn't have saved me a minute's trouble if I'd told 'em the whole thing at the very beginning?"

"No?"

"No. They wouldn't have believed me. What they wanted was a new weapon. Super-science from a super-race, to slap hell out of the super-race if they ever got a chance, or out of our own if they don't. All those brains," she breathed, with more wonder than scorn, "all that brass. They think 'super-race' and it comes out 'super-science.' Don't they ever imagine a super-race has super-feelings, too—super-laughter, maybe, or super-hunger?" She paused. "Isn't it time you asked me what the saucer said?"

"I'll tell you," I blurted.

> *"There is in certain living souls*
> *A quality of loneliness unspeakable,*
> *So great it must be shared*
> *As company is shared by lesser beings.*
> *Such a loneliness is mine; so know by this*
> *That in immensity*
> *There is one lonelier than you."*

"Dear Jesus," she said devoutly, and began to weep. "And how is it addressed?"

*"To the loneliest one . . ."*

"How did you know?" she whispered.

"It's what you put in the bottles, isn't it?"

"Yes," she said. "Whenever it gets to be too much, that no one cares, that no one ever did . . . you throw a bottle into the sea, and out goes a part of your own loneliness. You sit and think of someone somewhere finding it . . . learning for the first time that the worst there is can be understood."

The moon was setting and the surf was hushed. We looked up and out to the stars. She said, "We don't know what loneliness is like. People thought the saucer was a saucer, but it wasn't. It was a bottle with a message inside. It had a bigger ocean to cross—all of space—and not much chance of finding anybody. Loneliness? We don't know loneliness."

When I could, I asked her why she had tried to kill herself.

"I've had it good," she said, "with what the saucer told me. I wanted to . . . pay back. I was bad enough to be helped; I had to know I was good enough to help. No one wants me? Fine. But don't tell me no one, anywhere, wants my help. I can't stand that."

I took a deep breath. "I found one of your bottles two years ago. I've been looking for you ever since. Tide charts, current tables, maps and . . . wandering. I heard some talk about you and the bottles hereabouts. Someone told me you'd quit doing it, you'd taken to wandering the dunes at night. I knew why. I ran all the way."

I needed another breath now. "I got a club foot. I think right, but the words don't come out of my mouth the way they're inside my head. I have this nose. I never had a woman. Nobody ever wanted to hire me to work where they'd have to look at me. You're beautiful," I said. "You're beautiful."

She said nothing, but it was as if a light came from her, more light and far less shadow than ever the practiced moon could cast. Among the many things it meant was that even to loneliness there is an end, for those who are lonely enough, long enough.

*Perhaps the largest problem one encounters in attempting to investigate UFOs is the numerous frauds who bilk the field for money. What motivates people to earn their living in such a fashion? Is there any honesty within them? And what would happen if they actually met some flying saucers? These are the questions Theodore Sturgeon acidulously investigates in the following story.*

# FEAR IS A BUSINESS

## by Theodore Sturgeon

Josephus Macardle Phillipso is a man of destiny and he can prove it. His books prove it. The Temple of Space proves it.

A man of destiny is someone who is forced into things—big things—willy, as the saying goes, nilly. Phillipso, just for example, never meant to get into the Unidentified (except by Phillipso) Aerial Object business. This is to say, he didn't sit down like some of his less honest (according to Phillipso) contemporaries and say "I think I'll sit down and tell some lies about flying saucers and make some money." Everything that happened (Phillipso ultimately believed) just happened, and happened to happen to him. Might have been anybody. Then, what with one thing leading to another the way it does, well, you burn your forearm on an alibi and wind up with a Temple.

It was, on looking back on it (something which Phillipso
never does any more), an unnecessary alibi devised for inadequate reasons. Phillipso merely calls the beginnings "inaus-
picious" and lets it go at that. The fact remains that it all
started one night when he tied one on for no special reason
except that he had just been paid his forty-eight dollars for
writing advertising promotion copy for the Hincty Pincty
Value Stores, and excused his absence on the following day
with a story about a faulty lead on the spark coil of his car
which took him most of the night to locate, and there he was
stranded in the hills on the way back from a visit to his aging
mother. The next night he did visit his aging mother and on
the way back his car unaccountably quit and he spent most of
the night fiddling with the electrical system until he discovered, just at dawn, a—well, there it was. At a time like that
you just can't tell the truth. And while he was pondering
various credible alternatives to veracity, the sky lit up briefly
and shadows of the rocks and trees around him grew and slid
away and died before he could even look up. It was a temperature inversion or a methane fireball or St. Elmo's fire or
maybe even a weather balloon—actually that doesn't matter.
He looked up at where it already wasn't, and succumbed to
inspiration.

His car was parked on a grassy shoulder in a cut between
two bluffs. Thick woods surrounded a small clearing to his
right, a sloping glade sparsely studded with almost round
moraine boulders, of all sizes. He quickly located three, a
foot or so in diameter, equally spaced, and buried to approximately the same depth—*i.e.*, not much, Phillipso being merely
an ingenious man, not an industrious one. These three he
lifted out, being careful to keep his crepe-soled shoes flat on
the resilient grass and to leave as few scuff-marks and
indentations as possible. One by one he took the stones into
the woods and dropped them into an evacuated foxhole and
shoved some dead branches in on top of them. He then ran to
his car and from the trunk got a blowtorch which he had
borrowed to fix a leak in the sweated joint of a very old-
fashioned bathtub in his mother's house, and with it thoroughly charred the three depressions in the ground where
the boulders had lain.

Destiny had unquestionably been at work from the time he
had beered himself into mendacity forty-eight hours before.
But it became manifest at this point, for after Phillipso had

licked his forearm lightly with the tongue of flame from the torch, extinguished the same and put it away, a car ground up the hill toward him. And it was not just any car. It belonged to a Sunday supplement feature writer named Penfield who was not only featureless at the moment, but who had also seen the light in the sky a half hour earlier. It may have been Phillipso's intention to drive into town with his story, and back with a reporter and cameraman, all to the end that he could show a late edition to his boss and explain this second absence. Destiny, however, made a much larger thing of it.

Phillipso stood in the graying light in the middle of the road and flapped his arms until the approaching car stopped. "They," he said hoarsely, "almost killed me."

From then on, as they say in the Sunday supplement business, it wrote itself. Phillipso offered not one blessed thing. All he did was answer questions, and the whole thing was born in the brain of this Penfield, who realized nothing except that here was the ideal interview subject. "Came down on a jet of fire, did it? Oh—*three* jets of fire." Phillipso took him into the glade and showed him the three scorched pits, still warm. "Threaten you, did they? Oh—all Earth. Threatened all Earth." Scribble scribble. He took his own pictures too. "What'd you do, speak right up to them? Hm?" Phillipso said he had, and so it went.

The story didn't make the Sunday supplements, but the late editions, just as Phillipso had planned, but much bigger. So big, as a matter of fact, that he didn't go back to his job at all; he didn't need it. He got a wire from a publisher who wanted to know if he, as a promotion writer, might be able to undertake a book.

He might and he did. He wrote with a crackling facility (*The first word in thrift, the last word in value* was his, and was posted all over the Hincty Pincty chain just as if it meant something) in a style homely as a cowlick and sincere as a banker's nameplate. *The Man Who Saved the Earth* sold two hundred and eighty thousand copies in the first seven months.

So the money started to come in. Not only the book money— the other money. This other money came from the end-of-the-world people, the humanity-is-just-too-wicked people, the save-us-from-the-spacemen folk. Clear across the spectrum, from people who believed that if God wanted us to fly through space we'd have been born with tailfins to people who didn't believe in anything but Russians but would believe anything of them, people said "Save us!" and every crack on the pot dripped gold. Hence the Temple of Space, just to regularize the thing, you know, and then the lectures, and could Phillipso help it if half the congre—uh, club members called them services?

The sequel happened the same way, just appendixes to the first book, to handle certain statements he had made which some critics said made him fall apart by his own internal evidence. *We Need Not Surrender* contradicted itself even more, was a third longer, sold three hundred and ten thousand in the first nine weeks, and brought in so much of that other money that Phillipso registered himself as an institute and put all the royalties with it. The temple itself began to show signs of elaboration, the most spectacular piece of which was the war-surplus radar basket of a battleship that went round and round all the time. It wasn't connected to a damn thing but people felt that Phillipso had his eyes open. You could see it, on a clear day, from Catalina, especially at night after the orange searchlight was installed to rotate with it. It looked like a cosmic windshield wiper.

Phillipso's office was in the dome under the radar basket, and was reachable only from the floor below by an automatic elevator. He could commune with himself in there just fine, especially when he switched the elevator off. He had a lot of communing to do, too, sometimes detail stuff, like whether he could sustain a rally at the Coliseum and where to apply the ten-thousand-dollar grant from the Astrological Union which had annoyingly announced the exact size of the gift to the press before sending him the check. But his main preoccupation was another book, or what do I do for an encore? Having said that we are under attack, and then that we can rally and beat 'em, he needed an angle. Something new, preferably born by newsbeat out of cultural terror. And soon, too; his kind of wonder could always use another nine days.

As he sat alone and isolated in the amnion of these reflections, his astonishment can hardly be described at the sound of a dry cough just behind him, and the sight of a short sandy-haired man who stood there. Phillipso might have fled, or leapt at the man's throat, or done any number of violent things besides, but he was stopped cold by a device historically guaranteed to stem all raging authors: "I have," said the man, holding up one volume in each hand, "read your stuff."

"Oh, really?" asked Phillipso.

"I find it," said the man, "logical and sincere."

Phillipso looked smilingly at the man's unforgettable bland face and his unnoticeable gray suit. The man said, "Sincerity and logic have this in common: neither need have anything to do with truth."

"Who are you?" demanded Phillipso immediately. "What do you want and how did you get in here?"

"I am not, as you put it, in here," said the man. He pointed upward suddenly, and in spite of himself Phillipso found his eyes following the commanding finger.

The sky was darkening, and Phillipso's orange searchlight slashed at it with increasing authority. Through the transparent dome, just to the north, and exactly where his visitor pointed, Phillipso saw the searchlight pick out a great silver shape which hovered perhaps fifty feet away and a hundred feet above the Temple. He saw it only momentarily, but it left an afterimage in his retinae like a flashbulb. And by the time the light had circled around again and passed the place, the thing was gone. "I'm in that," said the sandy-haired man. "Here in this room I'm a sort of projection. But then," he sighed, "aren't we all?"

"You better explain yourself," said Phillipso loudly enough to keep his voice from shaking, "or I'll throw you out of here on your ear."

"You couldn't. I'm not here to be thrown." The man approached Phillipso, who had advanced away from his desk into the room. Rather than suffer a collision, Phillipso retreated a step and another, until he felt the edge of his desk against his glutei. The sandy-haired man, impassive, kept on walking—to Phillipso, through Phillipso, Phillipso's desk, Phillipso's chair, and Phillipso's equanimity, the last-named being the only thing he touched.

"I didn't want to do that," said the man some moments later, bending solicitously over Phillipso as he opened his eyes. He put out his hand as if to assist Phillipso to his feet. Phillipso bounced up by himself and cowered away, remembering only then that, on his own terms, the man could not have touched him. He crouched there, gulping and glaring, while the man shook his head regretfully. "I *am* sorry, Phillipso."

"Who are you, anyway?" gasped Phillipso.

For the first time the man seemed at a loss. He looked in puzzlement at each of Phillipso's eyes, and then scratched his head. "I hadn't thought of that," he said musingly. "Important, of course, of course. Labeling." Focusing his gaze more presently at Phillipso, he said, "We have a name for you people that translates roughly to *'Labelers.'* Don't be insulted. It's a categorization, like *'biped'* or *'omnivorous.'* It means the mentality that verbalizes or it can't think."

"Who are you?"

"Oh, I do beg your pardon. Call me—uh, well, call me Hurensohn. I suggest that because I know you have to call me something, because it doesn't matter what you call me, and because it's the sort of thing you'll be calling me once you find out why I'm here."

"I don't know what you're talking about."

"Then by all means let's discuss the matter until you do."

"D-discuss what?"

"I don't have to show you that ship out there again?"

"Please," said Phillipso ardently, "don't."

"Now look," said Hurensohn gently, "there is nothing to fear, only a great deal to explain. Please straighten up and take the knots out of your thorax. That's better. Now sit down calmly and we'll talk the whole thing over. *There,* that's *fine!*" As Phillipso sank shakily into his desk chair, Hurensohn lowered himself into the easy chair which flanked it. Phillipso was horrified to see the half-inch gap of air which, for five seconds or so, separated the man from the chair. Then Hurensohn glanced down, murmured an apology, and floated down to contact the cushion somewhat more normally. "Careless, sometimes," he explained. "So many things to keep in mind at once. You get interested, you know, and next thing you're buzzing around without your light-warp or forgetting your hypno-field when you go in swimming, like that fool in Loch Ness."

"Are you really a—a—an extraulp?"

"Oh, yes, indeed. Extraterrestrial, extrasolar, extragalactic—all that."

"You don't, I mean, I don't see any—"

"I know I don't look like one. I don't look like this"—he gestured down his gray waistcoat with the tips of all his fingers—"either. I could show you what I really do look like, but that's inadvisable. It's been tried." He shook his head sadly, and said again, "Inadvisable."

"Wh-what do you want?"

"Ah. Now we get down to it. How would you like to tell the world about me—about us?"

"Well, I already—"

"I mean, the *truth* about us."

"From the evidence I already have—" Phillipso began with some heat. It cooled swiftly. Hurensohn's face had taken on an expression of unshakable patience; Phillipso was suddenly aware that he could rant and rave and command and explain from now until Michaelmas, and this creature would simply wait him out. He knew, too (though he kept it well below the conscious area) that the more he talked the more he would leave himself open to contradiction—the worst kind of contradiction at that: quotes from Phillipso. So he dried right up and tried the other tack. "All right," he said humbly. "Tell me."

"Ah ..." It was a long-drawn-out sound, denoting deep satisfaction. "I think I'll begin by informing you that you have, quite without knowing it, set certain forces in motion which can profoundly affect mankind for hundreds, even thousands, of years."

"Hundreds," breathed Phillipso, his eye beginning to glow. "Even thousands."

"That is not a guess," said Hurensohn. "It's a computation. And the effect you have on your cultural matrix is—well, let me draw an analogy from your own recent history. I'll quote something: *'Long had part of the idea; McCarthy had the other part. McCarthy got nowhere, failed with his third party, because he attacked and destroyed but didn't give. He appealed to hate, but not to greed, no what's-in-it-for-me, no porkchops.'* That's from the works of a reformed murderer who now writes reviews for the New York *Herald Tribune*."

"What has this to do with me?"

"You," said Hurensohn, "are the Joseph McCarthy of saucer-writers."

Phillipso's glow increased. "My," he sighed.

"And," said Hurensohn, "you may profit by his example. If that be—no, I've quoted enough. I see you are not getting my drift, anyway. I shall be more explicit. We came here many years ago to study your interesting little civilization. It shows great promise—so great that we have decided to help you."

"Who needs help?"

"Who needs help?" Hurensohn paused for a long time, as if he had sent away somewhere for words and was waiting for them to arrive. Finally, "I take it back. I won't be more explicit. If I explained myself in detail I would only sound corny. Any rephrasing of the Decalogue sounds corny to a human being. Every statement of every way in which you need help has been said and said. You are cursed with a sense of rejection, and your rejection begets anger and your anger begets crime and your crime begets guilt; and all your guilty reject the innocent and destroy their innocence. Riding this wheel you totter and spin, and the only basket in which you can drop your almighty insecurity is an almighty fear, and anything that makes the basket bigger is welcome to you. . . . Do you begin to see what I am talking about, and why I'm talking to you?

"Fear is your business, your stock in trade. You've gotten fat on it. With humanity trembling on the edge of the known, you've found a new unknown to breed fear in. And this one's a honey; it's infinite. Death from space . . . and every time knowledge lights a brighter light and drives the darkness back, you'll be there to show how much wider the circumference of darkness has become. . . . Were you going to say something?"

"I am *not* getting fat," said Phillipso.

"Am I saying anything?" breathed the sandy-haired man. "Am I here at all?"

In all innocence Phillipso pointed out, "You said you weren't."

Hurensohn closed his eyes and said in tones of sweet infinite patience, "Listen to me, Phillipso, because I now fear I shall never speak to you again. Whether or not you like it—and you do, and we don't—you have become the central clearinghouse for the Unidentified Aerial Object. You have accomplished this by lies and by fear, but that's now beside the point—you accomplished it. Of all countries on earth, this is the only one we can effectively deal with; the other so-called Great Powers are constitutionally vindictive, or impotent, or hidebound, or all three. Of all the people in this country we could deal with—in government, or the great foundations, or the churches—we can find no one who could overcome the frenzy and foolishness of your following. You have forced us to deal with you."

"My," said Phillipso.

"Your people listen to you. More people than you know listen to your people—frequently without knowing it themselves. You have something for everyone on earth who feels small, and afraid, and guilty. You tell them they are right to be afraid, and that makes them proud. You tell them that the forces ranged against them are beyond their understanding, and they find comfort in each other's ignorance. You say the enemy is irresistible, and they huddle together in terror and are unanimous. And at the same time you expect yourself, implying that you and you alone can protect them."

"Well," said Phillipso, "if you have to deal with me ... isn't it so?"

"It is not," said Hurensohn flatly. " 'Protect' presupposes 'attack.' There is no attack. We came here to help."

"Liberate us," said Phillipso.

"Yes. No!" For the first time Hurensohn showed a sign of irritation. "Don't go leading me into your snide little rat-shrewd pitfalls, Phillipso! By liberate I meant make free; what you meant is what the Russians did to the Czechs."

"All right," said Phillipso guardedly. "You want to free us. Of what?"

"War. Disease. Poverty. Insecurity."

"Yes," said Phillipso. "It's corny."

"You don't believe it."

"I haven't thought about it one way or the other yet," said Phillipso candidly. "Maybe you can do all you say. What is it you want from me?"

Hurensohn held up his hands. Phillipso blinked as *The Man Who Saved the Earth* appeared in one of them and *We Need Not Surrender* in the other. He then realized that the actual volumes must be in the ship. Some of his incipient anger faded; some of his insipid pleasure returned. Hurensohn said, "These. You'll have to retract."

"What do you mean retract?"

"Not all at once. You're going to write another book, aren't you? Of course; you'd have to." There was the slightest emphasis on *"you'd"* and Phillipso did not like it. However, he said nothing. Hurensohn went on: "You could make new discoveries. Revelations, if you like. Interpretations."

"I couldn't do that."

"You'd have all the help in the world. Or out of it."

"Well, but what for?"

"To draw the poison of those lies of yours. To give us a chance to show ourselves without getting shot on sight."

"Can't you protect yourselves against that?"

"Against the bullets, certainly. Not against what pulls the triggers."

"Suppose I go along with you."

"I told you! No poverty, no insecurity, no crime, no—"

"No Phillipso."

"Oh. You mean, what's in it for you? Can't you see? You'd make possible a new Eden, the flowering of your entire species—a world where men laughed and worked and loved and achieved, where a child could grow up unafraid and where, for the first time in your history, human beings would understand one another when they spoke. You could do this—just you."

"I can see it," said Phillipso scathingly. "All the world on the village green and me with them, leading a morris dance. I couldn't live that way."

"You're suddenly very cocky, Mister Phillipso," said Hurensohn with a quiet and frightening courtesy.

Phillipso drew a deep breath. "I can afford to be," he said harshly. "I'll level with you, bogeyman." He laughed unpleasantly. "Good, huh. Bogey. That's what they call you when they—"

"—get us on a radar screen. I know, I know. Get to the point."

"Well. All right then. You asked for it." He got to his feet. "You're a phony. You can maybe do tricks with mirrors, maybe even hide the mirrors, but that's it. If you could do a tenth of what you say, you wouldn't have to come begging. You'd just . . . do it. You'd just walk in and take over. By God, I would."

"You probably would," said Hurensohn, with something like astonishment. No, it was more like an incredulous distaste. He narrowed his eyes. For a brief moment Phillipso thought it was part of his facial expression, or the beginning of a new one, and then he realized it was something else, a concentration, a—

He shrieked. He found himself doing something proverbial, unprintable, and not quite impossible. He didn't want to do it—with all his mind and soul he did not want to, but he did it nonetheless.

"If and when I want you to," said Hurensohn calmly, "you'll do that in the window of Bullock's Wilshire at high noon."

"Please . . ."

"I'm not doing anything," said Hurensohn. He laughed explosively, put his hands in his jacket pockets, and—worst of all, he watched. "Go to it, boy."

*"Please!"* Phillipso whimpered.

Hurensohn made not the slightest detectable move, but Phillipso was suddenly free. He fell back into his chair, sobbing with rage, fear, and humiliation. When he could find a word at all, it came out between the fingers laced over his scarlet face, and was, "Inhuman. That was . . . inhuman."

"Uh-huh," agreed Hurensohn pleasantly. He waited until the walls of outrage expanded enough to include him, recoil from him, and return to the quivering Phillipso, who could then hear when he was spoken to. "What you've got to understand," said Hurensohn, "is that we don't do what we can do. We can, I suppose, smash a planet, explode it, drop it into the sun. You can, in that sense, eat worms. You don't, though, and wouldn't. In your idiom you *couldn't*. Well then, neither can we force humanity into anything without its reasoned consent. You can't understand that, can you? Listen: I'll tell you just how far it goes. We couldn't force even *one* human to do what we want done. You, for example."

"You-you just did, though."

Hurensohn shuddered—a very odd effect, rather like that on a screen when one thumps a slide projector with the heel of one's hand. "A demonstration, that's all. Costly, I may add. I won't get over it as soon as you will. To make a point, you might say, I had to eat a bedbug." Again the flickering shudder. "But then, people have gone farther than that to put an idea over."

"I could refuse?" Phillipso said, timidly.

"Easily."

"What would you do to me?"

"Nothing."

"But you'd go ahead and—"

Hurensohn was shaking his head as soon as Phillipso began to speak. "We'd just go. You've done too much damage. If you won't repair it, there's no way for us to do it unless we use force, and we can't do that. It seems an awful waste, though. Four hundred years of observation. . . . I wish I could tell you the trouble we've gone to, trying to watch you, *learn* you, without interfering. Of course, it's been easier since Kenneth Arnold and the noise he made about us."

"Easier?"

"Lord, yes. You people have a talent—really, a genius for making rational your unwillingness to believe your own eyes. We got along famously after the weather-balloon hypothesis was made public. It's so easy to imitate a weather balloon. Pokey, though. The greatest boon of all was that nonsense about temperature inversions. It's quite a trick to make a ship behave like automobile headlights on a distant mountain or the planet Venus, but temperature inversions?" He snapped his fingers. "Nothing to it. Nobody understands 'em so they explain everything. We thought we had a pretty complete tactical manual on concealment, but did you see the one the U.S. Air Force got out? Bless 'em! It even explains the mistakes we make. Well, most of them, anyway. That idiot in Loch Ness—"

"Wait, wait!" Phillipso wailed. "I'm trying to find out what I'm supposed to do, what will happen, and you sit there and go *on* so!"

"Yes, yes of course. You're quite right. I was just blowing words over my tongue to try to get the taste of you out of my mouth. Not that I really have a mouth, and that would make a tongue sort of frustrated, wouldn't it? Figure of speech, you know."

"Tell me again. This Paradise on earth—how long is it supposed to take? How would you go about it?"

"Through your next book, I suppose. We'd have to work out a way to counteract your other two without losing your audience. If you jump right into line and say how friendly and wise we aliens are, the way Adamski and Heard did, you'll only disappoint your followers. I know! I'll give you a weapon against these—uh—bogeymen of yours. A simple formula, a simple field generator. We'll lay it out so anyone can use it, and bait it with some of your previous nonsense— beg pardon, I might have meant some of your previous statements. Something guaranteed to defend Earth against the—uh—World Destroyers." He smiled. It was rather a pleasant sight. "It would, too."

"What do you mean?"

"Well, if we claimed that the device had an effective range of fifty feet and it actually covered, say, two thousand square miles, and it was easy and cheap to build, and the plans were in every copy of your new book . . . let's see now, we'd have to pretend to violate a little security, too, so the people who aren't afraid would think they were stealing . . . hmmm."

"Device, device—*what* device?"

"Oh, a—" Hurensohn came up out of his reverie. "Labeling again, dammit. I'll have to think a minute. You have no name for such a thing."

"Well, what is it supposed to do?"

"Communicate. That is, it makes complete communications possible."

"We get along pretty well."

"Nonsense! You communicate with labels—words. Your words are like a jumble of packages under a Christmas tree. You know who sent each one and you can see its size and shape, and sometimes it's soft or it rattles or ticks. But that's all. You don't know *exactly* what it means and you won't until you open it. That's what this device will do—open your words to complete comprehension. If every human being, regardless of language, age or background, understood exactly what every other human being wanted, and knew at the same time that he himself was understood, it would change the face of the earth. Overnight."

Phillipso sat and thought that one out. "You couldn't bargain," he said at length. "You couldn't—uh—explain a mistake, even."

"You could explain it," said Hurensohn. "It's just that you couldn't excuse it."

"You mean every husband who—ah—flirted, every child who played hooky, every manufacturer who—"

"All that."

"Chaos," whispered Phillipso. "The very structure of—"

Hurensohn laughed pleasantly. "You know what you're saying, Phillipso. You're saying that the basic structure of your whole civilization is lies and partial truths, and that without them it would fall apart. And you're quite right." He chuckled again. "Your Temple of Space, just for example. What do you think would happen to it if all your sheep knew what their shepherd was and what was in the shepherd's mind?"

"What are you trying to do—tempt me with all this?"

Most gravely Hurensohn answered him, and it shocked Phillipso to the marrow when he used his first name to do it. "I am, Joe, with all my heart I am. You're right about the chaos, but such a chaos should happen to mankind or any species like it. I will admit that it would strike civilization like a mighty wind, and that a great many structures would fall. But there would be no looters in the wreckage, Joe. No man would take advantage of the ones who fell."

"I know something about human beings," Phillipso said in a flat, hurt voice. "And I don't want 'em on the prowl when I'm down. Especially when they don't have anything. God."

Hurensohn shook his head sadly. "You don't know enough, then. You have never seen the core of a human being, a part which is not afraid, and which understands and is understood." Hurensohn searched his face with earnest eyes.

"Have you?"

"I have. I see it now. I see it in you all. But then, I see more than you do. You could see as much; you all could. Let me do it, Joe. Help me. Help me, *please*."

"And lose everything I've worked so hard to—"

"Lose? Think of the gain! Think of what you'd do for the whole world! Or—if it means any more to you—turn the coin over. Think of what you'll carry with you if you don't help us. Every war casualty, every death from preventable disease, every minute of pain in every cancer patient, every stumbling step of a multiple sclerosis victim, will be on your conscience from the moment you refuse me.

"Ah, think, Joe—*think!*"

Phillipso slowly raised his eyes from his clenched hands to Hurensohn's plain, intense face. Higher, then, to the dome and through it. He raised his hand and pointed. "Pardon me," he said shakily, "but your ship is showing."

"Pshaw," said Hurensohn surprisingly. "Dammit, Phillipso, you've gone and made me concentrate, and I've let go the warp-matrix and fused my omicron. Take a minute or two to fix. I'll be back." And he disappeared. He didn't go anywhere; he just abruptly wasn't.

Josephus Macardle Phillipso moved like a sleepwalker across the round room and stood against the Plexiglas, staring up and out at the shining ship. It was balanced and beautiful, dusty-textured and untouchable like a moth's wing. It was lightly phosphorescent, flaring in the orange glow of the slashing searchlight, dimming rapidly almost to blackness just as the light cut at it again.

He looked past the ship to the stars, and in his mind's eye, past them to stars again, and stars, and whole systems of stars which in their remoteness looked like stars again, and stars again. He looked down then, to the ground under the Temple and down again to its steep slope, its one narrow terrace of a highway, and down and down again to the lamp-speckled black of the valley bottom. And if I fell from here to there, he thought, it would be like falling from crest to trough in the whorls of a baby's fingerprint.

And he thought, even with help from Heaven, I couldn't tell this truth and be believed. I couldn't suggest this work and be trusted. I am unfit, and I have unfit myself.

He thought bitterly, It's only the truth. The truth and I have a like polarity, and it springs away from me when I approach, by a law of nature. I prosper without the truth, and it has cost me nothing, nothing, nothing but the ability to tell the truth.

But I might try, he thought. What was it he said: *The core of a human being, a part which is not afraid, and which understands and is understood.* Who was he talking about? Anybody I know? Anyone I ever heard of? ("How are you?" you say, when you don't care how they are. "I'm sorry," you say, when you're not. "Goodby," you say, and it means God be with you, and how often is your goodby a blessing? Hypocrisy and lies, thousands a day, so easily done we forget to feel guilty for them.)

*I see it now,* he said, though. Did he mean me? Could he see the core of me, and say that? . . . if he can see such a marrow, he can see a strand of spider-silk at sixty yards.

He said, Phillipso recalled, that if I wouldn't help, they'd do nothing. They'd go away that's all—go away, forever, and leave us at the mercy of—what was that sardonic phrase? —the World Destroyers.

"But I never lied!" he wailed, suddenly and frighteningly loud. "I never meant to. They'd ask, don't you see, and I'd only say yes or no, whatever they wanted to hear. The only other thing I ever did was to explain the yes, or the no; they didn't start out to be lies!" No one answered him. He felt very alone. He thought again, I could try . . . and then, wistfully, could I try?

The phone rang. He looked blindly at it until it rang again. Tiredly he crossed to it and picked it up. "Phillipso."

The phone said, "Okay, Swami, you win. How did you do it?"

"Who is that? Penfield?" Penfield, whose original Phillipso spread had started his rise from Sunday feature writer; Penfield, who, as district chief of a whole newspaper chain, had of course long since forsworn Phillipso . . .

"Yeah, Penfield," drawled the pugnacious, insulting voice. "Penfield who promised you faithfully that never again would these papers run a line about you and your phony space war."

"What do you want, Penfield?"

"So you win, that's all. Whether I like it or not, you're news again. We're getting calls from all over the county. There's a flight of F-84s on the way from the Base. There's a TV mobile unit coming up the mountain to get that flying saucer of yours on network, and four queries already from INS. I don't know how you're doing it, but you're news, so what's your lousy story?"

Phillipso glanced up over his shoulder at the ship. The orange searchlight set it to flaming once, once again, while the telephone urgently bleated his name. Around came the light, and—

And nothing. It was gone. The ship was gone. "Wait!" cried Phillipso hoarsely. But it was gone.

The phone gabbled at him. Slowly he turned back to it. "Wait," he said to it too. He put down the instrument and rubbed water out of his eyes. Then he picked up the phone again.

"I saw from here," said the tinny voice. "It's gone. What was it? What'd you do?"

"Ship," said Phillipso. "It was a spaceship."

" 'It was a spaceship,' " Penfield repeated in the voice of a man writing on a pad. "So come on, Phillipso. What happened? Aliens came down and met you face to face, that it?"

"They—yes."

" 'Face . . . to . . . face.' Got it. What'd they want?" A pause, then, angrily, "Phillipso, you there? Dammit, I got a story to get out here. What'd they want? They beg for mercy, want you to lay off?"

Phillipso wet his lips. "Well, yes. Yes, they did."

"What'd they look like?"

"I—they . . . there was only one."

Penfield growled something about pulling teeth. "All right, only one. One *what?* Monster, spider, octopus—come *on,* Phillipso!"

"It . . . well, it wasn't a man, exactly."

"A girl," said Penfield excitedly. "A girl of unearthly beauty. How's that? They've threatened you before. Now they came to beguile you with, and so on. How's that?"

"Well, I—"

"I'll quote you. *'Unearthly* . . . mmm . . . *and refused* . . . mmm, *temptation.'*"

"Penfield, I—"

"Listen, Swami, that's all you get. I haven't time to listen to any more of your crap. I'll give you this in exchange, though. Just a friendly warning, and besides, I want this story to hold up through tomorrow anyhow. ATIC and the FBI are going to be all over that Temple of yours like flies on a warm marshmallow. You better hide the pieces of that balloon or whatever else the trick was. When it reaches the point of sending out a flight of jets, they don't think publicity is funny."

"Penfield, I—" But the phone was dead. Phillipso hung up and whirled to the empty room. "You *see?*" he wept. "You see what they make me do?"

He sat down heavily. The phone rang again. New York, the operator said. It was Jonathan, his publisher. "Joe! Your line's been busy. Great work, fella. Heard the bulletin on TV. How'd you do it? Never mind. Give me the main facts. I'll have a release out first thing in the morning. Hey, how soon can you get the new book done? Two weeks? Well, three—you can do it in three, fella. You have to do it in three. I'll cancel the new Heming—or the—never mind, I'll get press time for it. Now. Let's have it. I'll put you on the recorder."

Phillipso looked out at the stars. From the telephone, he heard the first sharp high *beep* of the recording machine. He bent close to it, breathed deeply, and said, "Tonight I was visited by aliens. This was no accidental contact like my first one; they planned this one. They came to stop me—not with violence, not by persuasion, but with—uh—the ultimate weapon. A girl of unearthly beauty appeared amidst the coils and busbars of my long-range radar. I—"

From behind Phillipso came a sound, soft, moist, explosive— the exact reproduction of someone too angry, too disgusted to speak, but driven irresistibly to spit.

Phillipso dropped the telephone and whirled. He thought he saw the figure of a sandy-haired man, but it vanished. He caught the barest flicker of something in the sky where the ship had been, but not enough really to identify; then it was gone too.

"I was on the phone," he whimpered. "I had too much on my mind, I thought you'd gone, I didn't know you'd just fixed your warp-what-ever-you-call-it, I didn't mean, I was going to, I—"

At last he realized he was alone. He had never been so alone. Absently he picked up the telephone and put it to his ear. Jonathan was saying excitedly, ". . . and the title. *The Ultimate Weapon.* Cheesecake pic of the girl coming out of the radar, nekkid. The one thing you haven't used yet. We'll *bomb* 'em, boy. Yeah, and you resisting, too. Do wonders for your Temple. But get busy on that book, hear? Get it to me in fifteen days and you can open your own branch of the U.S. mint."

Slowly, without speaking or waiting to see if the publisher was finished, Phillipso hung up. Once, just once, he looked out at the stars, and for a terrible instant each star was a life, a crippled limb, a faulty heart, a day of agony; and there were millions on countless millions of stars, and some of the stars were galaxies of stars; by their millions, by their flaming megatons, they were falling on him now and would fall on him forever.

He sighed and turned away, and switched on the light over his typewriter. He rolled in a sandwich of bond, carbon, second-sheet, centered the carriage, and wrote

THE ULTIMATE WEAPON
*by*
Josephus Macardle Phillipso.

Facile, swift, deft, and dedicated, he began to write.

*Thomas Burnett Swann was an English professor who produced approximately 20 books and 15 stories of fantasy before falling victim to cancer. Much of his early fame was obtained in England, and most of his work centers around Mediterranean myths and legends. The following story, however, is one of his few works of science fiction. It is a flavorful attempt to explain the motivation behind Hieronymus Bosch's most famous painting.*

# THE PAINTER

## by THOMAS BURNETT SWANN

They called him the merry painter. With his oils and ink, his canvases and panels, Hieronymus Bosch was quicker to sketch a bacchanalian frolic than a Last Judgment. They liked him, he realized, as one likes clever, engaging pets; because he performed for them. But at twenty-three, he had no wish to imitate his six older brothers and become a substantial burgher of Hertogensbosch. His parents were dead; his oldest brothers tolerated him in the family home because his drawings contributed to household expenses. At weddings, for example, he could sketch the bride and groom with amazing likeness, though afterwards he sometimes passed out from the wine, muttering that he, at least, would never entangle himself with a wife. It was one thing to paint a groom, another to marry and forgo his freedom. After he met the devils, of course, he changed his mind about many things; after that night in the barn when the great blue fish disgorged its appalling company.

To the wedding of the Vandermeers he had brought his younger brother, Jan, who worshiped him. While Jan watched admiringly over his shoulder, he had sketched the bride, a pallid dove of a girl with hair shaved high up her forehead, a tall headdress, and a veil fastened by one of those fashionable new pins shaped like butterflies.

Hieronymus slapped Jan on the back. "A few more years, and I'll be painting *your bride*."

Jan replied with a shrug: "Brides are for merchants. I am going to be an artist like you." A slender boy of fifteen, almost ethereal with his amber hair, he scarcely resembled the red-maned brother he adored. Unaccustomed to wine in large quantity, but unwilling to fall behind Hieronymus, he swayed tipsily.

Hieronymus, a trifle unsure on his own feet, led his brother towards a circle of guests engaged in animated conversation. The house which was merriest, the room which was liveliest, the group which was noisiest attracted him as an apple attracts a bee. People called him merry for his person as well as his manner. He refused to hide his hair in the tall black hats of a burgher, but combed it loose to his shoulders like a young Florentine painted by Botticelli (whose grave goddesses and sensual madonnas were delighting Europe).

Farmer Terburg was describing a fish he had seen, of enormous size, and, of all places, in the sky.

"I tell you I saw him," he said, disdaining an offer of wine as if to disavow its influence. "A fish as big as this house, with blue scales, and a smoking tail."

"A fish in the sky!" protested Hieronymus, who disliked for anyone to tell taller tales than his own. "And a fishing pole, I expect. The angels are having sport."

Farmer Terburg adjusted his blue spectacles. They had come from Brussels, and he was very proud of them. *"Your* stories," he said, "begin in a bottle. My fish does not."

Quick to defend his brother, Jan cried: "Hieronymus can hold his wine. Can you, Farmer Terburg?"

The farmer, absurdly overdressed in a black courtier's cape, glared at his accuser and opened his mouth to speak. But Hieronymus forestalled him:

"With fish about the sky, we should all get drunk. Then they will not distress us."

The group laughed and dispersed, flushed with wine and unresponsive to further fantasies. The hour was late, and town lay two miles away. Some had ridden in carts, others like Hieronymus and Jan had walked.

"One more glass apiece," said Hieronymus, "and home we go." But the one glass became four, and the brothers found themselves the last guests, forsaken even by their host, who, Hieronymus surmised, expected them to collapse on the red-and-cream tiles of the floor and sleep until morning. He stared at the cypress cabinet against the far wall, with its slender blue vases from the new Italian glass center in Flanders. He watched the light of a dying fire flicker along the encaustic tiles. The room was comfortable, the floor warm in front of the fire. He resented, however, his host's desertion. Pompous old farmer! He lifted the rectangular wicker basket which held his drawing tools—ink, reed pen, and a white panel like the one he had used for the bride and groom—and fastened it to his shoulders. Steering his brother through the door and into the fields, he tried gallantly to keep his balance—and Jan's.

Their route took them through an orchard whose apples glistened like Venetian goblets, twisting their fine-blown spheres to capture the moonlight. But Hieronymus, far from sobered by the brisk night air, felt increasingly sleepy, and Jan lurched against him, half asleep himself, and sighed:

"Is it much further?"

For at least a mile the fields lay unbroken by houses—orchards mingling with open pastures and dewberry brambles—but an old barn, a storeplace for apples which belonged to the bride's father, loomed invitingly ahead of them and offered the respite of a nap. Otherwise, Hieronymus feared that they would fall in the fields and grow chilled. He directed his brother into the barn, a rounded structure like a stemless mushroom, with a tower at the back and a cluster of gorse and juniper. The earthen floor overflowed with apples.

Hieronymus removed his basket and scooped out a nest in the rear of the barn. Their backs against the earth, they drew apples over their bodies for warmth. The place was redolent of fruit, and the apples, in spite of their lumpiness, felt not unwelcome to Hieronymus' wine-drugged body. A few thoughts flickered through his mind: the sketch he had made of the pretty, insipid bride (God spare him from such a spouse!); Farmer Terburg's tale of the fish in the sky, which he wished he had invented himself; and finally, the pleasurable nearness of his brother, whom he loved above all people. Jan's thin shoulder pressed against his own, and Hieronymus felt warm, strong, protective, with the fire of his hair and the ruddiness of his skin a shield between the vulnerable boy and the cold night.

He awoke with the feeling of having heard—or dreamed—a noise like a great object coming to rest, first a kind of whoosh, then a settling. When a light flickered through the wooden and wattle walls of the barn, he knew that he had not dreamed. The thought of Farmer Terburg's fish returned to him. If an enormous fish were to land outside the barn, it would have made such a sound. His first impulse was to rise and investigate. But his brain had cleared of wine, and a second impulse told him to remain where he was, far back in the apples and out of sight with Jan. A fish as big as Farmer Terburg's might go fishing for men.

Soon he had company. At first he took them for men of wildly differing sizes—some like the midgets who entertained in the great castles, some like the giants of the perilous East. There were six of them, and the first carried a round object which cast a green luminescence over the interior of the barn. Then he saw that they were not men. They reminded him of the devils above the door of the Autun cathedral, those inspired diableries of the sculptor Giselbertus. But they surpassed the horror of the sculptor's nightmares. Though they walked upright, their faces were bestial and twisted as if by leprosy. His first thought was to run for the door. But how could he waken Jan without discovery? Better to stay where he was and hope that Jan did not wake abruptly and betray them.

The creatures began to chatter in harsh, metallic tones. They seemed to be members of three races, banded together for devilish purposes; gods of three pagan lands, perhaps, reduced to the common denominator of devils. Two were tall, thin, rufous-bodied, with skinny tails; they wore cloth hoods on their heads but nothing on their bodies except belts which held unrecognizable implements of blue metal. They were snakes with limbs. A third, also nude, had the blue moist head of a rat. And the last three bulged enormous stomachs with prickly pears, walked on webbed green feet, and peered with sunken eyes through a tangle of hair like bleached seaweed; old men, they seemed, turned to beasts through lechery.

Jan's breathing was normal and even, but to Hieronymus's fear-sensitized ears it roared with the gush of wind along the dikes. Surely, he thought, the devils would hear the boy. He lay very still and regretted his sins—the girls he had kissed in the orchards with never a word of marriage, the wine he had drunk, the wicked unseriousness of his life. Had the devils been sent to punish him? Hardly, he decided, since they endangered his innocent brother as well. Doubtless they had come on their own, in spite of Christ and Our Lady, not because of them; everyone knew that devils liked to climb out of the earth and see what they were missing. To be sure, these seemed to have come down, not up. Maybe they had been deformed and cast out of heaven like Lucifer. Or maybe they had simply been exploring the sky in their fish.

One of the devils pointed toward the apples. He gesticulated and the others laughed (at least Hieronymus so interpreted their metallic raspings). Angrily he stooped—or rather, hunched, for this was a fat one—to the ground and thrust a large apple in his larger mouth. Rising, he smacked his lips noisily and struck a pose of self-satisfied contentment. Vanity seemed a characteristic of the creatures. But the green skin of his cheeks crinkled, the coarse white hair bobbed over his eyes, and bits of apple exploded from his mouth. The others roared in unison, and with great relief Hieronymus saw that they were preparing to leave. Their apparent leader, the rat, advanced toward the door.

Then Jan woke up and called out Hieronymus' name. The creatures stopped, turned, and stared at them with ghoulish curiosity. The rat motioned with his claw: they were to come forward. Hieronymus stepped in front of Jan.

"This is not your barn," he said stoutly. "It belongs to Farmer Valk."

The rat peered at him as if trying to understand his words. He spoke very slowly, in a metallic tone like the scraping of a horseshoe on stone, but unmistakably in Flemish. He had a curious way of substituting "n" for "m" at the start of a word:

"You question *ny* right to be here, ruddy one?" The others howled with laughter.

"Not if you leave us now," said Hieronymus, his hand restraining Jan, who tried to push beside him. He whispered a prayer to the Virgin. Enrolled last year in the Fraternity of Our Lady, he had always felt that she tolerated his vagaries much more than did her son. The prayer completed, he wondered how the devils had learned Flemish. In Hell there were perhaps Dutchmen to teach it to them. Or perhaps, cruising about in their fish, they had found ways to overhear conversations on earth, learn the language, and thus direct their machinations for Satan.

The rat lifted a small elongated instrument from his belt. He aimed it at the corner of the wall. A thin red line spat across the barn and bit a hole in the wall as large as a man's head. Jan's arms, behind Hieronymus, tightened around his waist. It was not a time for bravado. With such a weapon, the devils had nothing to fear.

"Then let us go. We mean you no harm."

"You could do us none if you wished. But . . . we have nade a long journey. We have grown fatigued and hungry." A red tongue thrust through his lips, poised in the air, withdrew into the dark cavern of his mouth.

"You didn't care for the apples?" Hieronymus asked, at a loss for less obvious words and with no intention of irony.

"We are not fond of fruits. We are fond of *neat*."

"Perhaps we could get you chickens at the farmhouse beyond the orchard."

"Perhaps," said the rat with a meaningful look at his friends. "But there is neat close at hand."

Like water invading a swimmer, horror flooded his body. Meat close at hand: Jan dismembered, his pale, thin limbs stripped of flesh by these creatures from Hell. I would kill him first myself, he thought. I would choke him with my bare hands. Our Lady would forgive me. She has known what it means for a child to be threatened.

Silent, he waited. The boy stood beside him now, his body shaken but staunch. Hieronymus pressed his shoulder.

The rat pointed toward Jan. "He is quiet. Has he nothing to say for himself?"

Hieronymus tried to speak, but Jan anticipated him. "This, you rat-faced devil. Go to Hell!" Then, as if amazed at his own temerity, he stood open-mouthed. The others laughed, the rat scowled. None of them could tolerate a blow to his vanity. He turned to the snake and spoke orders in his alien tongue. The snake's hand whipped out like a noose and circled the boy's throat. Jan gave a quick, muffled sob. The same instant, Hieronymus struck the snake in the face with the full strength of his large, knotted fist. A substance like flesh and gristle, quite boneless, crunched sickeningly under the blow. The snake howled and fell to the floor, clutching his ruined face. Hieronymus awaited retaliation. When the rat did not disintegrate them with the beam, he knelt beside his fallen brother and took the nearly garroted boy in his arms. He felt Jan's body quiver beneath his touch, and he wanted urgently to preserve him from these monsters. He looked up, wondering what delayed their destruction.

The devils were gazing at their wounded comrade, and they were laughing, silently at first, then with growing merriment, until the barn shuddered with laughter, and little particles of dust careened in the light of the green lamp. Truly they were devils, Hieronymus thought. They enjoyed the pain of their friends.

The rat turned to him at last. "You are droll," he said. "Laughter rests us from the journey. It is almost as good as food. Almost." He peered at the unconscious Jan, and the red tongue flickered from his mouth. A bead of thick saliva fell to the dirt and hissed like water in an oven.

"What can I give you to let him go?" Hieronymus said hopelessly. If, in the face of the beam, he hurled his body at the rat, would enough remain to injure or at least unbalance the creature? But Jan, still unconscious, could not seize the chance to escape.

"What have you to give me?" the rat sneered.

"What I am wearing."

The rat indicated a lapis lazuli ring, imported from Italy, on his left hand. He removed it only to have it struck from his fingers. The rat pointed to his turquoise cape, which met the same scornful treatment. Then his pointed wooden shoes. Then his trousers with vertical red and black stripes. Each time the response was identical. Soon Hieronymus stood nude and shivering in the cold night air. He is toying with me, the painter thought. He knew from the start that nothing I have could please him; if it could, he would take without asking. A brave man with clothes can face anything. How

much of his courage ebbs with his clothes! Naked, a man is
made Adam and burdened by original sin—and original fear.

The creatures could not restrain themselves. They pointed
at his bare reddish skin, and he guessed that they were
comparing it to disadvantage with their own blue, green, or
russet hides. To a man, a rat's skin looks gray and loathsome;
a snake's far worse. To the devils, Hieronymus' skin was
clearly no more to be envied. One of the round creatures,
eyeing the rat's weapon to make sure that he was well
covered, thrust a finger in Hieronymus' side as if to investigate the ribs which faintly outlined his well-muscled chest.
Apparently the creatures were little more than backbones
augmented by cartilage and Hieronymus' bone structure
astonished them. When the first thrust elicited no reaction,
the creature jabbed again, much harder, but the rat forestalled him from further experiments. The prisoner was his
to torment; he had not yet finished.

"What else have you to give me?"

Hieronymus shrugged wearily. "I have nothing."

The rat pointed to his wicker case, forgotten among the
apples. The painter retrieved it and displayed the contents—a
white panel, a red glass vial of ink, a reed pen—the tools of
his profession which he had carried to the wedding.

Casually the rat examined them. He was growing bored.
"Useless," he said, and prepared to throw them after the
clothes. Hieronymus stayed his hand. The rat brandished his
beam.

"Wait," Hieronymus said. He had remembered the creatures' vanity. "They are not useless. Let me draw you."

"With this?" sneered the rat, holding up the pen. "Where
are your brushes? Where are your canvases?"

"I don't need them."

The rat looked at his companions. Expressionless, they
awaited his decision. The wounded snake, neglected, had
recovered himself to slouch by the door.

"Draw me," said the rat. "But quickly."

Hieronymus sank to his knees, dipped his reed in the ink,
and began to draw, careful to allot space for six portraits. The
dim light gave an eeriness to the panel, and the figure which
began to materialize seemed born of that light. Never had
Hieronymus painted so quickly or with such assurance. Fear

for Jan gave power and certainty to his arm. Gone were the revelers, the lovers, the children at play who had once frolicked through his drawings. Line after line swiftly incised itself into the portrait (for the hideousness of the rat seemed to burn through his arm). The very features which made him shudder, he guessed, were those most precious to his model. He bared them in all their ugliness; indeed exaggerated them. A horror leered from the panel, a mouth like a fish's, a damp slimy skin, a knotted tail. A nightmare which was true. The rat watched with growing excitement. Angrily he motioned the others to allow the artist more room.

Hieronymus laid aside his pen. "It is finished," he said. The rat seized the panel in his paws and carried it under the lamp. His walk was the preening stride of someone who feels himself superbly complimented.

"Us, us," the others clamored, speaking Flemish for the first time, but without the ease of their friend. "Time for us."

Hieronymus pointed to Jan, conscious at last and crouching beyond the circle of watchers. "First you must let him go. Then I will paint you. If my brother comes back with friends, he knows you will kill me. Besides, your weapon is deadly. You have nothing to fear."

The rat shook his head, but the others scurried around him and shook their fists, shouting, no doubt, that now it was their turn. He raised his beam, but they knocked it from his hand and returned with the panel to entreat the painter.

Hieronymus, ignoring them, helped Jan to his feet. "Can you walk, brother?"

"Yes," the boy gasped with evident pain. "But I won't leave you."

Hieronymus embraced him with urgent tenderness. "You must," he said. "And don't come back until the fish is gone. I'll follow you when I can."

"No," Jan cried desperately. "I want to stay here." But Heironymus guided him past the creatures, who made no move, and through the door. Jan, accustomed to obedience, obeyed him now. Only when the boy had vanished into the orchards did Hieronymus turn to face his captors. He felt a curious buoyancy as he realized that Jan had escaped. Nothing they did could frighten him now. Still, he wanted very much to live and rejoin his brother.

\*    \*    \*

"Now I will paint the rest of you," he said. The rat stood apart, sulking; unwilling to share the panel. First, the snake, while the others waited, impatient. Then, one by one, the others, until the panel crawled with horror, with twisted shapes and reptile tails, lidless eyes and slimy skins, the loathsomest attributes of despicable animals. The models watched with pride at the truth of themselves in ink. When the panel bristled like a page from a bestiary, they wrested it from him and fought to hold it and trace their features. He turned, gathered up his tools and clothes (he dared not linger to dress), and realized that his limbs had grown numb from cold and exertion. When he steeled himself to move, he thought that they would stop him; that before he left the barn they would send a lethal red shaft into his back. But the panel held their attention; captivated them. It was not that they were grateful enough to let him go. He had simply given them a toy more pleasurable than torture. Soon they would tire of it. For the moment it served. Their minds were quick. They had built, at least they flew, the great blue fish which rested, Olympian, in the kindling dawnlight. But they had no hearts. That was why they were devils, not because they were ugly. . . .

In the coming years, when Hieronymus (married to a plump French girl) had ceased to paint his weddings and his revelers, and begun to paint grotesqueries not of this earth, and won a fame which extended even to the court of Spain, people would ask him where he had learned such horrors. Hieronymus would smile and say nothing. The people would turn then to Jan, and Jan catching his brother's eye, would answer:

"In Hell, where else?"

*F. L. Wallace is the author of one book and 24 stories of science fiction. He worked primarily for* Galaxy Magazine *during the 1950s and is perhaps best known for* Address: Centauri *(1955) and "Student Body." Currently, he lives in California and reports a desire to return to writing soon. But for now, at least, we must content ourselves with previously unreprinted stories such as the following one about a stowaway vampire.*

# THE DEADLY ONES

## by F. L. WALLACE

Rathsden. I'm sure the name means nothing to you. There are legends, of course—from old Germany and the greater Reich, colonial America even. But you can't prove anything very damaging or concrete with legends. And even when the story is otherwise correct, I've been careful to keep my name out of it. A clever person shuns publicity, though it may involve tampering with history. For all practical purposes the name Rathsden is unknown. I want it kept that way.

I can't remember when the inspiration came. Probably it had lain for a long time dormant in the back of my mind, like a mole hibernating in midwinter. Warmed by the proper circumstances, it emerged at last in its full vigor to claim my attention.

I've always worked hard, but lately what I got out of my

efforts you couldn't call a living. The Red Cross was largely responsible. You could never get me to say a good word for that agency—never.

Still, I have made use of them, and in this case they made their contribution, though it was an unwitting one.

I gave the idea careful thought. From the beginning I knew I needed help. I'm not superhuman, not in the strict sense, though I suppose I could give a good account of myself against Wells' Invisible Man, *Homo superior,* or the new crop of mutants that will spring up some day soon.

I needed help, and I carried the problem to a council of my fellows. We discussed it thoroughly, and in the end, though they didn't give me their blessing, they consented to aid me.

The problem was flying saucers, or rather how to force one to land. We debated the matter for a long time, but there didn't seem to be any way to do it. No jet could keep up with a saucer and present rockets were equally inadequate. Besides, we didn't have access to any of these machines.

Someone in the back of the council whose name I didn't catch suggested that if we couldn't force one to land, perhaps we could lure one down. It didn't matter how, as long as it remained on the ground for an hour or so, with its ports open. The rest would be up to me.

"Fine," I said. "What do you propose?"

"They're investigating, you know," he said, "in the western part of the country. Rocket bases, atom bomb sites, anything that indicates advanced technology. Let's give them another menace."

"Sounds good. What are they interested in?" He was a hard fellow to locate, and I didn't try to visualize his face. He came from Ireland, I believe.

"A spaceship," he said. "A very formidable creation, with an incredible drive."

There was nothing wrong with the basic concept. The ship wouldn't be real, of course. It would merely seem real from the air. We could accomplish that.

As for the drive, we could manage that too. In a little-investigated part of the spectrum we could create a low and steady output, suggesting that the drive was idling, ready for instant takeoff.

None of this was impossible for us.

We? Have I said that we're not human? We've existed for a long time on earth beside *Homo sapiens,* and he has only dimly guessed that we are here. The ordinary limitations of men don't apply to us.

A few of us working together could create an illusionary spaceship, and an intriguing drive to go with it. This was something flying saucers couldn't resist. They'd come down when they found they couldn't investigate from their customary high-level flights.

I nodded at the fellow I couldn't see. "Excellent. However, when the saucer lands you'll have to maintain the illusion. Logistics are involved too."

"That's easy," he said. "But what if it isn't manned by robots as you've assumed? You can get inside all right, but a living creature will discover you."

I looked at the blank spot where I thought he might be. "Really now. It *has* to be a robot. No living creature, except us, can stand the accelerations we've observed."

"But what if we're wrong?" he persisted.

"In that case we'll have time for one quick look," I said. "If it *is* living and we're no match for it, we'll run like hell."

There was general laughter and the fellow raised no further objections. For all I know, he went home. The meeting broke up and everyone except a few volunteers left. We continued to discuss ways and means.

When the plans seemed foolproof, I got up. "Just a minute," another fellow I didn't recognize interposed. "Suppose everything works the way you say it will. The saucer lands, and you succeed in getting inside. What makes you think it will go back to the home planet?"

"Don't overlook our fake spaceship," I said. "If the robot investigator from the saucer found a real spaceship, that would be important information. It would be important enough to warrant a quick trip back to the local base, wherever that may be situated.

"But when the robot can't locate anything, in spite of the evidence on the instruments, it will be dealing with *top priority* stuff. Logically it will have to report back to the prime evaluation center, on the home planet. I think I'm safe in anticipating a short journey."

"I hope so." He shook his head dubiously. "But what about us? We don't have to worry about humans, and probably those things out there haven't come close enough to learn about us. But they're pretty advanced. What if they should?"

"You think they can detect us when we're dematerialized?" I smiled. "Don't be naive. Anyway, nothing risked, you know."

I shouldn't have said that. I talk too much. "Nothing gained." He completed the sentence for me. He didn't look altruistic. "Just what do we stand to gain?"

The others hadn't thought of it, and neither had I, from that angle. I ad-libbed. "It's not been good here lately. There's too many factors against us, agencies that I don't have to mention.

"Feast or famine, mostly the last. And what are we going to do after an atomic war, when mutants come along? Are you sure we can compete with them? As bad as it is now, it can get worse." I paused to let the dire predictions sink in.

"Someone has to do it, and I intend to be the one to find new worlds for us," I said.

My confidence impressed the others, but not the heckler. "I can see that you'll find it for yourself. But how are you going to let us know?"

"Just now I can't communicate from here to Philadelphia," I said. "It's a harassing business, merely trying to stay alive. Here I haven't had time to practice mental communication. But there conditions will be ideal and I expect to develop myself so that I can reach out anywhere in the galaxy."

Objectively that was true. Subjectively I could have changed my mind about sharing my prize. They didn't think of that and I didn't mention it.

The last objection was silenced. They went about their preparations and I about mine.

We set up the decoy in Illinois. No real reason, I suppose, except that most of us are allergic to desert, the logical place to build spaceport and ships. Deserts are hot, dry and bright, and there are few humans there. In our own way we're fond of men, though they may not think so.

Illinois it was, and if there was a note of incongruity in it, so much the better. A spaceship looked strange in the middle of the flat cornfields? Very well, it did. Let the robot investigator find out why it was there.

The creation was not difficult. There was a haze in the air and the fields were green, and the spaceship pointed a sleek nose toward the sky. It was impalpable from below. A farmer plowed right through the stern tubes without knowing they were there. An inconvenience only; we blacked him out as seen from above. The farmhouse we converted into a control tower and the barn became a disembarkation structure.

There were side manifestations, of course. Dogs growled uneasily and barked, then ran away and hid in the woods. Roosters could not crow nor hens lay eggs. Milk curdled, in cows and cans, and all the butter turned rancid. Unfortunately we don't often use our entire minds—and when we do there are peripheral effects. However, no human in the area noticed us, and life went on pretty much as usual.

Radio reception was poor over all North America, and television was disrupted for a thousand miles. The disruption was deliberately planned. We had to attract the attention of the saucers, and that was the easiest way to do it. The radiation was supposed to represent a power leak from our hypothecated interstellar drive.

They came the second night, and it was good they did. The strain was telling on everyone in the project. It's not easy to keep up such a big illusion.

The flight of saucers wheeled across the sky, lights out and undoubtedly ready for action. They had located us all right, and they wanted to see just what it was we had. But they couldn't find out from the air no matter how many times they passed over.

It must have been quite a jolt. They had earth all pegged down to the last improvement in a self-locking nut. And suddenly here was something new which didn't belong.

Toward midnight, with five of them still skimming the clouds, the sixth came down. I was ready, and had everything I needed with me. The saucer landed in a field a half a mile away. The vegetation burned invisibly where it settled. A section of the saucer opened, and a much littler saucer came out.

The little saucer was a robot. I was sure of that the instant I saw it, mostly because it had wheels. There is nothing to indicate that a life form can't have wheels, but it does pose a nice problem of what a living creature will use for bearings. It was a robot then, and it came out and headed for our ship, which was still holding together splendidly, needle nose aimed at the sky.

It was time for me to go to work. I started toward the big saucer.

"It's coming closer." This was the thought of the individual who had created the ship out of his own dematerialized atoms.

"Put out a force field and keep it away." He sounded shaky and I thought a wry jest would help. The containers I was carrying were heavy.

The ship snorted. "I wish I could. But seriously, how long do I have to stay here?"

"Keep it up," I said. "I've got lots of supplies."

The terror in his voice was real. "I don't like that thing. It's snooping around."

"Waken the farmer. Maybe he'll kick up a disturbance and the robot will investigate."

With a shotgun the farmer couldn't do much, but a lucky shot might put a wheel out of commission. The robot wouldn't like that.

"I can't make the farmer open his eyes. The saucer put him to sleep and I can't touch his mind."

The saucers had a good brand of hypnotism, if that's what it was. We knew they had space travel, and now it was evident that they were equally advanced in other ways.

"Use your judgment," I told the ship. "Hold it as long as you can and then pretend to go out into space, or forward in time. Anything that will look good."

I needed time. I could have dematerialized where I stood, and rematerialized inside the saucer. But if I did, I would have to leave most of my supplies behind. A short journey, I had said. And that was true—short as far as interstellar distances were concerned. But it would be long by normal methods of reckoning, and I had to live through it. I couldn't abandon my supplies.

I succeeded in transporting all the food to a place just outside the large saucer before our ship disappeared. It didn't go out into space, nor into time as I expected. Instead it sank rapidly into the ground, and left no hole behind. This, I think, confused the robot. I heard it thrashing around in the cornfield, possibly in bewilderment.

I gathered some of the containers and carried them inside the saucer. It was lighted all right, and the lighting scheme was as weird as the interior. They used the spectrum below the red, and above the violet. Why this should be so I don't know. I merely report what I found. Apparently they didn't react to what we consider visible light.

I adjusted my eyes.

I found an empty space which I assumed was for the storage of specimens. I put my food in there. Outside I went for more, and then back again. I repeated my trips until everything was loaded. Unpalatable food, of course, concentrated and not tasty, but it would last until I stepped out on the planet at the opposite end. After that there would be other problems.

I went outside for the last communication with my fellows. The ship I could examine later. I looked around. The control tower and disembarkation structure were still visible, though they were wavering in the dim light.

"Are you there?" I thought.

"I am." The control tower thought back. "I wish I wasn't."

"It's just a robot," I said reassuringly. "It's not interested in a building."

"Maybe not," conceded the control tower. "But it's inside, examining sleeping people. I wish it would go away."

He was losing control of himself and that didn't suit my purpose. "It's just a machine. Hold on for a little longer."

He held on.

The robot left the illusionary control tower and headed toward the saucer. For a squat ungainly contrivance it covered the distance in an amazing fashion. I had barely time to get inside before it rumbled into the saucer. It was carrying something. We took off before I could see what it was.

We left earth smoothly, though any kind of takeoff would have suited me. Inertia had never been my problem. Neither was the possibility that the robot would discover me. I was certain I didn't register on light-sensitive cells, and I had other tricks I could use if I had to.

The robot had tentacles I hadn't noticed before because they had been retracted. They weren't retracted now, and they held a farmer. He was unconscious.

The robot was monkeying around with the farmer, but it was hardly the time to interfere. Needles stabbed the farmer in several places. Withdrawing the blood and storing it, probably inside the robot.

The first needles were jerked out, and replaced by others. Again this was logical: pumping a fluid into the farmer's veins with the intent of suspending the life force until they reached the home planet.

The whole procedure made sense. When the robot couldn't find the spaceship it had taken someone in the vicinity for questioning. They'd be surprised what they'd learn from the farmer, though. Absolutely nothing! We had protected ourselves too well. The farmer's ordeal had no bearing on the success of *my* enterprise. Nevertheless I became slightly ill at the waste involved.

The robot dropped the farmer in a place similar to the one in which I had hidden my supplies. Then it crouched down and became motionless, waiting. There was nothing for it to do.

Nor for myself either. We were out of the atmosphere and on our way.

The journey was six months of monotony. Avoiding the robot was easy because it didn't move. The ship was all mine but I couldn't make use of it. I puttered around, but there was nothing much to learn. The drive was in operation, and as long as it was, I couldn't get close. I had no idea of what it was nor how it worked, but the force that surrounded it was, for me at least, an absolute barrier.

The rest of the saucer was equally confounding. There were several low-ceilinged compartments which held instruments at whose functions I could not guess. There were no star charts anywhere, but I had to assume the ship knew where it was going.

Whatever our destination, we were approaching it faster than light. Occasionally I looked out of the vision ports, and what I saw didn't resemble suns, though of course they were. It was the light shaft which changed their appearance.

One day the saucer gave a lurch and we were simultaneously below the speed of light, and near our goal. Dead ahead was a multiple star system. Where it lay with relation to Earth I don't know. Within fifty to a thousand light-years I suppose.

For the first time in months the robot stirred, went to the farmer and began to work on him. I kept out of the way. It seemed the sensible thing to do. No matter how often I looked, I couldn't determine the location of the planet toward which we were bound. The ship knew, but I was in ignorance.

From behind, in the next compartment, came the labored sounds of the robot. Then there was another sound and it didn't come from the robot. I looked in. The farmer sat up, gazed around, understood some or little of what he saw. That understanding was enough for him. He collapsed. He was still breathing, though; in spasmodic gasps.

The revivification was a complete sucess. I decided to keep the man in mind. He was an important source of reserve strength.

My hopes leapt high when I saw the planet. It was something less than the size of Saturn, but much larger than Earth. It was large enough to support a tremendous population. I hadn't bargained for anything so good.

I had only a vague plan to go by. I had made the journey in complete safety, and that was most important. My next move would depend on circumstances. I could dematerialize myself off the ship, and onto the planet. With an extreme expenditure of energy I could even take the remainder of my food supply with me.

But it didn't seem worth the effort. I had done all right so far by remaining quiet, and letting events occur as they would. I decided to see it through on the same basis. I stayed in the ship, and let it land.

That was not my first mistake, landing with the ship. If anything, the error began a thousand years earlier, in my infancy, the first night I saw the light of the moon. No one asked me to come. I did it voluntarily, for reasons my total personality found acceptable. In my own mind I added up the advantages in leaving Earth, and then schemed until I found a way to do it.

I had been dissatisfied with the way things were going among men. I objected to blood spilled uselessly. And so I had contrived an escape. Greener pastures? Not exactly. I don't like salads. Still the saying conveys something of the way I felt. Long before the ship landed it was too late, though I didn't know it.

The robot scurried about the saucer, chirruping mechanically and creaking. When it finished the duties it picked up the farmer, and carried him out. The man was still unconscious, but he began to scream.

Soon after it left, other robots came into the ship. Slightly different from the kind I had seen, they must have been repair robots. They went about tasks that were unfamiliar to me, and they talked.

This was new. I couldn't understand what they said until I

found the speech center of one, and let my mind reach out, lightly.

"A master says there is a stowaway on one of the ships."

It was unforeseen. Nothing I had encountered could detect my existence without registering on my consciousness. These *masters* were going to be tougher than humans. I waited while the other replied:

"Do they know what ship he's on?"

My robot waved a tentacle. "There are ten thousand ships here, each waiting for a checkover before reassignment. Would they bother to search each ship?"

"Physically, you mean?" asked the other. "No. They will take him off as the ship leaves."

Getting me off was going to take some doing, though the *masters* didn't know it. They may have gauged humans correctly, but they hadn't met me. Nevertheless I was uneasy.

"Why does he stay on the ship?" asked my robot.

The other chuckled. "Maybe he's changed his mind, and wants to go home. He'll be surprised when he learns where he's bound for."

I'll admit I panicked then—because a robot chuckled. It's not the friendly sound you might think. And also because of what it said. I had no intention of going home, but I liked to think I could if I wanted to. Now I saw that, due to their system of rotating assignments, it was next to impossible to determine which ship was going back to Earth. I made up my mind quickly.

Several things happened simultaneously. I dematerialized myself where I was, and rematerialized tenuously inside the robot. At the same time I took control of its motor and brain centers.

I forced it away from the job, and commanded it to go to the storage space where the last of my food was hidden. The other robot didn't notice. I surmised they didn't take orders from each other but from someone above. For the moment *I* was above.

Out of the ship we went, and into the confusion of the repair shops. Nothing but ships and robots, and I'd had enough of these.

I needed a hiding place to rest, and plan my forays against the creatures of this planet. I rummaged hurriedly through the robot brain, and learned that we were near the edge of a large city. Without cataloguing all the information I received,

I forced the robot through obscure alleys toward the open plain that surrounded the city.

It was cramped and uncomfortable inside the robot even though I didn't exist as solid matter. And I had to operate blind. I couldn't adjust my sight to that of the robot, and had to function once removed from reality, through its incomplete senses.

The last alley we entered ended on the open plain. The robot rolled down it—and stopped. I couldn't see what was in front of us, but I could guess—one of the creatures of the planet, the things that made the flying saucers. Without hesitation I directed the robot to attack.

It didn't.

Its refusal was not unexpected. They would have been quite insane to build robots without installing some safe-guards. It meant, however, that the next step was up to me. I took it.

I dematerialized out of the robot and rematerialized facing my antagonist. On the average it takes me a few microseconds to evaluate a foe, and find his weakness. I looked longer than that. It was the first time I had seen anything that could destroy at a glance my confidence in my own survival capacity.

And there was no weakness.

What I did then was not cowardice, it was pure survival, the reaction of a nervous system shocked to the limits of endurance. I dematerialized myself from where I stood and rematerialized far out on the open plain. Twice I repeated the process until the city was out of sight over the horizon. The creature didn't follow, though it could have done so easily enough—if it had wanted to.

I know my strength. On Earth it's the source of legends—the shadowy half-believed stories of werewolves and vampires. Fact and fancy mixed together to chill the minds and hearts of men. For myself, and others like me, it's a distinct advantage to have our existence doubted. A victim paralyzed with fear, too shocked and demoralized to cry out, is easier to subdue.

But the strength I was so confident of is meaningless here. Crouched in the shadow of the boulder, the only shade on the arid plain, it suddenly dawned on me that the creatures who rule this planet knew about me from the beginning, when I thought I was hidden. It amused them, I think.

I can't go back to the city and find the farmer. He's their meat. And I have limitations. I can't dematerialize myself off this planet. A few drops of fluid are left in the container with the Red Cross stamp on it, my last link with Earth.

I was born knowing the facts of *my* life. For a thousand years I've taken my food where and how I could get it. But these creatures are different, not only in body chemistry. They are tougher than Teflon skin and have hydrofluoric acid in their veins. I've always killed for food, but they—kill for pleasure. And their appearance exactly coincides with their character. I ought to know.

But there's one escape they forgot about, and I will take it. When they come hunting, they won't find me. Self-destruction is preferable to meeting those horrors face to face again.

*Robin Scott Wilson is the president of the University of California at Chico and co-founder (in 1968) of the Clarion Science Fiction Writer's Workshop for aspiring writers. After publishing approximately 20 short stories and editing three Clarion anthologies, he terminated his involvement with the conference and seems to have ceased writing. Or could it be he's simply been recording further adventures of the West Virginian junkman who debuts below?*

# THE JUNK MAN COMETH

## by Robin Scott Wilson

### I

One day late in June of '86, I was sitting on the veranda of the family home in Ard County, West Virginia, trying to match the rapidly diminishing figures in my checkbook against the printing bills beginning to come in for the campaign posters I'd orderd.

It was getting pretty obvious that there just wasn't going to be enough money for even a halfway adequate senatorial campaign. I'd been out stumping around the state in earnest for the previous two weeks and I was tired. My conscience was troubling me too; I'd been neglecting my share of the work in the family junk business.

All this was on my mind when we got a call from a junk

dealer over near Morgantown asking us to bid in on a load of Army surplus MHD generators he'd just picked up and claimed he couldn't handle. His asking price sounded pretty good; I was tired of worrying about my own problems, and I told Pop I'd run over to have a look.

"Old Jacobs is a shady character," warned Pop. "Don't let him sell you no pig in no poke."

I agreed to be cautious, pocketed the company checkbook and drove the thirty miles to Morgantown in the pickup. The front rotor was acting up, and it took me the best part of half an hour on those country roads to make the trip.

But it was worth it, or at least I thought so at first. Jacobs had the goods. Two hundred canisters with the factory seals on them, each painted olive-drab and stenciled with the model number and other nomenclature appropriate to the generators. I checked them against the catalogue listings, and at Jacobs' price I figured we could make a pretty neat profit on them. I wrote out a check for sixty of them and headed for home.

The next morning, my brother Buzzy decided that he needed a haircut and would take the carryall and two yard hands to pick up the canisters at Jacobs' yard on the way back. Along about noon, Buzzy's wife Phyllis stuck her head out of the kitchen door to holler at me in my alfresco office on the veranda. Phyllis had reproduced herself twice and Buzzy three times, and what with the kids constantly getting lost in the junk yard, she has developed a pretty fine voice for such a little woman.

"PERCE," she bellowed from not more than ten feet away. "WHEN YOU LOOK FOR BUZZY TO GET BACK?"

"I don't know, Phyllis," I said. "But I expect he heard you inquire after him wherever he is."

She lowered her voice a couple of hundred watts. "He left here before eight and he should have been back by now. I've got to take these kids into Morgantown for their shots at one o'clock."

I looked at my watch and heaved myself to my feet. "Maybe one of the rotors on the carryall gave out on him. I'll take the pickup and see if I can find him."

I backed the pickup out of its shed, skirted a pile of tangled and rusty reinforcing rod and pulled out toward the road. Pop was coming back from the mailbox, and he hopped aboard to come along for the ride.

About three miles beyond Carson's Corners we found the carryall and Buzzy. He was still alive, and Pop got on the pickup telephone to the Morgantown State Highway Patrol—even while I was stripping off Buzzy's shirt to see what I could do for him. The Patrol ductor arrived in minutes, and Pop rode off with Buzzy to the hospital. I stuck around with the Highway Patrol and tried to make some sense of the scene.

The evidence was confusing. Both men with Buzzy were dead. Old Ed Vickers was cut clean in two and the two halves of his body were a hundred yards apart. Billy White—at least we assumed it was Billy—was burned beyond recognition. The carryall itself lay on its side, blackened and crumpled. Under it lay the flattened remains of what had once been a white Jaguar XS convertible. Although from the time and the heading of the carryall it looked like Buzzy had been on his way back to the yard, he must not have made it to Jacobs' to pick up the generators; the carryall—or what was left of it—was empty, and there was no sign of cargo spilled out along the road.

The Patrol sergeant set his men to taking measurements and looking for skid marks. He shot a few photos and then stood scratching his head.

"It don't make no sense, Congersman Sansoni. It looks kinda like maybe your brother plowed into that there Jag-u-ar, I wouldn't thought it'd flip a big ol' carryall like that." He stooped to peer under the wrecked carryall. "And what happened to the party drivin' the Jag?"

I shook my head and shrugged. It didn't make any more sense to me. "I agree, Sergeant. And where did the fire come from? Both vehicles are cesium-powered. And what happened to poor old Vickers? What could have cut him up like that?"

It was the Sergeant's turn to shrug. "Damn'f I know. Guess we'll just have to wait and see what your brother's got to say." I looked away from the Sergeant and swallowed a pretty good-sized lump in my throat. Right then it didn't look as though Buzzy would ever be able to say much of anything again.

One of the principles which had guided my father, Albert Sansoni, to a highly successful career as a junk dealer was to *Keep the Stock Up*. Pop would buy anything if the price was right and the quantity meaningful, always confident that somebody, somewhere would someday pay him a higher price for it. Well, West Virginia real estate was cheap, and there was no shortage of boondocks to hold Pop's acquisitions. And of course he was right. There was always someone, somewhere.

Still, we used to kid the old man a lot. I remember Buzzy once saying that if Pop had a chance to buy up all of the old 1972 calendars in '73 for a song, he'd do it just in hopes that '72 would come back again someday and he could make a killing. Somehow, with Pop's luck, I wouldn't be surprised if he couldn't come out on a deal like that, somehow, with somebody, someday.

Pop applied his principle of *Keep the Stock Up* in raising Buzzy and me. Buzzy, who pretty well shares the old man's genius for mechanics, for combining useless junk into something highly salable, picked up degrees in metallurgy, mechanical engineering and physics. He fought against it those years in school, but Pop is pretty persuasive, and he kept Buzzy at it.

"You never know when you might need to know some of that stuff, Buzzy," he would say. "I never had no opportunity like you got, and you damn-well better make the best of it." Buzzy would sometimes argue back and plead and protest. But Pop finally put an end to the worst of these arguments with a blasted: "All right! You go ahead and marry Phyllis! But after your honeymoon, you get yourself back up to the college or I'll stomp the tar out'n you!"

Phyllis was the girl Buzzy had dated since he came back from the Sino-Sov war. "The college" at that time was MIT.

As for me, I'm two years older than Buzzy and a good deal more independent. While I didn't inherit much of the family's mechanical aptitude, I got a full measure of the old man's stubbornness. Along about high school, I got hooked on politics, played football and earned myself a law degree at the University of Virginia. I then spent two years at Oxford under the posthumous patronage of Cecil Rhodes and—after the war—came back to West Virginia to become the youngest congressman the 14th District had ever sent to Washington.

All this stretched Pop's utilitarian philosophy a good deal, but I guess he is not the only man who considers politicians a pretty useless form of life. Still, he made the best of it, gave me what financial support he could for my campaigns and was—I think—secretly a little proud of me.

I like politics, and I was a pretty good congressman. After three terms in the House, I was making serious plans to enter the senatorial race in '84, when I faced one of those situations which confronts every politician at one time or another. And maybe because of Pop or because of Cecil Rhodes or just because I am built that way, I acted according to my conscience—which can be a very expensive luxury in politics.

I won't go into the details, but after the dust had settled, I found myself still reasonably popular with the West Virginia electorate, but banished from public life by the West Virginia Party machine. My hopes for the senatorial nomination went glimmering, and my place on the congressional ballot went to an old Party hack from Green County. As a result, at thirty-four, former Congressman Percival Sansoni could be found almost any fine morning in the spring of 1986 sitting on the veranda of the family home, studying the most recent issue of the *Metals Reclamation Monthly*.

That's how it was that I found myself—for a while at least—back in the family business.

II

From the way he had looked when we had loaded him into the State Highway Patrol ductor for transport to the hospital, I thought for sure old Buzzy had had it. But Buzzy turned out lucky. He had some pretty bad burns, mostly on his back, but when I finally got in to see him the next day along with the Patrol investigator, he was more angry than injured.

"Boy, wait'll I get my hands on those bums!" Buzzy was lying on his stomach, his chest supported by a couple of pillows.

"Who do you mean, Mr. Sansoni?" asked the investigator. He had his recorder running.

"The hijackers! The guys that bushwhacked us!"

"Hijackers?" I echoed stupidly.

The investigator leaned forward from his chair to bring the microphone closer to Buzzy.

"Why don't you start at the beginning, Mr. Sansoni, and tell us what happened."

As Buzzy told it, greatly interspersed with profanity and clouds of cigar smoke, he'd gone into Morgantown that morning and gotten his haircut as planned. Then he had driven to Jacobs' yard, and he and Billy and Ed had loaded the MHD generators on the carryall. They headed for home then and were just topping the grade out of Carson's Corners, when

Buzzy spotted the Jaguar parked across the road, pretty well blocking it.

The investigator interrupted at this point. "What was your speed when you first spotted the Jag, Mr. Sansoni?"

"Ah hell, I couldn't have been doing more than one-ten, one-fifteen. We were pretty well loaded, and we'd just come up the grade."

As soon as Buzzy had seen the Jaguar, he'd reversed thrust, dropped the carryall down on the ground-effect shrouding and come to a stop about fifty yards on down the road from where the Jaguar had been.

"We rolled over that Jag like it wasn't even there, but I heard the forward rotors tear into it and drag it along, and I knew I'd burned up the shrouds skidding along like that. I was mad enough to spit nails."

"Was there anyone in the Jag?" asked the investigator.

"Hell no! And at first I figured some damn fool had just left it sitting there. Busted a rotor or run out of catalyst or something. Then I found out different."

Buzzy had dropped out of the cab, cursing, and started to work his way in through the ruined shrouding to take a look at the forward rotor, when there had been a flash and he heard a man scream—either Billy or Ed—he didn't know which. The next thing he knew the carryall was flipped over on its side, and there was fire everywhere. The last thing he remembered was a big piece of tattered shrouding, stinking of smoldering rubber and fiber, dropping down on top of him. It probably saved his life.

Buzzy was worn out with so much talk, and the doctor shooed us out of his room. In the hall, the investigator rewound his tape and shook his head, clucking to himself.

"We haven't had a case of hijacking in this county for twenty years. Your brother must have had a pretty valuable and tempting cargo."

I stopped short, and for the first time I began to realize just how little sense the whole thing made. "What's a Jaguar like that worth?" I asked.

"They run about ten thousand new, and that one was new."

"Then it doesn't make any sense," I said. "Whoever hijacked that cargo destroyed ten thousand dollars worth of ductor to do it and got sixty generators at a junk price of two hundred bucks apiece. They made two thousand dollars and killed two people doing it."

The investigator looked hard at me. "Maybe three. The Jaguar was registered to a woman in New York. She hasn't been heard of since she left Morgantown yesterday morning."

### III

Although I grew up in one of the biggest junk yards in the East, it never occurred to me until pretty recently to really *think* about junk. I read the other day where some archeologist was calling for Federal funds to make a national memorial out of a big junk yard up in Rhode Island. Claimed it was a treasure trove for future generations of archeologists, a "many-layered record of the achievements of our society." Conspicuous consumption and so forth.

Maybe so. But—until recently—I never entertained such elevated ideas about junk; and if the elections go the way I hope they will this fall, I don't expect to give the subject much consideration in the future.

My father, being both a very successful junk dealer for over thirty-five years and something of an original thinker by natural bent, has a well-developed philosophy of junk. I can picture Pop—a skinny, tough little man with bandy legs, a face like a geologist's map and two bright eyes behind thick spectacles—Pop expounding this philosophy in his rough West Virginia speech to Mom (before she died) or to one of the neighbors or to anyone who would drink a beer with him and listen.

"The thing you gotta realize about junk," he would begin, "is that ever'thin' in the world is junk to someone, while at the same time, they ain't nothin' in the world that ain't worth *somethin'* to someone somewheres. It all depends on your pointa view."

This statement would usually earn Pop a quizzical look from his listener, and practiced as he was in exposition, he'd take a long pull on his beer to let the full dramatic effect sink in before continuing with his theory.

"Now to show you what I mean, you take your *A*-rab oil millionaire with his fifty Cadillacs and two hunert wives and jools and all, settin' in his hot ol' tent just wishin' them slaves'd work them fans a little faster, and you send him a nice shiny fuel-oil stove right out'n the factory."

Pop would pause again and fix his listener with a piercing

eye. "Why it's junk, ain't it! Far's that *A*-rab's concerned, it about as useless as teats on a boar hog!"

Then Pop would lower his voice to a conspiratorial tone: "On t'other hand, you go on out in the yard there and dig up a couple them sorry old magnetic heat-exchangers and some of them cruddy surplus blowers, and you hook 'em together and give 'em a coat of paint and send 'em off to that old *A*-rab, and he's gonna be *some kinda* happy! I know, 'cause I done it already."

After this, Pop would sit back as if exhausted from the force of his argument and suck down whatever was left of his beer. Then, if he was talking to me or to my brother Buzzy, he'd add some shrewd observation on the business of being a junk dealer as part of his continuing program which was intended to prepare us to take over the business from him someday.

As he talked he would sweep his arm comprehensively around the fifteen acres of crowded yard, taking in the old ground-effect cars, the rusting industrial machinery, the hulks of surplus military equipment, the rows of factory-reject appliances, the piles of bent ductor fans, the rolls of wire and heaps of industrial scrap, the stacks of crated electronic gear, the million and one bits and pieces which lay oxidizing quietly—each element in its own sure way—in the hot West Virginia sun.

IV

That night, after the Patrol investigator's interview with Buzzy, Phyllis cooked supper for the kids and Pop and me and then went off to spend the evening with Buzzy. Pop and I sat in the warm summer darkness out on the veranda, drinking beer and watching each other flip cigarette butts over the rail. There was a big, fat, lazy moon rising off the end of the airstrip, its yellow light silhouetting the steel spires and crags of the yard. The old M-70 tank Pop had stripped to bulldoze with looked like a war memorial. In fact the whole yard looked like a battle field in the moonlight, torn by shot and shell. During the day, with the bright wink of cutting torches, the raucous whine of the yard machinery, the squeals of Buzzy's kids as they clambered like mountain goats on the piles of scrap, the yard was a cheerful place. I'd grown up in that junk, and I knew what a wonderful fairyland it was for kids.

But at night, silent and deserted, the yard looked like a place where giants had wrestled, where great issues had been decided at high cost, leaving the wasted detritus conflict always brings.

Pop heaved his empty beer can out into the darkness. For a man of sixty, Pop can still heave pretty far. It took a long time for the distant clatter to come back to us. He peeled the top off another and propped his feet on the veranda rail. "Perce?" he said.

"Yeah, Pop."

"I run this yard more'n thirty-five years now. Ain't never been nobody hurt workin' for me here—until yesterday anyways."

"Yeah, I know, Pop. But it wasn't your fault."

Pop sighed and was silent for a moment. Then he snapped his chair back on the floor from its tilted position and stamped angrily to his feet.

"Listen, son. Ever'thin' about this yard is my fault! Somebody gits hurt workin' for me, I'm damn-well gonna find out why! I'm gonna git them bums that done it to Buzzy and Ed and Billy!"

"Now take it easy, Pop. That's what the police are for—"

"Police, hell! They ain't never gonna figure it out. They ain't even figured out *how* them hijackers managed to tip over a forty-five-ton carryall and burn it up thataway, much less *who* done it!"

"Or for that matter," I added, musing, "why?"

"What do you mean, 'why'?" Pop's voice grew quieter. "They was hijackin', wasn't they? Stealin' Buzzy's cargo!"

I shook my head in the darkness. "It doesn't add up, Pop. Why would anybody go to all that trouble, smash up a ten-thousand-dollar car, wreck a carryall and kill two men, just to get sixty surplus MHD generators worth maybe two-fifty apiece, tops?"

That stopped the old man for a minute. Another empty clattered in the darkness, and the flare of a match illuminated the old man's face, his heavy white brows drawn together in thought, his lined and seamed face etched with concern. Pop looks like an old white-haired Indian when he's worried about something. Other times he looks like a skinny Santa Claus.

"Perce, like I always say, the value of junk depends on how much somebody wants it. Them generators ain't worth more'n two-fifty to you and me, but somebody else must've wanted 'em pretty bad."

"Granted, Pop," I said. "But the surplus catalogues are full of brand-new generators. The government over-procured on them when it looked like that South Africa business was going to get nasty, and now they're all over the place. Maybe the guys who bushwhacked Buzzy would've had to pay three or four hundred for them—I got a pretty good bargain out of Jacobs—but they sure as hell didn't have enough to justify stealing them and killing people."

That stopped Pop again, but only for a minute. "What'd you say you paid old man Jacobs for them generators?" There was a note of excitement in his voice.

"Two hundred."

"And they was new? Factory-sealed?"

"The one I inspected was."

"One. You only looked at one?" Pop's voice held a familiar note of accusation.

"Heck, Pop. The others were all in sealed canisters. What would have been the point of—"

"Perce, I done told you to watch that Jacobs. He's a sharp one. He wouldn't let you have them generators for no two hundred bucks if there wasn't somethin' wrong somewheres." He snapped his fingers. "Sure, that's it. You bought yourself one surplus MHD generator *and fifty-nine somethin' elses!*"

I was chagrined. I knew what Pop said made sense, and maybe I *had* been taken. Somewhat sheepishly I said: "I suppose you're right, Pop. I guess I'm lucky I didn't take all two hundred of them."

Pop exploded. "You mean he had more of them at that price. Why in the name of heaven didn't you clean him out?"

"But Pop! If he was cheating me, it's a good thing I didn't!"

Pop was halfway down the veranda stairs when he turned back to inquire, "How many times I gotta tell you, Perce, *Keep the Stock Up!*"

## V

I took off after him. There was something wrong in the logic of Pop's argument, but I didn't care to pursue it further. He was headed for the shed with the pickup, and I ran after him. I knew where he was going. If what I had bought weren't two-hundred-and-fifty-dollar government-surplus MHD generators, *what were they?*

Were they—perhaps unknown to Jacobs—something valuable enough to kill for, as someone had quite obviously done? The answer just might lie on Jacobs' loading platform, where—forty-eight hours before—I'd seen two hundred of the now mysterious canisters standing in neatly serried ranks.

Pop beat me to the shed and backed the pickup out into the yard. He jumped down then and disappeared into the house, reappearing moments later with his arms full of weapons he'd salvaged at one time or another from junked military equipment and put into working order just for the hell of it. Pop didn't even own a hunting license, but he had enough death and destruction in his arms to outfit a banana-republic constabulary.

There was a BAR of World War II vintage, old but oiled and gleaming. There was a 55mm bazooka of somewhat later date, a fairly new lazgun, one of the high-frequency types like I'd used in Australia ten years before, and a 75-shot officer's-issue carbine which was still standard in the Army. He dumped his load with a clatter in the bed of the pickup and dove back into the house to reappear in a moment with a crate of bazooka shells, a couple of hundred rounds for the BAR and two spare power packs for the lazgun. He dumped his load in on top of the weapons and climbed up into the seat next to me in the cab. He wasn't even breathing hard.

I went to full thrust and negotiated the lane leading to the Morgantown road at top speed before I said anything. When we'd settled down to a nice even one-fifty, I shouted to Pop above the whine of the rotors: "Hey Pop! What's all the armament for? You got enough there for an army!"

Pop struck a match on the pickup door and swallowed a cloud of cigarette smoke. "Perce, you seen what a mess that carryall was and what they done to Ed and Billy—"

He didn't have to say anything more. I knew what the

weapons were for, and I was glad Pop had thought to bring them.

We sat in silence during the twenty-minute drive to Morgantown. The town was deserted; it was nearly midnight. Once through and on the other side, we whipped down the grade to Carson's Corners, where Buzzy had been waylaid the day before, and took the turn into Jacobs' access road with rotors whining and the outboard shrouding scraping clouds of dust from the dirt road.

The Jacobs yard was dark, but there was plenty of moonlight, enough to reveal the empty loading platform.

"They're gone, Pop. He must have sold them to someone else."

"Yeah." There was disappointment in Pop's voice. "But let's us talk to the old bum. Maybe we can shake outa him what was in them canisters."

I parked the pickup, and we walked up to the dark shed that was old Jacobs' combined bachelor quarters and office. Pop banged on the door, but there was no flare of light or answering stream of profanity. I left Pop on the front porch and walked around to the rear. Jacobs' yard wasn't anywhere near as big as ours; according to Pop, he specialized in junked ductors, making a good living out of reclaiming cesium oxide and now and again taking on a hot vehicle for illicit resale. Still, the same moon that shone on our yard shone on Jacobs', and there was the same sense of desolation and look of ended conflict in Jacobs' shadowed junk piles.

The illusion of a battlefield was heightened by Jacobs himself—as I found him that night behind his home. Or at least pieces of him. I don't know if they ever found all of him. There was enough, though, once I sorted it out from the blackened ruins of his pickup truck. There was a head and most of an arm still in the smashed cab. The rest was pretty widely distributed.

I threw up and then shouted for Pop. He's a tough old bird, Pop, but he got sick too when he saw what I was looking at. The empty platform and the carnage behind the house didn't leave much doubt as to what had happened. I still don't buy the hijacker theory, but I walked around the pickup and pulled the lazgun out of the clutter in the bed and strapped it on anyway.

I rejoined Pop, who was rather futilely trying to cover up

what was left of Jacobs with a piece of tarpaulin. He'd have needed several hundred square feet to have done the job properly.

"I guess we better give the Highway Patrol a call," I said.

"Yeah," said Pop. "But let's us look around a little bit first. Old Jacobs wasn't the sort to put all his eggs in one basket. There may be some more of them canisters stuck around here somewheres."

Pop got a flashlight out of the pickup, and we went hunting. After a quarter of an hour we found them, twenty of them, standing stacked two-high in the little shed Jacobs had used as his workshop.

"These like the ones you bought?" Pop gestured with his flashlight.

"Yes. Identical as far as I can see."

Pop bent to examine the canisters more closely. "They ain't Army canisters, Perce. I ain't never seen none like this before. Looky here. Look at this sealing band."

I looked and then realized I'd never seen a seal like that before either, except maybe for the sixty I'd bought the other day, when I hadn't really examined them closely.

"But Pop, it's stenciled right on them: 'ONE EA MHD GEN MOD 2 MARK IV U.S. ARMY DELPHOS DEPOT.' "

Pop directed the flashlight at the wall above Jacobs' workbench. There hung a stencil with yellow paint:

VI KRAM 2 DOM NEG DHM
AE ENO
YMRA .S.U
TOPED SOHPLED

"Old crook—rest his soul—sold you ringers, all right."

I went for the pickup and backed it up to the door of the workshop. We shifted our arsenal into the cab and loaded all twenty canisters onto the truck bed. It was hot work; each canister weighed the best part of three hundred pounds, and when we were finished the rear shrouding was belled out against the ground.

We got ready to leave, and the thought hit me. "Hey Pop, wait a minute! Last couple of times somebody tried to truck these canisters around, they got chopped into little pieces. Maybe we better think a bit."

Pop didn't hesitate. "You might be right, son. But we can't

do nothin' with these babies here, and maybe the guys that got old Jacobs will figure the same as we did and come back to see if there's any more."

I looked around the dark yard and shivered. Pop had a point. He fired the turbine and opened the door for me to climb into the cab beside him.

"No, Pop. You drive, and I'll ride shotgun in the back." Pop shrugged in that comical way he has when he's really under pressure.

"Okay. Choose your weapon, son."

I pulled the BAR out of the pile and took the belt of ammo he handed me. "Keep your eyes peeled, son."

I climbed in back and settled myself among the canisters. "You too, Pop."

I wanted to look brave and nonchalant, and I poked a cigarette in my mouth with the kind of tough-guy gesture I'd seen on 3-D. But my lighter was out of gas, and I had to be content to perch on the canisters looking every bit as frightened as I felt.

The rotors roared, and the heavily laden truck moved off onto the highway. We went through Carson's Corners wide open and whined up the grade outside of town at top speed. Once we passed the point where Buzzy had been bushwhacked, I began—foolishly—to breathe easier. Then we were in Morgantown, and Pop had to drop down to sixty-five to make some of the turns in town. Once again in open country, he really opened her up. I was beginning to think we were home free, when something large and dark appeared a few hundred feet above the moonlit road behind us, blotting out a segment of stars.

I started to shout a warning into the wind, but by that time Pop had spotted the tank-truck blocking the road ahead, and he reversed thrust and slewed off onto the berm. The heavy truck sat down hard on its shrouding, skidded crazily, and clipped a couple of small pines, but Pop managed to wrestle it off the road and bring it to a stop to one side of the stalled oil truck. I caught a glimpse of the driver's body, mangled and torn, lying half out of the open cab door.

Now clearly visible, the black shape—something like a flattened teardrop—slowed. A bright spot glowed high on its prow, and the tops of the pines along the road burst into flame. The beam from the strange craft swept across the oil truck. There was a massive blast and a wave of heat, and thick black billows of smoke began to pour across the road into the thicket which concealed us.

I shouted at the top of my lungs: "Take off, Pop! The smoke'll screen us." Hoping Pop would think I was still aboard, I rolled silently off the truck bed, the BAR cradled in my arms, and flopped to the ground. I opened up with the BAR. It was no match for whatever it was that had burned up the tank truck and the trees around us, but I figured it might give Pop enough cover to get away.

The BAR whacked away, although I had trouble keeping it elevated enough to bring the wavering stream of tracers onto the black ship. I heard the whine of rotors as Pop slid the pickup through the burning thicket and back up onto the road behind the burning oil. Then I came to the end of the belt, and I wished I had that 55 bazooka that was now—hopefully—rolling away from me at well over a hundred MPH. But I didn't. I pulled the lazgun and crackled away at the black shape now hovering closer and closer over me, and I thought of Pop and Buzzy and Phyllis and the kids and Oxford and the election and the girl I'd almost married, when I first went down to Washington in '78.

And then I don't remember any more. Not a thing.

## VI

The first thing I became aware of—how much later I don't know—was the fact that I was lying flat on my back, my head elevated from the hard surface under me by a lump on the back of my head the size of a turkey egg. It hurt like hell, and I rolled my head to one side to ease the pain. There was a quick rustling sound not far away, and I opened my eyes, expecting—I guess—to see some starchy nurse and maybe Buzzy on the next bed.

But it wasn't a hospital. Or if it was, I was blind. I contemplated that thought for a while and found little comfort in it. Then my other senses came into play, and I realized that hospitals don't smell of chlorine and hospital beds are not entirely constructed of cold, hard metal.

I sat up, eyes straining in the blackness, and there was another rustle, a frantic scuttling sound which my imagination quickly translated into something horrible. I was scared, and I sat motionless for a long while, breathing as quietly as I

could. There were no more rustlings, but I could hear something else breathing, something breathing in short, shallow
gasps, like a wounded animal.

*Something,* I thought, *with a high metabolism rate.*

*I should stay put,* I thought. *Nothing has hurt me yet,* I
thought.

And even as I thought it, my curiosity got the better of me.
Or maybe it was the fact that I can't stand fear and uncer-
tainty and prefer almost any resolution, even an unfavorable
one, to continuing in doubt. I stretched out a hand in the
darkness before me and touched something round and soft
and warm which seemed to shrink away from me with much
rustling and an intake of breath.

I checked the sensation of that touch against the card file of
touches every man has in his head and very quickly identified it.

"I beg your pardon, Madam," I said. "Could you be good
enough to tell me where we are?"

There was a gasp, much rustling, a fumble of arms around
my neck, and I found a sobbing girl pressing her head against
my chest. Her hair smelled good.

"Oh thank God! Thank God! I thought you were one of
them." The girl shuddered in revulsion.

I held her tightly until her sobbing stopped. Then, as if
suddenly aware of me as an individual and not just a pleas-
anter alternative to "them," she pulled away, and I heard more
rustling. There was the snap of a purse and the frustrated
rattle of lipstick and mirror. "Damn," she said. "I must look
awful." She sniffed once or twice as women do, when wiping
their eyes.

"I think you look just fine," I said, gallantly ignoring the
fact that we were in utter darkness. "Do you have any idea
where we are?"

"In their ship—I think."

"A big black job, kind of a flattened teardrop shape?"

"Uh huh." She slid over against me again and fumbled for
the security of my hand.

"How long have you been here?" I asked.

"I don't know. It seems forever. Since Wednesday morning,
however long ago that was."

I began to put two and two together. "You own a white
Jaguar?"

"Yes! How did you know?"

I told her about Buzzy and the carryall, about Jacobs and the canisters and our attempt to get what was left of them back to our yard.

"These canisters," she said when I had finished, "are they round, with rounded ends, like maybe sleeping-powder capsules?"

"Yes. That's a good description. But they're about the size of three fifty-gallon oil drums laid end to end."

"That explains it then. They can't talk, at least not so you can understand them, but they kept drawing pictures. I didn't understand what they wanted, but they drew a lot of pictures of those capsule-shaped things." The girl withdrew her hand—to gesture with I guess.

We sat in silence for a while, and some of the awesomeness of our situation began to sink in on me. Funny, you can talk blithely about creatures from outer space, about spaceships and first contact, and other esoteric matters. The reality is a hell of a lot more mundane, and its most striking aspect is more than that most simple and basic of human emotions: fear.

And then the girl told me how she had been driving along the Morgantown road, when the ship had appeared above her and settled on the road before her. She had stopped; a hatchway had opened in the side of the ship, and the next thing she had known, she had been lying in darkness, sliding about on the metal floor of our prison as the ship apparently went through violent maneuvers.

"There's light sometimes. Not much, a dim, red light, but enough to see by. They showed me their silly pictures, but I didn't understand them. Once they handed me the tablet and a funny-kind of pencil thing, and I wrote my name over and over again, but all they did was waggle their arms at each other and draw more capsules and meaningless pictures.

"Then it was dark and then it was that funny kind of dim red light again. And there was a lot of flying around. Three times since I came here."

"That would have been the attacks on Buzzy, on old man Jacobs and on Pop and me."

"But if what they want is those capsules—canisters—why didn't they just go get them from that man's junk yard? Why did they have to wreck your brother's carryall and kill that man and go after you and your father?"

I thought a bit. "I don't know, Miss . . ."

"Berenson. My name is Claudia Berenson."

". . . I don't know, Miss Berenson. Maybe it has something to do with the blackness in here. Maybe they can't see by the kind of light we see by. Maybe they can't tell where the canisters are until they're in motion, or something."

We were silent again for a moment. Miss Berenson—Claudia—snuggled up close to me again, and I put a protective arm around her. She could have been any age, in the darkness, and ugly as sin. But from what I could feel and the sound of her voice, I had a hunch she was no old crone.

Then, as much because we were afraid as anything else, we started to talk, to tell each other about ourselves. She told me what it was like to be a fashion buyer for a big chain of women's stores, about how her brother had died during the Australian campaign, about going to school in Albany, New York, about her first date and how funny it had been, about the apartment she shared with two other twenty-five-year-olds in Manhattan, about her unhappy love affair in '84.

Darkness is a wonderful aid to confession, and I found myself talking about Australia and Oxford and the Party and the junk business and about my unhappy affair with Julia in Washington, and I discovered all of a sudden that talking about Julia didn't hurt anymore. Despite the mystery and threat of our strange meeting, I found myself cheered at the absence of old pain and the promise of . . . something new.

I was almost disappointed when the dim red lights suddenly came to life. As my eyes adjusted I was able to see what our prison consisted of. We occupied a kind of transparent bubble enclosing a roughly hemispherical space, perhaps a dozen feet across at its widest point.

It looked like it had been jury-rigged from some sort of plastic material just to contain us; I could see where the edges of the bubble were crudely but effectively fused against the deck, against what I took to be the outer wall of the ship and against a rear transverse bulkhead. A cylindrical duct a few inches across led from the bubble to the ceiling, bringing sweet West Virginia summer air into us and offsetting the stench of chlorine.

The space into which our bubble intruded conformed roughly to the forward half of the flattened teardrop ship, I had last seen hovering over the Morgantown road. Perhaps thirty feet at its widest and sixty feet long, it tapered from a rounded prow back to the flat bulkhead, separating, I supposed, the crew's living and control area from that portion of the ship containing its drive mechanism and whatever cargo space could now be presumed to contain all but twenty of old man Jacobs' two hundred and twenty canisters.

There were no windows or ports, but a row of flickering screens on the inner side of the curved prow gave a curiously distorted picture of woodland and hill. The ship—if the screens were correct—seemed to be nestled into one of the wilder groves that dot the northern West Virginia countryside.

All of this, of course, I observed in detail later. My attention was initially riveted on the four figures now climbing down from crude wirelike racks suspended from the ceiling of the craft. Claudia shuddered beside me, and I gathered that these were "them."

I couldn't blame her for shuddering. They looked pretty bad, and I wouldn't have found them substantially more appealing even had I known they were all registered voters in the 14th district. Maybe eight or nine feet tall, they were vaguely human in that there was a recognizable head and trunk. But there the resemblance ceased.

There were far too many arms and legs, and each was tipped with a writhing collection of small, pulpy tentacles. These "fingers" and "toes" seemed to obey their owner's commands to grasp a stanchion or turn a dial, but when their services were not otherwise engaged, they danced and waved with a weird life of their own. It was hard to tell colors in the red light, but our wriggling captors seemed to be covered with some sort of hard, chitinous material, its shimmering surface broken only by two slashes of bright clothlike stuff, one draped across the chest and another bound about the uppermost "arm" on the left side. There is a kind of universal principle of clothing, and I would have bet my chances of ever getting out of there that one chunk of cloth indicated rank or status and the other covered whatever passed for pudenda among our chitinous friends.

As a sometime lawyer, I am not unschooled in the rules of evidence, the logical process of putting two and two together to make four, twenty-two, or 1,111, as the case and the nature of the jury demanded. Hence I was puzzled by the great discrepancy between the physical conformation of our captors and the ship and its outfitting. The chairs in front of the screens at the prow of the ship were man-sized, not "thing"-sized; there was a contour couch visible to us, and the contour was not that of a "thing."

So far as I could tell, the switches and knobs, the door handles and lock mechanisms, the height of various indicating instruments all seemed designed for some creature other than the "things." Specifically, it looked like the mysterious ship had been—or was designed to be—occupied by a two-legged two-armed biped, like, say, you or me. I puzzled over this for a bit. And then two and two added up to suggest that the "things" had not come by their ship honestly. I filed this assumption for future use.

## VII

My ruminations came to an end. One of our captors donned a transparent helmet, for all the world like an inverted fishbowl, and slipped his uppermost arms and one leg through a harness containing what must have been gas bottles of some sort. He passed out of our field of vision through a hatchway in the rear bulkhead and reappeared a moment later through a lock mechanism leading into our bubble from the same bulkhead, bringing with him a puff of chlorine. We coughed and choked for a moment until the lock had closed behind him. Claudia skittered behind me, as I rose to meet him. There was none of that "take me to your leader" business. Instead our visitor gave out with a scratching, whistling noise—like a fingernail across a blackboard—and looked at me expectantly with several wide-set, many-faceted eyes. When neither of us reacted to his greeting with a similar sound, he gave an unmistakable shrug—a gesture which also must be well nigh universal, but one which is formidable when performed by a column of three shoulders. Then came the tablet and pencil.

First there was a picture of the ship and under it a series of curved symbols unlike anything I'd ever seen. The thing in the helmet pointed to the ship with one set of bunched tentacles and drew another bunch, stiffly gathered into a pointer, across the line of symbols.

"Wheeskrick," it said.

I bowed slightly, stabbed a forefinger at my chest and said, "Percival Sansoni."

The Wheeskrick chattered and whistled and handed me the tablet and scriber. I'd read a lot of science fiction and I figured I knew just what to do. I drew a circle and ten smaller circles in orbit around it. With an air of triumph and a proud eye cast toward Claudia, I placed a large X through the third circle out from the center.

The Wheeskrick whistled and squeaked again, took the tablet and scriber from me with two jellyfishlike tentacles and lashed me a good one across the chops with a third. The language lesson was over, and he was impatient with my attempts at rudimentary cosmography.

I staggered back before him, mindful of the girl beside me and the necessity for belting him one in return. But I didn't know where to start in, and anyway, he was busy scribbling again. It was another picture of the black, flattened-teardrop ship, this time with a jagged hole in its side and little black Wheeskricks unloading canisters from a hatchway onto a neat stack under what was quite clearly a tree.

The Wheeskrick chittered and whistled; the picture disappeared and was replaced with another displaying a crudely drawn man loading canisters onto a carryall, while behind a straight line, apparently representing the side of the ship, four Wheeskricks lay supine in complex wire racks. I began to get the picture.

The Wheeskrick manipulated something on the tablet, and the picture disappeared again; he began to draw another: a carryall lying on its side, crumpled but recognizable, and two Wheeskricks loading canisters into their ship. Off to one side, the Wheeskrick painstakingly drew two stacks of canisters, each stack twenty-one canisters long and five high. He blacked in the last four rows of five with his stylus—the twenty canisters not yet recovered.

Whistling and screeching, he drew another series of inexplicable symbols under the twenty blackened canisters and translated them for me by reaching out with his middle-right-hand arm and belting me again, this time hard enough to knock me up against the inner surface of our bubble prison. Without so much as a parting whistle, he wheeled on three feet, tucked his tablet under his upper left-hand arm and exited through the lock, leaving us once again gasping and choking in the fumes of the atmosphere he entered.

Claudia knelt beside me and crooned over me, and although I wasn't really hurt by the Wheeskrick's blow, I groaned a little bit for effect. The dim light was perfectly sufficient to show me—besides the nature of our prison, the reaches of the interior of the Wheeskrick ship and the creeping horror of the Wheeskricks themselves—the delightful fact that Claudia Berenson was a real looker, the kind of girl men dream about crooning over them when they have fallen honorably (and not fatally) on the field of combat.

But that wasn't getting us out of there. I stopped groaning, sat up and started thinking. The Wheeskrick's pictures had been pretty clear. So had his blows. Old man Jacobs must have stumbled on the Wheeskrick's cargo, when they had off-loaded it to repair some trouble in their ship. He'd swiped it during one of the sleep periods, sold it the way he sold other hot goods—quickly and cheaply—and now the Wheeskricks were doing all they could to recover it.

I began to get curious about what was in those canisters, more curious than I had been before. Whatever it was, though, it was amply clear that the Wheeskricks wanted it back, wanted those other twenty canisters and were prepared to knock me around until they found out where they were.

Well hell! They could have them. They'd cost too many human lives already. The problem was, how do you let go of a tiger when he has you by the tail?

Claudia had been thinking too. She had been in our cage a lot longer than I, with nothing to eat or drink, and there was a note of panic in her voice.

"All they seem to want are their silly canisters. Can't you tell them where they are? Maybe they'll let us go then."

I thought about the possibility. Then I thought about what they had done to Ed and Billy and to the old man, Jacobs, and what they might do if they got to Pop's junk yard. I'd seen a lot of killing in Australia, some of it performed with the casual inefficiency of the aborigines, but nothing to rival the way old man Jacobs had looked. Or Ed Vickers.

I shook my head. "I don't think they'd let us go. I think we're like some kind of annoying wildlife to them; I think they'd as soon kill us as look at us. Those missing twenty canisters are the only reason you and I are alive now."

"But what can we *do?*" The panic in Claudia's voice advanced a half a dozen spaces toward "go."

"I don't know," I said. "Let me think."

While I was thinking, Claudia sat with her head back against the bubble, too frightened to sleep, too weary to look about her any more. I tested the walls, probing at the transparent plastic with my penknife. They were slightly flexible, and I could penetrate the surface with my knife. But all I got for my pains was a whiff of chlorine, and I realized that we'd suffocate long before I could chop a hole big enough to let us escape. And even then, we would escape only into the Wheeskrick's chlorine-filled control room.

In the meantime, our captors were busy. One of them cycled his way out through a lock in the wall opposite our cage—his helmet and gas cylinders in place—while two others busied themselves assembling dozens of small tripod affairs, each a hand high and two hands across the base. When they had finished, the two went back through the after bulkhead and reappeared with one of the canisters. One by one they tested the tripods by waving each toward the canister. There were bright blips on the screen before the fourth Wheeskrick.

An hour after he had left, the Wheeskrick with the helmet returned, a struggling calf in his arms. The Wheeskricks dragged the strangling animal over to our bubble and proceeded to disassemble it before our eyes. I had a sobbing girl, her head buried in my shoulder again, to contend with. The obvious instructional session of the Wheeskricks was not lost on me, and I began to think even harder.

But I didn't come up with anything. Not for a while. There was another sleep period of complete darkness and another period of dim red light, during which three of the four Wheeskricks disappeared through the outer lock, their arms loaded with the little tripod detection devices.

I could see what would lie ahead; I'd watched men break in Australia. There would be hunger and—judging from what had already occurred—some more abuse. Then would come the time when they'd start in on Claudia, maybe like the calf, and I'd begin to think that perhaps if I started doing some fancy drawing on their tablet for them they'd let us go and maybe not hurt Buzzy and Phyllis and the kids and Pop. Just take their damn canisters and go. That's what I'd begin to think after a while, and I knew I'd be wrong. The dim red light winked out for the second time, and I thought even harder.

I had long since assayed my pockets and found nothing other than some loose change, my penknife, and my fuel-less lighter. I gave Claudia a try.

"What do you have in your purse?"

"Why . . . I don't know. A few dollars, my comb, some cosmetics."

"Dump it out," I said, "and tell me item by item what's in it."

There was a clatter, like a slot machine paying off, and Claudia began to finger her possessions in the blackness to identify them.

"Let's see. There's a comb, lipstick, mirror, . . . uh . . . four, no *five* bobby pins, compact, eye pencil, one, two, three, four, five, six . . . six coins, a can of hairspray, billfold, a couple of . . . uh . . . stamps, I guess, a box of aspirin tablets, car keys, apartment keys, nail file, a screw thingumajiggy out of my radio that I've got to get a new one of, subway pass, handkerchief, two . . . three coughdrops, master credit card, and . . ." Claudia broke off.

"And what?" I asked. I should have known better.

"Uh . . . a box of . . . uh . . . contraceptive pills."

"Oh," I said.

It didn't look like a very promising collection, but I added it to my mental assay of my own pockets, and we lapsed into silence.

Then I had it. It was a long shot. I didn't know if it would work, or if it did, whether we would survive it or not. But I remembered that calf and old man Jacobs and Ed Vickers, and I figured it was worth the chance.

The dim red light came on again, and the Wheeskricks began to clamber down from their wire perches. I pulled Claudia to her feet.

"Pull your collar up around your ears and stand up as close to the outside wall as you can." I thought a moment and stripped my jacket off and draped it over her head. "I'm going to try to blow us out of here, and if it works, get a good lung full of air and get to that outer lock as fast as you can. I think the top button makes it open."

She nodded dumbly and did as she was bid. I watched the Wheeskricks. One of them had donned his fishbowl and tanks and was headed back toward the entrance to our bubble.

I fished the can of hairspray from Claudia's purse and depressed the plunger on top. The small bubble began to fill with scent and with finely atomized particles of highly flammable lacquer. I heard the inner lock door start to open just as the spray can fizzed out of gas. I joined Claudia at the wall, fished my fuelless lighter from my pocket, held it as far behind my back as I could, shouted "Hold your breath!" and thumbed the striker.

There was a whoosh of flame and a thumping explosion. The entering Wheeskrick never knew what hit him. The plastic walls of our prison blew out like an overinflated balloon, and the shirt sleeve over my right arm burned with a merry flame. I ignored it and propelled Claudia before me through the ruptured bubble toward the outer lock.

One of the Wheeskricks brushed past us, headed to aid his colleague in the ruined bubble lock, confident that his buddy— who was approaching us as only a nine-foot, six-legged Wheeskrick can—would make short work of me. I was pretty confident he could too, but I figured Claudia, at least, might make it. The fourth Wheeskrick never budged from his position in front of the detection screens, which shows the relative priority the Wheeskricks put on recovering the rest of those canisters.

Claudia reached the outer lock, hammered the uppermost button with her fist, and the door started to swing inward. I was making full speed toward her, my lungs bursting and eyes streaming from the chlorine, when a tentacled limb caught me on my burned right arm and the massive weight of the Wheeskrick brought me up short. I let his pull swing me in a short arc, and I brought my left fist around in an old-style haymaker, knuckle out, aimed for the center of the patch of yellow cloth on the Wheeskrick's chest. If Sansoni's Universal Theory of Clothing was wrong, I would do him little damage. You may wound a soldier in his pride if you shoot him in the epaulette, but you really stop him if you get him in the pants.

The theory proved correct. There was agonized screeching and whistling and I tore myself loose from his writhing grasp and leapt the last few feet to the open door of the lock. Claudia slammed the door behind me; the pumps cycled swiftly, and we lay gasping and choking in the sweet after-noon air. I was dizzy, but I figured the Wheeskricks couldn't open the inner lock door until the outer was closed, at least not for a while, and with the last of my strength I ripped one of Claudia's shoes off her foot and wedged its heel into the crack between the outer door and its jamb. I wanted to make sure that door stayed open until we felt like leaving there.

# VIII

We lay gasping and retching for several minutes in the mouth of the strange ship's airlock, and then it occurred to me that the Wheeskricks would soon be out after us. They had helmets and gas bottles, and no doubt there was some way of getting that inner door open without closing the outer one.

"Come on, Claudia, we've got to get out of here."

Claudia choked, slipped her other shoe off and slid with me over the lip of the lock and dropped the three or four feet to the ground. We'd taken only two or three steps toward the dense woods which surrounded the Wheeskrick ship when a bright pencil of light sprang from somewhere above and behind us and a fresh, green juniper a few inches before my nose burst into flame. I pulled Claudia back into the shadowed swell of the ship's flank.

"Looks like they don't want us to leave," I said. Claudia began to sob quietly. I felt a little like it myself. It looked as if we had jumped splendidly out of the frying pan and into the fire. I slid down beside Claudia on the grass, threw a welldone right arm around her quaking shoulders and started to think again.

I thought very hard. *We take three steps out of the shadow of the ship where their damn screens can pick us up, and ZAP, they burn us down. We wait here, and they'll come out after us, and this time—outside the ship—they won't be shy about using their weapons.*

We were damned if we did and damned if we didn't.

Then I remembered something out of OCS. The old, grizzled infantry officer who lectured us: "If you find yourself on foot against an enemy tank, the safest place to be is up on the tank. They can't get you there but there is always a chance you can get them."

I pulled Claudia to her feet and then in best platoon-leader style said: "Follow me!" We skirted around the swelling of the ship toward the rear, where the teardrop diminished to a series of blackened tubes, apparently the business end of the ship's drive mechanism. I boosted Claudia ahead of me, up the tube mouths, until we were both on hands and knees on the pitted upper surface of the ship. I could see the slightly elevated turret from which the ship's lazbeams were projected, but even if their basic sensor system was in the same turret, they would not dare fire at us without running the risk of scorching their own tail.

We advanced on the turret. I rather cavalierly swatted Claudia on the fanny when she let it elevate too much; we would be far ahead if we could take them by surprise. After a hundred feet of abrasive crawling we had reached the turret, and I could see the objectives of the ship's sensors. There were six of them, each—I would suppose—with a sixty-degree coverage of the area around the ship. We kept low, beneath the muzzles of the lazbeam projectors, and I pulled that precious, junk-laden purse from Claudia's shoulder. There was a lipstick, and it was only a moment's work to obscure the objectives of the ship's eyes with a thick, greasy layer of the stuff. Like Pop says, one man's junk is another man's salvation.

We took the quick way down, sliding and scraping across the sharp prow and dropping the last eight or ten feet to the grass of the clearing. We didn't pause. Three leaps and we were on the verge of the woods. Another scrub crackled into flame a yard away, and I turned to see one of the Wheeskricks in the lock entrance, a weapon in his hand. We ran on.

After ten minutes, Claudia was breathing like a broken piston, and I wasn't in much better shape. We went to ground, and I could hear the Wheeskrick thrashing around in the underbrush a hundred yards away. But now we were in our element, not his. We lay silently, and he passed us by, half blind in the high actinic light of our sun, laboring under the drag of his breathing apparatus.

We lay like that, Claudia's head pillowed on my shoulder, for hours. I figured with what I had observed of the Wheeskrick's vision, we weren't much better off in the night than in the day, but we needed the rest; Claudia—now three days without food or water—was in bad shape.

At dusk, while she slept, I worked my way slowly around to a thick wild grape growing up a nearby pine, severed a three foot chunk of it, and brought it back to her. She drank greedily from the hollow core and rested; I figured she would be good for an hour or two of travel. Our ace in the hole was those twenty canisters. As long as they weren't moved, the Wheeskricks couldn't find them—or so I hoped. And if Claudia and I could make the thirty miles to my home and Pop's ingenuity and those canisters, we might have a fighting chance.

We kept off the roads until we reached the outskirts of Carson's Corners, which are about a nine-iron shot from the inskirts. There is a truck stop in Carson's Corners, and I slicked my hair into some semblance of order and went in alone and bought a sack of hamburgers to go. We hunched together in the shadows behind the stop and ate greedily, while I watched for a chance to steal a ductor. I hated to do it, but I figured we could square it later, and my first assumption was that the Wheeskricks would be looking for two people on foot.

I toyed with the idea of calling the Highway Patrol, but when I thought of the problem of trying to convince anybody who hadn't seen the Wheeskrick ship that there was such a horror loose in the county, I gave up. Even if I could convince them, what could they do?

A middle-aged couple parked their '84 Buick with its turbine still turning and headed for the rest rooms. I bundled Claudia through the door and crept silently out of the parking lot and onto the highway. At the edge of town I waited until a trucker pulled out toward Morgantown and drove in the shadow of his tailgate into and through that metropolis. My second assumption was that the Wheeskricks could very well be up there a few hundred feet in the air, their black ship all but invisible, prepared to jump any single car going down that road alone.

Outside of Morgantown, the trucker turned off on the Washington Pike, and I drifted to the side of the road under a spreading maple. We waited until midnight, but nothing else came along. I could feel that black ship up there, detectors alert, waiting for something to pass down the road. Then somewhere behind us, on the outskirts of Morgantown I suppose, a drive-in theater let out. For a few minutes the road was crowded with ductors, and I swung out into the midst of them and let them convoy us all the way to Pop's yard. I parked the stolen ductor behind the pile of defective zinc coffins which graces the area between the road and the house, and sat there for a while, too weak to move.

After a bit, I helped Claudia out of the ductor and into the house. Buzzy was home and so was Pop. Phyllis came down in curlers and a robe.

We must have looked a sight. "Jeez! Perce," said Buzzy.

"My Lord, son!" said Pop.

"Oh you poor thing," said Phyllis, reaching out to Claudia.

"Pop!" I said, lapsing into my childhood West Virginia speech, "don't move them goddamn canisters! Not an inch!"

And then I dropped where I stood. I guess I was pretty tired.

## IX

The real secret of Pop's success as a junk dealer—apart from the philosophy and principles I have already described—lay in his genius for putting two or more pieces of useless machinery together into something that would bring a big price. Pop had a reputation all up and down the Eastern Seaboard, and the way it worked was this:

Suppose a widget manufacturer in Brockton, Massachusetts, gets a sudden rush order for a million biformed widgets with knobs on to be delivered (under time penalty) within sixty days. His production capacity is based almost entirely on the number of fully automated widget-making machines he has in service. And if he hasn't got enough to allow him to fill the lucrative order, or if one of his machines is broken down and can't be repaired in time, before he says "no" to the order, he gives Pop a call.

"Mr. Sansoni, can you haywire together a widget-maker with a 400-widget-per-hour capacity? I'll need it by Tuesday."

Maybe Pop has never heard of a widget, but he always answers in the same way. "Sure. Send me the prints and tell me how long it's gotta last." And that's Pop's secret. Send him the blueprints for a widget machine, and he'll make you a widget machine—out of junk. It may not be a very efficient widget machine and it may not last a hell of a lot longer than the requirements of the job (although it's surprising how many improvement patents Pop has sold—metaphorically speaking—to widget-machine manufacturers), but the widget man gets something that will do the job, and Pop turns low-cost junk into high-priced industrial machinery.

That's why we have an 8,000-foot landing strip out back of the yard. My earliest memories are of great cargo aircraft lumbering into that strip to pick up some complex piece of haywire Pop had spent the night crating for shipment. Of course, now the strip is mostly weeds and scrub pine; the flitters don't need anything like that kind of space to lift off from.

Anyway, as you can see from all this, I wasn't much use in the real operation of the family business. Sure, I could help out occasionally with a bit of wiring, and I wasn't bad with a cutting laser. But next to Pop and Buzzy I was all thumbs, and I didn't have that trick of seeing how you could take the turbine from a '79 Olds, two refrigeration units mounted back to back, the fusion chamber from a field generating plant, and most of the guts from a surplus radar set and put them all together into a workable widget-maker. Besides, I'd been gone too long and I didn't know where anything was anymore. And in a junk yard the size of ours, that's as important as anything else.

And that's why it was that I found myself working as combination bookkeeper and purchasing agent for the business, along with handling Pop's occasional legal problems. Pop didn't mind giving up the bookkeeping, but he hated to miss out on the fun of acquisition. Still, he and Buzzy had all they could handle right there in the yard, and I started running around to surplus auctions, plant dismantlings, and other junk yards—like old man Jacobs'—bidding on this and that, doing my bit to *Keep the Stock Up*.

I hadn't given up on my political career. Not by a damn sight. But my only chance was to run as an independent for the Senate seat that would be up for grabs in the fall of '86. I have a good name in the state, and I figured that if I could run a big enough campaign, I could be pretty sure to beat both the regular Party candidates, which would go a long way towards breaking the power of the courthouse gang that had tossed me out.

But such a campaign takes money, lots of it. I figured I had about a year to earn it, and a third share in the family profits—unfair to Pop and Buzzy as it was—seemed like the best way to go about it. I didn't really have much hope that I would be able to accumulate even half what I would need to do the job right, but I had to make the try with whatever resources I could muster.

Sometimes, after a long day passing out my own campaign literature to uninterested housewives at some shopping center or shaking hands with too many limp individuals at some surplus auction, I felt like I was more of a junk man than Pop ever was, trying to salvage something useful out of the old rags and bones that my political career had become.

Funny thing about the sleep of total exhaustion. When I awoke the morning after our escape from the Wheeskricks, my mind was full of campaign worries, thoughts about speeches and posters and 3-D time and how I was going to pay for it all. And then I came fully awake, heard voices outside my window, and the full memory of the events of the past three days came rushing in on me.

I dragged myself out of bed, a little surprised to find that I wasn't a good deal more stiff and sore than I was, and peeked out the window. A State Trooper was driving off in the ductor I'd swiped the night before, and I could hear Pop explaining to another Trooper something about "them no-good juvenile delinquents" and how they must have abandoned it here and so forth. Pop is not without imagination in a pinch.

I showered and shaved and went down to the veranda, letting my nose guide me to the stacks of flapjacks and bacon there. The kids were already off playing in the coffins in the front yard, and Pop was just coming in from his talk with the Troopers. Claudia, despite her three-day ordeal, looked fresh—like a million dollars in small, unmarked bills—and she was helping Phyllis turn out the flapjacks and bacon.

Funny thing. We didn't say anything at all to each other at first. She turned toward me from the stove and kind of lifted her arms, and before either of us quite knew what we were doing, I had my arms around her and she had hers around my neck and we kissed. I guess it lasted a pretty long time.

Buzzy was grinning. Phyllis looked like she was going to cry a little bit. Pop looked mildly disgusted. "When you're all done, Perce," he said, "I'd 'preciate it if you could tell us where'n hell you been since I last seen you on the Morgantown road."

I flushed a little bit and looked at Claudia. She was cool as a cucumber and went back to slicing bread and feeding it into the toaster.

I filled in Pop and Buzzy between bites of flapjack. I told them about the Wheeskrick ship and the Wheeskricks and how it looked like they didn't really *fit* in their ship somehow. I told them about how old Jacobs had swiped the canisters

and about my theory that the Wheeskricks couldn't see very
well in our light and depended on their detection system to
locate the canisters. I wound up by stating the problem as I
saw it: getting the canisters back to the Wheeskricks without
incurring a visit from them. I guess I had in mind some sort
of remote-controlled ductor we could send off down the road
loaded with the twenty canisters.

Pop's look of disgust deepened. "I ain't *about* to give them
things nothin'," he said. "Not after what they done to you and
Buzzy and poor Ed and Billy."

"But Pop," I said, "those canisters *belong* to the Wheeskricks.
And anyway, you can't very well call up the Highway Patrol
and expect them to believe anything as wild as this."

"I ain't goin' to call up nobody," said Pop. "And as far as the
canisters belonging to the Wheeskricks, didn't you say it
looked like they didn't really fit in that ship? Like maybe it
was built for someone else? I bet they hijacked that ship just
like they coldcocked Buzzy here."

I got legalistic and quoted something out of Blackstone to
the effect that two wrongs don't make a right and that even if
the canisters were stolen property (several times, that is: the
Wheeskricks stole them from some rightful owner, and Jacobs
stole them from the Wheeskricks), we still didn't have any
legal title to them.

Pop thought a minute. "All right, Perce. You want it nice
and legal. I know a little sumpin' about the Law. What do you
call it when a guy unloads cargo on your property and has to
pay for storage?"

"Demurrage," I said.

"Yeah," said Pop, a note of triumph in his voice. "And what
happens if he don't pay when he unloads his stuff?"

"Well," I said, "under the Law Merchant, the wharf owner
can claim up to the value of the goods for nonpayment,
providing . . ."

"See!" said Pop, fairly cackling in triumph. "Them's our
canisters until some court decides different, and I'll bet
anything it's up to the Wheeskricks to take it to court,
certainly not us."

"My God, Pop, you can't apply common law to a situation
like this."

Pop paid no attention. "And just think what them canisters
must be worth!"

The word "worth" struck a responsive chord in me, and the legalisms began to give way to shysterisms. I needed money, and this could be the windfall that would pay the printing bills and maybe buy some 3-D time, and . . . And maybe it was sheer rationalization, but the memory of that tank-truck driver suddenly arose in my mind. It seemed to be a fixed part of the Wheeskricks' *modus operandi* to set up a violently constructed roadblock whenever they wanted to intercept canisters on the move. My idea of a remote-controlled ductor would be almost sure to cost at least one more life.

I became very silent as Pop and Buzzy began to talk about ways and means of moving the canisters without activating the Wheeskrick detection system.

As they talked I became aware of Claudia again, and I broke into their technical plotting.

"All right," I said. "I'll go along with you. But you better figure from the start that the only way to get out of this in one piece is to suck those birds in and eliminate them, and if there's going to be that kind of rough stuff around here, we better plan on getting Phyllis and the kids and Claudia the hell out of here."

For a change, Pop and Buzzy agreed with me, and the three of us started to hatch plans which would get the women and kids off the premises.

Phyllis responded first with a sweet and dulcet: "Cut the crap, Buzzy, I'm not going anywhere."

Buzzy subsided meekly.

Claudia just looked at me and grinned. "Now Claudia," I said, "there's no reason in the world . . ." My voice trailed off.

Pop looked at Buzzy, and then he looked at me. The look of disgust on his face deepened. "When your mother was alive, why when I said something, she . . ." Pop stopped and shook his head. "Keerist," he said and went back to drawing diagrams on the table top. Claudia and Phyllis started cackling at each other and resumed their work at the sink. For a lawyer who was once pretty good at trial work, I was not batting very well that day.

X

By noon the Wheeskricks problem was still without a
solution, but Pop had shrouded the parked pickup containing
the canisters with several layers of copper screening, carefully grounded to the pickup frame, just in case the canisters
were radiating something the Wheeskricks could detect.

Pop and Buzzy argued most of the morning on the best way
to get the Wheeskricks. Buzzy was in favor of rigging the
pickup for remote control as I had suggested and then laying
for the Wheeskricks' ship with a couple of 75mm recoilless
rifles. But I piped up about the women and kids and said I
wouldn't have anything to do with a shooting match. Pop just
grunted and gave Buzzy his pitying look. "I ain't never had
no chance to get me a spaceship before and I ain't about to
shoot this one full of holes."

Then they debated running a heavy cable out into the
boondocks well away from the house and wiring the canisters
good and hot to ground. Pop almost bought that one, until I
pointed out that while we might fry the first couple of
Wheeskricks who caught the loading detail, it'd still leave
one or two inside to fight back, burn up the countryside with
their lazbeams or, at the very least, shag on out of there when
their buddies got cooked.

That stumped us for a while, and you could see the gloom
gathering. To lighten things a bit I suggested that maybe
what we needed to get all the Wheeskricks out of their ship at
once was a good supply of lady Wheeskricks. Nobody laughed.
Pop said: "The way you described 'em, how do you know
they ain't already lady Wheeskricks?"

He had me there, and the gloom deepened.

We sat there like three dummies while the women busied
themselves in the kitchen with lunch. I wanted to be done
with the whole thing, to take Claudia and shove off for far
places where there were no life-or-death problems. With
Claudia there, and the promise of what might be, I was even
losing some of my despair about the election. Some of it, but
not all.

Then Pop got his idea. Phyllis was pulling and heaving on
the long dining table on the veranda, trying to pull it apart
so that an extra leaf could be inserted. But the catch was in
an awkward position, and the slides were old and sticky. It

wasn't until Claudia came and got a firm grip on the far end that Phyllis was able to pull her end out enough to open up the space in the middle.

"See," said Pop. "There're just some things that take more'n one to do." He pulled an old envelope out of his pocket and began to sketch with the stub of a pencil. "Looky here, boys. We gotta build us something like this and drop it down over them canisters."

And by evening we were finished. Pop had welded up a kind of bottomless cage, a shallow affair made out of reinforcing rod and channel iron. It was just wide enough and long enough to fit down over the canisters stacked two high and ten long. In the center of the top of the cage was welded a cast-iron collar, part of the clutch housing from an '83 Ford, through which Pop had bored four radial holes. Out in the strip, half a mile from the house, Buzzy and I sank the massive piston from an old pneumatic lift into the ground and anchored it upright with a couple of yards of concrete.

Along the top of Pop's cage ran four spring-loaded rods designed to extend inward from each corner, through the holes in the collar, and into matching holes bored in the pneumatic piston and lined with insulating ceramic. Once lowered over the piston with the rods seated through the collar into the piston, there would be only one way to remove the cage and get at the canisters underneath: someone had to be at each corner to pull back the rod. Four corners meant four Wheeskricks. At least that's the way Pop had it figured.

But it didn't quite work out that way.

It was nearly dark when we had finished. Pop had run the old M-70 out to where we had planted the piston, the cage dangling from the M-70's A-frame. We stashed a thousand KVA MHD generator in a little patch of brush a hundred yards away and ran a heavy cable out from it to the cage. One lead Pop bolted to the cage; the other we tack-welded to the piston for a ground. The earth was moist from recent rains, and if the Wheeskricks were even halfway decent conductors, they should get a good jolt. At least that's the way we figured it.

Pop looked everything over and nodded with satisfaction. All that was left to us was to run the pickup full of canisters out, unload them under the dangling cage, and lower it into place. Judging from the time it had taken the Wheeskricks to detect us when we had driven from Jacobs' yard two nights before, we would have a good quarter hour before we could expect them, after we once moved the canisters.

Buzzy was all for going ahead with it immediately. But Pop wanted to give the concrete a little more settling time, and I reminded Buzzy about the Wheeskricks' vision. "We're going to need every break we can get," I said. I was feeling pessimistic and more than a little scared. I wished we could persuade Phyllis and Claudia to take the kids and leave.

We slept fitfully that night, and at five in the morning Pop was up and dealing out weapons from his store in the basement. I look one of the 75-shot carbines and looked longingly at the 55mm bazooka. But I remembered the hard, pitted surface of that ship and gave it up. Pop probably would have objected anyway.

As if we'd been practicing it for weeks, we drove the pickup out to the cage and off-loaded the twenty canisters in a matter of minutes. In my mind's eye I could see those Wheeskricks huddled in front of their detection screen whistling and chattering as the blips began to appear. Pop pulled the M-70 into position and lowered the cage down over the piston. The four rods sprang home with a solid snap. Buzzy cast off the winch line, and Pop took off in the M-70 for the brush patch with the generator.

Buzzy and I went to ground in a drainage ditch fifty yards away in the opposite direction and began to survey the sky in the direction of Morgantown.

It was just a little after sunup and a fine day. There were chicken hawks wheeling in slow, precise circles over the woodlot down by the stream. Cicadas were beginning to saw away in the heavy dew, and from somewhere way off to the north there came the faint, casual clank of cowbells as some farmer turned his herd into pasture. The faint whine of the MHD generator was the only other man-made sound.

Then right on time the Wheeskricks showed up. Their ship was low, not more than a couple of hundred feet off the ground, and it zigzagged slightly, like a hound coursing after scent. Then it locked on, flew swiftly to the strip and settled silently a few yards from the stacked canisters. There was an eerie silence, and then the turret winked into life, and the M-70 glowed cherry red and began to burn. Its fuel tank went off with a shuddering blast, and the A-frame crumbled into ruin. The turret winked off. Buzzy and I dug our noses deeper into the grassy bank of the drainage ditch. I hoped Pop had had sense enough to dig in in his brush patch.

The round hatchway in the side of the Wheeskrick ship swung open, and two came out, their goldfish bowls shining in the morning sun. They looked around carefully, saw no sign of life, and stepped down to examine Pop's handiwork. They heaved at the cage and jiggled it and then spotted the spring-loaded bolts. One of them loped around to the far side, pulled back one bolt and stretched to reach the other on his side. His waving tentacles were inches short.

He rejoined his fellow and waved three tentacled arms in a curious pattern. We could hear his whistling and screeching through the goldfish bowl and fifty yards away. There were two formidable Wheeskrick shrugs, and one of them did something to the top of his goldfish bowl and pointed a waving bunch of tentacles at the ship. The hatch closed and a moment later reopened. Two more Wheeskricks joined the first two and watched attentively as the first two gesticulated and wiggled their tentacles.

As the four took up their stations at the corners of Pop's cage, Buzzy dug me in the ribs. "We got 'em, Perce! We got 'em!"

I heard the faint whine of the generator deepen into a growl as Pop threw the breakers in.

The Wheeskricks went on about their business. They released the bolts and started to lift the cage up and off the piston. There was a flash of fire as the collar of the cage brushed against the piston. I heard the clatter of breakers going out and then being shoved back in manually. The cable leading to Pop's brush pile glowed red and broke into smoking flame. Whatever else they were, the Wheeskricks were dandy dielectrics, and if they felt anything at all from the jolt Pop was giving them, they didn't show it.

But the glowing cable showed *them* something. They pitched the cage to one side and opened fire at Pop's brush patch. I got the carbine in position and started plugging away; Buzzy blasted with his lazgun. I took my time and aimed for fishbowls. I shot two, and two Wheeskricks lay rolling and gasping on the ground. Buzzy's lazgun hung on a third until he went screeching and whistling toward the rear of the ship, stumbled, and fell rolling, his fishbowl and tank bouncing away from his grasp.

The grass in front of us flared, and Buzzy cursed. His hair was burning, and he dropped the lazgun to beat out the flame. The remaining Wheeskrick made a dash for the open hatch, and without really thinking I was on my feet and running through the burning pastureland to intercept him.

Wheeskricks are faster than people, and he beat me by a good ten yards. I snapped a few rounds from the hip as I ran and saw him spurt rusty fluid and drop pulpy tentacles, still writhing, on the ground. Then I was at the hatchway, thrusting the carbine barrel into the rapidly diminishing gap between hatch and jamb. The barrel glowed red, and the stock began to smolder; but it was good steel, and the Wheeskrick abandoned his attempt to burn it out of the doorway. I heard the inner lock open and choked at the rush of chlorine. I took a deep breath, pried with all my might on the ruined carbine and plunged into the red dimness within.

The Wheeskrick lay just inside the inner door, viscous fluid pouring from one ruined shoulder. His five remaining arms scrabbled at the lock on the door, trying to shut it. Blinded by the chlorine, I flailed at the figure before me. Something hard smashed me in the face, and I felt teeth loosen. I jabbed with the carbine, caught a glimpse of yellow and jabbed again. Something pulled my feet out from under me, and I fell heavily, swinging as I went. There was a crunch of plastic, and then fire flared in my face, and I saw the fire envelop the Wheeskrick and my own clothes start to burn. As I started to take a deep breath, I felt hands—not tentacles—dragging me back toward daylight.

## XI

Claudia was giving me mouth-to-mouth resuscitation, when I came to a quarter of an hour later. I kept my eyes tightly closed and enjoyed the treatment. But she must have been able to tell from my more regular breathing that I was on the mend, and she stopped. I opened my eyes, looked up at her tear-stained face and the blue sky and the chicken hawks beyond.

"Oh Perce!" she said. I smiled and winked one bloodshot eye.

We went back to the resuscitation treatment.

After a bit, I thought about Pop and sat up. Three

Wheeskricks lay where they had fallen around the canisters and at the rear of the ship; the fourth was hanging dead, half out of the hatchway. Pop was cursing in a steady monotone as Phyllis rubbed some kind of salve onto his burned neck and shoulder. Buzzy was holding a handkerchief over his nose and peering in over the dead Wheeskrick at the interior of the ship. I got to my feet and hobbled over to them.

Buzzy looked around as I approached. Most of his hair was missing, and the bandages on his burned back were singed black. "You okay, Perce?"

I felt for the burned places on my cheek and forehead. "Yeah, but I'm glad I had my campaign pictures taken before this started."

Buzzy turned back to his inspection of the ship. "It's going to be a while before we can get in there to look around."

"I'm in no hurry," I said. "I been in there too much already. All I want to know is how much dough we can get for it." Buzzy, who at the moment was full of the purest scientific curiosity, looked blankly at me. "Oh yeah. Your campaign."

We walked to the canister pile, but Pop was already ahead of us. He had horsed one of them free from the pile and was examining the sealing band. "Here, Buzzy. Take a look. I'll be dipped if I can figure out how this thing opens."

Buzzy bent over the strip to inspect it and then pulled a pair of pliers from his coverall pocket. He got a good grip and pulled. His face grew red and his knuckles white. The end of the strip didn't budge. He stopped and wiped his hands on his coveralls. "Maybe this isn't a sealing strip," he said. "Maybe there's something else."

Together the three of us rolled the canister over and over, examining every inch for some means of opening it. "No wonder old man Jacobs sold you these things so cheap, Perce," said Pop. "He couldn't figure out how to open the cotton-pickers."

I thought back to Jacobs' yard. "He must have opened one," I said, "or found one already opened. There was the one he'd put the MHD in."

"Say," I said, "that one wasn't open along the end at all, come to think of it. It was split right down the middle."

Pop got down on his hands and knees and took his glasses off. Without his glasses, Pop has about four-power magnification in his nearsighted eyes.

He found the hair-fine crack that ran the length of the canister, and midway along it he found a slight indentation. "Looky here, boys," he said, laying his thumb in the indentation.

There was a soft, chiming sound and the quiet hum of delicate machinery. Pop sprang back in surprise, and the canister slowly split open along its seam, the two halves swinging slowly back from each other until they both lay horizontal.

From where I was standing I could see only one half; it was packed with a fantastically complex mechanism, like three running yards of swiss watch, digital computer and heart-lung machine all carefully fitted together. All that had been covered by olive-drab Army packing paper at Jacobs', but I marveled at Jacobs selling the canisters off as he did. He must have known the Wheeskricks would be coming after the canisters and unloaded them in sheer panic.

I looked at that canister and saw dollar signs and campaign posters and 3-D time. I looked up at Pop, across the canister, and saw shock. I moved toward him and looked back at the canister.

A man lay in the other half. An old fellow, maybe sixty or so. His eyes were open, and he was grinning at us. He was naked as a jaybird.

He sat up, did something to the maze of instruments in the canister's other half and climbed to his feet, stepping gingerly out onto the grass. He looked about him, taking in the ship, the dead Wheeskricks and the five of us. Then he bowed to Pop, crooked his elbow and swung it in a short circle in some sort of ceremonial gesture and said something like "Sally Constantinople." Pop, who has dealt with a lot of odd ones in his life, didn't blink an eye. He crooked his elbow and waggled it in the same sort of stiff gesture and answered: "Sally Constantinople to you, buster."

The naked old man laughed, a nice human laugh, and walked with a quick and springing step to the hatch of the ship. The chlorine had pretty well dissipated now, and we all crowded in after him. He looked at the jury-rigged sleeping rack of the Wheeskricks with a frown of disapproval and then strode to the complicated control area, seated himself in one of those very human-looking chairs and began to examine various instruments with practiced sureness, occasionally snapping a switch or turning a dial, nodding with satisfaction at the results he read off.

He rose then, and we followed him back outside to the pile of canisters. He carefully picked over them until he found what he was looking for and began to heave one clear from the others. He was an old man, and Buzzy and I leaped to help him. In the same way, he found two more, and we helped him line up all three on the grass.

He thumbed all three open. Out of two stepped men, one middle-aged and one who looked about as old as Buzzy. From the third came a girl

Funny thing about women. Neither Claudia nor Phyllis had said a word during all this, exhibited no surprise at the masculine nudity, but when that girl rose, displaying firm breasts and smooth shanks to the West Virginia sun, both women started off for the house. "I'll bet they're hungry," said Phyllis, eyeing Buzzy with a speculative look. "Yes," said Claudia. "And cold, too. We'd better get that poor girl something to cover up with." It was at least eighty by that time in the morning!

Well, that was the end of the business. We helped the three men and the girl carry the canisters into the ship and stow them in the after cargo compartment with the other two hundred. We helped them tear out the Wheeskricks' makeshift sleeping racks, and we brought up a couple of milk cans full of spring water to top off their tanks. They ate the sandwiches Phyllis and Claudia brought, but declined the offer of clothing with polite smiles.

Then we had a session with a pencil and one of my yellow legal pads, and they drew pictures much as the Wheeskricks had done, explaining how they had been underway for a long time, maybe even hundreds of years—the time symbol was confusing. As passengers on the ship, they had no way of knowing just how it had happened, but the evidence they now had suggested that the Wheeskricks had somehow taken over the ship at some way-station, killed the regular crew (Jacobs' empty canister?) and stolen the ship and its encapsulated passengers. I couldn't understand why the Wheeskricks wanted the passengers so much, and the pictures that appeared when I tried to ask didn't help much.

But that was the end of the business anyway. By noon, all four had waggled their elbows at us and said "Sally Constantinople" to us several times and had smiled great appreciative smiles as they presented Pop with a small ceramic vase—a real work of art, I'm sure—and entered their ship, which now, with new inhabitants, didn't look nearly so formidable and frightening as it had before.

There was a shimmer of air under the ship, a faint whine and then a rapidly diminishing dot in the sky. The chicken hawks stopped their circling for a moment to watch and then went back to work. The spot disappeared, and I stopped craning my neck and lowered my gaze to more mundane things.

Claudia and Phyllis were gathering up paper plates and empty beer cans and shooing the children back toward the house, just as if they'd finished a perfectly ordinary picnic in the State Park over at Olney. Pop was bent over a spade, excavating a grave for one of the Wheeskricks. Buzzy slumped over toward us, the doleful look on his face matching mine.

Pop finished his work and pried the dead Wheeskrick into its shallow grave. He looked at me, and then he looked at Buzzy. "What's the matter, boys? You both look so down in the mouth you'd think you been eatin' baby ducks." Pop cackled at his own wit, but neither of us cracked a smile.

Buzzy shook his head in sorrow. "I don't know, Pop. Just disappointed I guess. When I think what we could have learned from that ship, from anything in that ship! If they'd just have given us anything but that damn vase."

Pop said: "The trouble with you, Buzzy, is you just ain't no art lover." He had something up his sleeve, but I was too depressed to notice it. He looked at me. "And what about you, Perce. What's got you so unhappy?"

I shook my head. "I guess I'm just disappointed too, Pop. I should be thankful that we all got out of this business more or less healthy, but I guess I was kind of counting on getting something out of it, something we could raise a fast buck on." I felt ashamed of myself. My motives weren't anywhere near as honorable as Buzzy's pure love of science.

"I guess I wanted that Senate seat pretty badly," I said. "And all we've gotten is four dead Wheeskricks to bury."

Pop leaned on his spade and gave us that "how-did-a-smart-old-man-like-me-get-such-stupid-sons" look. He stripped the lid off a fresh can of beer and downed half of it at a gulp. Then he strode toward the brush patch, beckoning Buzzy and me to follow. He pulled back the limbs of a scrub cottonwood and there in the weeds lay four canisters.

Buzzy said: "Jeez, Pop. How'd you manage that?"

"I snuck 'em back off the ship while they was eatin' Phyllis' sandwiches and drawin' pictures for you boys."

I felt sick inside. "Pop," I said. "Don't you know that there are four human beings in there? You can't *do* this!"

Pop took a long pull on his beer and heaved the empty can off into orbit somewhere up near the chicken hawks.

"Aw heck, Perce. What do you think I am?

"I'm a junk dealer, Perce.

"These here are the empties."

*Since 1953, Robert F. Young has published three books and approximately 150 short stories of science fiction. His exclusive concentration on shorter lengths has caused him to be shamefully neglected, and that is too bad, since much of his work is excellent and a "Best of" collection would be stunning. He is fascinated with romance and myth, and often manages to combine both, as in the following story of a woman torn between dreams and reality.*

# FLYING PAN

## by ROBERT F. YOUNG

Marianne Summers worked in a frying-pan factory. For eight hours every day and for five days every week she stood by a production-line conveyor and every time a frying pan went by she put a handle on it. And all the while she stood by one conveyor she rode along on another—a big conveyor with days and nights over it instead of fluorescent tubes, and months standing along it instead of people. And every time she passed a month it added something to her or took something away, and as time went by she became increasingly aware of the ultimate month—the one standing far down the line, waiting to put a handle on her soul.

Sometimes Marianne sat down and wondered how she could possibly have gotten into such a rut, but all the while she wondered she knew that she was only kidding herself, that she knew perfectly well why. Ruts were made for untalented people, and if you were untalented you ended up in one; moreover if you were untalented and were too stubborn to go home and admit you were untalented, you stayed in one.

There was a great deal of difference between dancing on TV and putting handles on frying pans: the difference between being graceful and gawky, lucky and unlucky, or—to get right back to the basic truth again—the difference between being talented and untalented. No matter how hard you practiced or how hard you tried, if your legs were too fat, no one wanted you and you ended up in a rut or in a frying-pan factory, which was the same thing, and you went to work every morning and performed the same tasks and you came home every night and thought the same thoughts, and all the while you rode down the big conveyor between the merciless months and came closer and closer to the ultimate month that would put the final touches on you and make you just like everybody else. . . .

Mornings were getting up and cooking breakfasts in her small apartment and taking the bus to work. Evenings were going home and cooking lonely suppers and afterward TV. Weekends were writing letters and walking in the park. Nothing ever changed and Marianne had begun to think that nothing ever would. . . .

And then one night when she came home, she found a flying frying pan on her window ledge.

It had been a day like all days, replete with frying pans, superintendents, boredom and tired feet. Around ten o'clock the maintenance man stopped by and asked her to go to the Halloween Dance with him. The Halloween Dance was a yearly event sponsored by the company and was scheduled for that night. So far, Marianne had turned down fifteen would-be escorts.

A frying pan went by and she put a handle on it. "No, I don't think so," she said.

"Why?" the maintenance man asked bluntly.

It was a good question, one that Marianne couldn't answer honestly because she wasn't being honest with herself. So she told the same little white lie she had told all the others: "I—I don't like dances."

"Oh." The maintenance man gave her the same look his fifteen predecessors had given her, and moved on. Marianne shrugged her shoulders. I don't care *what* they think, she told herself. Another frying pan went by, and another and another.

After a while, noon came, and Marianne and all the other employees ate frankfurters and sauerkraut in the company cafeteria. The parade of frying pans recommenced promptly at 12:30.

During the afternoon she was approached twice more by would-be escorts. You'd have thought she was the only girl in the factory. Sometimes she hated her blue eyes and round pink face, and sometimes she even hated her bright yellow hair, which had some of the properties of a magnet. But hating the way she looked didn't solve her problems—it only aggravated them—and by the time 4:30 came she had a headache and she heartily despised the whole world.

Diminutive trick-or-treaters were already making the rounds when she got off the bus at the corner. Witches walked and goblins leered, and pumpkin candles sputtered in the dusk. But Marianne hardly noticed.

Halloween was for children, not for an embittered old woman of twenty-two who worked in a frying-pan factory.

She walked down the street to the apartment building and picked up her mail at the desk. There were two letters, one from her mother, one from—

Marianne's heart pounded all the way up in the elevator and all the way down the sixth-floor corridor to her apartment. But she forced herself to open her mother's letter first. It was a typical letter, not essentially different from the last one. The grape crop had been good, but what with the trimming and the tying and the disking and the horse-hoeing, and paying off the pickers, there wasn't going to be much left of the check—if and when it came; the hens were laying better, but then they always did whenever egg prices dropped; Ed Olmstead was putting a new addition on his general store (it was high time!); Doris Hickett had just given birth to a 7 lb. baby boy; Pa sent his love, and please forget your foolish pride and come home. P.S.—Marianne should see the wonderful remodeling job Howard King was doing on his house. It was going to be a regular palace when he got done.

Marianne swallowed the lump in her throat. She opened the other letter with trembling fingers:

DEAR MARIANNE,

*I said I wasn't going to write you any more, that I'd already written you too many times asking you to come home and marry me and you never gave me an answer one way or the other. But sometimes a fellow's pride don't amount to much.*

*I guess you know I'm remodeling the house and I guess you know the reason why. In case you don't it's the same reason I bought the house in the first place, because of you. I only got one picture window and I don't know whether I should put it in the parlor or in the kitchen. The kitchen would be fine, but all you can see from there is the barn and you know how the barn looks, but if I put it in the parlor the northwest wind would be sure to crack it the first winter though you'd get a good view of the road and the willows along the creek. I don't know what to do.*

*The hills behind the south meadow are all red and gold the way you used to like them. The willows look like they're on fire. Nights I sit on the steps and picture you coming walking down the road and stopping by the gate and then I get up and walk down the path and I say, "I'm glad you've come back, Marianne. I guess you know I still love you." I guess if anybody ever heard me they'd think I was crazy because the road is always empty when I get there, and there's no one ever standing by the gate.*

HOWARD

There had been that crisp December night with the sound of song and laughter intermingling with the crackling of the ice beneath the runners and the chug-chugging of the tractor as it pulled the hay-filled sleigh, and the stars so bright and close they touched the topmost branches of the silhouetted trees, and the snow, pale and clean in the starlight, stretching away over the hills, up and up, into the first dark fringe of the forest; and herself, sitting on the tractor with Howard instead of in the hay with the rest of the party, and the tractor lurching and bumping, its headbeams lighting the way over the rutted country road—

Howard's arm was around her and their frosty breaths blended as they kissed. "I love you, Marianne," Howard said, and she could see the words issuing from his lips in little silvery puffs and drifting away into the darkness, and suddenly she saw her own words, silver too, hovering tenuously in the air before her, and presently she heard them in wondrous astonishment: "I love you, too, Howie. I love you, too. . . ."

She didn't know how long she'd been sitting there crying before she first became aware of the ticking sound. A long time, she guessed, judging by the stiffness of her limbs. The sound was coming from her bedroom window and what it made her think of most was the common pins she and the other kids used to tie on strings and rig up so they'd keep swinging against the windowpanes of lonely old people sitting alone on Halloween.

She had lit the table lamp when she came in, and its beams splashed reassuringly on the living-room rug. But beyond the aura of the light, shadows lay along the walls, coalesced in the bedroom doorway. Marianne stood up, concentrating on the sound. The more she listened the more she doubted that she was being victimized by the neighborhood small fry: the ticks came too regularly to be ascribed to a pin dangling at the end of a string. First there would be a staccato series of them, then silence, then another series. Moreover, her bedroom window was six stories above the street and nowhere near a fire escape.

But if the small fry weren't responsible for the sound, who was? There was an excellent way to find out. Marianne forced her legs into motion, walked slowly to the bedroom doorway, switched on the ceiling light and entered the room. A few short steps brought her to the window by her bed.

She peered through the glass. Something gleamed on the window ledge but she couldn't make out what it was. The ticking noise had ceased and traffic sounds drifted up from below. Across the way, the warm rectangles of windows made precise patterns in the darkness, and down the street a huge sign said in big blue letters: SPRUCK'S CORN PADS ARE THE BEST.

Some of Marianne's confidence returned. She released the catch and slowly raised the window. At first she didn't recognize the gleaming object as a flying saucer; she took it for an upside-down frying pan without a handle. And so ingrained was the habit by now that she reached for it instinctively, with the unconscious intention of putting a handle on it.

"Don't touch my ship!"

That was when Marianne saw the spaceman. He was standing off to one side, his diminutive helmet glimmering in the radiance of SPRUCK'S CORN PADS. He wore a gray, form-fitting space suit replete with ray guns, shoulder tanks, and boots with turned-up toes, and he was every bit of five inches tall. He had drawn one of the ray guns (Marianne didn't know for sure they were ray guns, but judging from the rest of his paraphernalia, what else could they be?) and was holding it by the barrel. It was clear to Marianne that he had been tapping on the window with it.

It was also clear to Marianne that she was going, or had gone, out of her mind. She started to close the window—

"Stop, or I'll burn you!"

Her hands fell away from the sash. The voice had seemed real enough, a little on the thin side, perhaps, but certainly audible enough. Was it possible? Could this tiny creature be something more than a figment?

He had changed his gun to his other hand, she noticed, and its minute muzzle pointed directly at her forehead. When she made no further move, he permitted the barrel to drop slightly and said, "That's better. Now if you'll behave yourself and do as I say, maybe I can spare your life."

"Who are you?" Marianne asked.

It was as though he had been awaiting the question. He stepped dramatically into the full radiance of the light streaming through the window and sheathed his gun. He bowed almost imperceptibly, and his helmet flashed like the tinsel on a gum wrapper. "Prince Moy Trehano," he said majestically, though the majesty was marred by the thinness of his voice, "Emperor of 10,000 suns, Commander of the vast space fleet which is at this very moment in orbit around this insignificant planet you call 'Earth'!"

"Wh—why?"

"Because we're going to bomb you, that's why!"

"But why do you want to bomb us?"

"Because you're a menace to galactic civilization! Why else?"

"Oh," Marianne said.

"We're going to blow your cities to smithereens. There'll be so much death and destruction in our wake that you'll never recover from it. . . . Do you have any batteries?"

For a moment Marianne thought she had misunderstood. "Batteries?"

"Flashlight batteries will do." Prince Moy Trehano seemed embarrassed, though it was impossible to tell for sure because his helmet completely hid his face. There was a small horizontal slit where, presumably, his eyes were, but that was the only opening. "My atomic drive's been acting up," he went on. "In fact, this was a forced landing. Fortunately, however, I know a secret formula whereby I can convert the energy in a dry-cell battery into a controlled chain reaction. Do you have any?"

"I'll see," Marianne said.

"Remember now, no tricks. I'll burn you right through the walls with my atomic ray gun if you try to call anyone!"

"I—I think there's a flashlight in my bed-table drawer."

There was. She unscrewed the base, shook out the batteries and set them on the window sill. Prince Moy Trehano went into action. He opened a little door on the side of his ship and rolled the batteries through. Then he turned to Marianne. "Don't you move an inch from where you are!" he said. "I'll be watching you through the viewports." He stepped inside and closed the door.

Marianne held her terror at bay and peered at the spaceship more closely. They aren't really flying *saucers* at all, she thought; they're just like frying pans . . . flying frying pans. It even had a little bracket that could have been the place where the handle was supposed to go. Not only that, its ventral regions strongly suggested a frying-pan cover.

She shook her head, trying to clear it. First thing you knew, everything she saw would look like a frying pan. She remembered the viewports Prince Moy Trehano had mentioned, and presently she made them out—a series of tiny crinkly windows encircling the upper part of the saucer. She leaned closer, trying to see into the interior.

"Stand back!"

Marianne straightened up abruptly, so abruptly that she nearly lost her kneeling position before the window and toppled back into the room. Prince Moy Trehano had reemerged from his vessel and was standing imperiously in the combined radiance of the bedroom light and SPRUCK'S CORN PADS.

"The technical secrets of my stellar empire are not for the likes of you," he said. "But as a recompense for your assistance in the repairing of my atomic drive I am going to divulge my space fleet's target areas.

"We do not contemplate the complete destruction of humanity. We wish merely to destroy the present civilization, and to accomplish this it is our intention to wipe out every city on Earth. Villages will be exempt, as will small towns with populations of less than 20,000 humans. The bombings will begin as soon as I get back to my fleet—a matter of four or five hours—and if I do not return, they will begin in four or five hours anyway. So if you value your life, go ho— I mean, leave the city at once. I, Prince Moy Trehano, have spoken!"

Once again the bow, and the iridescing of the tinselly helmet, and then Prince Moy Trehano stepped into the spaceship and slammed the door. A whirring sound ensued, and the vessel began to shake. Colored lights went on in the viewports—a red one here, a blue one there, then a green one—creating a Christmas-tree effect.

Marianne watched, entranced. Suddenly the door flew open and Prince Moy Trehano's head popped out. "Get back!" he shouted. "Get back! You don't want to get burned by the jets, do you?" His head disappeared and the door slammed again.

Jets? Were flying saucers jet-propelled? Even as she instinctively shrank back into her bedroom, Marianne pondered the question. Then, as the saucer rose from the window ledge and into the night, she saw the little streams of fire issuing from its base. They were far more suggestive of sparks from a Zippo lighter than they were of jets, but if Prince Moy Trehano had said they were jets, then jets they were. Marianne was not inclined to argue the point.

When she thought about the incident afterward she remembered a lot of points that she could have argued—if she'd wanted to. Prince Moy Trehano's knowledge of the English language, for one, and his slip of the tongue when he started to tell her to go home, for another. And then there was the matter of his atomic drive. Certainly, Marianne reflected later, if the bombs his fleet was supposed to have carried were as technically naive as his atomic drive, the world had never had much to worry about.

But at the moment she didn't feel like arguing any points. Anyway, she was too busy to argue. Busy packing. Under ordinary circumstances Prince Moy Trehano's threatened destruction of the cities of Earth would never have been reason enough to send her scurrying to the sticks. But Lord, when you were so sick of the pinched little channels of blue that city dwellers called a sky, of the disciplined little plots of grass that took the place of fields, of bored agents who sneered at you just because you had fat legs; when, deep in your heart, you wanted an excuse to go home—then it was reason enough.

More than enough.

At the terminal she paused long enough to send a telegram:

DEAR HOWIE: PUT THE PICTURE WINDOW IN THE KITCHEN, I DON'T MIND THE BARN. WILL BE HOME ON THE FIRST TRAIN.
MARIANNE

When the lights of the city faded into the dark line of the horizon, Prince Moy Trehano relaxed at the controls. His mission, he reflected, had come off reasonably well.

Of course there had been the inevitable unforeseen complication. But he couldn't blame anyone for it besides himself. He should have checked the flashlight batteries before he swiped them. He knew well enough that half the stock in Olmstead's general store had been gathering dust for years, that Ed Olmstead would rather die than throw away anything that some unwary customer might buy. But he'd been so busy rigging up his ship that he just hadn't thought.

In a way, though, his having to ask Marianne's help in the repairing of his improvised motor had lent his story a conviction it might otherwise have lacked. If he'd said right out of a clear blue sky that his "fleet" was going to bomb the cities and spare the villages, it wouldn't have sounded right. Her giving him the batteries had supplied him with a motivation. And his impromptu explanation about converting their energy into a controlled chain reaction had been a perfect cover-up. Marianne, he was sure, didn't know any more about atomic drives than he did.

Prince Moy Trehano shifted to a more comfortable position on his matchbox pilot's seat. He took off his tinfoil helmet and let his beard fall free. He switched off the Christmas-tree lights beneath the Saran Wrap viewports and looked out at the village-bejeweled countryside.

By morning he'd be home, snug and secure in his miniature mansion in the willows. First, though, he'd hide the frying pan in the same rabbit hole where he'd hidden the handle, so no one would ever find it. Then he could sit back and take it easy, comforted by the knowledge of a good deed well done—and by the happy prospect of his household chores being cut in half.

A witch went by on a broom. Prince Moy Trehano shook his head in disgust. Such an outmoded means of locomotion! It was no wonder humans didn't believe in witches any more. You had to keep up with the times if you expected to stay in the race. Why, if he were as old-fashioned and as antiquated as his contemporaries he might have been stuck with a bachelor for the rest of his life, and a shiftless bachelor—when it came to housework, anyway—at that. Not that Howard King wasn't a fine human being; he was as fine as they came. But you never got your dusting and your sweeping done mooning on the front steps like a sick calf, talking to yourself and waiting for your girl to come home from the city.

When you came right down to it, you *had* to be modern. Why, Marianne wouldn't even have *seen* him, to say nothing of hearing what he'd had to say, if he'd worn his traditional clothing, used his own name and employed his normal means of locomotion. Twentieth-century humans were just as imaginative as eighteenth-century and nineteenth-century humans: they believed in creatures from black lagoons and monsters from 20,000 fathoms and flying saucers and beings from outer space—

But they didn't believe in brownies. . . .